PALM BEACH COUNTY
LIBRARY SYSTEM
3650 Summit Boulevard
West Palm Beach, FL 33406-4198

NO
STONE
UNTURNED

ALSO BY ANDREA KANE

FORENSIC INSTINCTS NOVELS:

THE GIRL WHO DISAPPEARED TWICE
THE LINE BETWEEN HERE AND GONE
THE STRANGER YOU KNOW
THE SILENCE THAT SPEAKS
THE MURDER THAT NEVER WAS
A FACE TO DIE FOR
DEAD IN A WEEK

OTHER SUSPENSE THRILLERS:

RUN FOR YOUR LIFE
NO WAY OUT
SCENT OF DANGER
I'LL BE WATCHING YOU
WRONG PLACE, WRONG TIME
DARK ROOM
TWISTED
DRAWN IN BLOOD

HISTORICAL ROMANCES:

MY HEART'S DESIRE
DREAM CASTLE
MASQUE OF BETRAYAL
ECHOES IN THE MIST
SAMANTHA
THE LAST DUKE
EMERALD GARDEN
WISHES IN THE WIND
LEGACY OF THE DIAMOND
THE BLACK DIAMOND
THE MUSIC BOX
THE THEFT
THE GOLD COIN
THE SILVER COIN

ANDREA KANE

NO STONE UNTURNED

ISBN-13:   9781682320396 (Hardcover)
              9781682320426 (Trade Paperback)
              9781682320402 (ePub)
              9781682320419 (Kindle)

LCCN: 2019949608

No Stone Unturned

For questions and comments about the quality of this book, please contact us at:
CustomerService@bonniemeadowpublishing.com.

www.BonnieMeadowPublishing.com

Printed in USA

Publisher's Cataloging-in-Publication

Names: Kane, Andrea, author. | Kane, Andrea. Forensic Instincts novel ; 8.
Title: No stone unturned / Andrea Kane.
Description: Warren, NJ : Bonnie Meadow Publishing LLC, [2020]
Identifiers: ISBN 9781682320396 (hardcover) | ISBN 9781682320426 (trade paperback) | ISBN 9781682320402 (epub) | ISBN 9781682320419 (Kindle)
Subjects: LCSH: Jewelers--Fiction. | Murder--Fiction. | Assassins--Fiction. | McKay family--Fiction. | Forensic sciences--Fiction. |
    LCGFT: Thrillers (Fiction)
Classification: LCC PS3561.A463 N6 2020 (print) | LCC PS3561.A463 (ebook) | DDC 813/.54--dc23

To Mischief—always by my side, forever in my heart.

1

Slowly, Rose Flaherty made her way over to the front window of her Greenwich Village antique shop, leaning heavily on her cane as she did. Preoccupied with the ramifications of her research findings, she barely took note of the passersby on Bedford Street, most of them headed home for the evening. A few of them glanced in her window, their unpracticed eyes seeing none of the beauty attached to the treasure trove of antiques and antiquities, instead seeing only the dusty surfaces, the random pieces, and odd assortment of furnishings that bespoke unwanted junk from the past.

At seventy-nine years old, Rose had long ago stopped caring what people thought. She knew who and what she was. And she knew it was no accident that her established clientele, many of whom were wealthy and educated in the realm of ancient civilizations—including Egyptian, Etruscan, Roman, Byzantine, Greek, and her beloved Celtic—came to her for her expertise as well as her one-of-a-kind offerings. Her knowledge was vast, her list of contacts vaster still.

The levels of research she performed were always a labor of love.

However, her current project was even more than that. It was a thrilling adventure, a fascination of possibilities that transcended anything she'd dealt with in the past.

She couldn't wait to delve deeper.

Impatiently, she squinted at her watch, barely able to make out the hands without the aid of her glasses, which she'd left somewhere. Ah. Five fifteen. Forty-five minutes to go.

Given the magnitude of her findings, there was just one way to pass the time.

She limped her way over to her Chippendale desk, sliding open the bottom drawer and pulling out the bottle of rare, old Irish whiskey she kept on hand for special clients. It was sinfully expensive. How fortunate that one of her prominent clients, Niall Dempsey, was a wealthy real estate developer who also appreciated fine Irish whiskey and who had been kind enough to gift this to her.

She poured the whiskey into a glass, making sure to put out a second for her client. They certainly had something to toast to. She would just get a wee bit of a head start.

"Rose?" Glenna Robinson, Rose's assistant, poked her head out of the back room. Glenna was studying archeology at NYU and thoroughly enjoyed her part-time job at the shop. The fragile, white-haired owner was an intellectual wonder. Learning from her was an honor—even if she was becoming a bit more absentminded as she neared eighty. Absentminded about everything except her work. In that precious realm, her mind was like a steel trap.

"Hmmm?" Rose lifted her lips from her glass and turned, initially surprised to see Glenna was still here. Ah, but it wasn't yet five thirty, and Glenna never left before checking in, so she should have expected to see her shiny young face. Such was the level of Rose's absorption with the task at hand. "Yes, dear?"

Glenna's gaze flickered from the glass in Rose's hand to its mate, sitting neatly beside the whiskey bottle on the desk. "Do you need me to stay late? You mentioned an evening appointment, obviously an important one… even if it's not in the calendar."

"It was last minute." Rose smiled, giving a gentle wave of her hand. "There's no need for you to stay. This is a meeting, not a transaction.

If you'd just collect the mail and drop it off, you can go and enjoy your evening."

Glenna smiled back, trying not to look as relieved as she felt. Her friends had invited her to join them for pizza and beer. After a long week, that was exactly what she needed. But she wouldn't leave Rose in the lurch.

"Are you sure?" she asked.

"Positive. Now run along."

"Thank you. See you tomorrow afternoon." Glenna blew Rose a kiss, then retraced her steps into the small back room—the business office, as she and Rose laughingly called it. It was barely larger than a closet, but it served its purpose. Glenna used it to answer phone calls, schedule appointments, email invoices, do reams of paperwork, and keep track of the countless Post-its Rose stuck on every inch of available surface space. She called it Glenna's to-do list, but Glenna was well aware that the reminders were really for Rose, not for her. All part of Rose's charm. The Post-it-spotted room contained a jam-packed file cabinet, a rusty metal desk, an on-its-last-legs photocopier, and a computer that Glenna had nicknamed Methuselah because it was older than time. Still, it was enough for their needs and Rose didn't know how to use it anyway. That was part of Glenna's job. She'd been doing it since she was sixteen, and she had no desire to go elsewhere.

She scooped up the stack of mail and was about to leave when she spotted a manila envelope propped up against the outbox with the name of the addressee penned on it in Rose's neat hand. No street address. No postage.

Typical forgetful Rose.

Recognizing the client's name, Glenna quickly scanned their contacts list, found the requisite address, printed it on a label that she adhered to the envelope, and carefully marked the parcel: *hand cancel*. She'd take care of the postage at the post office. Jimmy would move the process along. He was an efficient postal worker with a wild crush on her. She'd be in and out in a flash.

After tucking the envelope beneath the rest of the mail, she shut down Methuselah for the night, then grabbed her lightweight jacket and left the shop.

The tinkling sound of the bells over the door echoed behind her.

Twenty minutes later, they tinkled again.

Rose had been sitting in a chair midway in the shop, her back turned to the entrance as she sipped her whiskey and stared idly at the marble fireplace that stayed lit year-round to ward off dampness and mildew. Hearing the bells, she reached for her cane and came to her feet, surprised but delighted. Her client was early.

She turned, a greeting freezing on her lips.

It wasn't a client who had come for her.

2

Fiona jogged the three-quarters of a mile from her place in SoHo to Rose's antique shop. It was a cool September evening, the sun had yet to set, and besides, she needed the exercise and the time to clear her head. She'd been so focused on the final details of the ring she'd been crafting for her new collection that, had it not been for the alarm she'd set on her iPhone, she'd probably have missed the appointment. Time was not her friend these days. She was always rushing to keep up. Not that she could complain. The initial pieces of her new Celtic line, Light and Shadows, were selling like crazy and she'd already begun a major marketing campaign for the next wave.

Thank heavens for her mom's memory box. That's where she'd found the tapestries that were the inspiration for her latest work. And that's why she'd gone to Rose for assistance. No one loved exquisite Celtic treasures as much as Fiona did—other than Rose. And when it came to historical knowledge and international contacts on all things Celtic, the gentle woman was the quintessential source.

Fiona had given Rose a full-page print of the photo she wanted her to start with—the largest and most intricate one. The rest would follow. And since she was basing her whole line on the exquisite images woven into the fabric—both the traditional symbols and the symbols she'd never before seen—she wanted to know all there was to know about them.

She found herself becoming excited again, just as she'd been weeks ago when she first asked Rose for her help.

Jogging lightly across the street, Fiona stopped long enough to admire the latest antiques displayed in Rose's bay window. An Egyptian perfume bottle, a Waterford crystal vase, and a pair of Renaissance statues. All finely detailed, the vase a complex and ornate pattern of Celtic symbols. It even had a fresh bouquet of flowers in it—that would be Glenna's touch.

With a sense of homecoming, Fiona pulled open the door and stepped inside, her eyes searching the cluttered room she'd visited so many times since she'd started making her own jewelry, back in her teens. Rose had been the one to sell her original pieces—sterling silver earrings with intricately pieced Celtic patterns in the center—crafted in her parents' basement when she was just beginning her career. That had been nine years ago—nine years of what had become a valued professional relationship. Fiona would be forever grateful to Rose for giving her that crucial start.

As always, the shop was the essence of clutter. It was dimly lit by a single crystal chandelier, and the fine layer of dust that covered everything made it look as if it hadn't been touched in thirty years. Stacks of papers and old magazines were piled high on the Chippendale desk, behind which were a trio of odd tables haphazardly placed and crammed full of objets d'art—miniature Egyptian statues from three-thousand-year-old tombs, candlesticks from medieval castles, inkwells once belonging to Charles Dickens, and dozens of Celtic stone carvings. Three of the four walls were covered with African masks, ancient scabbards, pieces of Italian frescoes, old rifles, mosaics from Pompeii, and dark Rembrandt-like paintings in gilded frames. Floor-to-ceiling bookshelves lined the fourth wall, holding hundreds of worn leather-bound books on archeology, painting, ancient art, and art history. The bottom shelf held a long row of thick three-ring binders, each one filled to the brim with plastic page-protectors holding photocopies of pages from obscure texts that Rose found especially intriguing.

Fiona's gaze darted back to the desk, noting the bottle of whiskey and sole empty glass sitting on it. Was this going to be some kind of celebration?

"Rose?" she called out, somewhat surprised that the elderly woman hadn't come out of the back room at the first sound of Fiona's arrival. Whatever she'd discovered in her research had her so excited that she didn't even want to discuss it over the phone. She'd practically ordered Fiona to show up at the end of the business day so they could talk in private. And she'd put out her vintage whiskey. According to the antique clock on the wall, it was two minutes past six.

Clearly, this was not a meeting Rose had forgotten, absentminded or not.

This time Fiona yelled louder… and waited. "Rose?"

Something about the silence was unnatural, and it totally creeped her out. She glanced instinctively behind her, not sure what she was expecting to see.

Nothing.

She'd been watching way too many crime dramas.

With a self-deprecating shake of her head, Fiona took a deep, steadying breath—one that ended up making things worse. Yes, her nostrils were accosted by the usual musty smell. Only this time that smell was mixed with another odor, one that was nauseatingly metallic.

The strange feeling slammed back full-force, accompanied by an innate sense of fear.

"Rose." This time Fiona said her name quietly, tentatively, moving forward as she did. She eased her way around the desk, reached the tables… and tripped. Looking down, she saw Rose's cane. Why was it there? Slowly, with an eerie sense of reluctance, she raised her head. And what she saw made her stop dead in her tracks, her hands flying to her face to stifle a scream.

At the back of the shop, maybe thirty feet away, Rose was lying, crumpled on the floor, her head against the marble hearth of the fireplace, a stream of blood seeping from beneath her skull and pooling all around her.

For a long instant, Fiona froze, just staring at her friend's oh-so-still body.

Then she acted. Grasping wildly at her purse, Fiona pulled out her iPhone and punched in 911.

"I'm at Fifty-seven Bedford Street," she told the emergency operator. "The owner of the shop is on the floor. There's blood pouring out from under her head." Tears welled up in Fiona's eyes and she forced out her next words. "She's not moving and it doesn't look like she's breathing. I think she's dead. Oh, God, I think she's dead."

Fiona sat numbly while the professionals did their jobs. Two uniformed officers arrived simultaneously with a beat cop who'd been three blocks away when the call came in. One of the officers immediately got on his radio and Fiona heard snippets: *bleeding profusely... we need bus... we need squad....*

EMS, Fiona thought idly. *And a detective squad.* At least that's who always showed up in TV police procedural shows.

Shortly, a city block of Bedford Street was taped off. The same officer who'd radioed in now made a phone call, providing more thorough details to his precinct and asking, "Who's catching tonight?"

EMS burst in. It took them little more than a moment. Rose was declared dead. They then backed off, attempting to not disturb the body further.

Two plainclothes detectives entered the scene, one man and one woman. From the woman's take-charge manner, Fiona assumed she was the catching detective tonight. Right behind them came a team of four other detectives. The take-charge woman scrutinized the scene for a few minutes, after which Fiona heard her call for Crime Scene and a medical examiner.

Why? Fiona wondered. *Why Crime Scene?*

Before her dazed, grief-stricken mind could process more, the woman approached her.

"I'm Detective Alvarez," she said in a calm, straightforward tone. "You're the person who made the 911 call…" She paused, waiting for something.

My name, Fiona thought stupidly. *She wants my name.*

Slowly, she raised her head and removed her hands, the heels of which she'd just pressed against her eye sockets. "Fiona," she whispered.

"Okay, Fiona. So you found the victim and called it in?"

A nod was all Fiona could muster.

Up close, the woman looked even more solid and authoritative, but she gave Fiona a compassionate look. "I'm going to need you to come down to the Sixth Precinct and answer some questions. It's just procedure. I know you're very upset right now, and I'm sorry about that. We'll do our best to make you comfortable and get you out of there as soon as possible."

Again, she paused.

Fiona forced herself to nod.

"Good. The squad car will take you to the precinct. I'll follow shortly to interview you."

Responding on cue, Fiona stood. Almost against her will, she turned her head and—for one brief instant—stared at the hideous sight of Rose's contorted body, now an impersonal object waiting to be examined and removed. The elderly woman's cane lay sideways near the chair, where Fiona had tripped over it. Fragments of glass were scattered around the cane with rivulets of whiskey interspersed among them.

Quickly averting her gaze, Fiona took a step and swayed on her feet. She steadied herself in time for one of the officers to come over and assist her to the car.

***

At the precinct, she was settled in a bare-bones interviewing room and offered coffee. Her stomach was in knots and she was trembling like a leaf. Coffee was the last thing she needed. In the end, she took a Sprite. No caffeine but plenty of sugar, which was necessary given how dizzy she felt. It was close to seven thirty, she hadn't eaten dinner, and the shock of finding Rose's body was taking its toll.

Detective Alvarez arrived forty-five minutes later. The hour and a half that followed was a Q and A blur.

Where were you coming from? What route did you take to the shop? Did you know this woman? For how long? How often do you go to her shop? Did you have an appointment? What was the nature of your business with her today? What time did you get there? How do you know it was that time? What do you remember seeing in the block or two before you got there? Are you familiar with her clientele? What family does she have? What's their contact information?

Fiona blinked at the last few questions. The only person she knew who might be able to supply all those details was Glenna. She herself hadn't a clue if Rose had family or close friends. She gave Detective Alvarez Glenna's information, hoping that Rose's assistant could help where she couldn't. Poor Glenna. Not only would she have to cope with the horrifying news of Rose's death and be subjected to a lengthy interview, but she'd have to personally reach out to all the numerous clients and colleagues who knew and loved her boss. There'd be a wake and a funeral to arrange. Fiona would share that responsibility with Glenna and any living next of kin. That much, at least, she could give to Rose.

Detective Alvarez was scribbling down Glenna's data. "I'll call her right away and find out where she is. What time does she regularly leave the shop?"

"Five thirty," Fiona replied woodenly. "I think she takes classes at NYU in the morning and works at Rose's shop until after closing time."

"Then she might very well be the last person to have seen the victim alive," the detective said. "Plus, she'll be familiar with the clients who visited and called today and she can give us a list of the victim's contacts. Hopefully, she'll also be able to supply us with the name of the next of kin."

Tears dampened Fiona's cheeks. "Glenna adores Rose. She's been with her for five years. Please be gentle when you tell her."

"I'll inform her in person, not on the phone. After that, I'll bring her in to be interviewed." The detective rose. "Thank you very much for your cooperation. I have your contact information if we need to talk to you again. Meanwhile, my partner will drive you home, or wherever you want to go."

Fiona stared at her for a long moment.

Home? Her roommate was out of town. And she couldn't bear to be alone with the horrifying images still flashing through her mind. She could go up to her parents' house, but she wasn't sure she could handle the emotional scene that would erupt.

She needed support, not hysteria.

Suddenly, she knew exactly where she wanted to go.

3

Ryan McKay's bed was in shambles—and so was he.

With a groan of pleasure, he rolled onto his back, thinking that nothing, not even penetrating a highly secure corporate firewall, could come close to the high he felt when he had Claire Hedgleigh under him.

Hot as hell, their connection was made more intense by the fact that they were polar opposites. Ryan was the tech king, the gym rat, the robotics expert. Claire was all about yoga and herbal tea and was, in her words, a *claircognizant*, which to Ryan meant some kind of a psychic, although Claire described it as just inherently knowing things with no tangible explanation as to how. Ryan had been a skeptic from day one, but since then, he'd seen Claire in action enough times to make total disbelief an impossibility.

They were colleagues at Forensic Instincts, a high-profile investigative company that boasted, in Ryan's opinion, the most awesome team members with a crazy number of skills to go around. Their success rate spoke for itself.

At work, Claire and Ryan argued about pretty much everything.

In bed, they were in total accord.

Which meant the past hour had been a roller coaster of pleasure.

Ryan raised the back of his head from the pillow just long enough to fold an arm beneath it. Claire didn't even do that much. She was now lying on her side, her arm draped across his chest, her breathing still erratic.

"I *was* pretty amazing, wasn't I," Ryan said, a statement not a question.

Claire's hand balled into a fist and she gave his chest a light punch. "Not bad. I'll give you an A-minus."

"What did I lose points for?"

"Lack of humility."

Ryan chuckled. "I'll keep that in mind for next time." He tugged at her arm, intending to pull her over him. "Which, by the way, is now."

He was startled when Claire's hand abruptly flattened against him, pushing lightly as she moved away and sat up. "No."

"No?" Ryan sat up, too, looking totally baffled. "Why not?"

"I'm not sure." Claire was already on her feet, pulling on her yoga clothes. "But something…" She gave a puzzled shake of her head. "We can't."

"What the hell do you mean, we can't? We just did."

"We can't… now."

"Why not now?" Ryan was throwing back the covers, fully intending to coax Claire back into bed.

Claire didn't give him time, nor did she answer his question. Leaving him gaping, she walked out of his bedroom, combing her fingers through her long, tangled blonde hair, somehow needing to make herself look presentable.

She realized she was heading for Ryan's front door.

Without pause, she flipped the lock and pulled open the door.

A stunning young woman of about her age, maybe a couple of years younger, was standing there, her finger poised to ring the bell. Tall, with long wavy black hair and intensely blue eyes, she could have been a model. She was in a visibly distressed state, although she looked startled to see Claire there, doing a double take as she gazed from Claire to the doorbell, then back to Claire again.

"Who are you?" the woman asked. "And how did you know I was out here?" Without waiting for an answer, she peered past Claire, scanning the all-purpose room that was the heart of Ryan's domain. Light on furnishings, devoid of people. Ryan was a minimalist—at least at home.

"I... I need to see Ryan right away." She started to step around Claire and into the apartment.

Reflexively, Claire blocked her way. The woman was a stranger—a very beautiful, very territorial stranger who was clearly tight with Ryan. Claire felt a surge of angry betrayal. She and Ryan might never have assigned a name to what they had, but they'd long since agreed they were exclusive. And now, still warm from his bed, she was standing face-to-face with this female who was obviously very much an existing factor in his life.

What the hell?

She took a few deep, cleansing breaths—and abruptly pinpricks of insight began sparking in her mind, growing in number as they interspersed with her anger. They expanded into a kaleidoscope of contradictions, descending on her in a heavy cascade, awareness clashing with her jealousy.

She had to stem the jealousy and let the energy flow. Something was going on here, something she hadn't been able to connect with because of her own emotional involvement. Forcibly, she shut down her hurt and channeled her insights. This woman needed to be here. She emanated an aura of intense upset and pain. And, yes, she had a powerful connection to Ryan, but it was one that bound her to him in a way that had nothing to do with romance or sex.

"Please," the young woman reiterated, her voice quavering. "I have to see Ryan."

The connection snapped into place, and it was Claire's turn to do a double take. Stunned though she was, she knew that, whatever its purpose, this visit was imperative.

Without further thought, she stepped aside and let the woman enter. "I'm Claire," she said, answering the original question. "And you are?"

"Fiona." A single word, one that seemed to require no explanation. Yet, after looking at Claire and recognizing, on some dazed level, that an explanation was needed, she provided one. "I'm Ryan's—"

"Fee?" Ryan emerged from the bedroom, wearing sweats and looking surprised and irritated. "What are you doing here? You're supposed to call first if you plan on dropping by, remember?"

Nodding, Fiona swallowed hard and dragged a hand through her hair. "I'm sorry. It's just that something happened and I needed to see you." She looked back at Claire, unnerved in a way that had nothing to do with her original shock by Claire's foreknowledge of her arrival. She seemed to have totally forgotten about that in the wake of something far more significant. "I apologize for interrupting," she said in a wooden tone—an apology uttered almost on autopilot.

Ryan seemed oblivious to the fact that Fiona was totally freaked out. He was watching Claire, quickly telling her what he thought she needed to know. "Fee is—"

"Your sister," Claire finished for him. Even if she hadn't felt it in her bones, she'd know it was true. Seeing them together, the resemblance was as striking as the realization. Those same drop-dead Black Irish good looks. She hadn't even known Ryan *had* a sister, much less that she lived in New York. But even though Claire had a million questions, now was not the time to ask them.

She gestured at the cushioned sofa facing the screen of Ryan's prized 4K OLED TV, which was mounted on the opposite wall. "Please. Come sit down."

Fiona needed no second invitation. She made her way through the all-purpose living-dining-workroom. Other than the two-tiered coffee table that stood between the TV and the sofa and a ginormous workstation packed with tech equipment, the only other piece of furniture was Ryan's pride and joy: a large homemade table, built of two oak casks that had once contained aged whiskey and an old mahogany door placed across them. The uneven, pock-marked surface always presented a challenge when trying to balance a glass on top. Ryan got a huge chuckle watching guests struggle and then give up as their glasses teetered across the surface, spilling beverages in their wake. But that table had served for years as Ryan's office desk, workbench, and dining table. And he wasn't about to trade it in for some IKEA thing made of sawdust and glue.

"Would you like something to drink?" Claire asked.

A faint smile touched the corners of Fiona's lips as she sank down into the cushy sofa. "I hate beer. So I guess water."

"There's Chardonnay," Claire replied, glad she kept a bottle here for herself. "I'll get you a glass."

As she headed into the tiny kitchenette, she heard Fiona start to cry. Stopping in her tracks, she turned. Tears were gliding down the girl's cheeks—tears she dashed away with shaking hands. As much as Claire wanted to go to her, she knew that wasn't what, or who, Fiona needed right then. She also knew that the person she did need was about to get the picture.

Sure enough, this time Ryan got it.

"Fee? What is it?" He crossed over and squatted down in front of her. "Are you hurt?" He was starting to sound alarmed. "Did someone do something to you?"

She shook her head. "Nothing like that. I just… I just…" Her jaw set and she got herself under control. "A little while ago, I found a dead body. There was so much blood, and… Ryan, it was horrible. There were cops and emergency responders and detectives who called for Crime Scene and a medical examiner. They said it was strictly procedural. Then they took me down to the precinct and asked me a million questions and… I kind of freaked out. So as soon as I could, I ran to my big brother. Pretty lame, I guess. It's just that you work for a place that deals with this stuff.

And I..." The bravado disappeared as quickly as it had come, and Fiona began openly weeping. "I didn't know what else to do."

"You found a dead...? *Shit.*" Ryan reached over and put his arms around her, pulling her closer and pressing her head to his shoulder. "Hey, it's okay now. I'm here. Tell me what happened."

Very quietly, Claire reappeared, handing Fiona her wine. "I'll take off now so the two of you can talk."

"No." Fiona drew back and shook her head. "Please stay. I didn't mean to screw up your evening." She accepted the glass and took a sip, her trembling having subsided with Ryan's presence. Abruptly, her brows went up. "Now I know why you look familiar. I saw your photo on the Forensic Instincts website. You're the"—she paused, searching for the word—"claircognizant."

"I guess your resemblance to Ryan ends at the physical." Claire strove for a drop of levity to ease what this poor young woman was going through. "He still hasn't memorized that term."

Thankfully, Fiona gave a small laugh. "I'm not surprised. My brother's not the metaphysical type. He still thinks that if a tree falls in the woods and he didn't hear it, the standard question is irrelevant; it still fell." She patted the cushion beside her. "I'd really like it if you stayed. Maybe you'll pick up some positive energy that will tell me she didn't suffer. I could really use that."

"She," Ryan repeated as Claire sat down. "So this dead body was a woman?"

"She wasn't 'this dead body,'" Fiona corrected. "She was Rose Flaherty, an antiquities expert I've worked with since college. She was my professional go-to source, more a mentor than a colleague. I had an appointment to meet with her. When I got to her antique shop, she was lying in a pool of her own blood." A shudder. "I knew she was dead. She was so, so... still. Unnaturally so."

"That's horrifying." Claire brushed her fingers across Fiona's cold hand—and flashes of darkness slammed through Claire's head. "So you knew Rose well. That makes this experience even harder. Walking into that kind of scene—a frail and elderly woman, a fatal head injury, that amount of blood—of course you're a wreck."

Ryan picked up on the new details Claire had provided, and he addressed them with his sister. "I take it that Rose Flaherty was old and that she died by hitting her head on the floor."

"The fireplace hearth," Fiona replied, visibly impressed by Claire's awareness. "And, yes, she was nearing eighty. But there was still so much life left in her. This shouldn't have happened. I don't know why it did. She was using her cane."

"Was it broken?"

"No. It was just lying there. I tripped over it right before I found her. She must have taken a misstep. The whole thing makes me ill."

"She didn't suffer," Claire said quietly. "She died on impact."

Fiona looked relieved.

Claire wasn't. From the small contact she'd made with Fiona's hand, she'd been besieged by heightened images and feelings—Rose backing away from danger... the icy sense of her sheer terror... and the agonizing pain from the impact of her head striking the hearth. Then... nothing. A fall? Yes. But an accident? Definitely not. Any more than it had been an accident that Crime Scene was called and that Fiona had been grilled with so many questions.

Claire didn't doubt that Ryan was thinking similarly, even if he arrived there by different means. But like her, he knew that now was not the time to drop the bomb on Fiona. She'd had enough of a shock for one day. But Claire planned to talk frankly with him as soon as she could get him alone.

"I called 911," Fiona was saying. "And the whole world descended. I was driven to the precinct and I answered all the detective's dozens of questions. I doubt I gave her anything worthwhile. I didn't see Rose fall and I was such a mess that all I could do was give stilted answers and cry. Poor Glenna, her assistant. I have to call her later, since I'm sure she'll be a wreck. And I want to help with the preparations for the wake and the funeral." Fiona broke off, shaking her head. "I can't believe I'm saying all this. I can't believe Rose is gone."

She picked up her glass of wine, pausing to stare vacantly at it. "There was a splintered glass on the floor," she murmured, "and some of Rose's prized whiskey was splattered around it. She'd put out a second glass, clearly for me. That bottle was worth a fortune and she only took it out on special occasions. She was obviously waiting for us to celebrate something. Now I'll never know what."

Ryan's brows knit in question. "Was she a drinker? Could that have dulled her senses?" His question was targeted, trying to determine if Rose had been in any condition to struggle. But he asked it offhandedly, so that it didn't raise any red flags for Fiona.

"Absolutely not," Fiona replied emphatically. "She never drank. That's why the whiskey was so special. Not just because of its price tag but because of its significance. Like I said, it was for celebrating huge successes."

"You don't mean monetary successes, do you?" Claire asked.

Again, Fiona shook her head. "Money wasn't Rose's thing. She was all about connecting the right piece with the right person, or coming up with incredible findings in her research."

"And she was researching something for you."

"The background and significance of a specific tapestry. The largest of thirteen, eleven of which I found in my mom's memory box."

Again, Claire placed a gentle hand on Fiona's arm, stopping her from going on. Ryan's sister was exhausted and still in shock. There was a long story about to come out. And there'd be plenty of time for discussion later.

The instant she touched Fiona's arm, Claire was once again besieged by an onslaught of painful auras—auras she was determined to put on hold. She shifted her hand and the feelings were exacerbated by her contact with a thick, hard object. She looked down, her eyes widening in awe at the breathtaking, and obviously uber-expensive, bracelet Fiona wore.

It was a wide, hammered gold cuff bracelet with a Celtic knot design around it in a three-dimensional raised pattern. Between each knot was a tiny round emerald, the color of the green gemstones against the bright gold striking and unforgettable.

"What a stunning bracelet," Claire said.

"Thank you." Fiona smiled. "It's one of my high-end pieces that's part of my new collection—Light and Shadows. It's twenty-two-karat gold. I had to sell off a lot of my other gold pieces in order to afford making it, but it was worth every cent."

Claire's brows drew together in question.

"Oh, sorry. Judging from your earlier reaction, it's clear you didn't know I existed. So how would you know what I do?" Another pointed glare at Ryan. "I make jewelry. I'm a goldsmith, as well. And I specialize in Celtic design with a contemporary twist." She gave a light shake of her wrist. "For example, for this I used an ancient technique called chasing and repoussé. I won't bore you with the details. But the combination of metals and techniques I use would probably not be combined in ancient times. I also stylize the pieces to make them more appealing to today's audience."

"I'm totally blown away." Claire was studying the design more closely. "I recognize the Celtic knots. As for the rest—you're unbe-lievably talented."

"Thank you." Fiona looked flattered—and wiped out. "I try."

"Why don't you lie down?" Claire suggested. "It's almost ten. Have you eaten?"

Fiona shook her head.

"Put your head down for a while. I'll order some takeout in an hour or so and wake you when it gets here. We can talk while we eat."

"That would be great." Relief and gratitude flashed across Fiona's face. "I've been flying on adrenaline for hours." She slumped back against the cushions. "I think I'm about to crash."

"Is the sofa okay?" Ryan asked, looking like a hopeful puppy.

A twinkle of amusement lit Fiona's eyes, and she was the spitting image of Ryan at that moment.

"Why the sofa?" Fiona asked, her expression the picture of innocence. "Is the bed wrecked?"

Ryan's eyes narrowed. "Not funny."

"But true. I really did interrupt, big-time, didn't I?"

"Actually, yeah, you did." Ryan went to the hall closet and returned to toss her a blanket. "But I forgive you. Extenuating circumstances." Reflexively, he glanced toward his bedroom, visibly remembering what had been going on before Fiona arrived.

The gesture did not go unnoticed.

Fiona's gaze slid from her brother to Claire and back again, sizing things up with a woman's intuition and a mixture of surprise and curiosity. "Why didn't you tell me you had a girlfriend? As in *singular*?"

Claire inclined her head in Ryan's direction, wondering how he was going to respond. He and she had never assigned an official label to what they had. And that tidbit aside, she had the same question about radio silence that Fiona did.

She spoke up, adding her voice to Fiona's. "And while we're at it, why didn't you ever mention you had a sister?"

Ryan shot each of them an aggravated look. "I didn't realize I had to report in. Fine. Fiona, I have a girlfriend, as in singular. Claire, I have a sister, as in family. And two brothers, too, while we're at it. Anything else either of you needs to know about my life?"

Both women were reeling. Claire from the *girlfriend* word and Fiona from the emotionally charged reaction.

"Wow," Fiona said, recovering first. "This really is a first. Ryan McKay with a serious girlfriend. Should I tell Mom to set an extra place setting at our next family dinner?"

"I'm not laughing, Fee," Ryan said in a warning tone. "I feel bad about what you went through, so I'm being tolerant. But keep prying and I might toss you out. And don't even think about mentioning this to Mom."

"My lips are sealed," Fiona replied, not looking the least bit worried.

She did, however, back off, more, Claire suspected, out of fatigue than out of being bested. No, Claire was quite sure that Fiona McKay gave as good as she got.

On a yawn, Fiona settled herself on the couch and tucked the blanket around her. "Just give me an hour before you order the food. I probably won't be able to sleep anyway."

Thirty seconds later, she was out cold.

4

"Poor kid," Ryan muttered, his underlying affection for his younger sister blatantly obvious, despite his best intentions to act otherwise. "Finding a corpse is something no one should have to go through. And the rest of it—it hasn't sunken in yet. But when the shock fades, it will."

Claire gestured toward the bedroom. "I need to talk to you alone," she said quietly. "And I do mean *talk*."

Ryan sighed. "Yeah, I kind of assumed that's what you meant. Rain check?"

"Many rain checks."

A corner of his mouth lifted. "Then talk time it is."

They went inside the bedroom and shut the door.

Ryan propped a hip against the wall, his gaze no longer playful. "You realize Rose Flaherty was murdered. There was nothing 'simply procedural' about the handling of her death."

"Yes. I know." Claire was moving restlessly around the room. "Listening to Fiona and then touching her hand… I'm getting all kinds of images. Rose's cane wasn't next to her body; Fiona tripped over it halfway across the shop. And Rose wasn't just shoved. There was a struggle—a struggle over something. I don't know what. The position of the body, with one hand out as if she were reaching for something or pushing something or someone away… not to mention the contusions on the back of her head rather than on the side or the front..." Claire waved a frustrated hand in the air. "I realize I'm babbling."

"You're not babbling. You're just combining things I know with things I don't. What else?"

"I'm not sure. I..." Claire broke off, a faraway look coming into her eyes—a look Ryan was beginning to know well. "The broken whiskey glass and its contents were in the middle of the room," Claire murmured. "Rose dropped it before she reached the fireplace. That's as telling as the location of the cane. If she'd just stumbled at the hearth, the glass would have shattered right there and the cane would have toppled nearby. Neither of those things happened. Both the pieces of glass and the cane were a good distance from the body."

"Fiona never said where on the floor they found the pieces of glass. And she certainly wouldn't know the location of the head contusions." Ryan paused. "You're sure?"

Now clear-eyed, Claire met his gaze. "Yes. I'm also sure that had Fiona arrived twenty minutes earlier..."

"She would have walked in on the murder—and the murderer."

Claire nodded, looking even more troubled than she had a few minutes ago. "There's more, Ryan."

He tensed. "Go on."

"When I touched Fiona's hand, I got a strong aura of darkness. The feeling intensified when I came in contact with her bracelet. I'm not sure if that darkness was rooted in the emotional experience she just went through, the pain of what the next few days will bring... or something more."

"More? What kind of more?"

Claire gave a helpless shrug. "Again, I don't know. I'm just... unsettled. Something doesn't feel right. Fiona had a six o'clock appointment with Rose. She arrived on time. Rose's assistant left at five thirty. That provided a convenient half-hour time frame when Rose was alone. I don't see that as a coincidence."

"If you're saying that the killer kept track of Rose's daily routine, and maybe even knew her appointment schedule—that's a reach. We're talking about things like surveillance, possibly even phone tapping."

"I know. It's farfetched. But I still can't shake this feeling. And if it has merit, then the killer might have known that Rose's six o'clock appointment was with Fiona."

"And if he did?" Ryan frowned. "How is that significant?"

"Let's just say it creeps me out."

"What difference would it make who Rose was meeting? Unless… Are you saying that Fiona is in some kind of danger?"

"I can't see why she would be. I don't know what to attribute this feeling to." Claire dragged her fingers through her hair. "I wish I could get inside the antique shop. That way, I might be able to pick up on something more substantial—something that would put our minds at ease."

"Not happening and you know it." Ryan stopped her right there. "The shop will be taped off and designated a crime scene."

Claire nodded. "Obviously, the detectives saw the location of the glass shards and the cane, and they drew the same conclusion I did. I'm sure they've also made note of the body position. Between the forensics and the ME's report, Rose's death will be labelled a homicide."

"And that means you're not getting anywhere near the shop until Crime Scene releases it." Ryan rubbed his chin thoughtfully. "The only good thing is that the police have opened a case file on this by now. So I can hack into the system and get eyes on it. This way, I'll know whatever they know."

Claire nodded, not even questioning Ryan's abilities to do just that.

"In the meantime," she asked, "how much do you want to tell Fiona?"

"Good question." Ryan blew out a breath. "She'll realize on her own that Rose's death was no accident. But the rest? Logic dictates that she's a grown woman and needs to be aware of your insights right away."

"Logic does dictate that," Claire agreed. A faint smile touched her lips. "But—heaven forbid—emotion dictates something else. She's your kid sister. You want to protect her."

"Yeah."

This time Claire laughed. "You don't have to sound like you're confessing to a crime. It's okay to care about someone and to admit it. It doesn't make you any less of the bionic man you are."

Ryan shot her a look. "Very funny."

"How many years younger than you is Fiona?"

"Four. My brother Nolan is the oldest. Garret came along two years later, followed by me in a record eleven months. Then Fee."

"And I take it that all of you live somewhere in the state, including your parents?"

By now, Ryan was moving around restlessly and looking annoyed. "You're the claircognizant. You tell me."

"I have no idea." Claire ignored Ryan's defensiveness. She got it, just as she got him—more than he realized. "I'm not a walking crystal ball. But the way Fiona referred to setting a place at your parents' dinner table, I got the feeling that the table was a large one and that family dinners didn't happen only on holidays."

"Okay, fine." Ryan waved his hands in frustration. "My parents live in the Bronx—Woodlawn. My father's a teacher at the Bronx School of Science. His IQ is off the charts, and he's heavily into technology. My mom's a homemaker—literally. She invented the word *family*. If she had her way, we'd have Sunday dinner every week, probably every day of the week. My brothers share a law practice in White Plains. You know about Fee. Anything else?"

Claire digested the information she'd just reluctantly been given. It wasn't just that Ryan was so private. There was something more going on here.

It was something that echoed inside Claire, something she herself had felt not so many years ago.

"Your father's disappointment hurt," she said quietly. "That's why you're so reluctant to discuss your family. You're distancing yourself emotionally."

Ryan arched a brow. "I thought you said you weren't a walking crystal ball."

"I'm not. I've just felt that hurt myself. You've read my dossier. You know I come from Grosse Point, and how affluent and socially prominent my parents are. You can guess how they reacted to my... gift. It had no place in their world. So I left. I haven't been back since, nor have I received an invitation. But, in my case, my family was never close. Yours is pretty tight."

"I guess." Ryan shrugged.

"It sounds like you take after your dad."

"Nope. He's all about academics. As opposed to me, who dropped out of MIT after two years. You'd think I committed a cardinal sin. And, yeah, before you continue with your insights, he and I have gotten past it. Sort of. Now can we stop with the touchy-feely stuff?"

"Okay." Claire kept a straight face as she added, "But you can't blame me for asking a few personal questions. After all, I am your girlfriend. As in *singular*."

To her surprise, Ryan grinned. "Damn lucky, aren't you?"

"I guess. Given how good you are in bed. But not as lucky as you are."

"Because?" Ryan prompted.

Interesting. He obviously needed this affirmation, too.

Claire gave it to him. "Because if I'm your girlfriend, that makes you my boyfriend. Pretty scary, saying this out loud, isn't it?"

"It didn't freak me out as much as I thought it would."

"Same here. But you'd better not become a slacker in bed. Because if you do, then all bets are off."

Ryan threw back his head in laughter. "Now *that's* never going to happen. It's you who'd better keep up your stamina. Speaking of which..." His gaze flickered to the bed.

"Forget it." Claire gave an adamant shake of her head. "Not until we're alone. And I don't think Fiona is in any condition to go home tonight. Where does she live?"

"SoHo. She shares a townhouse with a friend she met in college. Her friend's family is loaded. They bought the place a bunch of years ago as an investment. It sure paid off. That area is gold."

"It's also a long subway ride away," Claire reminded him. "You might still be in Brooklyn, but Park Slope is farther away than DUMBO."

Claire was right. DUMBO—short for Down Under the Manhattan Bridge Overpass—was a spit throw to Manhattan. Ryan had lived there until six months ago, when he'd started complaining that the area had become too upscale for his tastes. Park Slope wasn't exactly cheap, but Ryan had found an apartment that was affordable because it was on a main drag and directly over a laundromat. The entire FI team had helped him move.

"Yeah, you're right." Ryan nodded. "She'll have to crash here. If she wanted to go to my parents' place, she would have gone there first. My guess is she needed a level head. That's not my mom. She's going to be a wreck when she hears about this. She'll probably be pressuring Fee to move home for a while. And even though Fee is a mess right now, she's pretty independent. So that's not going to fly." He paused, weighing out a decision.

"Let her call them herself," Claire advised him. "And not tonight. Let her eat and talk as she needs to. She'll call your parents in the morning."

"Thanks for letting me off the hook."

"I wasn't. I just think we should allow your sister to take the lead in her own life." A pause. "Which means we have to get into the real circumstances of Rose's death tonight, as soon as we wake Fiona up. Because we both know the detectives will be descending on her tomorrow to see if she's remembered anything else."

"Yeah. Great. This is going to be tough."

"I know." Claire chewed her lip. "Let's leave out any conjectures about her being in danger. I have no basis for that theory and there's no point in scaring her unless there's a reason to."

"Agreed."

Claire kept chewing her lip. "I'm not sure if I should stay or leave."

"Leave?" Ryan nearly choked on the word. "You can't leave. Fee likes you. You calm her down, just like you do everyone else. And I'm no good at this stuff. You are."

Claire didn't dispute that. "Fine, I'll stay, but only if you give up the idea of anything happening in this room tonight other than sleeping. Otherwise, you're taking the sofa and Fiona can share the bed with me."

A corner of Ryan's mouth lifted. "I can keep my hands to myself—for one night," he clarified. Abruptly, his grin faded. "Thanks for doing this, Claire."

"You're very welcome." Claire took out her iPhone. "Now let's decide what we're eating."

***

Niall Dempsey strode down Third Avenue and pulled open the door to Kelly's Irish Tavern, the 1870s pub where his old life still existed, if only in its shadows. The place was as authentic as they came, right down to the dust on the floor and the distressed wooden booths and bar counter—not to mention the old-world whiskey and the best shepherd's pie in the city.

Niall didn't pause for food or drink. The coded phone call he'd received had set off alarm bells in his head. Ignoring the crowd, he stalked across the room, turning only to signal Donald Kelly, the sixty-five-year-old bar owner who was his connection to whatever he needed, or had needed, since coming over from Ireland as a twenty-year-old, thirty-five years ago.

Donald nodded, tossing down his towel and instructing his young bartender to handle things alone. The place was busy but not unmanageable. Most of the patrons were eating as well as drinking, so the tables were more filled up than the barstools, and Donald had plenty of servers to wait on the customers. Confident that things were well under control, he quickly followed Niall, who'd never broken stride, to the back room of the pub.

"Shut the door," Niall said, his Irish brogue remaining strong even after all these years in the US. Some things you couldn't erase. Nor did he want to. Niall was proud of his Irish birth and of his cause.

His request was reflexive but unnecessary, given that Donald was already doing just that. He was a pro at this, his life choices dictating that most meetings he had were conducted in private.

Donald knew everything there was to know about Niall Dempsey—or Sean Donovan, as he'd once been. Born in the town of Lurgan, County Armagh, Northern Ireland, Sean had been a troublemaker of a lad, fascinated rather than intimidated by the parades of loyalists who marched through the streets, their fifes and drums a prelude to the skirmishes in the streets. By ten years old, he'd be sneaking out to watch what looked to him like action movies—ones he was itching to be a part of, although he had no understanding yet of the Troubles—a turbulent time in history in which the Irish were bitterly fighting the British for a unified Ireland—nor did he have any real idea of who the IRA or the Ulster Defence Association were.

His mother was having none of his shenanigans. She scooped up her two sons—Sean and his brother, Kevin—and moved to Dundalk, County Louth, in the Republic of Ireland, where Sean wouldn't be exposed to the burgeoning violence taking place in the North.

But his mother's efforts hadn't squelched his interest. He'd met Peter Walsh, his best mate, in Dundalk, when they were barely into their teens. Both of them restless, they smoked stolen cigarettes and looked for more exciting diversions. One evening, they rode their bikes down to the docks and discovered a stash of stolen Irish whiskey that some dockworkers who loaded containers headed for the US had helped themselves to and hidden in an old rusty barrel behind a trash can. The two lads made good use of their find, snatching a few bottles and climbing into one of the cars that were packed like sardines at the docks, where they drank their fill and laughed about stealing what had already been stolen. Those trips became a weekly ritual for years, inspiring a strong bond and shared secrets.

One night, Peter confided in Sean that his father, Gerard, was not a mere fisherman, but an active member of the Provisional IRA, or Provos, traveling frequently to the North to act as a getaway driver for IRA assassins. At fifteen, Peter himself, who was already a nimble car thief, was recruited via his father, and began stealing cars for the Provos—cars that would be transporting weapons to the units in the North.

Sean had felt a surge of nationalistic pride, hearing the stories Peter told about his fight for a unified Ireland. He'd prevailed upon his friend to bring him into the fold. And Peter had accomplished just that. By the time he was sixteen, Sean was part of the IRA, and the entire course of his life changed.

He started out in a six-man Active Service Unit, building bombs in Peter's basement. After a few scary close calls—the last one nearly blowing off his hand—he was ready for a change. His talents as a marksman had been evidenced during training and were well known by the IRA. So were his smarts. He'd been moved to another unit, this time working solo as a sniper. So successful was he that he developed a reputation as the most feared IRA sniper, lethal with his Barrett .50 caliber sniper rifle, anonymous and known only as Silver Finger. No one but the highest-level IRA agents knew his real identity—them and his brother, Kevin, who'd joined up with him as a spotter on his hits.

He was at the height of his glory when, abruptly, his world fell apart. Somewhere among them existed an allegedly loyal member of

the IRA, an operative whose job it was to interrogate potential trai-
tors—duplicitous bastards who informed on their own IRA brothers
to the Royal Ulster Constabulary. It turned out that he was a traitor
to the IRA, using his position as an enforcer to become an RUC
asset. Other informants like him existed, touts as they were called,
but this one, known only as Cobra, was inarguably connected at the
highest levels. Somehow he figured out Sean's identity and reported
it to the RUC, together with the details of his upcoming assignment
to drive North and assassinate a high-ranking British soldier. Kevin
had been with him on that mission, with Sean lying prone in a Pinto
hatchback with the hatch rigged to optimize his ability to take the
single kill shot and Kevin acting as both driver and spotter. Through
binoculars, Kevin studied their target for his older brother, preparing
to tell him precisely when to take the shot. But before he could, they'd
heard the approaching sounds of the RUC helicopters and frantically
abandoned their mission, with Kevin leaping into the car and peeling
off, desperate to save their lives.

Bullets had flown from the skies, and Sean had returned fire—until
he heard Kevin let out an agonized groan, collapsing at the wheel. Sean
had jumped forward from the back and leapt into the passenger seat,
leaning over to steer the car off the road.

They'd thudded through the mud and Sean had used his left foot
to brake as hard as he could.

The car came to a halt.

He'd grabbed hold of Kevin, who was bleeding profusely from the
head and chest. Sean tore off his own shirt, which was blood-stained
from the bullets that had grazed his neck and arms, and pressed it tight
against Kevin's chest, desperate to stem the bleeding. Kevin muttered
something unintelligible and then slumped over, utterly still.

He died in Sean's arms.

It was only then that Sean felt the stabbing pain in his right calf
and realized that he, too, had been hit. He'd barely had time to transfer

the shirt to press against his own wound when the whirring sound of approaching RUC helicopters reached his ears.

With one last look at his brother, he flung down his shirt and bailed—abandoning the car. He ducked down and hobbled into a housing estate, staying between buildings, where the helicopters couldn't reach him. In one of those buildings was a trusted family he'd known since childhood. They took him in without asking questions and did a makeshift job of patching him up. He'd made a coded phone call from there, reaching out to the high-level contact who'd given him this job. Soon after, a delivery truck arrived, presumably dropping something off, but instead extracting Sean from hiding.

He was taken to a safe house, where he was tended to by an IRA medic, fed, and kept for a week while plans were put into place.

He knew he was a marked man. He couldn't even attend his own brother's funeral. He'd never gotten over that.

The IRA machine moved quickly. Without a word to anyone, Sean vanished. He was put on a fishing trawler, disguised as a low-level crew member—a lad who washed dishes and kept to himself. He jumped ship in Newfoundland, having memorized what he'd been given: his contact source's name, the vehicle he'd be driving, and the necessary code phrase he'd use to confirm his identity. Donald met up with him at the border and drove him into New York State by way of the Mohawk Nation at Akwesasne, where it was easy to cross over without dealing with Customs.

They'd made the eight-hour drive to Donald's summer house in Long Island, where Sean was told to remain for the time it took for Donald to set up a whole new identity for him. He took Sean's picture for a passport photo, and a few days later, he returned, this time with a birth certificate, social security card, driver's license, passport, and union card—all made out in the name of Niall Dempsey.

Niall's new life had begun, and Donald, the ultimate IRA-sympathizer, had been his facilitator ever since.

He'd used Niall's carpentry skills to get him a union job framing houses at a decent-sized construction company, and Niall had jumped into his new life with both feet. He'd worked tirelessly, with great skill and care—simultaneously moonlighting, doing side projects until he managed to accumulate enough money and referrals to start his own business doing both building and remodeling. The business grew into a substantial construction company. Then the real estate boom happened in the early 2000s, and his business exploded into an enormous entity, making him a millionaire.

Niall never forgot his roots, though, always making sure to hand over large amounts of money to Donald so he could send the funds on to the Provos back in Ireland. And he still carried a rage inside him that ate him alive. He knew from Donald that it was that bastard Cobra who'd made him and resulted in Kevin's death. He'd sworn on his brother's soul that he would find Cobra and put a bullet through him, watching as the bastard's head exploded like a pumpkin. Niall had hired international resources, all of whom were invested in figuring out Cobra's true identity and tracking him down. Last word was that the pig had left Ireland and was living under an assumed identity, but where was still unknown. Niall intended to find out, exacting his revenge on the traitor who'd killed his brother and betrayed them and their cause.

But today's visit to Kelly's wasn't about his past. It was very much about his present.

Donald sat down with Niall at the large booth at the far end of the room.

Niall folded his hands in front of him in a death grip. "I'm here. Tell me what went wrong."

Donald looked ripping pissed. "Our guys. That's what went wrong."

By *our guys*, Donald was referring to the recruited twentysome-things from Queens who had been working for Niall via Donald since their mid-teens. Niall never met with his hires in person. It was a risk he couldn't take. Donald did all the middle-manning.

"What did they do?" Niall looked coiled to strike.

"According to them? They got to the shop at the scheduled time. The old woman was lying on the floor in the back, blood everywhere. They took off."

Niall swore under his breath. "In other words, they screwed up and are lying to cover their asses. Did you get them to talk?"

Donald shook his head. "They were too scared of what you'd do to them. They cried, pissed their pants, and swore on their mothers' graves that they were telling me the truth."

"Do you think they got any useful information out of the old woman before things went wrong?"

"Not a prayer. Not after my handiwork. With broken fingers and kneecaps and a gun pointed to their heads, they would have given up anything they had."

"Then get rid of them."

"Already done. We'll have new guys in place by tomorrow."

Niall acknowledged that with a nod, although the disposal of their hires was the least of his concerns. "So we're not sure she's dead."

"I'm waiting for a call. We'll get answers."

"We'd fucking well better. Because if she's alive, she's telling the police what really went on and what the interrogating was all about. That can't happen."

His words were interrupted by the buzz of Donald's private cell phone—a number few people had.

Donald glanced down. "This is the call I've been waiting for." He pressed the accept button and held the phone up to his ear. "Yeah." A long pause, during which time Niall studied his expression. It never changed. "Before or after the cops showed up?" Another pause. "Okay. Stay close to the investigation."

Donald disconnected the call. "Rose Flaherty was DOA. Never talked."

"Is the death being ruled accidental?"

"Suspicious. After Crime Scene finishes, it'll probably move up to homicide. Our guys weren't trained killers. There's bound to be evidence they didn't clean up."

"Which means there'll be a full-scale investigation. Shit!" Niall slammed his fist on the table, wincing at the pain caused by the scars on his off hand. The markings had faded into dull white patches, but they still ached after all these years, as did the swollen joints on his fingers. "Now what?"

"Now nothing. You wait for the news to officially reach you. You pay your respects. You find another way to get what you're after—a careful way. The NYPD can't get you in their sights. Let me stay on top of things. I'll call you when I hear something. Now go home and get some sleep."

5

Fiona, Ryan, and Claire gathered around the coffee table, cartons of Chinese takeout covering most of the glass surface. Claire had over-ordered and she knew it, but Fiona was badly depleted and needed to eat. The more food options, the better.

Sure enough, despite being traumatized, Fiona gobbled up three-quarters of an order of sesame chicken, along with a bowl of egg drop soup and a spring roll. Whatever she left on her plate, Ryan polished off, together with most of the other dishes, automatically leaving the vegetarian fried rice and steamed vegetable dumplings for Claire.

With a sigh, Fiona leaned back against the sofa. "I'm about to explode."

"Yeah, well, you swallowed a ton of food without breathing," Ryan said.

"Coming from the guy who ate everything that wasn't moving," his sister retorted. "Too bad the cartons aren't edible."

"Have you checked?"

"I thought I'd leave that to you. You're the vacuum cleaner, not me."

"I work out for two hours every morning. When was the last time you saw a gym?"

"I run five miles a day. Gyms cost money."

"I'll pay for your membership. You'll crap out after two visits."

"I'll take you up on that. Give me six months. Then we'll do a circuit together to find out who's in better shape." Fiona paused, her eyes twinkling. "Although you're obviously getting extra workouts at home." A quick sideways glance at Claire. "Sorry."

"No you're not," Ryan countered. "Sleeping and eating just restored you to your usual nosy, pain-in-the-ass self."

"And proud of it."

"Don't be. My personal life is off-limits."

"Since when?"

"Since now."

Claire took another bite of her vegetable dumpling, utterly fascinated by the easygoing insults flying between siblings. She was used to Ryan's banter at work. But this was different. The affection underlying his and Fiona's back-and-forth was a whole new realm for her. And not just because she herself was an only child. But because this was a softer side of Ryan she rarely saw, other than in unguarded moments with her.

"I really am sorry, Claire," Fiona was saying. "That just kind of slipped out. Although it's the first time Ryan's cared. He must be in pretty deep."

"Fee." There was a warning note in Ryan's voice.

"Okay, okay." Fiona held up both hands, visibly trying to control her laughter. "I'll respect your boundaries."

"Yeah. Right."

"Don't worry about it," Claire replied, stepping in like monkey-in-the-middle. "I've long since abandoned any hope of staying the private person that I am. Nothing is off-limits when it comes to Ryan."

Fiona's brows rose and she might as well have said *until now*. But she refrained from giving voice to her thoughts. To the contrary, she fell silent for a moment, her expression saying that her mind had gone in a different direction, one that was devoid of any levity.

"Did you call Mom and Dad?" she asked Ryan.

He shook his head, all banter having faded at his end, as well. "I wasn't sure if you wanted to do it yourself or if you really wanted them to know right away. I figured tomorrow morning was soon enough."

"Thanks." Fiona was clearly relieved. "I wouldn't have been able to handle a huge emotional scene and a hundred questions, not tonight. You and Claire have been great, exactly what I needed to get me through this." A quick glance at the time on her iPhone. "Which reminds me, I'd better head for the subway so I can let you guys have the rest of your night."

"Nope." Ryan shook his head. "You're staying here. It's already midnight. And I don't want you to be alone, not after witnessing what you did."

Surprisingly, Fiona didn't argue. "Thanks, Ry. I'll just hang out on the sofa and take off first thing tomorrow."

"Let's wait and see about the timing. I want to be with you when the detectives follow up."

"Follow up?" Fiona rubbed her fingers nervously against the sofa cushion. "Why would they? I told them everything I could. I…" She stopped, her face white as she stated the obvious. "I accepted what Detective Alvarez said because I wanted to. But I can't block out the truth no matter how horrifying it is. They're investigating Rose's death as a potential homicide, aren't they?"

Claire and Ryan exchanged glances, and Ryan nodded, gesturing for Claire to take the lead.

"We believe so, yes," Claire replied. In a calm, soothing voice, she went on to fill Fiona in on the insights she'd had: the location of the glass shards and splashes of whiskey, as well as the cane. The position of the body and the placement of the contusions. And lastly, the struggle Rose had put up before she fell.

"Oh my God," Fiona said in a whisper, her palms pressed to her cheeks. "Why would anyone want to hurt that wonderful woman?"

"Remember what I said," Claire added. "Death was instantaneous. After the initial blow, Rose didn't linger."

That accomplished what Claire had intended. Fiona nodded, lowering her hands and taking a deep, calming breath. "So when Detective Alvarez calls me tomorrow, it will be to jolt my memory, to see if there are any other details that I recall."

"Yeah, that's what cops do," Ryan said. "So hang around for breakfast. I'll even make waffles."

"You mean you'll burn waffles." There was as much gratitude in Fiona's voice as there was teasing.

"If I do, you'll never know it. I'll drown them in maple syrup."

"What if she doesn't call by then? I can't move in here."

Ryan leaned back on the sofa. "My suggestion? You should be proactive, go to them and ask something innocuous, like if they found out the name of the next of kin since you want to plan the wake and the funeral. Detective Alvarez won't give you any specifics, but at this point she'll probably tell you they're investigating this as a potential homicide. Then, she'll use the opportunity to question you again. The direction of that questioning could give us a hint as to where their heads are."

"*Us?*"

"Yup. Like I said, I want to be in on the follow-up. So I'll go with you, see if I can read anything between the lines. Just introduce me as your brother. No first name necessary. That'll keep my being there personal."

"Because the Forensic Instincts team is pretty well known?"

"Especially by law enforcement, yes. And this isn't an FI investigation, nor do I imagine she'd welcome one."

"I see your point." Fiona nodded thoughtfully. "I actually do need to get enough information to plan things. Did Rose have family? Were they told? How long will the ME have to keep her body in order to"—Fiona's voice quavered—"do an autopsy?" She swallowed and continued. "I also have to see Glenna. I'm sure she won't be going to her classes tomorrow. But she lives in the Village, not too far from the Sixth Precinct. If I call her and she says that it's okay, I want to head straight to her apartment after we leave the police precinct."

"Good idea. But I wouldn't call her until morning. She's probably still being interviewed. Remember, she knew more about Rose's life and her schedule than anyone. She might even know of her family. The detectives are going to keep her for hours. She'll probably go home and collapse. If she needs you tonight, she'll call you."

"You're right. I'll wait."

Claire was studying Fiona carefully, getting a handle on whether or not she was up for a different line of conversation. Even though she didn't want Fiona to know about her suspicions concerning the link between Rose's death and the timing of her meeting with Fiona, she did need to find out what she could.

Fiona was sipping tea with steady hands. Her freaked-out demeanor had eased. And she clearly wasn't dazed or tired.

Claire went for it, using her own genuine interest to achieve her goal.

"I'd love to hear more about your work," she said, settling herself in lotus position—soothing for both herself and those around her. "Where can I see photos? Do you have a website?"

Fiona smiled. "Yes, and thank you. It's FionaMcKayJewelry.com. I sell primarily through my site and through specific online stores and specialized boutiques that feature my collections. I do postcard mailings, advertise on social media, and go to trade shows, exhibitions, art museums—you name it. It can get pretty overwhelming, but I love the process, the research, and hopefully, the end results. So it's worth it."

"Wow." Claire exhaled in a rush, fascinated by the extensiveness of the process. "You do all that by yourself?"

"Most of it. I do have a marketing manager. Jay Mehta. I met him at a trade show and he's awesome. I'm way too scatterbrained to do the organized stuff. I'm all about the creative process. He created a brand for me, he handles the mailings of my postcards and flyers, and he controls my social media presence. I stick to my precious metals and gemstones, fulfilling sales, and going to the trade shows."

Claire was getting more and more drawn in—enough so that she had to remind herself of what she needed to extract from this conversation. "I'm so impressed," she said, inching things along. "What inspires you, or have you been asked that question a hundred times?"

"I think every artist has. Sometimes it's a tangible, physical object or artifact. Sometimes it's just a flash of insight. Either way, I take the inspiration and move on to the research. That brings a whole new depth and dimension to the final product."

That was the opening Claire had been waiting for. "What do you research—the history of the stones and the symbols?"

Fiona made a wide sweep of her arm. "Their history, their meaning, even the legends behind them. Celtic art is rich in those."

Claire wet her lips with the tip of her tongue. "I hope my bringing up Rose's name doesn't upset you, but earlier this evening, you mentioned something about her helping you research tapestries you found at your parents' house. Was that an independent project or did it relate to your jewelry making?"

A bittersweet expression flashed across Fiona's face. "It's okay. Talking about Rose and her abilities makes me feel like I'm honoring her. She was the ultimate antiquities expert with a ton of international contacts to confer with. Celtic art was her passion. And, yes, the tapestries totally tie to my work. I'm basing my whole new line on them, including the emeralds on this bracelet. The tapestries are breathtaking, with the most exquisite and unusual patterns woven around classic Irish imagery, like landscapes and architecture. And they include some traditional symbols and visuals that I don't recognize. There are thirteen panels in all, each of them eighteen inches by eighteen inches except for one larger one that's thirty-six inches by thirty-six inches. If you place the smaller ones randomly along the perimeter of the larger one, they form one overwhelmingly beautiful piece of artistry. Rose was researching the larger panel for me, since I see that as the central focus. I wanted to know everything there was to know about its historic, artistic, architectural, and cultural representations. Then I was hoping to move on to do the same for each of the smaller panels."

Claire was soaking up all this information, formulating her next question as things began to resonate in her mind.

"And you found these in your mother's memory box, you said?"

"It's not a box, it's a trunk," Ryan amended wryly. "My mom keeps everything related to and made by the McKays, dating back a millennium. My father's an only child, so my mom inherited it through marriage. Lucky her."

Fiona arched her brows. "You're just jealous because the *trunk* is passed down generationally, but only to the McKay *women* because of our superior creative talents."

"Jealous?" Ryan's laughter was real. "Do I look to you as if I want that humongous thing cluttering my place? Now, if it had decades of technology in it or manuals on robotics through the ages or even a bottle or two of whiskey, I might put up a fight. But diaries, frilly placemats, wall hangings, and blankets? No, thanks. You and Mom can have it."

Claire totally ignored Ryan. "When you say *creative talents*, do you mean all your female ancestors contributed something to this box—something handmade?"

"For three generations, four if you count me," Fiona replied. "And they're far from placemats and blankets." She glowered at Ryan. "They're exquisite, rich with beauty and history. The tapestries. A needle-tatted set of antique lace doilies. And a gorgeous Irish chain quilt. I've already started working on my contributing piece—a silver Celtic knot medallion—and it had better come out incredible.

I can't even imagine matching the level of talent possessed by my great-grandmother, grandmother, and mom."

"Who wove the tapestries?"

"My great-grandmother." Fiona sighed. "That's the most frustrating part. If she were alive, I would ask her what she'd based her designs on. But unfortunately, she's not. I've even pored over her diary, seeing if she made specific references to the tapestries. But I can't find any details."

"Would your grandmother be able to help?"

"She's gone, as well, as are both my great-grandfather and grandfather. It's just my parents, my brothers, and me. So I'm on my own, especially now that Rose is gone."

Claire's brows drew together in puzzlement. "I'm missing something here. You said the memory box was passed down from one generation of McKay women to the next. But your grandmother married. So how did the name McKay continue on to your father?"

Fiona's eyes twinkled. "Another story I've been told dozens of times and never tired of hearing. My grandmother and grandfather shared the last name McKay. They attended the same schools from elementary school up. Thanks to alphabetical order, they sat next to each other every year. They were friends as kids and wound up falling in love and getting married. True childhood sweethearts. Isn't that romantic?"

"Very," Claire replied with a smile. "It's like fate intended it that way."

"That's what my mom always says." Fiona waved her hand. "Sorry to digress. You were asking about the memory box."

"You didn't digress. I asked. And I loved the story," Claire reassured her. She then picked up where they'd left off. "You said there are thirteen tapestry panels, but only eleven are in the memory box."

Fiona nodded. "Two of them are hanging in my parents' house. I can't blame my mom for doing that. They're too unique not to have at least a few of them on display. Actually, one. It's in the living room. The other one is hanging in their bedroom. It's my mom's personal favorite."

"You'll have to show me photos of all these treasures," Claire found herself saying, completely drawn, at this point, into the artistic talents of the McKay women.

"I can. But frankly, photos don't do them justice. I'd rather show them to you in person. If Ryan can't get over himself and bring you over to meet my folks, I will. My mom would be ecstatic to meet you and to show you the family heirlooms."

"Now *that's* not happening." Ryan was sitting straight up now, looking distinctly unhappy.

"Why not? I won't even mention you. I'll just say that Claire is a friend."

"A friend who happens to work at Forensic Instincts, a company you've never set foot in, but where I happen to shine?"

"Works for me," Fiona said. She grew sober, and her brows knit. "In fact, it better than works. It would make a very painful day a lot more bearable." She met her brother's eyes. "Ry, I have to go there tomorrow to tell them about Rose. Mom isn't going to take this well. Not only is she going to be a wreck about me, she's going to be upset about Rose. She knew her from church, remember?"

"Yeah, I remember." Ryan blew out a breath. "And diverting her by asking if she'll show Claire the stuff in that memory box will calm her down. So will Claire. She's the walking definition of soothing. Fine. We can all go there tomorrow after you're finished with the police and with Glenna." A quick glance at Claire. "If that's all right with you."

"Of course." Claire was surprised, but she was even more touched. Ryan was opening a door for her to meet his parents—a reality that was even more un-Ryan-like than announcing she was his girlfriend. Of course, there were extenuating circumstances, but he could easily have ducked this visit and let Fiona finesse it on her own. The truth was that, in addition to supporting his little sister, he was allowing Claire deeper into his life.

"Are you okay with this, Claire?" Fiona asked, interpreting Claire's momentary silence as discomfort. "I know it's a big favor. You and I met a nanosecond ago, and here I am asking you to act as a cushion for me and my family."

"I'm absolutely fine with it," Claire reassured her. "I was just thinking that we should wait until evening, when your father is home, too. That way they can both hear the news together. They'll each play a different role in supporting you."

Fiona swallowed a smile. "You're very tactful. What you mean is that my dad is the solid presence that will keep my mom from going to pieces."

"Something like that. Also, while you and your mother are sharing the memory box with me, Ryan can fill your father in on any ugly particulars you'd rather your mother not hear—at least not right away. He'll have a chance to talk to her later and cushion whatever grizzly details the press is soon going to report."

"Good idea." Fiona nodded. "The evening's better anyway. Glenna and I have a lot to plan and not a lot of time to do it in—unless the police delay the process." Her mouth set in a grim line. "Today was a nightmare. And it doesn't look like tomorrow is going to get much better."

6

It was nine a.m.

The Tribeca brownstone that served as the headquarters of Forensic Instincts was crackling with energy as the team settled into the main conference room on the second floor.

The room was as impressive as the FI team members themselves. The decorating had been done by FI's president, Casey Woods, and like Casey, it was pure class. Polished hardwood floors. A plush Oriental rug. A gleaming mahogany conference table and matching credenza with its JURA Professional coffee station and built-in fridge and wine cooler. French doors led to a terrace that overlooked a small but professionally landscaped garden.

Then came the crucial technology infrastructure, which was pure Ryan—light-years ahead of its time in both design and operation. Unlike the stunning furnishings, it was all hidden from view. Only the gigantic video wall was visible, covering the longest side of the room and allowing Ryan to assemble a dizzying array of information into a large single image or several smaller, simultaneous data feeds. Videoconferencing equipment, a sophisticated phone system, and a personalized virtual workstation available to each member of the group completed the elaborate system.

This room was the team's central meeting point and think-tank location—the place where all new cases were discussed and all major developments reviewed. Casey had scheduled this morning's meeting to do a quick wrap-up of their just-closed case and to start the selection process on their next one. Given their reputation and success rate, their pile of prospective cases was always sky-high, and it was up to them to choose the one that seemed the most pressing and the most suited to their skills and passions. There was always some debate among the members, but it was rare that they wholly disagreed about the ultimate selection. Some cases were just more urgent than others.

As always, Casey sat at the head of the table, with Hero, the bloodhound who was the team's human-scent evidence dog, stretched out at her feet. Patrick Lynch, retired FBI and now FI's security expert, sat beside his boss. He'd been predictably early, a quality he and Casey shared. Marc Devereaux, former Navy SEAL, former FBI Behavioral Analysis Unit, and Casey's right hand on just about everything, was on-the-dot punctual. Emma Stirling, former pickpocket, now honest and reformed—unless FI required that she not be—showed up two minutes past nine.

There were two glaringly empty seats at the table.

"Where are Claire and Ryan?" Emma asked, her blue eyes wide with interest as she helped herself to a chocolate croissant from the breakfast tray. As the one-time personal assistant to the group, now graduated to full-fledged team member, she was the one who'd ordered the continental breakfast. So, of course, chocolate croissants were always on the menu.

Casey hid her smile. It was no surprise that their outspoken newbie was the one who blurted out the question that was on everyone's mind. Everyone save Casey's; Ryan and Claire had both called her and explained what was going on, getting her okay to do what they felt was necessary.

"Wow," Emma continued, speculating aloud. "Did they do something cool like run off and elope?"

Marc nearly choked on his coffee as he snorted with laughter. "What movies have you been watching? We're talking about no-commitments Ryan and always-level-headed Claire. They still pretend they're not together."

"I know, but they've never *not* been at a team meeting. Never. And since they're *both* out..."

"Enough, Emma." Casey gestured pointedly at the chair Emma should be occupying. "Ryan has a family situation. Claire is assisting him."

"Is everyone okay?" Patrick's brow furrowed. He wasn't prying. That just wasn't Patrick. But he was the father figure of the group, and often their grounding force. "Nothing serious, I hope?"

Casey interlaced her fingers in front of her. The FI team was like family. They all cared about each other. But up until now, the personal details of their lives had been in closed files reserved for her eyes only. Anything they chose to reveal was up to them. Given how close they'd all become, it was an antiquated arrangement, one she planned to address at this meeting. However, with regard to Ryan's current situation, it was moot. When he'd called in, he'd given her the go-ahead to share. Plus, news of Rose Flaherty's death would now be public information, and some unethical reporter was bound to dig up the name of the witness who found the body—and to identify her online. So Casey was about to give everyone a little more insight into Ryan McKay.

"An elderly antique dealer died under suspicious circumstances in her Greenwich Village shop yesterday," she said. "The person who discovered her body was Ryan's sister."

Patrick's brows rose. "Sister?"

"Yes. Her name is Fiona. She walked in on a bad scene—a dead body, lots of blood, lots of law enforcement. She was interviewed at length and left the precinct pretty freaked out. She went straight to Ryan. He's helping her navigate further police questioning and sharing the news with their parents."

"Which is where Claire comes in." Marc nodded in comprehension. "I get it."

"Well, I don't." Emma looked positively affronted. "Why didn't I know that Ryan has a sister?"

"The same way you never knew I had a brother," Marc said, reminding her about his older brother, Aidan, whose global skills Emma had now seen firsthand. "Our personal files are just that. Personal. Casey is the only one with access to that information."

"Right." Patrick looked amused. "Except for Ryan, who's hacked into all our files and knows more about each of us than we do."

"I stand corrected," Marc acknowledged with an offhand shrug. "Some of us respect boundaries."

"That's true." Casey used the opportunity to broach the subject on her mind. "However, we were strangers when I put that rule into place. Now, we're family. There's very little we don't know about each other anyway. So I'm suggesting we ditch the secrecy about our personal lives."

"I'm fine with that," Marc said.

"As am I." Patrick nodded.

"Well, my life's an open book," Emma muttered. "You all knew everything about me when I was hired."

"Comments and evaluations are mine and mine alone," Casey continued, "and I've ensured that those file addendums are encrypted and protected by two-factor authentication, the details of which no one has but me. That has been done, am I correct, Yoda?"

Yoda was Ryan's homegrown AI system that ran everything at Forensic Instincts. Seemingly half human, Yoda kept track of all their cases—ongoing and closed, always at the ready when an authorized user would simply ask him to do some research or analysis.

In response to Casey's question, an entire wall of floor-to-ceiling video screens began to glow. A long green line formed across each panel, pulsating from left to right, and Yoda's voice replied, "Yes,

Casey, you are correct. No one can bypass the encryption process, not even Ryan."

"Good. Then I'll run all this by Claire and Ryan and we can get rid of the archaic nonsense. In the meantime"—she interrupted Emma's next question—"anyone who wants to know more about Ryan's situation can ask him directly. He and Claire will be here for a few hours this afternoon. We can bring them up to speed on this morning's case wrap-up."

Patrick folded one leg across the other. "Do you still want to go ahead and select our next case? Or do you want to wait until we're all together?"

"I'd rather wait," Casey replied. The unwritten FI rule was that the entire team contributed to this process and made the ultimate decision. "I've read through all the case possibilities—which I'm sure you all have—and nothing is life-or-death. We can bandy around some ideas, but we'll put off making any final decision until tomorrow."

Everyone nodded in unison.

Casey's fingers were poised over her keyboard. "Then let's get started on our wrap-up."

***

By the time Fiona had finished up at both the police precinct and at Glenna's apartment, she was so drained that all she wanted to do was to sleep. As Ryan had predicted, Detective Alvarez had pressed her for any additional details she'd recalled about last night, providing Fiona only with the fact that this was now a homicide investigation. But no clue about the direction the investigation was taking, no information about when the ME would be releasing the body, and no answers about whether or not they'd discovered the name of Rose's next of kin—assuming she had any.

Detective Alvarez had taken it a little easy on Fiona, seeing how pale she was and how pronounced the dark circles under her eyes were—not to mention the fact that she'd needed to bring her brother with her for emotional support—so the questions had been asked in a less intense manner than they had been during last night's interview. Still, all they'd accomplished was to rehash what had already been discussed, and Fiona had left the Sixth Precinct totally frustrated. So had Ryan.

Fiona had gone to Glenna's alone, after Ryan had advised her that he and Claire would pick her up at her townhouse around four so they could head up to the Bronx. They'd done rock, paper, scissors, and Ryan had lost, so it was his job to call their parents and announce their visit, if not its basis.

Glenna had been in even worse shape than Fiona had imagined.

She'd opened her apartment door, her eyes red-rimmed and her face splotchy from crying. Her hair was tied back, damp from a shower but with loose hairs dangling chaotically around her face in a way that mirrored the emotional mess she was. She looked dazed and faraway, as if she was shell-shocked. And why wouldn't she be? After her lengthy interview with Detective Alvarez, she was only too aware of the fact that Rose's death was being ruled a homicide. She was as horrified by that as Fiona was—and just as clueless as to why anyone would want to hurt such a gentle old woman.

By unspoken agreement, they'd avoided having a prolonged discussion on the subject. It simply hurt too much, and they had nothing but questions, no answers.

Instead, they'd talked about happy memories, each of them recalling their favorite Rose stories. It gave them some sense of peace to celebrate her life rather than dwell on her death. But eventually, the nuts and bolts needed to be addressed.

Glenna started out by filling Fiona in on the fact that Rose had no living relatives; her eighty-five-year-old sister had passed away in a Florida nursing facility two years ago. She'd told that to Detective Alvarez, who'd thanked her and said the NYPD would do a search to confirm that no other living relatives existed. Glenna had asked if she could claim the body for a proper funeral, only to be told that, assuming no next of kin existed, the state of Florida would have jurisdiction since Rose's sister had died there. Glenna would have to contact a Floridian attorney, supply him with a letter from the NYPD stating the fact that this was a DOA, and have him appear before a judge with that letter and the proper legal documents. If everything was in order, the judge would provide the attorney with signed papers allowing Glenna to claim guardianship of Rose's body.

"I don't know where to turn," Glenna had said, chewing on her lip with a helpless expression. "I don't know any lawyers, much less one who practices in Florida. Finding one… getting this done… who knows how long that will take and how much it will cost? I don't know where to start."

"I do." Fiona had whipped out her phone and called her brother Nolan, laying out the dilemma for him while omitting the part about her being the one who found the body. The last thing she needed was another family member worrying about her. Nolan had listened carefully and said that he'd attended law school with a buddy who was now an attorney in Florida. He assured his sister that he'd contact him and Detective Alvarez right away and make sure this all happened as quickly as possible—maybe even in a day if his friend knew the right judge. A few faxes, an in-chambers meeting, and the legal document with the judge's raised seal and signature could be overnighted to New York.

Both Fiona and Glenna had heaved a sigh of relief.

Once legal channels had been surmounted, Glenna and Fiona would then make all the wake and funeral arrangements. Rose, like Glenna and the McKays, belonged to the Basilica of Saint Patrick's Old Cathedral. Located in Nolita, an eclectic neighborhood between Canal and Houston Streets in New York City, it was a historic treasure. Tomorrow, Glenna and Fiona would meet the funeral director at the parish office and see what they could arrange with their limited funds. In the meantime, Glenna planned on spending the rest of that afternoon and evening calling all of Rose's contacts to personally tell them the news and to tactfully ask if they'd like to contribute to a special Mass and funeral for the beloved antiquities expert. Many of those contacts had been customers for years and would hopefully contribute even a small sum.

Fiona had offered to make some of the phone calls, but Glenna had thanked her and said no, that she felt obligated to contact the patrons. Since she was Rose's assistant, they all knew her, so it was best that it was her voice they heard when they were told the upsetting news. And she intended to jump right on those calls in the hopes of reaching as many people as possible before the NYPD beat her to it.

Fiona had understood. So she made plans with Glenna for tomorrow and left.

Back at her place, she curled up on the sofa, covered herself with one of her mother's beautiful quilts, and fell fast asleep.

She was awakened by the ringing of her cell phone. Damn. Why hadn't she turned off the ringer? She groped for the phone and stuck it under her ear. "Hello?" she mumbled.

"Fee? Where the hell are you?" Ryan demanded. "I'm double-parked outside your townhouse and Claire has been ringing your doorbell for five minutes."

Fiona bolted to a sitting position. "Shit. I fell asleep. What time is it?"

"Time for us to get going unless we want to sit in Midtown rush-hour traffic for who knows how long."

Fiona had already jumped to her feet and was combing her fingers through her hair as she hurried to the door. "I'm really sorry. I'll let Claire in. Give me five minutes to get myself together."

Seven minutes later, they were all on their way.

7

Woodlawn was a predominately Irish-American community at the northern-most tip of the Bronx, only a forty-minute drive from SoHo. They could have taken mass transit. But Ryan loved driving his new high-tech baby—a black BMW i3s electric car that he'd affectionately named Evie, as in EV, meaning an electric vehicle. Whenever he got the slightest chance, he was behind the wheel, reveling in the ride.

It was good that he was occupied, because Fiona wasn't in a chatty mood. The next few hours were going to be very difficult. She hadn't heard from her parents, nor had they said anything to Ryan when he called, which meant they hadn't yet spotted Rose's obituary and the small article about her suspicious death that had appeared in a nondescript section of the newspaper. That elicited a feeling of both worry and relief. Relief because they hadn't been slapped in the face with the tragic news and worry because she was the one who was going to drop that on them—plus a whole lot more.

"Are you okay?" Claire asked from the passenger seat, twisting around to study her.

"As okay as I can be, I guess." Fiona met Claire's understanding gaze. "I'm glad you're coming. This is going to be rough. My mom's very protective of her kids."

Claire nodded. "Plus what you're about to tell her is major. Of course, she'll be badly thrown. But it will be okay. You'll see."

"Thanks, Claire. I don't know what Ryan did to deserve you, but he's one lucky guy."

"Okay, Fee. I hear you." Ryan rolled his eyes. "You're now Claire-voyant's number one fan."

"Claire-voyant?" Fiona blinked. "You've got to be kidding me. *That's* what you call her?"

Claire gave a dismissive wave of her hand. "That's your brother's idea of a term of affection." She paused. "Actually, I stand corrected. It started as a put-down. As you know, he's not exactly a believer."

"Yeah, but I've softened up since I've seen you in action," Ryan corrected. He grinned. "Still, I do kind of like the nickname. So it sticks."

"I give up," Fiona muttered. "Are you sure *I'm* the baby of the family?"

"Yup," Ryan confirmed. "And you're about to be reminded of that." As he spoke, he pulled off Route 87 North and turned onto East 233rd Street.

Minutes later, Ryan arrived on his parents' street. The two rows of small, two-story shingled houses were modest but impeccably kept, with awnings overhanging the front doors and ivy-covered chain-link fences. The homeowners clearly took pride in their residences, and there was a certain peaceful charm that pervaded the block.

"This is lovely," Claire said as Ryan pulled into the driveway of a light gray house with brick stairs leading up to the front door and a small garden out front. She glanced from Ryan to Fiona. "You both grew up here?"

"Born and raised," Fiona replied. "All four of us."

Ryan was already shutting down Evie and getting ready to go in. He paused to look quickly over his shoulder at Fiona. "We'll back you up, Fee. No worries."

She gave him a weak smile. "I'll need it."

They all climbed out and Ryan made triple sure the car was locked. No matter how safe the neighborhood, he wasn't taking any chances. He was no different when he left Evie in the Park Slope parking lot.

"This is home, Ryan," Fiona said. "There hasn't been a car theft, or any theft, on this street in as long as I can remember."

"Yeah, I know." Having reassured himself, Ryan joined the two women and headed toward the house.

The front door opened before they reached the steps, and a slim, middle-aged woman with short light brown hair, a smattering of freckles, and a light-up-her-face smile that was identical to Ryan and Fiona's stepped outside. "A rare visit from two of my favorite children," Maureen McKay said, hugging Fiona and giving Ryan a peck on the cheek. "I feel honored." She turned to Claire, a quizzical expression on her face.

"Mom, this is Claire Hedgleigh," Fiona said. "She's a good friend. She also works with Ryan at Forensic Instincts. I invited her to join us."

Maureen accepted that without further inquiry, extending her hand and shaking Claire's. "Lovely to meet you, Claire."

"And you, as well." Claire took an instant liking to Ryan and Fiona's mother. She was straightforward, clearly loved her children very much, and yet didn't intrude in their lives. Her entire demeanor stated that whatever they wanted her to know, they would tell her.

"Come in. My husband just got home a few minutes ago." She led them inside, down a narrow hall, and into a small living room with heavy dark wood furniture, lace curtains, and on the side tables, porcelain vases with green shamrock designs. But Claire's gaze was immediately drawn to the strikingly beautiful tapestry on the wall. It portrayed a flock of sheep, grazing in the greenest of fields, under the bluest of skies, every detail exquisitely captured. In the top right corner was a symbol Claire had never seen before—a one-line drawing that began with a spiral that spun out into a tunnel-shaped arch of some kind. The border of the panel was a gentle Kelly green—the perfect complement to the tapestry itself—with rows of Celtic symbols woven in, including the knots Claire recognized from Fiona's bracelet. The tapestry was held up by padded clips that a decorative rod had been glided through—an obvious way to avoid cutting holes in the fabric.

Before Claire could comment, a tall man, whose dark hair and deep blue eyes smacked of Ryan's and Fiona's, rose from the sofa.

"This is a nice surprise," he said, hugging Fiona as she went straight to him. "Hello, son," he addressed Ryan, extending his hand.

"Hi, Dad," Ryan replied, meeting his father's handshake in an uncharacteristically formal way.

Claire didn't need her gift to feel the strain between father and son. The undercurrent of love was there, but the past still weighed heavily on their relationship.

How sad, she thought. *Something has to bridge this gap, no matter how many years it's been.* She tucked that thought away for later.

"This is Claire Hedgleigh," Maureen was saying, introducing Claire to her husband. "She's a friend of Fiona's and works with Ryan. Claire, this is my husband, Colin."

Ryan's father's brows arched slightly in surprise at this unexpected addition to Fiona and Ryan. "Hello, Claire, welcome to our home," he said, shaking her hand, as well.

"Thank you." Claire smiled politely. "I can see where Fiona and Ryan get their vivid coloring."

"Yes, that and a stubborn streak a mile wide." Colin's stiffness eased as he spoke. "We McKays are known for both." He gestured toward the love seat and club chairs. "Please, have a seat."

"I'll put on a kettle for tea," Maureen announced. She looked questioningly at Claire. "Or do you take coffee?"

Claire suppressed her grin. Ryan's mother made the word *coffee* sound blasphemous. "Tea would be wonderful, thank you," she said.

A broad smile was her response. "Good. I'll bring some sandwiches, as well. It's near dinnertime. You must be hungry."

Fiona shook her head. "The tea is great, Mom. But we're really not up for food. I need to talk to you."

Maureen hesitated, torn between concern over the sobriety of Fiona's tone and her responsibilities as a hostess.

"Just some cake then." She scurried off to the kitchen.

It was only when everyone was settled, sipping their tea, that Fiona quietly broke the news to them of Rose's death and how she'd been the one to discover her lifeless body. She left out any mention of a homicide investigation. Ryan would discuss that with his father when they were alone. This was more than enough to drop on her mother.

As predicted, all the color drained from Maureen McKay's face, and she gasped in horror, clapping her hand over her mouth with a soft, shocked cry. An instant later, maternal instinct took over, and she hurried to her daughter's side, leaning down to hug her fiercely.

"My poor lovey," she said. "How excruciating for you. To walk into something like that. And what tragic news. Rose was a kind and gentle soul. To die so painfully. And all alone. My heart goes out to her." She tipped up Fiona's chin. "And you, I'm so worried about you. Judging from how pale you are and the dark circles under your eyes, I'm guessing you haven't slept at all. Or if you have, you've been having nightmares. My poor Fiona." She gently stroked her daughter's hair.

Fiona hadn't expected to start crying again. But just the tenderness of her mother's caress brought on the tears. She squeezed her eyes shut, once again trying to block out the memory of Rose's body and all that blood.

"I'm sorry," she murmured, totally embarrassed by her loss of control in front of the whole group. "I guess I'm having a harder time with this than I realized."

"Well, you're not going to deal with it alone." Maureen wiped Fiona's tears away with gentle fingers. "To begin with, you'll move home for a few weeks, maybe a month."

"No, Mom, I can't—although I'm very grateful for the offer. I need to have access to my workroom and my equipment. Staying busy will be good for me. But if I have bad moments, I promise I'll come straight to you and Dad."

Her mother didn't look happy about Fiona's decision, but she didn't push. "I'll contact the church and see if I can help with the provisions that need to be made," she said instead.

Fiona hesitated. She obviously couldn't tell her mother that those provisions were dependent upon when Rose's body was released. So she settled for filling them in on her call to Nolan and the legal issues that needed addressing.

"Good," Maureen said. "I'm glad you reached out to Nolan. He'll speed things up so we can move forward."

"Glenna wants to make the necessary phone calls herself," Fiona said honestly. "She's also making arrangements for the wake and the funeral, with a little help from me. I'm not sure what else there is to do. I'm sure there'll be a repast of some kind afterwards."

Maureen nodded. "The funeral director will handle that. But not all the congregants, or Rose's friends and colleagues, will be there to pay their respects. I'll hold a gathering at our house a few evenings later. Everyone who knew Rose will be invited so that we can properly honor her."

"That would be great, Mom," Fiona said, truly relieved. A gathering like that was her mother's forte, not hers. "Rose would have loved the gesture—and the party."

"Since she didn't have family, I agree with your mother," Colin said. "It's up to us."

"What a horrible, horrible accident," Maureen said quietly, visibly bringing herself under control for her daughter's sake. "I'll say a prayer for Rose tonight." She gave Fiona's hair one more gentle stroke and then reflexively checked everyone's teacup to make sure they were filled. That only partially satisfied her, since the cake she brought in hadn't been touched. "Please eat. Rose would want us to go on."

At the word *accident*, Fiona had shot Ryan a quick look. He nodded, his gaze shifting to Claire.

Claire reacted at once, turning to stare at the scenic tapestry on the wall, this time studying it for a long, pointed moment. "Mrs. McKay, I've been admiring that exquisite tapestry. May I ask who wove it?"

Maureen's eyes lit up. "That would be Colin's grandmother. Isn't it lovely? It's one of my favorites, which is why I hung it here for everyone to see and to admire. Those are Galway sheep; they're indigenous to Ireland. See the bob of wool on their heads and wool on their legs? That's a characteristic only to them. And the Celtic symbols are traditional to Ireland so they're a perfect blend with the Irish countryside." She warmed to her subject. "Even though this is one of my personal favorites, the other tapestries are equally striking."

Claire seized her cue. "Fiona mentioned there were others and that she was basing her new jewelry line on them. Given the brilliance of the colors and the significance of the symbols, I can see why. And if this one is any indication of your grandmother-in-law's talent, I can only imagine how breathtaking the others must be."

"Would you like to see them?"

"I'd love to." Claire's eagerness wasn't feigned. There was something almost poetic about the tapestry, as if it were a page out of its creator's life. "Fiona mentioned a memory box that was passed down to the McKay women?"

Maureen smiled. "And that included me, by the sheer luck that Colin was an only child so I was the only McKay woman to be gifted it by marriage and not by blood." Her eyes twinkled. "In truth, the word *box* is a misnomer."

"I told them it was more of a trunk," Ryan inserted.

His mother gave him a tolerant look. "Ryan is right. We Irish tend to keep everything that tells a story about family. This box goes back many generations. There are countless stories to be told over that many years. I've added more than my share of journals and family photos. The box is near bursting." She glanced at her husband. "Can you and Ryan entertain yourselves for a while so I can show Claire the tapestries?"

There was a momentary awkward silence before Colin said, "Of course." He looked over at Ryan. "Let's switch from tea to a Guinness since the ladies won't be present."

"Sounds good." Ryan was intent on making this conversation work. He had details to share with his father—details that transcended any tension that existed between them.

"Then it's up to the attic with us, ladies," Maureen said, already leading the way. "And Colin—one pint apiece; Ryan has to drive back to the city."

Ryan perched at the edge of his chair, waiting for the women's footsteps to fade away. His father walked over to his prized kegerator, reached up to the shelf above, grabbed a pint glass, and filled it with Guinness. He set the glass down, grabbed a second glass, and did the same for Ryan.

"Here you go, son." Colin headed back and handed the glass over to Ryan, sitting down on the sofa across from him and taking a long swallow of his brew. "I'm glad you were there for Fiona. She's a lot more tenderhearted than she realizes."

"Which is why I needed this chance to talk to you alone," Ryan replied, pausing only long enough to take a belt of his own beer. "There's more to Rose Flaherty's death than Fee just led you to believe. We didn't want to upset Mom any more than we had to. But she's going to find out soon, either through another member of the church or from reading about it herself. Fee's only seen one newspaper article. But I've spotted more. The crime beat reporters are already on this."

Colin's brows knit. "Crime beat reporters? Exactly what is it that Fiona didn't tell us?"

Ryan frowned. "That Rose was murdered. An investigation is underway. NYPD Crime Scene was called in and the area around

Rose's shop is taped off. The medical examiner hasn't released the body, which obviously means an autopsy is being conducted. And there are substantiating details in the police file that haven't been released."

Colin just stared at his son. "*Murdered*... Dear God. They're sure?"

"Unfortunately, yes. The file is still thin. But it'll grow."

Colin's penetrating blue gaze delved into Ryan's. "Details that haven't been released, a thin file... You've hacked into the NYPD's computer system," he stated flatly, this time without judgement but with certainty.

Ryan didn't avert his gaze. "I'll do what I have to do to protect Fee."

Colin paused and then nodded, visibly accepting the fact that, in this case, the end justified the means. "Why would anyone want to kill Rose?" he asked.

"Now that I don't know, at least not yet. But I'm worried. She was researching something for Fee right before she died. And her last appointment of the day was with Fee—an appointment that never happened because of her death. Is that a coincidence? Could be. Could also not be. But if Fee is caught in something ugly, I'm not sitting by and doing nothing."

"Of course not." Colin cleared his throat. "Is your investigative agency taking this on as a case?"

Ryan rolled the glass between his palms. "I haven't approached them with it yet. I don't have enough hard-core facts, or certainty that Fee is in danger. Right now it's just an unsolved murder."

"But you will go to them if it comes to it."

"In a heartbeat."

"Is there anything else I should know?" Colin asked.

"Not yet." Ryan wasn't planning on getting into Claire's insights and her gift.

If Ryan was a doubter, his father would be a full-blown disbeliever. And arguing about metaphysical abilities was the last thing he needed right now.

Colin cleared his throat. "I'm not going to pry into your work. But anything that impacts Fiona—I'm asking that you share those findings with me. I'll talk to your mother and give her the facts as gently as I can. But she's a strong woman. She wouldn't want to be protected from anything that threatens her children. And neither would I."

"I'll keep you in the loop on anything that relates to Fee," Ryan replied.

"Keep her safe, Ryan. Do whatever it takes."

"Count on it."

***

Upstairs in the attic, Fiona had urged Claire to have a seat on the wood floor with her mother while she went across the room to push over what definitely qualified as a small trunk.

"Fiona loved to play up here when she was a little girl," Maureen said with a reminiscent smile. "And not with dolls or toys, mind you. She liked to try on all her grandmother's and my costume jewelry. We kept a collection of it all in a big box, and it was the first thing she went to whenever she climbed her way up here. And she never just put the pieces on willy-nilly. She examined each one thoughtfully and selected certain clip-on earrings that she decided she liked with a specific bracelet or necklace, or both. I remember the way she'd model them for me, turning side to side so I could see what she'd done. I should have known then where her talents would lie."

"Mom," Fiona called out. "I'm sure Claire doesn't want to hear about my childhood antics."

"Actually, I think it's really sweet," Claire said. "You were already on a career track when you were…" A quizzical glance at Maureen.

"Four," Maureen proudly supplied.

"Most of us don't know what we want to be when we grow up until after the fact." Claire smiled. "You knew in preschool. Pretty impressive."

Fiona grinned at the assessment, simultaneously pushing the trunk toward her mother and Claire.

Just before she reached them, Maureen spoke quietly to Claire, gratitude and awareness in her tone. "Thank you for coming. Fiona needs emotional support. I realize you're offering her that. You're a good friend." She gave Claire's arm a quick squeeze, then released it just as Fiona joined them.

"Our memory box," Fiona said with pride, sitting down with Claire and her mother and lifting the lid. "It's a work in progress, including all the family photos and journals my mom keeps adding."

Claire looked down into the neatly organized history of the McKays. There were diaries and journals that filled one section, handmade creations like finely detailed lace doilies and handmade quilts in another, and a good third of the trunk devoted to the tapestry panels. Fiona leaned forward, reverently lifting each panel for Claire's inspection. Like the panel hanging in the living room, each panel had the slim Kelly-green border with Celtic symbols and the unusual spiral and arch drawing in the upper right-hand corner. And each one portrayed a facet of the McKay history—from rich, traditional Irish themes to the story of their journey to the US to religious depictions that clearly factored prominently in their lives. Some of the themes were more abstract, things Claire couldn't understand the meaning of. That didn't make them any less magnificent. But this was clearly a very private, meaningful collection to the McKays and she had no intention of prying.

That didn't mean she wasn't dying to ask—or to be invited to hold the panels, feel their texture, and see if any flashes of insight came of that process.

While Claire was still admiring the quality of the weaving, Fiona took out and unfurled a much larger square—obviously the three-by-three panel she'd spoken of. This one made Claire's jaw drop.

It was entirely different from the others. Its border, while slim, was far more elaborate. It was made up of a continuous pattern of delicate, intertwined rectangular symbols along each edge. Precise and symmetrical, the border itself was a work of art. This complex pattern continued along all four edges of the square, interspersed only with four of the curious arched spiral symbols—one in the center of each of the four sides—and four simple three-lined symbols, one at each corner. Those Claire recognized as the Celtic Awen symbols, the signs for the three rays of light.

Inside the border was a stunning, breath-catching design.

Woven over a soft forest-green background were the images of what appeared to be a throne on which flourished the Tree of Life. Above the throne was a large golden crown set with precious gemstones.

The entire effect was dazzling.

"I'm speechless," Claire said, still staring at it. "I mean, the whole collection is exquisite. But that one—wow."

"I told you it was amazing," Fiona said. "That's why you had to see the real thing, not just a photo or even a print. They're all inspirational, but the craftsmanship on this one is unbelievable."

"So is the impact. I can understand why you'd want to base your new jewelry line on these. Obviously, the symbols. But the gemstones on the bracelet you were wearing last night remind me of the ones on that crown—vivid, rich—set in twin Awen symbols. Incredible."

Fiona smiled. "I'm so glad you see the influence of the tapestry, and that you like it so much. I've also made matching earrings that are back at my studio. And I have a few additional ideas for more elaborate pieces I'll be making for Light and Shadows."

"I'd love to see the ones you've completed, the ones yet to come, and your entire line."

Claire meant every word. But she was still itching to touch the center panel, to see if she picked up on any present-day energy that might help her understand what Rose had unearthed for Fiona and if it had any link to her suspicious death. But without holding the panel in her hands, sitting in a quiet, dark place by herself, and letting the images come at will—assuming they came at all—she was stymied.

But again, she restrained herself. These were family heirlooms. They were being displayed for her, not offered for tactile exploration.

On that thought, Fiona's iPhone trilled.

"I'm sorry," she said, pulling it out of her pocket. "I left this on in case Glenna needed to reach me." She glanced at the caller ID. "It's her," she confirmed. "Everything okay?" she said into the receiver. She listened for a moment and Claire could see the look of surprise on her face. "You have no idea who?" Another pause. "That's odd, but certainly a blessing. Now we need to find out when we can make those arrangements. I'll let you know the minute I hear from Nolan."

Fiona disconnected the phone and gazed with puzzlement at her mother and Fiona. "The church called Glenna. Apparently, an anonymous donor left ten thousand dollars in cash there along with a note asking that the funds be put toward a private Mass in Rose's honor and an urn to be buried in the church's columbaria."

Maureen gasped. "That's a fortune! Who did Rose know who's that wealthy?"

"I have no idea. But whoever it is, we're so grateful. Glenna and I could have managed the Mass donation, but we could never have raised the kind of money necessary for a burial like that."

"Yes, it's a true blessing," Maureen agreed. "Let's accept it as such."

Claire's brows drew together. "I don't mean to sound ignorant, but what are columbaria and why is it so costly to be buried there?"

"You don't sound ignorant," Fiona replied. "A columbarium is a room with niches—places for funeral urns to be stored. Saint Patrick's Old Cathedral has a limited number of those niches available, although they're building more. Purchasing one costs close to the ten thousand dollars our anonymous donor left. Nothing would be more meaningful to Rose than being buried at our church."

Claire inclined her head in question. "I didn't know the Catholic Church sanctioned cremation."

"As of the 1960s, yes, they do. It's not the Church's preferred method of burial, but it is sanctioned." Fiona's smile was soft. "And Rose believed in the spirit, not the body. We had many religious talks, especially given how much the Church factors into Celtic art. Knowing Rose as we do, Glenna and I could pick out the perfect urn together. Rather than having Rose's body present at the special Mass, we can arrange for the cremation to take place first so the urn holding Rose's ashes will be there. Afterwards, the urn will be brought to the niche and both of them will be blessed as the urn is placed inside. There's only room for twenty mourners to be present during that ceremony."

Maureen was nodding. "All the more reason we should have the gathering at our home. Here, everyone can be here—the congregants, as well as Rose's friends and colleagues."

Claire was absorbing all this with great interest. "You said Saint Patrick's Old Cathedral. I take it that differs from the New York landmark I know of."

"Yes. The church's full name is the Basilica of Saint Patrick's Old Cathedral and it was the original Saint Patrick's, built in 1815," Maureen informed her with pride. "The grand cathedral in Midtown wasn't built until 1878. Since Colin's family came over from Ireland in 1920, every generation of McKays has belonged to Old Saint Patrick's. It's smaller but equally beautiful."

"And it has the coolest Sunday evening Masses," Fiona added. "They're geared toward a young crowd, since fifty percent of the congregation is between eighteen and thirty-four. Lots of great-looking professionals come to meet friends. And there are wine and beer tastings in the courtyard after the Mass. You'll have to come with me. Just once. You'll really enjoy it." A twinkle lit Fiona's eyes. "One paper actually referred to Old Saint Patrick's as the 'sexy church.'"

Laughter bubbled up in Claire's throat. "Now that's an adjective I never thought I'd hear applied to a church. I'd love to go with you."

"Don't count on Ryan joining us."

"It never occurred to me that he would."

"Ryan is a good man," his mother said loyally. "He just doesn't feel the same way about the Church as we do."

Fiona patted her mother's hand. "We're not criticizing Ryan, Mom. Just acknowledging who he is—and isn't. You know how much I love and admire him. That's why I ran straight to him after I found..." Her voice trailed off.

This time it was Maureen who covered her daughter's hand with her own. "We'll get through this, my Fiona. Now that we received that generous donation, we can start making plans."

Fiona felt Claire's gaze on her, and she knew exactly what she was thinking.

There'd be no getting through this. Not until they knew who'd killed Rose—and why.

8

Fiona was almost sorry for the bravado she'd displayed at her parents' house.

She spent a sleepless night in her townhouse, quaking in her bed, as the word *murder* slammed at her brain. Who in the name of heaven would want to kill Rose? A robbery? Doubtful. Rose's pieces weren't cheap. She took mostly credit cards. She didn't keep a drawer full of cash. Plus, Glenna deposited the shop's profits in the bank daily. Had any of the more valuable antiques been missing when Fiona arrived? She didn't think so, but she'd been so fixated on Rose's body that she hadn't exactly taken inventory. She did recall that there'd been no physical upheaval, so clearly the killer hadn't trashed the place. Had Rose surprised him before he could take anything? Had she confronted him? But why would her cane and shattered whiskey glass be so far from her body?

After endless hours of driving herself crazy, Fiona gave up any thought of sleep. She was out of bed and pounding away at her five-mile run by five thirty. Back home, she showered, dressed, and headed straight upstairs to the third-floor loft that was her studio—the only place where she could find a shred of solace. She was in mid-project anyway and wanted to complete the ring she was designing for her collection.

As always, she lost herself in the process, moments slipping by unnoticed. Finally, with a surge of pride, she turned off her torch and sat back to scrutinize her handiwork.

Like all her other pieces, the design was steeped in Celtic traditions but infused with a style that was her own unique blend of cultures. This new ring consisted of Celtic spirals and interlacing triangles along the band, topped with a stunning bezel-set ruby. All she had left to do was set the stone and give the ring a soft going-over with a brass brush for a lovely satin finish.

The whole process still filled her with a sense of awe, and she found herself thinking back on the work of ancient goldsmiths who produced exquisite gold filigree and decorations with tiny gold beads using the technique of granulation. It was hard for her to imagine working without the extensive tool collection she had at her disposal.

Abruptly, she became aware of just how much time had passed.

She glanced at the time on her iPhone. Nine forty-five. She was meeting Glenna at the parish office at ten. Good thing she only had a five-minute walk. Otherwise, she'd be screwed.

She put all her jewelry-making equipment in order and left the townhouse.

***

Casey pushed the Forensic Instinct team's nine o'clock meeting until ten. She made that decision at eight thirty, when she came down from her apartment on the brownstone's fourth floor only to hear banging and swearing coming from the basement, which they all referred to as Ryan's lair.

She'd descended the steps, found the door ajar, and stepped inside to the compartmentalized workroom that Ryan had created for himself.

Just inside the room was his tech center—a massive rectangular desk with a thirty-two-inch NEC UHD monitor. Ryan always bought the best equipment that money could buy, and Casey was always generous about supporting him. On the back wall were a series of Liebert MCR mini computer room enclosures, cabinets with built-in air conditioning and backup battery systems, which simultaneously housed and protected Forensic Instincts' critical command and control gear. Emanating from inside the locked enclosures was a powerful thrum of communication gear and Dell PowerEdge servers that powered Yoda. Ryan barely noticed the background noise any longer. It was just part of his normal work environment.

At the other end of the basement was a small machine shop—compact lathe and mini vertical milling machine and welding equipment, along with a wall filled with hand tools, measuring devices, and accessories for the machine tools. As a result, Ryan could design and build anything smaller than a motorcycle.

In the center of the basement was his arena, as he liked to call it, in which he would test his latest robotic incarnation against a variety of challenges—obstacles, flames, circular saws. In the corner were swept-up pieces of his experimental designs that failed in combat.

At the moment when Casey walked in, he'd been squatting over some robotic thing that obviously wasn't living up to his expectations. He was slamming parts around and muttering profanities at the metal contraption as if it were a living creature. Which, to Ryan, it probably was.

"Hey," Casey greeted him. "You're in early. Was the gym closed?" The entire FI team knew how much Ryan valued his sleep and how cranky he got when he lost out on it. He didn't do his morning workout until seven and rarely showed up at the office until after nine—unless he was knee-deep in solving a case.

He looked up at the sound of Casey's voice and rose to his feet. "Nope. I got my workout in early and did a fair amount of damage to the equipment, actually. Just didn't sleep well. It was one of those nights."

Casey had studied him thoughtfully. She was a behavioral expert and Ryan was so easy to read. He was more on edge than Casey had ever seen him, his jaw tight, his gaze darting about restlessly, and his mind somewhere far away from his failed robotic project.

"What's up?" she asked.

Ryan glanced at the time. "I'm not late for the meeting. I'll be there."

"I pushed it back an hour. I wanted to talk to you."

"About?"

"First of all, I need your notes substantiating the huge chunk of money you're requesting for Yoda's update. You were supposed to get those to me when you got home from your parents' house last night."

"You're right. Sorry." Ryan was trying to get his head in the game. "I'll have them to you by the end of today, okay?"

"Fine." Casey was still watching him. "Second—which is absolutely ridiculous for me to ask you, since you've hacked into the entire team's personal files—I need your permission to share yours with the rest of the team. Everyone else has consented to this, and I think it's only fair for you to do so, as well. And by the way, my comments and reviews have been encrypted and protected by two-factor authentication by Yoda so that even you can't gain access. And even if you could, I'd count on your integrity and loyalty to me not to. It's time we made this a level playing field."

That made Ryan chuckle. "I hear you, boss, and I'd be a real prick to refuse. Sure." He gave a dismissive wave of his hand. "It's not much of a concession on my part. Over these past few days, my life seems to have become an open book anyway."

Casey's brows drew together in question. "Meaning?"

"Oh, just that Claire was pissed that she didn't know I had a sister and Fee was pissed that she didn't know I had—in her words—*a girlfriend, as in singular*. Between that and the visit to my parents, Claire knows my whole family history and Fiona knows that Claire and I are together."

Amusement flashed in Casey's eyes, although she hid her surprise at Ryan's *finally* stating the obvious reality about him and Claire. It had sure taken him long enough.

"Those aren't the real reasons I pushed back the meeting," she said. "As I asked, what's up? You were barely here for an hour yesterday and you're clearly not yourself today. That will affect your work, so it gives me permission to ask."

Ryan's jaw tightened again. "You know why I wasn't here. You okayed it."

"Yes, I did. But I assumed you'd resolved things. If I was wrong, let me know."

"I offered Fee my support. Claire provided much-needed backup. That doesn't mean anything got resolved."

Casey sighed. "Ryan, let's stop playing games. Your sister went through a traumatic experience. I understand you being there for her and asking Claire to bring some calm to the chaos. But you're not just upset. Your tension level is through the stratosphere. So I'm asking you, is there more to this than I know?"

Ryan walked over to the futon against the short wall and dropped down onto it, sighing as he did. "I think so, yeah. I just don't know so."

"Care to share?"

"As a matter of fact, yes." Ryan looked relieved, as if he'd been waiting for this opportunity to unload. He laid it all out for Casey—what he'd found by hacking into the NYPD case file, about Claire's flashes of insight, and about the uneasy feeling he had regarding Fiona's place in all this.

"It could be circumstantial bullshit," he said. "But I have a bad feeling. Honestly, so does Claire, which worries me even more."

Casey heard him out, chewing her lip thoughtfully. "You think that the research Rose Flaherty was doing for Fiona is tied to her murder?"

Ryan shrugged, that strained look back on his face. "That's the problem. I'm not sure. So far, I have nothing solid to go on. If I did…"

"Then you'd be bringing the case to FI," Casey finished for him. "Which you should." She tucked an errant strand of red hair behind her ear. "Dig as deep as you have to. Include Claire as you need to. When the team meets at ten, tell them what you just told me. I guarantee you they'll vote unanimously to defer taking on a new case until we're clear whether or not we've already got one."

***

Fiona took a minute to stop at the church itself before heading across the street to the parish office. She wasn't particularly religious, but there was something about visiting Saint Patrick's Old Cathedral that drew her in and brought her a sense of peace and calm.

The outside of the church was understated, in sharp contrast to the spectacular interior, and especially in light of the sanctity and importance of the Basilica, or the Pope's church in the history of Catholicism in America. Constructed of beige brick and surrounded by a black wrought iron fence, the church needed no fancy sculptural features or gargoyles. Instead, it beckoned you in with a sense of warm invitation.

Fiona entered and walked straight to the entrance of the chapel, pausing to take in the full effect of its beauty.

What looked unassuming from the outside was stunning on the inside. The chapel had an elegant symmetry in its soaring gothic arches, and a grand stained glass window behind the altar that echoed the slender beauty of the arches in the nave. More stained glass windows graced the sides of the room. Beneath the main stained glass window were elaborately carved niches, each holding a colorful statue of a saint. These niches spread out like wings from the central painted archway, which was decorated in rich blues and golds, like a starry sky. Each niche was carved in the same pointed gothic shape as the arches in the nave, so when one looked down the aisle, there was a cohesive continuity of shape, form, and color. Flanked on each side of the altar were two tall candlesticks, as if they were standing guard. Six wrought iron chandeliers were suspended by chains that seemed to disappear into the lofty vault, bathing the room in an ethereal light.

The overall affect was one of serene beauty and calm.

Letting the sense of peace pervade her, Fiona felt more ready to deal with the difficult process she and Glenna were about to face. Finishing her prayers, she left the church.

Her phone rang as she turned onto Prince Street, and she answered as soon as she saw Nolan's number come up. Thankfully, his attorney friend in Florida had taken care of everything and had just left the judge's chambers with the signed papers in hand. A fax had already been sent to the NYPD, and the original would arrive by FedEx tomorrow.

Fiona had thanked her brother profusely and promised him a steak dinner at Peter Luger's.

She'd just hung up the phone when she rounded the corner on Mulberry and spied Glenna stepping out of the parish office.

"Hi. I thought you were running late," she said, looking as pale and tired as Fiona did.

"Sorry. I spent a moment inside the church. It helped."

Glenna nodded in understanding. "The funeral director is waiting for us."

"Okay. But before we go in, I just heard back from Nolan. Everything is set. Once the ME releases the body, you can take custody of it."

"Oh, bless your brother," Glenna breathed. "That takes a huge burden off my shoulders. It also explains the call I just got from Detective Alvarez."

"What did she say?"

"That the medical examiner had completed his autopsy and that, if the requisite document was received tomorrow, I'd be able to claim Rose's body."

Fiona's relief was a palpable entity. "Then we can actually discuss specifics with the funeral director. Not only what our wishes are for Rose's Mass and burial, but also the timing of everything, including the wake." She gave Glenna's hand a gentle squeeze. "Let's go in and honor Rose the way she deserves to be honored."

***

This time the entire Forensic Instincts team was present at the conference room table for the morning meeting. And they all listened carefully to what Ryan had to say. He made sure to elaborate further, explaining the nature of the research Rose had been doing for Fiona and how it tied to her current jewelry line.

"It's hard for me to be objective," he concluded. "I could be way overreacting."

"No, you're not." Claire gave an adamant shake of her head. "Something is definitely off. There's a darkness about Fiona's involvement here that transcends the ugliness of her finding Rose's body. I'm not sure what it is, but I do think it ties to the research Rose was doing for her. I sensed it when I touched her hand, even more so when I touched her bracelet—which just happens to be based on the tapestry designs." She sighed in frustration. "I wish I could have held those tapestries. But they're almost sacrosanct to Ryan's mother, so I just couldn't bring myself to ask. And the poor woman had taken about all she could handle for one day."

"She wasn't much better this morning," Ryan said. "She called me, since Fee turns off her phone when she's working. My dad had told her about the fact that Rose's death was being ruled a homicide. She was pretty unhinged, not only about the murder but about how it must be affecting Fee."

"Let's get back to these tapestries." Marc steepled his fingers in front of him in the way he always did when he was concentrating. "Tell us more about them."

Ryan looked over at Claire. "You saw them. I didn't. Can you take this one?"

"Not a problem." Claire went on to explain.

"Intricate symbols, pictorial representations, and panels that line up together—this sounds pretty complex," Patrick said. "And the large center panel with the symbols of royalty is clearly divergent from the others."

Claire nodded. "It's beyond impressive, and, yes, it's unique in its design. It also happens to be the panel Fiona was having Rose research, which she was clearly doing right before her death."

"Then there's the celebration Rose was planning," Casey reminded them. "That implies she'd found something of significance—something she didn't live long enough to share with Fiona."

"I don't disagree with the direction you're all taking," Marc said in his usual level-headed manner. "I'm not comfortable with what I'm hearing, either. The problem is that this is all conjecture, so I can see why Ryan is spinning in neutral. There are a lot of maybes that suggest Fiona might be in the middle of something that's over her head. But there's not a shred of concrete proof. And there are only two people who could fill in the blanks—one is dead and the other is the killer."

Ryan nodded. "So you see my dilemma."

"Well, *I* see that you're trying to protect your sister, which is very cool," Emma said, putting in her two cents. "And I think we should help you. If you want me to lift anything from the crime scene, get me into that shop. Yellow tape can't stop me."

"Forget it, Emma." Casey put the kibosh on that idea right away. "You're not contaminating a crime scene. Besides, there's nothing there that could help us. Law enforcement undoubtedly confiscated anything that smacked of evidence." She paused, glancing around the table. "But I do agree with Emma about our helping to investigate. I realize we don't know what our next step should be, but if a step is necessary, it will be necessary soon."

"Too soon to take on another case," Marc agreed. "In my opinion, we should hold off starting anything new for a few days. Just in the event that we're needed."

"Without question," Patrick said. "We're talking about one of our own. That takes priority. Period."

"Well, you know the way I feel." Claire stated the obvious. "My aura is so unsettled that I can't shake it. I'm convinced Fiona needs us."

"Then that settles it," Casey said. "We wait on a new case and treat this like an impending one."

Ryan glanced around the table, looking as touched and humbled as Ryan had ever looked. "Thanks, guys," he said simply. "This means a lot."

"No thanks necessary." Casey gazed straight at Ryan, not insulting him by softening her words. "Whoever killed Rose Flaherty wanted something. If that something relates to Fiona, she *is* in danger. Because in order to get what he wants, he'll be willing to kill again to get it."

9

Niall Dempsey's office took up the penthouse of one of his most sought-after Upper East Side luxury high-rises. All polished teak built-ins along the walls, marble floors, and chrome and glass accessories, the place proudly boasted all that Niall had become—all he'd *made* himself become.

Right now, he wasn't admiring his surroundings. He was standing at the panorama of windows, hands clasped behind his back, wishing Donald would contact him with an update. Whatever the police had found couldn't be traced back to him. That was a given. But what *had* they found and what secrets had Rose Flaherty died with?

Most unsettling of all, had she shared her findings or shown that print to anyone before the stupid guys he'd hired had screwed up and killed her?

His relationship with Rose had been carefully built over time. Meeting her hadn't been an accident. He'd done extensive research into the qualifications and experience of other antiquities experts in New York City before homing in on her. Not only was she more knowl-edgeable than all the others about ancient civilizations and timeless relics, she had a vast network of equally knowledgeable international colleagues. She also had a love of all things Celtic, which was a passion he shared. Given all that, he'd become a regular customer at her antique

shop, making certain to ingratiate himself with her in the hopes that
if anyone, however unaware of the information she possessed, might
know something to aid in his quest, that someone would be her.

His revelation had come in the form of Fiona McKay's tapestry
panel.

Oh, how excited Rose had been to show him that print, and to tell
him she was researching its history and for whom. After all, how could
she know it was a hidden secret too coveted and precious to discuss?
But Niall *had* known, from the moment he'd studied the details of the
panel. And to hear there were twelve more related ones yet to come?

The question was, how much had Rose learned? What did
the symbols mean? At the end, she'd become more closemouthed,
responding to Niall's questions by saying she couldn't say more until
she'd completed her work and reported everything to Fiona, but it was
clear from her demeanor that her findings were fascinating.

He couldn't settle for that. So he'd taken action.

But to what end? To spin in neutral? Not a prayer.

He was following Donald's advice and keeping a low profile. For
now. But investigation or not, he was going after what he wanted.

"Mr. Dempsey?" Niall's PA, George Cullen—hand-picked, vetted,
and hired by Donald—entered the room, repeating his employer's
name twice and then clearing his throat to get Niall's attention.

"What is it, George?" Niall didn't turn.

"The doorman just informed me that Peter Walsh is here to see you."

That news brought a smile to Niall's face. He and Peter had been
reunited in New York three years ago, totally by chance. Peter had left
Ireland long after Niall and flown to the Big Apple, hoping to make a
life for himself. As luck would have it, a few years ago, he'd come upon
a news story written about Niall and his meteoric rise as a millionaire
real estate developer. The article had come complete with Niall's photo.

Peter had recognized his old mate instantly and sought him out.
The reunion had been heartfelt and emotional—two middle-aged

men who'd been kids together, whispered confidences together, and joined the IRA together.

Sadly, life had taken a huge toll on Niall's best mate. His last years in Ireland had been dark ones, with him being squeezed out of the Provos because better-connected drivers were sought, and his other skills weren't outstanding enough to impress the higher-ups. His father had been a real son of a bitch, too, reminding his son that if he were a better shot, he could have been more, done better, made a success of himself.

Peter hadn't wept when his father was killed during an IRA operation that the RUC ambushed.

Nor had he wept when he bid Ireland good-bye forever.

But he was haunted by shadows. He was bitter. He drank way too much. And since his Visa had expired six months after he'd arrived in the US, he'd never been able to get a decent job. Niall treaded lightly on the subject, since Peter's ego was so fragile. Peter insisted he was doing fine as a large-scale bookmaker, raking in tons of cash. But Niall knew the streets all too well. And he'd long since figured out that Peter was no bookmaker, he was a bagman who collected sports gambling bets from runners and brought them to the actual bookmaker, getting a pittance of a cut for his efforts.

It was a shit of a life, and Niall spent long hours thinking of ways he could help his friend without putting himself at risk. He couldn't sponsor him; that might uncover his own identity. And he couldn't officially hire him for the same reason. The last thing he needed was to have the authorities poking around in his life and finding anything that tied him to a past he'd so carefully erased. What he did do, repeatedly, was to ask Peter for alleged favors—like making sure his slew of under-construction Manhattan high-rises were properly locked up for the night. Niall always made sure it came across as a huge favor, adding that he knew it was inconvenient for Peter to check on them. Accordingly, he gave Peter more money than he deserved for his efforts. They both knew what Niall was really doing, but neither said a word. They were as close to brothers as they could be, and Niall knew that Peter would do the same if their situations were reversed.

Today's visit would be social, as always. They'd share a pint—or several, in Peter's case—and relive happier times. But beneath the surface would lie the reality that Peter needed cash. He'd never ask for a loan outright, nor would Niall allow him to humiliate himself by doing so. That meant that Niall had about three minutes to come up with a plausible "chore" that needed to be done.

His mind was already racing through the possibilities as he acknowledged George's announcement.

"Have the doorman send him up."

"Yes, sir." George complied, then disappeared promptly, well aware that the meetings between these two men were off-limits to him.

Niall opened the door wide, welcoming his friend with a warm hug. As always, seeing Peter was both a joy and a heartache. His build was still square and solid and his hair was still full, although, like Niall's, it was now salt-and-pepper. But unlike Niall, Peter's features were sunken in from a hard life and too much drinking, and his eyes held irreparable darkness that no amount of time could erase. True, Niall had shared the younger years of that life, but he was stronger, harder, more of a survivor than Peter.

"Niall," Peter greeted him as the two men hugged. When they'd first reunited, Niall had told Peter only that he'd left Ireland with his life in jeopardy—enough so that he required a new identity. Peter had never once asked questions and never again called his friend "Sean." That alone spoke to the depth of their friendship.

"I'm glad you came by," Niall said once the two men were settled in the twin leather club chairs, glasses of Guinness in their hands.

"Hope I'm not interrupting," Peter replied, lifting his glass in a toast to his friend before taking a few healthy gulps. It was barely noon and Peter looked as if he'd already drunk away the morning. "Lunchtime is usually a good time for you."

Niall chuckled. "That's because the rest of the world eats and I don't." His brows drew together in question. "But I'd be glad to make an exception if you want to take a run down to Quinn's."

Quinn's was their pub and restaurant of choice. Located in the East Village, Quinn's was, like Kelly's, as authentic as you could find outside Ireland. Niall hadn't found the place by chance. Donald had pointed him in that direction, not only because of the great food, drink, and atmosphere, but because it was far away from Kelly's—the spot where Niall went only when he needed to meet with Donald.

At Quinn's, he was Niall Dempsey, with no ties to Sean Donovan.

Peter's face lit up. "Can you spare the time?"

"I can use the break. My mind is too crowded with business." Short, sweet, and loosely true.

Other than his identity as Silver Finger, Niall kept only one secret from Peter—that being his relentless quest for an incomparable find. Once that find was made, it had to belong to him and him alone.

By the time the two men reached Quinn's, settled themselves in their regular booth, and ordered their usual Irish stew flavored with Guinness, Niall had come up with an idea for helping Peter.

"I've been meaning to bring this up for a few weeks now, but I didn't want to make you feel obligated," he began, drinking his Guinness slowly. He wasn't used to having two drinks by this time of day, especially since he'd eaten nothing but half a donut at six thirty. And he needed to keep his wits about him, given that he was walking a fine line here.

Peter set down his glass, his brows drawn together quizzically. "Obligated? You know that whatever you need is as good as done."

"Which is exactly why I haven't mentioned it. I knew you'd say yes. I want to make sure you have the time."

Peter gave a bark of laughter. "I work bat hours. Trust me, I have the time."

"That's the thing. It involves bat hours. I've held off asking you to act as an actual security guard because of your business. The problem is that I need one. Not full-time, just two nights a week, one at my Midtown location and one at my Upper West Side location. I'm short-staffed, and I don't trust anyone the way I trust you. On top of that, I'm about to start construction on two new high-rises, both in Brooklyn—Williamsburg and Fort Greene. That means added sites for you to check out and make sure everything is locked down. You'll be running all over the city, plus giving up two nights a week. I'm a shit to ask this of you and I want you to say no if you have to. But if you could manage it—"

"I'll manage it," Peter interrupted. "We just have to work out how many hours you need and on which nights. I have to make it a consistent schedule so I can arrange things at my end. I keep a tight leash on my bagmen and runners. They show up when and where I tell them to." He rubbed his glass between his palms. "And even though it's a regular thing, it would still have to be off the books, just like my bookmaking operation."

"Of course, cash only, as always," Niall agreed, never batting an eye at the bald-faced lie of a life Peter had concocted. "That's good for us both. As for payment, you name your price. You'll be doing me an enormous favor. The only perk I can think of to offer you to make things easier is a company car. That way, you can get around faster."

Peter hid his elation behind a thoughtful nod. "That makes sense. The way your company is growing, I'll be covering all five boroughs soon. If I try to do that by subway, I'll never get to all your jobsites."

"Done." Niall was quite pleased with the way things had turned out. He'd put much-needed money in Peter's pockets and have top-notch security. A win-win.

With that, their stew arrived, and Niall dug in and savored his first mouthful. "Nothing like the taste of home," he said. "At least the home of our childhood." He raised his glass. "To happy times past, and better times to come."

Peter raised his glass, as well, that dark look flickering in his eyes. Demons from the years they were apart and that gnawed at his guts. Niall often wanted to ask him about them, but he held back. If his friend wanted to talk, he would. And Niall would listen.

Ironically, when Peter did speak, his words dug into Niall's throat like talons, clawing until he could barely breathe.

"Word has it that Cobra is in New York."

Niall fought the talons, swallowing hard—once, twice—as he battled to mask his reaction and to physically bring himself under control.

With the greatest of efforts, he succeeded.

"Where did you hear that?" This was impossible. Niall had men scouring the globe for that bastard. How was it that Peter could have that kind of information when Niall didn't?

Peter shrugged. "I didn't burn all my bridges. I still have friends back home. Connected friends. They pass along things that might interest me. I figured this one would interest you, too, since I'm sure you lost people because of him."

Niall scrutinized Peter's face for any indication that he knew about Kevin and the way he'd died. But Peter had a different expression on his face. More of a smirk.

Totally taken aback, Niall spread his hands apart in noncomprehension. "I know your bitterness toward the Provos. But this isn't about them, at least not the high-ups. It's about our friends, the mates we grew up with. Cobra set them up to die. He's scum." A thought darted through Niall's mind. "Do your contacts know his real name?"

"That's still a big question mark." Peter was now eating his stew with gusto.

That did it. "Why are you so fucking detached about this?" Niall demanded.

Peter's head came up. His smirk was gone, but his gaze was as hard as his words. "I'm not detached. I hate the man as much as you do for what he did to our friends. But for me, there's more to it."

"More—how?"

A swig of Guinness, as if Peter were medicating himself. "You didn't really know my father. He was a heartless shit. Beat my mother until she was too weak to fight. Once she was gone, he turned his rages on me—and it wasn't just with his fists. That's why I started screwing up with the Provos. I was a mess. And when things started going downhill, he threatened to turn me in to the RUC. He would have done it, too, if he hadn't died first. Having him gone was a blessed relief. So no matter how much I hate Cobra, I also owe him a debt of thanks for killing the son of a bitch who raised me."

Niall blinked, shocked by everything he was hearing about Peter's life, but even more shocked by the last revelation. "Cobra ambushed your father's operation?"

"Not only ambushed it. Tortured my father and killed him in his signature style."

That took Niall aback. Cobra wasn't just the RUC's top informant. He was a sick, conscienceless fuck who lived by his own soulless set of rules.

Niall knew all about Cobra's signature style—one shot behind the ear using a .22 caliber long rifle round. The bullet ricocheted through the victim's head, causing unendurable pain and blood-curdling screams, lodging somewhere inside the skull without ever exiting. The mere mention of Cobra's name made the IRA quake.

The RUC expected Cobra to spare the lives of real RUC touts and accepted that occasionally he had to kill an IRA member to protect his cover with the RUC. But Cobra killed for a more fundamental reason—it gave him immense pleasure. He relished the whole process of grilling IRA members, torturing and breaking them until they begged to die. And die they would, in the most horrific way possible.

Cobra would then report back to the IRA leadership that a traitor had been eliminated. Those who heard the victims' screams would spread the word about what Cobra would do to an IRA traitor, making him more feared within the IRA, more useful to the IRA leadership, and more valuable to his RUC handlers.

But Peter's father being one of his victims? Niall had never even suspected. All he'd known was that Gerard had died in an ambush. No further details were provided. But now Peter's reaction, no matter how chilling, made sense.

Niall watched Peter eat, pushing away his own meal as nausea squeezed his stomach. "Why didn't you tell me all this was going on?"

"What could you have done? My scum of a father would have turned his rage on you, too. I wasn't having that." Peter signaled the waitress for another Guinness. "It was my problem. And Cobra took care of it for me." He looked at Niall as if he were preparing to see condemnation on his face. "I can only imagine what you're thinking, what a monster your best mate turned out to be. But the truth is, you wouldn't understand. Your mother was a good woman. You never knew your father. You're probably better off."

Niall was reeling in a way that Peter could never find out. "I'm not judging you," he said. "And you're right, I can't understand. But that kind of torture…"

"I try to block out that part. I focus only on the fact that he's dead. And all I feel is relief."

"That I can understand. It eats at me to know what you had to live through." Niall chose his next words carefully. "How are your friends so sure he's in New York?"

"I don't know if they're sure. But their information is always solid, so I'm betting they're right. And if they are, they'll find him and he'll wish he was never born."

"How will they do that if they don't know who it is they're looking for?"

Peter took his next glass of beer and half downed it in a few swallows. "They'll figure it out. Count on it. And if I get word, I promise to give you a front-row seat."

10

The chapel at Saint Patrick's Old Cathedral was filled with Rose's friends, colleagues, and patrons, as well as with her fellow church congregants. The special Mass that followed was beautiful and meaningful—exactly what Rose would have wanted.

The cremains were laid to rest in the columbarium at the church, and both Fiona and Glenna were among the small number of people present during the Rite of Committal, where they bid good-bye to their dear friend, tears mixed with prayers.

Afterwards, there was a small repast, a lovely gesture that was open to all who wanted to attend. Still, Fiona was grateful for the gathering her mother had arranged for the night after next, so that everyone who couldn't attend the Mass or who wanted the chance to celebrate Rose's life with good food, good drink, and good stories could do so.

The only damper on the day was the presence of Detective Alvarez and her partner, Detective Shaw, at the church. Fiona had winced when she saw them. And even though they kept a low, respectful profile, and even though almost no one knew who they were, Fiona and Glenna did. Just as they knew the detectives were checking out all the attendees, following up on whatever avenues they were pursuing.

Fiona gave them a curt nod as she left the church—which she did alone. Despite her mother's gentle protests, she explained to both her parents and to Glenna that she wanted some time just to walk and think.

She strolled through Nolita, stopping for a cup of coffee and then continuing on her way. She could go home, but she didn't want to. She wanted to be outside with the falling leaves and the cool September breezes. Somehow that made her feel closer to Rose.

She brushed her hair off her nape, and with one fingertip, she touched the earrings she'd chosen to wear, a soft smile coming to her lips. She'd spent days making them as another tribute to Rose and her research. Round silver disks dangled from eighteen-karat gold handcrafted ear wires, hovering about an inch below Fiona's earlobe. The earrings were framed by thin twisted wire that looped all around the disks. Small gemstones were scattered on the back. And on the front were the crown and the iconic Tree of Life, cut from gold sheet and soldered to the silver base. Tiny gemstones—ruby, emerald, and diamond—were set on the tree and points of the crown. It was a mini replica of the center tapestry. Later, Fiona would incorporate it in her new line. But for now... *Rose*, she thought, *these are for you. Maybe they'll bring you the peace that you deserve.*

A cold chill invaded her heart. There could be no peace until Rose's killer was caught.

Squeezing her eyes shut, Fiona stopped walking and took another sip of her coffee.

She didn't notice the guy behind her. Or the way he raised his cell phone to take pictures of her and her earrings.

***

Marc was in his office at FI, reading an article about current research on the sociopathic mind, when Ryan poked his head in.

"Busy?"

"I've got time. Come in." Marc saved the article on his computer to read later and waved Ryan in. He'd been expecting this visit; it was just a question of how long it would take for Ryan to reach the point where he'd show up at Marc's door.

The point had obviously arrived.

"What's up?" Marc asked.

Ryan dropped into a chair. "The detectives are blowing through Rose Flaherty's contacts. So far, everyone's checked out. No motives, all alibis verified—in short, a complete dead end." Ryan bristled. "They're actually investigating Fee as a possible suspect, doing all kinds of digging into her life."

Marc didn't look surprised, nor would Ryan had he any objectivity on the matter. "That's routine, Ryan. You know that. Fiona found the body. She was alone at the shop and has no alibi before her 911 call."

"And no motive."

"They'll figure that out." Marc's gaze was steady and his reaction was factual. Sheer habit from his years with the FBI's Behavioral Analysis Unit. Listening. Watching. Waiting people out so the silence made them uneasy enough to talk. Of course the latter part wasn't the case with the FI team. They, and his wife Madeline, were the only people he was totally himself with. But in this case, Ryan needed the voice of reason to lead him where he needed to go. And Marc was supplying it.

"Did you tell Fiona she was being investigated?" he asked.

"No." Ryan shook his head. "She's gotten about as much honesty as she can handle. I'll tell her things on—to use your favorite phrase—a need-to-know basis. The whole thing just really pisses me off."

A corner of Marc's mouth lifted in a half grin. "You don't *have* to hack into the NYPD's database. Not a requirement."

"It *sure as shit* is. Fee is strong, but she's also unexposed to this kind of stuff. I've got to look out for her!" Ryan blew out a breath. "Sorry. I guess I just needed to vent."

Marc made a wide sweep with his arm. "Vent away." Then, giving Ryan one more thing to chew over, knowing exactly where this conversation was leading, he said, "You know, there is an upside to this."

"Which is?"

"If the cops are checking out Fiona, they'll also be checking out the research Rose was doing for her. Maybe something will show up in the file that interests you."

"Point taken." Ryan mulled that one over. "The more they learn, the more I learn. They're investigating a murder. I'm making sure my sister isn't a target. Our goals are different, but our needs for information are the same, at least about this. If they figure out that Rose's research for Fee is the motive for her murder, they'll put together as detailed a record as they can as to why." His jaw hardened. "And then they'll be back to grilling Fee."

Marc watched as Ryan came to the exact place he knew he would.

"I'm not tagging along behind the NYPD," he exploded. "I lead. I don't follow. This passive bullshit won't work."

"Then maybe it's time to discuss a way not to be passive."

That made Ryan's head come up—as Marc knew it would. The two men had different temperaments, different ways of attacking a problem, and different maturity levels—given that Marc had more than a half dozen years on Ryan. But when they worked together, they made things happen. Ryan was the rocket and Marc the seasoned igniter.

"How?" Ryan demanded.

Marc leaned forward in his chair. He and Casey had gone back and forth about this game plan for the past two days now. Casey had been right on Marc's wavelength, and she'd given not only her approval but her full support of how things should be handled. Ultimately, though, they had to wait for Ryan to get out of his own way and come to them, probably to Marc. Well, here he was. Time to get into it.

"You've got to be willing to change tactics," Marc said bluntly. "Cut out the tunnel vision, divert your efforts, and expand your resources."

"Be more specific."

"You're focusing only on Fiona and any potential danger she might be in. Flip it around. Instead of Fiona, focus on everyone else. Rose's killer is out there. He or she had a motive. Maybe it's time to start investigating the murder, not just hovering over Fiona.

"As for expanding your resources, time to bring in FI. Turn the reins over to Casey and get the team involved. Whatever the police can do, we can do better. And faster. Download that contact list. We can divide it up and go through the people, one by one. Do a background check on Rose herself. Maybe she has a skeleton in her closet that no one knows about. Use Claire's talent; maybe she'll pick up something from our findings. Use Casey's talent; she has a way of seeking out persons of interest at their local Starbucks and walking away with information they never knew they disclosed. Have Patrick put security on Fiona—just one guy, and just in case—so that you can focus on *doing* rather than *waiting*. We've just been sitting on our hands. Let's use the time productively and proactively."

Ryan's eyes had narrowed as reality hit home. "You and Casey brainstormed this out. I hear her voice in all this."

"Yup."

"But at the team meeting, all she said was—"

"That was then. This is now. Days have passed and we're still spinning in neutral. Not our speed. Certainly not *your* speed. But Casey wanted to make sure you wanted this badly enough to relinquish control. She's our boss. If we make this our case, she's in charge."

Ryan nodded in understanding. "I hear you. I hear you both. A few days ago I wasn't ready. Now I am. I'll go to Casey. We'll make this our case, whether or not Fee is a target."

"And we'll catch a killer."

***

It was midafternoon when Fiona arrived home. She collected her mail and let herself into her townhouse.

The walk hadn't done much good. If anything, her heart was heavier now than it had been before. She couldn't stop thinking about the detectives' presence at the Mass and the fact that Rose's killer was still out there.

Slipping out of her jacket, Fiona hung it up on the coatrack and tossed the mail on the corner table in the hallway. A full-size Tyvek envelope peeked out from beneath the usual bills and correspondence. It immediately caught her eye—and the return address on it made her catch her breath.

Rose's antique shop.

With trembling hands, Fiona picked up the envelope and glanced at the postmark. It was mailed on the same day as she and Rose were set to meet. So why had Rose sent it rather than placed it right in Fiona's hands? And why was Fiona's name handwritten when her address and the return address were printed on labels?

With a sense of foreboding, Fiona opened the envelope and removed the contents.

The print of the center tapestry Fiona had given her. Two plastic-sheathed pages, photocopied from two different archeology textbooks. Just looking at the copies, Fiona could tell that the original pages were yellowed and brittle with age, the printing faded. She could almost smell the musty aroma that emanated from these typical pages from Rose's binders.

One plastic sheet holder had a Post-it on it, with Rose's scribbled handwriting. Fiona would need some decent lighting to read it.

She walked into her living room, flipping on the overhead lights, and sank down on the sofa. She planned on poring over everything. But she began with the Post-it, which read:

Reminders: Shield. High Irish king. Symbol reference obscure. Still researching. Require other tapestry panels. Crucial tie to imperceptible imageries.

Other than that, there was no further explanation, nothing. Fiona's brow furrowed, floundering as she read and reread the staccato phrases. Knowing Rose, she understood that she'd affixed the Post-it here in case she forgot to get into detail with Fiona on this subject.

But now Rose wasn't here to explain, and Fiona was totally lost. What shield? What high Irish king? What imperceptible imageries?

Maybe the enclosed pages would offer some insight.

Fiona leaned forward on the sofa cushion, focusing intently on the first page, realizing at the same time that a paragraph on each page was highlighted. And both highlighted paragraphs had photos of that unknown spiral symbol that appeared on every one of the tapestry panels.

The words on the first page were small, typed next to the symbol itself:

The "light at the end of the tunnel" symbol goes back hundreds, maybe thousands of years and was originally seen among the common Celtic symbols. Its usage diminished in the last three hundred years and has now become so obscure it's known mostly to scholars and to people living in Ireland for many generations. The symbol simply consists of a one-line drawing, starting with a spiral that becomes a tunnel-shaped outline. The spiral signifies light and the upside down U signifies a tunnel or a dark place.

That was it—other than the photo of the symbol alongside the paragraph.

Fiona turned to the second page, which had a similar photo of the symbol, along with the following paragraph:

This spiral and tunnel-shaped symbol is quite rare, and while scholars are in agreement that, when used, it appeared to have significant meaning, the meaning itself has been disputed. Overall, the following appear to be the most prominent interpretations:

Ancient interpretation: light after the dark, better days to come.

Religious interpretation: ascension to heaven after hard life on earth.

Most currently discovered interpretation: light at the end of the tunnel.

Thus the name "light at the end of the tunnel" has been assigned to this hard-to-trace Celtic symbol.

Fiona reread the paragraphs on each page several times, ascertaining that they were the only mention of this symbol at all. But in both cases, the paragraphs were capsulized segments of a longer page about obscure Celtic symbols.

Frustrated, Fiona slipped the page-protected sheets and the print back into the envelope, placing it on the coffee table in front of her.

Rather than answers, Fiona now had only more questions. Why did her great-grandmother focus on this symbol? What tunnel? What light? Was she describing their life in Ireland versus their life in New York? And Fiona's initial questions remained. What shield? What imperceptible imageries? And what high Irish king?

She squinted at the print, then shook her head. She'd have to go back to her parents' house right away and carefully study the actual center panel, not some paper replica. That had to hold some answers. But there were still so many questions.

For the easiest one, though, she was about to get her answer right now.

She took out her iPhone and called Glenna.

"Hi," Glenna answered. "Are you okay?"

"As okay as I can be. You?"

"Same."

"Glenna, I just got home and found a Tyvek envelope waiting for me. It's from Rose. My name is handwritten on it, but my address and the return address are printed on labels. And it was mailed to me on the same day I was coming into the shop to meet with Rose. I don't understand."

Glenna blew out a breath. "I'm so sorry. I forgot all about that envelope. Rose had set it aside for you. Obviously, she meant to give it to you in person, but I didn't realize that and printed labels and mailed it to you. Why? Is it significant?"

"I have no idea." Fiona stared at the envelope. "But if it is, I'm grateful you mailed it to me. Otherwise the detectives would have confiscated it at the crime scene." She paused, her mind racing. "Did you see my parents leave the church?"

"Yes, they left about a half hour before I did. I stayed to talk to some of Rose's clients who were understandably shaken by the news and by the phone calls they'd gotten from the NYPD. A lot of them plan on coming to the gathering at your parents' house. Niall Dempsey was kind enough to offer to provide accommodations for out-of-town guests—"

"That was really nice of him," Fiona replied, only half listening at this point. She was eager to hop on the train and get to Woodlawn. "Glenna, I don't mean to cut you off, but I want to check in with my mom and dad. I want to make sure they're okay and also to see what dishes I can bring with me to the gathering."

"Of course, go. Please ask them what I can bring, as well. I know a few of Rose's favorite dishes. I'd be happy to make them."

"Perfect. I'll let you know. Thanks."

Fiona was about to head out when she glanced down at the coffee table, her gaze focusing on the envelope.

Scooping it up, she tucked it in her tote bag and left the townhouse.

An unseen pair of eyes watched her leave.

11

As luck would have it, Fiona's parents weren't home when she got there.

Her father had probably gone directly to work, and her mother was undoubtedly already food shopping for the upcoming gathering. That meant she could do what she came here to do without having a cup of tea and chatting about how lovely the special Mass had been. She adored her parents, but sometimes she just had to get things done without fanfare.

This was one of those times.

Fiona let herself into the house and went straight up to the attic. She knelt down beside the memory box and lifted the lid. Carefully, she took out the largest tapestry panel and spread it out on the floor. Next, she pulled the Tyvek envelope out of her tote bag and placed the plastic-sleeved pages beside the tapestry for easy reference.

She'd done some quick research on her iPhone during the train ride. Yes, in fact, there had been high Irish kings. But they dated back to medieval times, with the last one being recorded in the twelfth century, and many of them were only legendary. As for shields, she'd researched both kinds of shields: weaponry and coats of arms. The latter didn't date back as far as the twelfth century and—even after they began to appear—neither they nor the weaponry shared any of the tapestry's images. Besides, why would her great-grandmother be weaving images from ancient times? It just didn't make sense.

She leaned forward and began studying every inch of the tapestry from top to bottom. Obviously the crown and throne-like image holding the Tree of Life spoke of royalty. Maybe it was symbolic rather than actual. But a real high Irish king? What could Rose have dug up?

Fiona's gaze shifted farther down, down the Tree of Life—and abruptly she was stopped by two tiny images she'd never noticed before. They were almost an identical color with the background, so much so that they blended together, and, unless one was studying the design as closely as she was right now, they would miss them altogether.

She squinted one eye to see them more closely.

Just below the Tree of Life, there was a tiny fist clutching what looked to be a trophy or a goblet of some kind. The depictions were so small that it would take some major zooming in to make out any further details. These had to be the imperceptible images Rose had been referring to. Did they have some special meaning? Was that part of what she was still researching or had she already gotten her answers?

Using the camera on her iPhone, Fiona zoomed in as close as she could and took a few pictures. She then sat back on her heels and studied the photos she'd taken. They were good, but certainly not of professional quality. Plus, they, just as the print, were blurred by the woven texture of the tapestry. She'd need to have someone capture all the nuances she was missing.

And then what?

She dragged both hands through her hair, feeling both anxious and frustrated. It was no longer a mere supposition that Rose had vital information to share with her, nor was there any doubt that there was more to this tapestry than just its beauty.

Fiona took out all the other tapestry panels and spread them out on the attic floor. True, Rose hadn't seen any of these. But maybe there were more imperceptible images on them that would relate to the ones she'd just found. Maybe there'd be a tie that she could build on.

That led to an obvious thought. She needed a new antiquities expert. No one could replace Rose, but she had to talk to Glenna and find out who Rose generally consulted with on matters such as these. Maybe she could even figure out the exact professionals she'd gone to about the tapestry panel she'd already researched. If so, Fiona would follow up with them; she didn't care if it was here or in Dublin. She'd call and ask for their help, also asking for any information they'd already passed along to Rose.

For now, she'd take the necessary photos and forward them to Ryan. Maybe he could find a way to smooth out the texture of the woven tufts and make the photos clearer. Then she'd have something more than just Rose's Post-it and the pages she'd sent her to share with the contacts she hoped to make.

Then there was the problem of photos versus the genuine objects. Fiona needed access to the tapestries themselves. She couldn't keep relying on pictures to capture the details she needed. And she couldn't keep running back and forth to her parents' house to see and hold the panels themselves. She'd have to get her mother's permission to borrow the tapestries—which would require an explanation she'd have to be ready to offer.

That could wait a bit. For now, she had her work cut out for her.

Still clutching her iPhone, she bent over the smaller panels and began her scrutiny.

***

Ryan was downstairs in his lair, intently researching Rose Flaherty's background and life, when his cell phone *bing*-ed. And *bing*-ed. And *bing*-ed.

A series of texts from Fee.

Quickly, he opened them. A bunch of photos along with the message: *Tapestry images, zoomed in as much as I could. Clarity sucks. Can you enhance these to make them look more like drawings than blurry photos of tapestry panels?*

Ryan frowned. He didn't like the fact that Fiona was doing her own investigating.

The sooner he took this out of her hands, the better.

I can do anything, he typed back. *Give me an hour or two.*

Upstairs in FI's third-floor yoga room, Claire was sitting quietly, the lights turned down low, her mind flitting from image to image—each tapestry she'd seen, every detail she could recall—as she desperately sought an awareness that was just not coming, not without physical contact.

Her eyes flew open as a dark, dark energy slammed into her consciousness, flowed through her like poison.

Something was wrong. Very wrong. It was happening right now.

And it involved Fiona.

She jumped to her feet and raced out of the room.

***

The sun was already setting when Fiona got back home.

She was feeling pretty wiped. She'd spent long, tedious hours in her parents' attic, after which she'd spent a while with her mom, who'd arrived home. Fiona hadn't gone into details, just saying that she'd taken some additional photos of the tapestries for her jewelry line. She didn't mention borrowing the tapestries—not yet. She was still pondering the best way to approach this so the answer would be yes. To get her mother to lend her anything from the memory box—much less these revered tapestry panels—would take a lot of convincing, and just saying that having them in her hands was for creativity purposes wasn't going to cut it.

Scrutinizing and taking photos of the tapestries had been a long and tedious task, and she'd sent Ryan everything she had in the hopes of coming up with a starting point. Not that there'd been anything new on the smaller panels. No fists. No trophies. But she still wanted sharp photos of them for when she approached whoever she hoped would help her further research this.

Ryan, of course, had cheerfully told her he'd accomplished what she wanted in record time—typical oh-so-modest Ryan—and he'd both texted and emailed her the finished photos, adding that she should forward him anything else she needed—and to let him run with any future adventures she planned on taking.

He was protecting her. She got that. It wouldn't stop her from acting on her own. Still, she might be taking him up on his offer to help.

Fitting her key in the lock, she pushed open the door, stepped inside, flipped on the pale hall light, and froze.

The place had been trashed. Drawers hanging open, sofa cushions torn apart, lamps overturned. The living room looked like a bulldozer had plowed through it. And from the doorway, she could see that the same applied to the dining room and kitchen.

For one long, heart-pounding minute, she just stood there, gaping. Then she ran outside, shaking on the sidewalk as she pulled out her phone.

First, she called 911. Then she called Ryan.

He answered on the first ring, and he sounded totally freaked out. "Claire just burst in here. Are you okay?"

"Ryan, someone broke into my house." Fiona could hear the panic in her own voice. "The place is trashed."

"Did you get the hell out of there?" he demanded. She could hear the feet of his chair squeal loudly and she knew he was already in motion.

"Yes. I'm outside. And I called 911."

"He could still be in there. Go down the block. I'm on my way."

Ryan screeched up to Fiona's townhouse in the FI van, having made the short but congested trip in just over five minutes. He'd zigzagged through traffic, blown through every yellow light, and ignored the drivers who gave him the finger.

He jumped out of the van—paying no attention to the fact that he'd parked willy-nilly with the back end jutting halfway into the street—slammed the door, and broke into a sprint. A white van with the bold lettering *Crime Scene Unit* was sitting prominently in front of the building, which meant they were already on the scene, dusting for fingerprints and collecting evidence. Flashing red lights also told Ryan that a patrol car from the First Precinct was here, as were—no surprise—Detective Alvarez and her partner, Detective Shaw. Both the First and the Sixth Precincts were part of the First Division of Manhattan South, which meant the same dispatched calls reached cops from both precincts. No doubt, Alvarez and Shaw had been out investigating the murder and had picked up the dispatch, thus shooting right over to Fee's.

This should be a great party, he thought grimly, pacing up the sidewalk to where Fiona stood, arms wrapped around herself to ward off the shock. *The First Precinct and Alvarez. Who could ask for more?*

The First Precinct served Tribeca as well as SoHo, so the cops there were acutely aware of Forensic Instincts and their habit of pushing the boundaries of legal protocol. And now Alvarez would learn that Fiona's brother was *that* Ryan McKay.

Well, screw them. All he cared about was Fee.

His sister sagged with relief when she saw Ryan, and she hurried away from the police to get to him.

"Thank you for coming," she managed as she reached his side.

"Are you okay?" Ryan wrapped her in a huge hug.

"I don't think so. I don't know." She drew back, visibly trying to get a handle on her emotions. "You and I both know that, whoever did this, it's no coincidence. It has to do with the tapestries and Rose's murder. There can't be any other explanation. Something she uncovered triggered all this. Oh, God, what if I'm responsible for her being killed?"

"Cut it out." Ryan gave her a gentle shake, more worried about the ramifications to Fiona's well-being than anything else. "You're not responsible for the actions of a killer." Glancing over his head, he saw Detective Alvarez glaring at him, tapping her foot impatiently. "What have you told the police?"

Fiona's jaw set. "Nothing. I don't have concrete answers and I'm not about to get into my suspicions. They asked me to call my roommate, which I already did. Lara will be on the next flight from Paris. She sounded pretty hysterical. And her parents aren't going to be too happy. After all, this is their place."

"We'll deal with that later," Ryan said. "What did the cops say is next?"

"They want me to walk through the house with them after the Crime Scene detectives are finished to see if I notice anything missing. In the meantime, Alvarez and Shaw just keep grilling me. They want answers I either don't have or am not ready to give. So I've just leaned on the fact that I'm in shock—again—and am clueless about their questions. Which isn't far from the truth."

"Smart girl." He draped a brotherly arm around her shoulders. "Let's stick to that approach—at least for now. You and I can talk later, once law enforcement is gone."

"Will they let me move back in? I've got a cleanup disaster to tackle. I only saw the first floor. That leaves the second-floor bedrooms and my entire third-floor loft. God only knows what they did to that."

"They'll let you in after CSU leaves. But if the place is as bad as you say, you'll stay with me for a few nights. I'm sure Lara will stay with her parents or a friend. I'll arrange for a cleanup crew."

"Mom and Dad will order me home," Fiona reminded him. "They were upset enough when I didn't move back in after the murder. Now I'm somehow targeted. They're going to flip out."

Ryan nodded. "Yup. But they'll be okay if they know you're with me. And even if you go out without me, you won't be alone. That's been taken care of." He waved away Fiona's oncoming question. "Not now. I'll get into it when it's just us."

"Okay." Fiona didn't look thrilled to be kept in the dark about her life, but she acquiesced, realizing the timing of this conversation sucked.

Together, she and Ryan walked back to the group of police gathered around.

Unfortunately, Ryan recognized one of the uniformed cops who was perched just outside Fiona's townhouse—a cop he wasn't on the best of terms with. Ryan had acted on a lead in FI's most recent case that had bypassed NYPD involvement.

"So the name McKay isn't a coincidence after all," Officer Colby said, his mouth set in a grim line. "No wonder our victim called her brother to the scene." He waved his arm toward Detectives Alvarez and Shaw. "Meet Ryan McKay—of Forensic Instincts fame."

Alvarez processed that with a tight nod and a glance at Fiona. "And here I thought you were just bringing your brother into the precinct for emotional support."

"That's all she was doing, Detective," Ryan said. "I specifically asked Fiona to leave out my first name so you didn't think Forensic Instincts was encroaching on your investigation. I was strictly there to hold my sister together. I'm sure you can imagine the kind of state she was in. And now this." He pointed at the townhouse.

"So I'm supposed to believe that your team isn't involved in this case?"

"Originally, we weren't. Now—things have changed. If Fiona chooses to retain our services, then we have a client and, yes, we'll be involved." Ryan continued, striving for a note of comradery, knowing he was lying even as he did, "If that happens, we won't work at odds with you. We'll try to dovetail our investigation so we're all on the same page."

"Yeah," Colby said in disgust. "Right."

"What do you know about what's happened?" Alvarez demanded.

"Exactly what you do. Fiona had an appointment with Rose Flaherty the other night and instead walked in on a murder scene. Now her place was just trashed. It doesn't take a genius to figure out there's a link between the two crimes."

"And you have no idea what they were looking for?"

Murky waters. "Nope," Ryan replied. "But whatever it was, they obviously want it badly. Fiona said the place is a disaster." Quickly, he turned the tables around so he was the one doing the asking. "Have you determined the point of entry?"

"No broken or open windows," Alvarez replied. "No visible tampering with the front door. Which suggests to me we're dealing with an accomplished bypass team."

"So they picked the lock." Ryan looked less than happy. "Pros. Great. Are you going to request the precinct gives this address special attention by the patrol force?"

"Of course."

"What does that mean?" Fiona asked.

"It means that a uniformed patrol car will make a pass every hour—for your protection." Ryan didn't bother mentioning the twenty-four-seven security Patrick had already placed on Fiona. That would keep her safe. The hourly pass would ensure that no one else paid the townhouse a visit. It was a comforting plus.

"I appreciate the precaution," Fiona said in a tight voice. "Thank you."

Ryan glanced at Fiona, who was clearly both scared and grateful but, at the same time, furious. And rightly so. Her personal space had been invaded. After long hours of detective work at their parents' house, how much did she know about the why?

Time to find out.

"Detective, my sister has taken all she can," he said. "The Crime Scene Unit will be in there for at least an hour, maybe two. It's getting cold out. I'll buy coffee for everyone. But let Fiona drink it in my van and try to relax. She'll have an easier time with the walk-through procedures if she's calm."

"I don't have a problem with that," Detective Alvarez said. The slightest hint of humor. "And if you buy me coffee, I'll try to overlook the fact that you're illegally parked."

Once all the cops had been plied with caffeine and were hunkered down in their respective vehicles, Ryan settled Fee in the van and hopped back into the driver's seat.

"What were those photos I enhanced?" he asked without preamble. "And what else don't I know?"

Fiona eased the Tyvek envelope out of her tote bag and slid it over to Ryan's lap, keeping it flat and low so the police wouldn't spot anything. "This came for me in the mail." As Ryan glanced over the material, Fiona explained everything that she'd discovered today.

"That's all I know so far," she concluded.

"So whatever all this means, whatever your friend Rose found, it clearly ties to something valuable. And whoever killed her thinks you have the key to that something." Ryan blew out a breath and whipped out his cell. "I'm asking Casey to call a late team meeting. Once you and I finish up here, we're going to FI."

Fiona blinked. "We can't just spring this on her."

"We damn well can. FI moves fast. Besides, she's already up to speed. So is the rest of the team. And to answer your earlier question, Patrick assigned security detail to you right after we agreed to treat this as a case. Now he'll assign it to your townhouse, as well."

"You did all this before the break-in?"

"Yup."

"Wow." Fiona acknowledged that with wide eyes. "You really are *the* Ryan McKay, aren't you?"

Ryan chuckled. "The very one."

12

It was close to two hours before the Crime Scene van pulled away from the curb with whatever evidence they'd bagged.

Ryan glanced up from behind the steering wheel. "That's our cue. Let's see how bad the damage is."

Fiona nodded bleakly, polishing off the last of her now-cold coffee and getting out of the van.

The police had all re-congregated outside the building. Detectives Alvarez and Shaw were poised and ready to move.

Fiona and Ryan joined them.

"How does this procedure work?" Fiona asked. "I want to get started right away. I need to see what they did to my house."

"We have three floors and a number of rooms to cover, so this won't be quick," Detective Shaw said. "We ask that you take your time, scrutinize everything carefully, and tell us what you know, or even suspect, is missing. Your roommate will have to do the same when she gets home."

"Okay." Fiona shot Ryan an imploring look.

"I want to go with you," he said, addressing the detectives, while simultaneously responding to Fiona's request for guidance and support. As strong as she was, this was going to be really tough.

"Why?" Alvarez asked. "Last I heard, you weren't exactly Forensic Instincts' go-to guy for police procedure."

Ryan ignored the barb. "I'm not. But I'm familiar with a lot of my sister's stuff. Plus, I'm less freaked out than she is. If she and I do this together, maybe I can help spot something missing."

Alvarez rolled her eyes and gestured toward the door. "Fine. Let's go."

Ryan gave Fiona's arm a gentle squeeze and the two of them followed the detectives into the townhouse.

Fiona hadn't been exaggerating. And it wasn't just the ground floor that had been ransacked. Both bedrooms on the second floor had been torn up, mattresses turned upside down, clothing emptied from the closets. Even the bathroom had been searched, as was evidenced by the scattered pharmaceuticals and makeup jars hanging out of the open drawers.

By the time they headed up the staircase leading to Fiona's third-floor loft, she looked white as a sheet.

She felt her insides twist as soon as she saw the door slightly off its hinges. She had a sickening feeling about what lay behind it.

Detective Alvarez pushed the door open.

"Oh, no," Fiona breathed as they stepped inside, the room still lit by the Tiffany lamps that the Crime Scene Unit had left on. Tears filled her eyes as she took in the damage.

Her bright, airy, and spotless workspace was destroyed.

The beautiful antique chest of drawers where she kept her tools had been rummaged through, tools tossed everywhere. Her normally neat wooden jeweler's workbench—which contained one shelf and racks for pliers, and small drawers on the right for hand tools—was totaled, and her current project had been tossed to the floor and crushed under a heavy foot. The L-shaped set of tables holding her soldering equipment was turned on end, everything on it dumped on the floor. Her torch was knocked over and her dental-like tool, the flex shaft, was knocked off its holder. Books were thrown off bookshelves, flung everywhere, their pages torn and their bindings broken.

Her gaze went reflexively to the always-locked glass cabinet where she kept her precious metals and gemstones. The cabinet had been jimmied open, with all its contents strewn about randomly.

Immediately, Fiona squatted down and began taking inventory of the valuable pieces. She knew every single one by memory.

It took her a while to collect it all.

Amazingly, nothing had been taken.

Nevertheless, she sank to the floor and began to cry.

"Can you tell what jewelry is missing?" Detective Alvarez asked in as gentle a tone as Fiona had ever heard from her.

"None of it," she managed, dashing at her cheeks as she tried to stem the tears. "Every single piece is here."

"You're sure?"

"Yes." Fiona forced herself to rise, turning to take in the overall destruction of her precious loft—the artist's haven she'd designed herself—from the floor-to-ceiling windows near her jeweler's bench, where she could take advantage of the natural light when she worked, to the bright LED light over the workbench, to the rolling mill on a stand that she used for fabricating metal sheet and wire for her creations. In the far left corner were double doors leading onto a small oval balcony. How many times had she taken a break from her work and sought creativity by going outside with a cup of tea and taking in the spectacular view of Lower Manhattan?

And now it was all a pile of debris. How long would it take to restore it? Worse, how long would it take her to feel safe in her private haven again?

While all this was going on, Ryan had made his way over to the other corner, where the computer station he'd set up for Fiona was located. Odd that nothing had been disturbed and that the laptop hadn't been taken. There had to be a reason. But for now, it was a big plus for him.

The Crime Scene detectives hadn't disturbed anything, other than to doubtlessly dust it all for fingerprints. Alvarez might routinely question Fiona about what she kept on there, but even if she asked for a look, she wouldn't find anything of interest.

But Ryan might.

He'd given Fee his "old" thirteen-inch MacBook Pro with a twenty-seven-inch Thunderbolt Display when she'd started her business. He'd feigned a need to upgrade his gear, even though he wasn't fooling Fiona, who knew he'd just bought all of it last year. Even though he was always buying the latest and the greatest stuff, to Fiona, Ryan's gift was like brand-new, and he still remembered how excited she'd been when he showed up with it.

She loved her monitor. It was nothing short of amazing, letting her see the beauty of her designs in detail. The MacBook Pro had enough horsepower to respond quickly when she created her jewelry designs in Photoshop, and when she needed to meet with a client at their place of business or home, she could take her Pro with her.

Ryan's trained mind was racing. Originally, this had been his computer. And when he gifted it to Fee, he hadn't removed the security logging application he'd added to the operating system—an application that would tell him exactly what had happened on this computer. Because something in his gut told him it had. Anyone who took the trouble to do all this damage, be painstakingly thorough enough to cover all their bases in search of something, wouldn't ignore the possibility that information might be stored on a computer. Not when they were obviously pros. And leaving the laptop here was a big unknown that was part of the overall equation he'd have to solve.

Right now, he was two steps ahead of the detectives. They didn't know anything about the tapestries or the details of Rose's research. And they weren't going to know—not unless it became impossible to keep it a secret without being accused of withholding evidence. But as long as anything to do with the tapestries was still speculation, the information would belong solely to FI. If they knew, Alvarez and Shaw would be all over Fiona, checking out her Photoshop content, and maybe even taking the tapestries with them to the precinct as possible evidence.

Right now, they were focused solely on Fiona's jewelry. That didn't mean it would stay that way. Ryan had to get this computer to his lair *now*, before it became an item of interest.

Using all his skills, he'd do a total sweep.

And all of his instincts doubted he'd come up empty.

For now, he kept his mouth shut, leaving the computer station before his being there aroused police interest, and walked back over to Fee, doing his best to calm her down.

It wasn't easy. She'd really reached the end of her rope. And Ryan was itching to get the cops out of there so that he could take Fee and her computer back to FI.

After what seemed like an eternity, Alvarez brought the evening to a close. "Since you're obviously not staying here tonight, where will you be?" she asked Fiona.

Fiona's expression was glazed. "I'll go home with Ryan."

"You'll keep your cell phone on?" It wasn't really a question.

A nod.

"And you'll be available as needed?"

"Obviously, Detective," Ryan answered for his sister. "Fiona and I want this case solved as badly as you do."

"And I'm sure you'll do whatever it takes to make that happen." Alvarez's statement might as well have been an accusation. "I expect immediate updates from you if your team comes up with a lead."

"You'll have them."

The detective looked less than convinced, but she didn't push the issue. "We'll be at your parents' house tomorrow evening for the gathering they've arranged. We'll be respectful and just observe the guests and pay attention to the conversations. We won't interfere in any way."

"That's considerate of you," Ryan said dryly.

Alvarez bristled. "Then we'll take off now."

"We'll leave as soon as Fiona's picked through her clothes and packed what she needs."

Alvarez didn't argue the routine request.

"If you discover anything missing that you didn't see during our walk-through—"

"I'll call you right away," Fiona said. She dragged a hand through her thick masses of hair. "Please, Detective, can that be enough for tonight?"

"Yes." Alvarez planted herself there for one last moment. "Remember how serious this is. For some reason, you've become a target. We need to figure out that reason. Don't impede our investigation."

"I don't plan to."

"Good. Then we'll clear out of here. You get some rest. We'll be in touch. And with you, as well, Mr. McKay."

Ryan had to fight to keep from rolling his eyes. "I'll be expecting your call."

Fifteen minutes later, Fiona had finished packing her stuff up. Ryan had spent that time peering out the window. Once he was sure the entourage of law enforcement was gone, he packed up a separate tote bag with Fiona's laptop. To any patrol car passing by, it looked like just another bag of Fiona's things that she was bringing with her.

Ryan loaded up the car, got Fiona settled, and drove off for the FI brownstone.

13

Casey and the team were all waiting in the downstairs conference room when Ryan brought Fiona in. As always when a client was distraught, Casey chose this room, rather than the more formal upstairs one, to conduct business. It was far more casual and homey, with its swivel tub chairs and cushy love seats.

Fiona stood in the doorway like a wide-eyed fawn, reeling from the events of the evening and trying to retain an element of composure when meeting Ryan's renowned colleagues.

Claire made it easier, going straight to Fiona and giving her a hug. "I'm so sorry you're going through yet another trauma," she said. "But we'll help make it right. That's what we do."

Ryan gave Claire a subtle nod of thanks and eased Fiona into the room, introducing the team members she had yet to meet.

Casey was already on her feet, and she walked up to Fiona and shook her hand. "It's a pleasure to meet you, even under these circumstances. You look just like Ryan. I hope you don't behave like him."

That had the desired effect, and Fiona couldn't help but laugh. "I hope not, too. I might be the baby of the family, but he's the brat."

"Tell us about it," Marc muttered, but he was smiling as he shook Fiona's hand. "We put up with him every day."

Fiona's gaze shifted to the official-looking bloodhound, who was watching her intently from his prone position on the floor. His head was up as he assessed the stranger in their midst.

"Hi, Hero," she said, squatting to stroke his head. "You must keep my brother humble by being so much better-looking."

Ryan rolled his eyes. "Thanks, Fee. Comparing me to a bloodhound? That's a real boost to my ego."

"Your ego doesn't need boosting," she replied.

"You can say that again," Claire echoed.

"But you're an amazing brother and I'm so grateful to you... to you all." Fiona made a wide sweep of her arm. Her gaze stopped on Patrick.

"Hello and welcome, Fiona," he said with a warm smile.

"Hi," she replied. "I hear I already have something to thank you for. I appreciate you putting a security detail on me. I never would have thought I'd need it. Now I'm changing my mind in a hurry." She gave Patrick a curious look. "Whoever you chose, I'd like to meet him."

"And you will," Patrick assured her. "His name is John Nickels, and he's one of the best and sharpest guys I have on my team. He's parked outside the building. After we finish up here, I'll have him come in. You're in the best of hands. John's about six foot three and is built like a linebacker. He worked homicide for the NYPD for twenty-five years. He's also a great guy. You'll like him—as long as you follow his instructions."

"I get it." Fiona nodded. "Believe me, I'll do whatever he says. I'm not going to play with fire when it comes to my life."

"Then you and John will work just fine together."

Emma had stayed quiet—at least until now. "You're gorgeous," she blurted out, having stared at Fiona the whole time the rest of the team members were greeting her. "And so's your jewelry. I looked at your website. If I could afford it, I'd buy it all."

Fiona's whole body relaxed. That kind of bluntness and enthusiasm felt really good about now, especially since it referred to anything other than murder and impending danger.

"That's ironic," she replied. "When I was growing up, I always wished I was blonde and petite. Like Alice in Wonderland. You look just like her, so right back at you about the gorgeous part. As for my jewelry, you just pick a piece and it's yours."

Emma's eyes widened. "Are you kidding? Most of your stuff costs thousands of dollars." She paused. "Although there's a thin bangle bracelet with three tiny sapphires that I love and it's a lot less. But it's still a few hundred dollars. Are you sure?"

"Positive. Consider it yours. That one would look beautiful on you."

"Oh my God! Thank you soooo much." Emma looked as if she'd won the lottery.

Casey shot her a that's-enough look, although she was visibly biting back laughter. Anything that diverted Fiona or calmed her down right now would be welcome. And Emma's bouncy enthusiasm always had that effect on people—unless, of course, she was on an assignment or picking someone's pocket. Then, she was all business and her targets didn't like her much.

"Why don't you sit down?" Casey indicated one of the caramel-colored tub chairs. "We ordered in some sandwiches, because I'm sure you haven't eaten a thing." She waved away Fiona's protest. "This isn't only about making sure you're fed. We need you clearheaded and alert, since you're about to go through yet another battery of questions. Only ours are more specific since we have more facts than the police do."

"Plus, I haven't eaten yet, either," Ryan announced. "I'm starved."

"Of course you are." Casey gestured toward the door. "So why don't you go upstairs to the kitchen and bring down the platter. We've got everything else we need in here—a coffee station that brews everything, a fridge filled with water, juice, soda, you name it, and a wine cooler. So there's something for everyone."

Ryan paused in the doorway. "I'll go get the food. But I'm going to wolf down a sandwich in the kitchen and then take a few more to my lair after I drop off the platter. I want to start analyzing Fee's computer immediately. If the guys who broke into her townhouse did manage to get into it and pull any data, I want to get a head start."

"Good idea." Casey nodded. "Besides, you're totally up to date on everything Fiona's about to tell us. So your talents are best served elsewhere. Just don't forget to bring the platter of food down here—without taking half of it for yourself—before you lose yourself in your techno world and your poor sister starves."

"No worries." Ryan glanced quickly at Fiona. "You okay?"

"Fine. I'm with your awesome teammates." She waved him away affectionately. "Go stuff your face."

"On my way." Ryan disappeared toward the staircase.

Once Fiona was settled, nibbling on a turkey sandwich, and more relaxed, Casey gave her a quick update before bringing up the immediate things FI needed to know.

"Ryan's conducting a full background check on Rose Flaherty, just to see if there was anyone in her life, past or present, who had motive to kill her. So far, he's found no red flags. We've also divided up Rose's contact list and are running through it to see if there are any possible suspects on it. Again, so far nothing's jumped out at us."

Fiona's brows rose. "You really got a head start on this. I'm so grateful." She fidgeted a bit. "We haven't talked about payment. Ryan's sister or not, I'm a client and I want to compensate you. How does this work? Do I sign a contract? Write you a check up front?"

Casey gave a dismissive wave of her hand. "We'll work something out. Right now, we need to figure out who's targeting you."

"But—"

"I'll take it out of Ryan's salary," Casey said dryly. "And you can sign the standard contract after this meeting. Now let's get down to business. The night of Rose Flaherty's murder, Detective Alvarez interviewed you at length. What did you tell her about the research

Rose was doing for you? Think hard before you answer. Fortunately, the print you gave Rose wasn't at the scene. But I want to be sure there was no mention of the tapestries."

"There wasn't," Fiona said, shaking her head. "Detective Alvarez asked me what the nature of my business with Rose was and I said that she was doing some research for me that related to my new jewelry line, things like Celtic symbols and images. I never said anything about the tapestries. I'm not sure why. Maybe because I was in shock. Maybe because I inherently knew it was something I wasn't ready to share. But the only people who know the full extent of my research are all of you and, of course, Rose."

"Okay, good. Let's keep it that way. We obviously know there's a link between the tapestries and whoever killed Rose and trashed your place. The criminals who did these things want something, and I'd be willing to bet that Rose had a good idea what that something might be."

"So we retrace Rose's steps," Marc said. "We now have the text pages and the Post-it note she sent you. Time to figure out who she consulted with to expand her knowledge base. Can her assistant help you with that?"

Fiona nodded. "I was planning to go to her for that very thing. I don't have to give her a reason that will creep her out or reveal more than I want to. I'll just tell her part of the truth—that I still need help with the Celtic symbols Rose was researching for me for my new line, and ask who Rose's go-to people were for that sort of thing. Glenna will probably know the answer off the top of her head. If not, she'll check out the contact list and give me a bunch of possibilities."

"Good."

"I need the tapestries themselves," Claire told Fiona. "I don't know how you're going to convince your mother that you need to borrow them, but we're going to have to come up with something. Because I *know* I can pick up energy from them. And maybe some of that energy will give us avenues to pursue." A frown. "I was in my yoga room all night. Obviously, the break-in at your house broke through all my other thoughts. But I went in to focus on that center panel. Something about it is really troubling me. We're missing something vital. I just don't know what."

"I do," Fiona replied. She filled Claire in on the tiny fist and trophy or goblet images woven into the fabric, as well as Rose's cryptic phrase about them on her Post-it message.

"I never noticed either of those images." Claire was still frowning. "But that's all the more reason I need to feel the tapestries in my hands, hold them up close."

Fiona sighed, leaning back against the chair and taking a sip of tea. "I've been wrestling with that already. As it was, I needed those tapestries to create the rest of my new line. And now, with everything that's happened and what you're saying, getting our hands on the panels has become urgent." She rubbed her forehead. "I've already got to tell my parents about the break-in. They're going to be way too upset to focus on anything else. And the gathering for Rose is tomorrow night. Everyone will be asking questions. I'm not sure how to field them."

"That's what we're here for," Casey replied, thoughtfully drumming her fingernails on her coffee mug. "How would your parents feel about a few more guests? Claire and I would be the best choices. Claire already met your mom and you introduced her as your friend, so that's not a problem. You could easily have met her—and me—at Forensic Instincts. After all, that's where your brother works. It's not a reach that we'd be there to offer you emotional support. Marc and Patrick will stay behind and start tracking Rose's research. And I'm sure Ryan will be locked up in his lair. He's on a tear right now, and besides, a social gathering honoring a murder victim who belonged to your church doesn't sound like his speed."

"Definitely not." Fiona had to smile. "As for you and Claire coming, my mom would be relieved—especially after I call her tonight and tell her about what happened. I know it's late, but I can't risk her finding out from the police. She needs to hear from me and know that I'm really okay." A quick glance at the wall clock. "Would you mind if I took a minute and made that call now? I won't mention the tapestries—it's the wrong time—but I have to tell them the police believe the break-in is tied to Rose's murder. Detective Alvarez is going to make that crystal clear anyway. Besides, they're not stupid. They're going to come to that conclusion even without the detectives telling them."

"Of course, go ahead." Casey rose. "I'll take you up to the den that's across from Claire's yoga room. It's great for relaxing or crashing for the night. You can have privacy to make your call. I'm also thinking you might want to use the sofa bed and stay over. I know Ryan said he'd take you to his place, but I'm pretty sure that tonight, 'his place' is going to mean his lair. This way, he'll be with you. So will I, because my apartment is on the fourth floor. And John will be camped out at his post. So you can sleep easy. Is that okay with you?"

Fiona stood up and gave Casey an impulsive hug. "I don't know how to thank you. Ryan's right—you guys are amazing."

Casey returned her hug. "Let's save the accolades for after we solve this case."

***

Niall was perched at the edge of his sofa when his private cell phone rang.

"Talk to me."

"Yes," Donald replied tersely. "We'll take a walk."

Niall sucked in his breath. *Yes* meant the job was done, but *we'll take a walk* meant there were only preliminary things to report. Otherwise, Donald would have said, *We'll be flying out tonight.*

Still, he was out the door five minutes later, heading for Kelly's and for an update.

***

Kelly's was still hopping when Niall walked in, wearing his customary canvas jacket with the collar turned up and his Yankees cap. Donald signaled him into the back room and finished serving a customer before joining him.

He shut the door firmly behind him.

"The cops swarmed the place," he began without preamble. "Not just the local precinct and the Crime Scene Unit, which we were expecting. The detectives handling the murder case charged in at the same time as the patrol car. Plus, of course, the girl's brother, who showed up five minutes later."

"Yeah, the Forensic Instincts tech genius." Niall scowled. "We're fighting the clock with him in the mix. We know he's good. We just don't know if he's as good as advertised."

"We do know the computer kid I hired is supposedly a whiz kid," Donald replied. "So I'm pretty confident that he'll turn something up."

"What'd he take from the house?"

"Nothing, as you ordered. He copied the hard drive. Kid kept laughing that the stupid girl had a Post-it with her password stuck to the back of one of the papers on the desk. The computer itself looks like it's never been touched. He said something about needing to crack some password before he can get at the photos you want. He babbled a bunch of other stuff in computer-ese. I have no idea what it meant, but bottom line: it's going to take some time before he has anything to report."

"Shit. How much time?"

"He doesn't know. It depends on how lucky he gets and how fast the spyware he installed pays off. We're going to have to sit tight."

Niall's jaw set in impatient frustration, and he rubbed his scarred palm. "What'd the other two kids find?"

"Only the jewelry. They followed your orders: take photos, then leave it all where they dumped it. They texted the photos to me after I called you. I'll forward them to you now."

Niall nodded, ignoring the series of *bings* that told him the texts had arrived. He'd get to them later. What he really wanted wasn't the jewelry, it was the inspiration for it. "Nothing else?"

Donald shook his head. "No tapestries." He looked Niall squarely in the eye. "Are you ever planning on telling me what these tapestries mean and what they'll lead you to that you're so determined to find?"

Niall fell silent. He'd never kept anything from Donald before. This man was responsible for saving his life and giving him a new one. "Once I have them in my hands, I'll tell you. Just you. Not another soul."

"Then not another soul will ever know."

Niall turned his attention to the other loose end. "Anything on the investigation?"

"The cops have gotten nowhere yet. They're questioning everyone on their list, but they've turned up nothing on the details of what the old woman was looking into. Given what you've told me, they're not going to—not unless the girl says something."

"She won't. Not with Forensic Instincts in her corner. Anything she has to confide, she'll confide in them." Niall scowled. "Let's not make the mistake of underestimating them. They'll be more of a problem than law enforcement."

***

Ryan was hunched over Fiona's laptop, periodically munching on a roast beef sandwich. At this point, it was purely for sustenance, not for savoring. His concentration was focused solely on his work. He punched in Fiona's usual password—*feefihohum*—the nickname Ryan had given her as a little girl when she said that the giant in *Jack and the Beanstalk* was talking about her. But no time for childhood memories—it was time to see exactly what had gone on with Fee's computer.

When he'd originally configured this laptop, he'd formatted the large SSD using Mac OS X extended. This enabled journaling on the hard drive. All read/write operations were logged for review at a later time. Ryan's monitoring software regularly connected to the FI servers and uploaded the journal files for analysis, should that be necessary.

Now it was necessary.

He took another bite of his sandwich and prepared himself for a long, long night.

14

Casey poked her head into the den, checking on Fiona before she went upstairs.

"I'm assuming you reached your parents," she said. "Was the conversation very rough?"

Fiona had just finished making up the sofa bed. She turned and sighed.

"My mom is probably still crying. My dad sounded ready to call the National Guard. The only thing that kept them from insisting I come home was the fact that I was not only with Ryan but here at Forensic Instincts. Even though they were completely freaked out, I think they were clearheaded enough to realize I'd be safest here. I told them I hired you. I hope that's okay."

"Of course it's okay." Casey leaned against the doorjamb. "Did you mention the idea of Claire and me coming tomorrow night?"

"It's all set. They were relieved. *I* was relieved, too, not only because you'll be at the gathering but because I was able to reach my folks tonight before Detectives Alvarez and Shaw did. The only thing that would have made this situation worse was if the two of them had knocked on my parents' door to ask if they knew anyone who'd want to hurt me. I'm sure that's in the cards. Both detectives were at the Mass we held for Rose. So they're aware of the fact that my parents knew her. It's not a reach that, after a break-in at my house, they'd want to question them." Fiona grimaced. "Detective Alvarez was pretty snarky when she left my place. I don't think she's too fond of Ryan."

Casey's lips twitched. "Not a surprise. Ryan does things his own way. That means that police procedure gets in his way. Sometimes he tolerates it. Sometimes he doesn't."

"Yeah, that's my brother," Fiona said wryly, although affection laced her tone. "He's been breaking rules since he was a kid."

"Now why doesn't that surprise me?" As she spoke, Casey waved her hand toward the sofa. "Anyway, you get some sleep. Oh, and don't get alarmed if I run downstairs and bring a tall, take-charge kind of guy up with me. It's my boyfriend, Hutch. He's FBI, so you can feel even more secure about staying here. But don't expect him to be chatty. He's not too crazy about FI's boundaries—or lack thereof."

"Hutch?" Fiona asked curiously.

"Supervisory Special Agent Kyle Hutchinson," Casey clarified. "He's a keeper."

"Got it." Fiona nodded. "I won't strike up a conversation. Besides, I doubt I'll even hear him, that's how zoned out I am." She yawned. "It's been another nightmare of a day."

***

Casey was in bed, studying Fiona's photos of the tapestries, when Hutch texted to say he was on her doorstep. She hurried downstairs and deactivated the Hirsch pad to let him in.

She didn't have time to greet him before he pulled her into his arms and gave her a kiss she felt down to her toes.

"I missed you," he said against her mouth. "Let's go upstairs."

Casey's lips curved into a smile. For a man who epitomized the word *reserved*, Hutch managed to take charge without even trying. He had an air of command about him—from the power of his build, the innate confidence he exuded, and those sharp blue eyes that missed nothing. His natural, compelling presence always filled the room and yanked everyone's gaze his way.

Marc had introduced them. The connection was instant.

"Bed," he muttered. "Or would you prefer right here?"

"Bed is perfect." Casey let him back her toward the staircase, unbuttoning the top few buttons of his shirt as she did. "I haven't seen you in three days or spoken more than two dozen words to you."

"Yeah, rough case," was all he said. Hutch was squad supervisor of the FBI's New York field office's NCAVC—the National Center for the Analysis of Violent Crime. He'd transferred from Quantico, where he'd work the BAU's crimes against adults, and was now the BAU coordinator and head of all the New York field office's Violent Crimes squads. It was a high-level, coveted leadership job, which Hutch handled with the same expertise and commitment he'd handled being a BAU agent and, before joining the bureau, a DC police detective.

His and Casey's relationship had blossomed from a long-distance affair to a serious involvement to something deeper and more long-lasting. The word *permanent* hung out there, along with everything that word conjured up, and both of them knew it and felt it.

Right now, all they wanted to feel was each other.

Hutch's hands were under her blouse, reaching around to unclasp her bra, as they rounded the third-floor landing.

"Wait," Casey murmured, putting a restraining hand on his forearm. "We have an overnight guest." She tipped her head toward the den.

Hutch didn't as much as glance in that direction. "Fine. Then run."

She turned around and scooted up to her apartment. Hutch was right behind her.

They were both laughing as they tumbled into Casey's bedroom and fell on the bed.

Hero's head came up. He'd been chilling in his pet bed when all the excitement erupted. His tail began wagging when he saw Hutch.

"Hey, boy," Hutch said as he worked off his clothes. "We'll wrestle later."

"*Much* later," Casey qualified, shimmying out of her thong.

Much later turned into *much, much* later, when she and Hutch both sank into the bed, breathless and sated, with Casey's head pillowed on Hutch's chest.

"I love you," Hutch said, his lips brushing the crown of her head.

"I love you, too." Casey draped a leg over his, giving a contented sigh. "Three days isn't happening again. Even two isn't great."

"You know if I had my way we'd be living together." He wrapped a strand of her tangled red hair around his finger. "But you love this place and I can't move in here."

Casey didn't answer right away. She'd been thinking about this a lot—more than Hutch realized. She knew the roadblocks. Hutch was FBI. He couldn't live at the FI brownstone, not when so much of what the team did was outside his comfort zone. He knew when they were about to step over the line, and he knew that meant it was time for him to stay away. As it was, he'd pushed the boundaries in the past when it came to Casey's safety. But, other than that, it wasn't happening. Nor would Casey ask it of him. So he'd taken over the lease on Marc's former apartment in Bensonhurst when Marc married Madeleine, and Casey spent many nights over there. The distance from Brooklyn to Tribeca was a hell of lot shorter than the distance from Quantico to Tribeca.

But it still wasn't short enough. Not anymore.

Thanks to the trust fund her grandfather had left her, Casey owned the brownstone. That meant this apartment would always be hers—when she needed it.

"I'll have to stay here sometimes. We both understand why," Casey replied softly. "But that doesn't mean I can't have a real home somewhere else."

She felt Hutch's body tense in reaction. His fingers tipped up her chin so their gazes locked.

"You'd move in with me?" he asked, half question, half demand.

Casey's fingertips traced the jagged scar across his left temple—a souvenir of his days as a DC police detective. "Not into Marc's place, no. But into a place of our own, one we chose together? Yes, I'd move in with you—happily. That is, if you're asking."

"*Asking*?" Hutch hauled her even closer against him, kissing her with a consuming intensity that spoke to the depth of her decision. Before she could catch her breath, he scooted her away. "Get your laptop. We're doing some looking right now. And first thing in the morning, I'm calling a Realtor."

***

Casey was up at five thirty, long before her iPhone alarm sounded.

She resisted the urge to wake Hutch up in all the ways that would keep them in bed for hours. Instead, she took a quick shower, got dressed, and took Hero out to do his business. Once he was resettled, she went into the kitchen to put a K-cup in her Keurig and brew a mug of coffee.

She was sitting at the counter, sipping it and reflecting on the monumental decision she'd come to last night, when Hutch walked in. He was wearing a pair of the sweats he kept at Casey's and he looked sexy as hell, five o'clock shadow and all.

"Morning, beautiful." He crossed over and gave Casey a long, deep kiss. "You're up early. Do you have time to share a cup with me before I shower and take off for work?"

"I'll make time." She waited while Hutch brewed himself a mug of the dark roast he preferred and straddled the stool beside her.

"Too bad Realtors don't start work at six," he said. "Otherwise, I'd be on the phone."

"I never doubted it." She smiled. "Our challenge won't be finding a place. It'll be coordinating our schedules in order to check out the listings."

"I'm a pro at coordinating schedules. I'll make it happen. Count on it." Hutch took a belt of coffee. "You mentioned an overnight guest. Should I be jealous?"

"Never. It's our client. She needed a safe place to spend the night. And she needed to be close to Ryan."

Hutch's brows rose. "Now *that* sounds intriguing. What can I know?"

Casey didn't have to weigh that one out. The basics were public information. "An antique dealer named Rose Flaherty was killed in her Greenwich Village shop a few nights ago. The person who found her body is Fiona McKay, Ryan's sister and our client."

"*Sister.* That's news to me."

"It was to everyone, except me." Casey took another sip of coffee. "And the reason she's here is because someone broke into her town-house last night and trashed it. Ryan wanted her to stay at his place, but he spent the night in his lair furiously analyzing her computer, which the intruders left behind. So I invited Fiona to crash here."

Hutch's expression didn't change. "Finding the body was obviously just the tip of the iceberg. Fiona is somehow connected to the murder, which makes her a target."

"Exactly."

"That's all I'll ask."

"That's all I'd tell."

"I know." Hutch polished off his coffee. "If you need help, I'm here." A corner of his mouth lifted. "For anything legal, that is."

"Thanks." Casey squeezed his arm. "I've got to get downstairs, check on Fiona, and see what Ryan's turned up."

"Has Hero been out?"

"Just for the basics."

"Then I'll take him for a run." Hutch pushed back his stool and rose. "He needs the exercise and I need to get my blood pumping so I can shower and be productive at work." A teasing grin. "You wore me out."

"Get used to it." Casey grinned back, a grin that rapidly faded. "Please don't tell me it's going to be another three days before I see you."

"Just the opposite. Don't be surprised if I call you later and tell you to drop everything and meet me. Realtors aren't dawdlers. And you and I have places to see and decisions to make."

They'd already discussed some of those decisions. They'd stay as close to work as possible, which was equidistant for them both, since Tribeca was a quarter of a mile from Federal Plaza. They knew that real estate prices in that area were obscene, so compromises would have to be made. Together, they'd choose which compromises were doable.

"I can't wait to hear your voice," Casey said, hopping off her stool, as well. She gave him a soft kiss. "And make sure pets are allowed."

15

Fiona was up, dressed, and pacing around the "guest room," staring at her phone when Casey knocked and walked in.

Seeing Fiona eyeing her phone, Casey snapped into high-alert mode. "Did you get a call?"

Fiona raised her head and what Casey saw on her face was annoyed indecision rather than fear.

"No, I guess even the detectives don't plan on bothering me at seven a.m. I was trying to decide whether to go bother my brother or not. He was going to arrange for a cleanup of my apartment. I want to start right away, so I'd like to get on the phone and make it happen. But he's buried in the guts of my computer, and if there's a specific company he has in mind…"

"We do have one we've used as needed," Casey said. "They're very thorough and very responsive." She nixed the idea of offering to make the call. Fiona needed to feel in control of her own life, especially now, when it was near impossible to do. Even something as small as running the show about her house restoration was imperative. "I'll text you their contact information right now." She whipped out her cell. "Just mention that you're our client. It'll move things up on their priority list."

Fiona gave her a grateful smile. "Great. Thanks so much." She waited while Casey sent the text, glancing at the phone as soon as she heard the receiving *bing*. "Is it too early to call?"

"Nope. Go ahead." Casey turned. "I'm going to see how far Ryan's gotten anyway."

"You're braver than I am."

"You're his sister. I'm his boss. He can't ream me out." Casey tossed the words back over her shoulder. "By the way, there's tons of food in the fridge, so make yourself some breakfast. I'll join you in a bit."

Fiona was already making the call as Casey reached the staircase.

***

Ryan was staring at his monitor when Casey stepped into the lair.

"How's it going?" she asked.

"Oh, it's going, but not in a good way," he replied in a grim tone.

"Go on."

He gripped the arms of his chair, swiveling it around to face Casey. "Whenever I set up MAC OS X, I always turn on journaling so I can see what's happening after the fact. The MacBook Pro I gave Fee had that feature intact. The journal log revealed that whoever broke into her apartment made a copy of everything on her hard drive. My guess is that they're combing through her entire life looking for clues to whatever they're searching for and whatever Rose Flaherty was digging into that got her killed."

Casey stayed silent as Ryan's body language told her he had more to say.

"And that's just the tip of the iceberg," Ryan confirmed her intuition by continuing. "I found some nasty little keystroke logger—as in major spyware—that the intruders installed. Apparently they weren't satisfied with just copying all Fee's information, they wanted to keep tabs on her and whoever she talks to going forward."

His lips thinned in anger. "The spyware captures and sends Fiona's keystrokes to a remote server, where what she types is logged. It also secretly sends copies of her emails to the same remote server. And the lucky bastards get a bonus in the process—they get to see Fee's text messages, courtesy of OS X's tight integration with iOS. She set up her laptop so that her text messages display on her MacBook as well as her iPhone. So her texts are also relayed to the same remote server. All that explains why the scumbags left the laptop at her townhouse, rather than ripping it off."

"Wouldn't you have to enter a password to gain access to a Mac?" Casey asked.

"Absolutely. Somehow these guys knew her password. I need to talk to Fee to find out how they knew hers."

"Okay." Casey studied Ryan's body language, heard the uncharacteristic emotion in his explanation. "Can't you just disable the feature you're describing so that her text messages stay private?"

"Yeah, I could, but then those scumbags would know we're onto them. So, like it or not, we have to let them spy on Fee and wait until we can turn the tables on them."

Casey chose her next words carefully.

"Ryan, you're very personally involved in all this—and I don't blame you. We're talking about your sister. But I need you to stay focused and professional. Given all you just told me, what would you advise us to do and what would you advise Fiona to do if she were a client with no emotional ties to you and, by association, us?"

Ryan ran his hands through his hair, as if to clear the cobwebs clouding his normally logical mind—a mind that was now consumed with Fiona's safety.

"First, I need to figure out how Fiona's password was compromised. Fortunately, Macs prevent you from using the same password for iCloud and access to your Mac. At this moment they are probably combining Fiona's Mac password with other details of her life to see if they can get lucky and score her iCloud password. We need to shut them down now or they will have access to all her photos, including ones of the tapestries."

He steepled his hands in front of his face, intensifying his concentration. Abruptly, his head came up. "I know what to do after that," he said with absolute certainty. "It means giving Yoda instructions right now. Can I run with it?"

Casey waved her hand. "Go ahead."

"Yoda," he called out. "Please make a bit-by-bit copy of the SSD in Fiona's MacBook Pro. I want this treated as a normal forensic investigation. Next, I want you to make another copy that we can analyze. Start by sorting all the files on the drive by content type. Photos in one folder. Word documents, Photoshop files with Fiona's designs, iMessages—if they're not encrypted—and emails into separate folders. Build a timeline that references each one of those objects so that if we want to get a reverse chronological view of Fiona's life, we can do that."

"Initiating now, Ryan," Yoda responded.

Casey, seeing where this was going, added her unique viewpoint and expertise into the mix.

"Yoda, in addition to Ryan's requests, please build another view of the data based on a threaded conversation. Focus on Fiona's first contact with the murder victim, Rose Flaherty. Then add content to enrich both the text and email messages. I want us to be able to understand these two women from the perspective of when their relationship started, how it progressed both personally and professionally."

"Yes, Casey," Yoda replied.

Ryan frowned. "Casey, I'm the first to boast Yoda's skills. But as his creator, I've got to stress that AI isn't one hundred percent accurate. We still need hands-on work. The entire FI team has to sift through Fiona's digital life searching for clues. We're starting off way behind the bad guys in one respect. They know what they're looking for and why. We *have* what they're looking for but haven't the vaguest idea why they're important."

"Understood." Casey paused, considering the best course of action. "Yoda," she added, "please send messages to the entire team instructing them to pack overnight bags and plan on camping out here for as long as it takes. We'll set up our own War Room to handle this as if it were a crisis." All the FI members were familiar with the term *War Room* and knew what it meant: a tight location where the team would come together, brainstorm and develop ideas, and, using their collective skills and creativity, solve a complex problem in an impossibly short time constraint.

Again, Yoda responded in the affirmative.

Casey turned back to Ryan. "Claire and I will focus on the threaded conversation view. Between us, I think we'll be able to understand the two women and what they were thinking leading up to the murder. I want Marc and Patrick to drill in on the timeline. They're our best and most experienced investigators and will see both the pattern of what's there as well as what elements are missing. Fiona can be pulled into each sub-team to answer questions as needed. And you'll keep analyzing the hard drive for anything we're missing. The only time there will be absentee teammates is tonight, when Claire and I are going to your parents' house. We'll keep it to as short a time frame as possible. But Fiona needs us there, and so does our investigation. So we're going. Does all that work?"

"Yeah, but it's not enough." Ryan barely heard the last part of what Casey said. His mind was already racing ahead to the next step of his plan. "I want to set a trap for these bastards. I think I can create a proxy computer that would act as a filter between the real world and Fee's compromised MacBook. I can decide what information is allowed to pass from the proxy to the MacBook and ultimately to those scumbags who are spying on her. They'll have no way of knowing I'm maneuvering their process. They'll think Fee is trying to put her life back together and that she's unaware they're watching and listening in on every move she makes. The reality will be that we'll be feeding them bullshit when we need to. And when the time is right, I'll send those fuckers right into a booby trap with me and Marc waiting for them."

"Hold on there, cowboy," Casey said. "I'm fine with everything but the last part. I don't need you killing people and spending the rest of your life in jail. Let's wait and see how this plays out. Detectives Alvarez and Shaw are already up our asses. If we blatantly sidestep them, it won't be pretty. We'll do whatever's necessary to protect Fiona. But she wouldn't want you to do anything stupid, and neither would I."

"And Fiona is standing right here, agreeing with everything Casey is saying."

Both Casey and Ryan turned to see Fiona perched in the doorway, her arms folded across her chest. "I just arrived, so I only heard the tail end of this conversation, and I only understood pieces of it. But it sure sounds to me like you're putting yourself in danger and, secondarily, that you're cutting me out of the equation. I appreciate everything you're doing—that you're all doing. But if what you're saying is that *you'll* be deciding what can and can't be sent through my computer, I think I should have a say in that. You can handle the bad guys. But I have a life, Ryan, and a profession. I can't stop living while this case is being solved. There are people I need to communicate with—clients, my marketing manager, new prospective buyers."

Ryan rolled his eyes. "I didn't say you couldn't communicate with anyone. Only that I'll have to see and approve anything you send. Your life's on the line."

"I get it." Fiona clearly understood. She just as clearly disliked what she was understanding. "And what am I going to do when I visit clients? I need to take my laptop with me, to take them through my designs step by step, even change them on the fly."

"That ain't happening." Ryan sliced the air with his palm. "Your computer and the proxy will go home to your place once it's cleaned up—and they'll stay there. There's no other way to do this. So use that creative mind of yours to come up with another way to dazzle your clients. This won't be forever, Fee. If you let us do our jobs, it'll be over soon—and you'll be safe."

"And you? Will you be safe?" Fiona demanded. "Bursting in like James Bond to taunt the bad guys? That's sheer insanity."

"I agree," Casey said. "So, at the finish line, if we can get law enforcement involved, that would be best."

Ryan shot her a look. "When has that ever been best?"

"At times like these. We're effectively working a murder case because that's what Fiona's caught up in. And that means the NYPD. We can cross only subtle lines, not blatant ones. Nothing out-and-out illegal. I'm serious, Ryan. And you know it. You also know I'm right."

"Yeah, I know." Ryan blew out an exasperated breath. "We just do things so much faster and better."

"Then let's do what we *can do* faster and better. We're already walking a fine line about withholding evidence. The minute the detectives put Fiona in a position where she has to mention the tapestries, they'll be firmly linked to the crimes, and we'll have to share everything we know. The more we accomplish before that happens, the more control we have."

Ryan gave a tight nod. "Yoda should be finished in an hour or so. Then we'll move." Abruptly, his eyes widened in an uncustomary show of panic, as he recalled the rest of what was going on around him. He stared at his sister, scrutinizing her as if to ascertain her well-being. "I've been here all night. Where did you sleep? Shit. If you stayed at my place, you were alone. Unless Claire was with you? Shit."

"I'm fine, Ryan," Fiona said gently, seeing the level of his distress. "Thanks to Casey, I stayed here last night. Also thanks to Casey, I just hung up with your cleanup crew. I'm meeting them at my place in an hour so we can start getting it back to normal. And John Nickels, who I met last night and is awesome, will be right there safeguarding me. So it's all cool."

Ryan gave Casey a look of sheer gratitude. "Thanks, boss." His gaze shifted back to Fiona. "I really screwed up on the personal front. I got so laser-focused down here…"

"I expected that. It's your job. I'm fine." A hint of a grin touched Fiona's lips. "I love you, but I also know you. That's why I let Casey step in. So no harm, no foul."

Abruptly, her grin transformed into a worried frown. "Ry, if these guys have access to my texts, that means they have the whole slew of the texts I sent you last night when I was still at Mom and Dad's—the ones asking you to refine the tapestry images. I sent you photos of all thirteen tapestry panels, including the two hanging in the house."

Ryan waved away her concern. "We may have gotten lucky here. Those photos are in a shared album in iCloud. Remember I set that up for you? So in order to access the photos, someone needs your iCloud password, which they don't have, at least right now. Speaking of passwords, the bad guys needed to log in to your Mac to clone the hard drive and install a keystroke logger. How did they know your password?"

Fiona thought and an embarrassed flush rose to her cheeks. "I'm sorry I'm such a ditz when it comes to remembering computer stuff—especially passwords. I wrote my password on a Post-it that I left somewhere on my desk. I guess they found it."

Ryan squelched his annoyance. "Well, there's nothing we can do about that now. What's your iCloud password?"

"Feefihohumgold. Why?"

"Shit. They have eighty percent of it already. One lucky guess on their part—adding *gold* to the end of your Mac password and they have access to all your photos. Shit. Shit. Shit. And if I change your iCloud password, they'll receive an email notifying them of that. They'll know we're onto them."

Fiona dragged a worried hand through her hair. "I really messed things up. Isn't there anything we can do? What if I call Apple and explain all this?"

"They can't do anything, Fee." A fleeting hope entered Ryan's brain. "Wait. What email address are you using for your iCloud account? Is it fiona@fionamckayjewelry.com?"

She nodded. "Yes."

"Bingo. I can fix this. First I'll change the routing of your email server so emails to your account go to a dummy account first. Then I can decide what emails to allow to pass and what emails will be deleted. The security email from Apple announcing a change in iCloud password will be deleted. The bad guys trying to hack into your iCloud account will never know." He shot her a pointed look. "And Fee, I'm choosing a new 16-character random password for your iCloud account once everything is in place. Oh, I'll also need your iPhone and iPad to update your Keychain passwords."

He angled his head toward Casey, who looked pretty grim at the revelation. "I doubt these guys have my expertise. Still, I can't know for sure that they haven't already hacked into Fee's iCloud account. So as soon as Yoda's finished, we need to review the texts and the photos before we go on to anything else, see how much worse it might be if we are wrong and they have access to all the photos."

"There's just one glimmer of hope, if you want to call it that," Casey said. "If those photos and texts you two sent each other last night give the bad guys whatever they need, maybe they'll leave Fiona alone."

"Do you really believe that?" Ryan demanded, his tone utterly dubious.

"No, and neither do you," Fiona answered for him. "Photos, no matter how professionally enhanced, don't compare to the real panels. And I'm their link to those. So, as much as I appreciate Casey trying to calm me down, it's not going to work. We have to find these guys, figure out what they want, and then make sure they're locked away for

Rose's murder." Abruptly, she paled. "Ry, they know the tapestry panels weren't at my place. What if they guess they're at Mom and Dad's?"

"Shit, you're right." His gaze darted to Casey. "Can Patrick…"

Casey already had her phone out, checking the time before pressing the button for Patrick's number. "He's probably about to hit the Holland Tunnel by now." Patrick hated mass transit. He drove in from his house in Hoboken every day. "Let me try to catch him before the reception becomes spotty." She held up one finger as Patrick picked up his phone.

"Hey," she said. "We need security at Fiona and Ryan's parents' house in the Bronx. Woodlawn. Who do you have near there?" She listened. "Close enough. Can you get one of the two of them to the address I'm about to text you ASAP? Sorry about the no-notice. But we're afraid the killer might guess the tapestries are at the McKays', which would put them both in danger. Hang on." Holding the phone away from her ear, Casey sent the text, then asked Patrick, "Did you get that?"

She gave Fiona and Ryan a quick nod. "Call me when things are in place. You also got Yoda's email? You can make a quick trip home after rush hour tonight and pack a bag. We need all hands on deck." Another pause. "Thanks. See you in a few."

She disconnected the call. "It's done. Patrick will have someone at your folks' place within the hour."

"That fast?" Fiona was gaping. "How can he do that?"

Casey smiled. "Patrick's network is wide. After thirty years with the FBI, twenty-five of them spent at the New York field office, he's amassed tons of contacts. A substantial number of them are now retired and work security. He recruits the best of the best."

"And they show up before he has time to hang up the phone," Ryan added, clearly proud of his teammate. "He's one of a kind—just like we all are."

Fiona rolled her eyes. "Keep working, Ry. We already know how good you are. And if we dare to forget, you remind us."

"That's me." Ryan turned back to his screen. "Speaking of which, time to tap into the NYPD's database and see if they've come up with anything new on the case. Doubtful. But by that time, Yoda should have what we need."

16

It was early evening and the gathering at the McKays' had scarcely gotten underway. Still, Casey could only drive halfway down their street in Woodlawn due to the number of cars parked along both sides of the road.

"Wow, I didn't expect this," Claire said, scanning the groups of people on the sidewalk, all making their way to Ryan's parents' house, carrying everything from cakes and pies to casseroles and other hot dishes. She glanced over her shoulder at Fiona, who was sitting in the back. "From what you said, I knew that Rose Flaherty was loved, but I didn't expect this kind of turnout."

"Neither did I." Casey parked at the first available empty space and turned off the ignition.

"Well, I did." Fiona didn't look a bit surprised. "Rose was a very special and very endearing person. Add to that the fact that the church congregation knows what a great cook and hostess my mom is, and you get a crowd like this." She looked from Casey to Claire. "I don't know how you two can look so energetic. I feel like I've been hit by a bus."

From the moment Yoda had completed his tasks, the entire day had been filled with intense work and analysis. Everyone was aware this was a matter of life and death. Ryan had secured Fiona's iCloud account. What damage had been done was capped. The whole team had closeted themselves in the War Room, where they had plenty of space to operate. Each team member was assigned a folder—photos and texts taking the lead and reviewed by them all—followed by the individual categories of emails, Word documents, Photoshop files with Fiona's designs, and iMessages.

The interactions with Yoda involved asking him to display all items in that folder and, once he had complied, going through the tedious process of saying, "next, next, next" until something of import was spotted on a particular slide, or "back, back, back" if a previous slide required re-examination. The process became too overwhelming and random, so each folder was further divided into sub-folders, labeled under specific headings, such as *Celtic design, specific collections, e.g. Light and Shadows,* and *personal versus business* when it came to texts and emails.

Yoda's multitasking abilities had astounded Fiona. Clearly, her brother's AI system was even more brilliant than she'd realized. Ryan truly was a genius and Yoda was a wizard.

Meanwhile, she did her own share of multitasking. She was pulled into every teammate's work, to answer questions, clarify the importance or lack thereof of a specific slide, and to identify anything potentially critical.

The most upsetting item had turned up right away, during the analysis of the photos. Not only were all of her and Ryan's exchanges from the previous night there, but a photo dated a few months back showed a picture of Fiona and her mom, standing together in the living room, smiling, and with the Galway sheep tapestry hanging prominently in the background.

It wouldn't be hard to guess whose house the photo had been taken in. Not with the homey feel that emanated from the entire scene.

Fiona had never been more grateful than she was at that moment, knowing that Al Sheppard, Patrick's security guy, was safeguarding her parents. Al was both a former FBI agent and a former NYPD homicide detective.

"Where's Al's car in this zoo?" she asked now, glancing nervously around.

Casey looked calmly down the street and into the McKays' driveway. Sure enough, the maroon Corolla Patrick had told her to look for was parked just a few feet from the garage door.

"His car is practically inside your house," she replied lightly, determined to calm Fiona down. "Remember, he's been here since early morning. None of the guests had even started baking their casseroles yet."

"You're right." Fiona looked sheepish. "I'm sorry I'm so on edge. Between worrying about my parents, worrying about my own safety, and worrying about how I'm going to answer the thousand questions waiting on the other side of that door, I'm a dead-on-my-feet nervous wreck. Plus, Lara and her parents landed right before we left the brownstone, and I'm not looking forward to the reaction to *their* townhouse being trashed—especially since I'm the reason for it. I only hope the cleanup team got a lot done today."

"On all counts, things will be fine," Claire said with gentle reassurance. "And by the way, I love your earrings. Are those part of the Light and Shadows collection?"

Casey slid a quick sidelong look at Claire. Obviously, she had the same idea about trying to calm Fiona down.

Sure enough, Fiona's entire demeanor changed. Her fingers went reflexively to her earlobes, touching the white teardrop pearls hanging from the gold Celtic triquetra symbol. "Yes, these are my Trinity knot earrings," she said with pride. "I finished them earlier this week, and I grabbed them, and all my jewelry, when Ryan and I left my house last night. I took everything—just in case. The place is like an open house while it's being cleaned up, and anyone could walk in. I wasn't taking any chances."

"Well, those are sheer elegance." Claire studied the stylized Trinity knot with utter fascination. Fiona had taken the symbol down to its bare contours and turned it on its side so one tip was pointing down, and it was from that tip that the pearls hung. The entire outline of the gold earrings themselves was embellished with tiny balls of gold that literally shimmered with light. "Ancient and modern at the same time," Claire murmured. "I don't know how you do it."

"Thanks, Claire. I really needed some positive energy right about now." Eagerly, Fiona leaned forward in her seat. "And speaking of positive energy, was that what you were picking up on when you said everything would be fine?"

"In this case, what I said was based on my faith in Forensic Instincts and my faith in you." Claire never lied about her gift. Nor did she make promises to clients that she couldn't be sure she could keep. "Right now, just concentrate on this gathering. Casey and I will be right there to back you up."

"I know. You're both wonderful." Fiona attempted a smile. "I'm half tempted to announce to my parents that you're Ryan's girlfriend, as in singular."

"Uh, I'd shelve that idea if I were you," Claire replied, smiling back. "I don't think your brother would appreciate it."

"He'll tell them himself—sooner than he expects," Fiona said with an innate knowledge of her brother. "He's crazy about you, you know."

Claire wasn't sure how to reply to that. Her feelings, like Ryan's, were complex and inexplicable—certainly not ready to be assigned a name other than the girlfriend-boyfriend one they'd just come to.

"You don't have to say anything." Fiona picked up on Claire's reticence. "Things will just play out on their own." She looked down at the huge tray of pastries that was on the seat beside her, both hers and the FI team's contribution to the gathering. "I wish I could have made some of Rose's favorite dishes. Glenna had to do all that since my kitchen is unusable. I would have begun with—"

"The pastries are great, and you're procrastinating," Casey interrupted. There was a big difference between calming Fiona down and letting her put off the inevitable. "Aside from admiring your exquisite earrings, we've now discussed the crowd, Claire's love life, and your lack of ability to cook for the occasion. Time to go in."

Fiona frowned. "You're *too* good at what you do."

"No major skills involved. You're as easy to read as your brother." Casey opened the car door. "I'll introduce you to Al when we go in. He'll be blending in with the crowd, saying he's one of Rose's clients. Once you see how capable he is, you'll feel better."

The three women walked up the street and were about to head up the path to the house when something caught Casey's eye.

"Hang on," she said. "I think Al is sitting in his car."

"What?" Fiona looked puzzled and more than a little uneasy. She hurried along with Casey and Claire as they went straight to the Corolla.

Al saw them before they even approached, and he opened his window. He looked frustrated but alert and ready to act on a moment's notice. "Hello, Casey, Claire—and you must be Fiona. I'm Al Sheppard."

"Nice to meet you," Fiona replied automatically. But she was clearly thrown by this unexpected turn of events.

Casey looked from Al to the bowl of stew in his lap to the untouched pint of Guinness placed on the floor of the passenger side of the car. "What's going on? Why are you out here?"

He cleared his throat, visibly trying for diplomacy. "I was inside the house all day. As for this evening? I'm lucky I got this close. Mrs. McKay is a rather strong personality. She informed me that there'd be no guard dogs in her home during her party. She ordered me out. On the other hand," he added quickly, seeing the stricken look on Fiona's face, "she's been back and forth to my car three times, bringing me a continuous supply of food. Oh, and this pint of beer, which she instructed me to place somewhere flat where it wouldn't spill. I told her I don't drink when I'm on duty, but she said I was relieved of duty until the guests had all gone. Sorry, Casey, but I'm not FBI anymore. I have no authority to force her to let me stay."

"Oh, Mom." Fiona rolled her eyes, then spoke directly to Al. "I apologize for my mother's behavior, Mr. Sheppard, well-intentioned or not. If I had my way, I'd bring you in as my escort. But the fireworks that would cause would compromise what you're really doing here. So I'll just thank you and ask for your patience and vigilance."

A corner of his mouth lifted. "Please call me Al. And no apologies necessary. I've eaten more good food in the past hour than I have all week." With that, he sobered. "Casey has my cell number. Text me if there's even the slightest hint of something being off. I'll be inside in a heartbeat. Although I wouldn't worry too much. Your detective friends have been in there for half an hour."

"Alvarez and Shaw showed up?" Casey's brows rose.

"Going by Patrick's descriptions and their official demeanor, I'd say yes. And after last night's break-in at Fiona's, I'm not really surprised. They're scoping out the guests to see if anyone on their potential list of suspects approaches her."

"Great, just great." Fiona glanced nervously around.

"It'll be fine," Al assured them. "No one is stupid enough to accost you in a crowd. Just pay attention to anyone who's interested in asking you a suspicious number of personal questions pertaining to this case. You have two of the finest investigators to help you." He indicated Casey and Claire.

"I know." Fiona turned to look at the house. "I just wish my mother had let you stay. Alvarez and Shaw don't exactly put me at ease."

"We'll handle them," Casey said. "Thanks, Al."

"Aren't you cold?" Claire asked him, wrapping her fall jacket around her. "It's kind of nippy out here."

Al held up his bowl. "I have my stew to keep me warm."

The McKays' house was a whirlwind of activity, people chatting, eating, drinking, and flitting around to socialize. There was a bit of a hush when

Fiona stepped into the hall, but she pretended not to notice it, instead scanning the area until she spotted her mother just inside the living room.

"In there," she murmured to Casey and Claire, and they all eased their way in that direction.

Fiona greeted people as she walked, but she didn't linger. As it was, far too many pairs of eyes were focused on her as she and her two-woman support system wove their way through the crowd and toward the living room. In those eyes were reflected many things—curiosity, sympathy, concern—you name it. That reaction only became more widespread, since the predominant number of guests were crammed in the living room and adjoining dining room. As those guests became aware of Fiona's presence, they turned to scrutinize her, to see what kind of shape she was in after the trauma of the past few days.

Her mother pivoted around as she approached.

"Fiona." Maureen embraced her daughter, holding on to her for an extra minute before easing away to assess Fiona's physical and emotional state as only a mother could. Clearly, she didn't give a damn what the guests were thinking. "Oh, lovey." She held Fiona's cheeks between her palms, her eyes growing damp. "Thank God you were here with me when this happened. Otherwise..." She broke off with a shudder.

"I'm really fine, Mom." Fiona said it loudly enough for the nosy guests to hear. She knew their hearts were in the right place. Still, she felt like the star attraction at a circus, with a rapt audience following her every move.

Casey leaned around to place the tray of pastries on the long buffet table, after which she reached out to shake Maureen's hand. "I'm Casey Woods, Mrs. McKay. Thank you for having us."

"It's such a pleasure to meet you," Maureen replied. "Ryan speaks so highly of you."

"I do the same of him. Your son's a genius. Just don't tell him I said so lest his ego become too big to fit in our brownstone."

Maureen chuckled, and the heightened tension of the previous few minutes dissipated, just as Casey had hoped. Most of the guests went back to what they were doing, although Casey had no doubt that they'd all seek Fiona out when she became available. By now, they all knew that she'd been the one to find Rose's body. But Casey had a strong suspicion that they also knew about the B and E at her place last night. The McKays' circle of friends and fellow church congregants was very tight, and news of an event of that magnitude would pass quickly from cell phone to cell phone.

"Claire." Maureen was now squeezing Claire's hands. "I'm so glad you're here. You have a kind and loving soul like Rose did. You two would have gotten along famously."

"I'm sure." Claire smiled. "Is there anything we can do to help?"

Maureen gave both Claire and Casey a pleading look, one that said: *Just take care of my daughter.*

Casey gave an indiscernible nod. "We'll let you get back to your guests," she said. "We're fine on our own." She turned to Fiona. "Introduce me to your dad. Then we can taste some of this delicious food your mom has prepared."

"Not just me," Maureen replied with a sweep of her arm. "Almost everyone who's here. Rose had generous friends and we have a generous congregation. But please do taste everything and help us celebrate Rose's life. That's what this evening is all about."

Maybe, Casey thought to herself with a quick scan of the area. *Maybe not.*

17

Fiona had just managed to introduce her father when Glenna appeared at her side, also giving her a big hug.

"I just got here. Are you okay?" she asked anxiously. "I talked to your mom earlier. She told me about the break-in."

"I'm fine," Fiona assured her. "It's just my townhouse that isn't." She turned to Casey and Claire. "These are friends of mine, Casey and Claire. They've helped me out a lot since last night. Thanks to their referral, my house is being put back together." She went on to complete the introductions. "This is Glenna Robinson, Rose's assistant. She was as dear to Rose as if she were her granddaughter."

"It's nice to meet you, Glenna," Casey said. "We're so very sorry for your loss."

Glenna's eyes glistened with tears. "Thank you. I still wake up each morning and expect to go to the antique shop after my classes and see Rose's smiling face. I can't believe she's gone—and in such a horrible way." She blinked back her tears. "But this is supposed to be a celebration of her life. She'd want it that way. So no more tears. Time to eat, drink, and share stories about—" She broke off, this time her eyes widening with dismay. "Oh, no. Not again. And not here."

Casey didn't even follow Glenna's gaze. She didn't need to. She'd sensed the detectives' presence and their scrutiny since she, Claire, and Fiona had walked in the door.

Fiona, evidently, hadn't. She looked confused, glancing around just as Alvarez and Shaw headed their way.

"That's right; I forgot they're here." She swore under her breath. "I'm *so* not in the mood for this."

"Hello, Fiona," Alvarez said as they reached her side. "Glenna." She nodded at Rose's assistant. "Fiona, how are you holding up?" she asked, her voice unusually quiet.

"As well as can be expected." Fiona's reply was terse. "I'm also here to honor my friend. So, with all due respect, any additional Q and A will have to wait."

"That's not why we're here," Shaw quickly responded, his voice equally soft.

"I know. You're just doing your jobs. I apologize." Fiona blew out a breath. "I'm just very, very weary."

"We understand." Alvarez was already assessing Casey and Claire. "We're just guests, paying our respects." Her point to Fiona was clear and explained their subdued manner: *Don't blow our cover.*

They were there on a mission—to figure out if the murderer would show up. It wouldn't be the first time a seasoned killer would come back to admire the aftermath of his handiwork, especially if he or she was an insider.

"Lucia Alvarez." The detective reached out her hand to shake Casey's and Claire's—and to find out who they were. "And this is my friend, Harry Shaw."

"Casey Woods," Casey replied. "And this is Claire Hedgleigh." She watched the comprehension on both Alvarez's and Shaw's faces as handshakes were exchanged all around.

"We're also here as guests, and as Fiona's friends, to support her at such a difficult time." Casey met Alvarez's stare directly. Now was not the time to get into a pissing match. It would be bad for all of them.

"A pleasure," Alvarez replied, clearly on board with the arrangement. Whatever probing she planned to do with FI, she'd do at another place and another time.

With that in mind, the four of them exchanged a few more pleasantries and then went their separate ways.

"That was unexpectedly painless," Glenna said, her brows drawn together in noncomprehension. "I assumed they'd... Why didn't they ask us more about—"

"Because they want to fly under the radar," Casey interrupted her quietly. "And we have to help them do that. If they have a lead on someone who's here or even if they're just taking people's temperature, they'd hit a stone wall if anyone knew who they were. So let's just think of them as Lucia and Harry, at least for tonight."

"Okay." Glenna gave a shaky nod.

"I didn't even know they had first names," Fiona muttered. "But I'm thrilled that they're leaving us alone. And I'd be even more thrilled if they actually turned up something—or someone—here tonight." She glanced around. "Although it's very hard for me to imagine any of these people wishing Rose harm, much less killing her."

"People aren't always what they seem," Casey replied. "Lucia and Harry are just covering all their bases—as they should."

Claire touched Fiona's arm. "Let's change the subject. I think the four of us should get some food. Glenna, show us which of Rose's favorite dishes you made. I want to try those first."

Across the room, Niall watched the entire scene with interest, even as he polished off his Guinness—only his second, since he had every intention of staying sharp. Pointedly, he avoided approaching Fiona right away. No sense in looking too eager. Plus, he wanted to wait for the right moment—a moment that wouldn't come until the barrage of guests had anxiously questioned her about her well-being. Even reaching her side would have to be done with casual grace, given the watchful eyes of the two detectives milling around and the obvious presence of the two women flanking Fiona on either side. Idly, he wondered who they were. Close friends? Probably. There for emotional support? Doubtless.

Fiona was shaking her head, and a glint of light shimmered from her earlobes. Earrings. Good. Maybe these would have a connection, as well. He'd have to get close to see every detail.

In the meantime, he continued with his social pleasantries, letting the evening unfold.

A couple of hours passed.

The crowd was thinning out, and the detectives were chatting with the remaining guests. Niall had rather enjoyed answering their subtle questions about his relationship to Rose. Given he was one of her best clients, it wasn't hard to offer both knowledgeable praise and deep sorrow. And given his well-known standing as a millionaire real estate developer and connoisseur of the arts, the cops had barely spent five minutes with him before they decided he wasn't even a blip on their radar. They'd graciously excused themselves and continued on their mission.

In the meantime, Fiona had been fielding ongoing questions from the crowd. She looked totally worn out. She'd be relieved to speak with someone who didn't pry into her life. And she was momentarily alone, other than her two friends, who weren't about to disappear any time soon. They were all chatting and nibbling on pieces of Irish soda bread.

Niall disengaged himself from the group of church congregants he'd been chatting with and walked toward them.

Fiona was chewing reflexively, barely aware of what she was tasting. It had been an eon of *Yes, finding her like that was horrible, No, I'm holding up fine, No, nothing was taken,* and *I have no idea why any of this happened.* Hugs and hand squeezes and offers of help—all the gestures were lovely but making Fiona panic all the more. If it weren't for Casey and Claire's support—steering conversations in a different direction, suggesting that they all grab something more to eat, or just drawing out the introductions—Fiona would have had a total meltdown. As it was, she was feeling trapped and freaked out about how much longer she'd have to stay.

"Hang on," Claire murmured. "A half-dozen people have already left. Stick it out for a little while longer and then we'll say our good-byes. Your parents will understand; they've been worrying about you all evening. I can see it in their eyes."

Fiona nodded, her anxiety easing a bit. She couldn't wait to get into the car and head for home—wherever home would be for the night. "Okay."

"Hello, Fiona." A deep voice with an Irish brogue interrupted their brief conversation.

Fiona turned, once again forcing a smile to her lips. "Niall. Hi."

"I'm sorry for what you've been through," he said simply. "But I'm glad you were up to coming tonight to celebrate Rose's life. We both know what a fine human being she was, as well as how brilliant she was in her field. She'll be dearly missed."

Fiona nodded, bracing herself for the next round of questions.

Niall surprised her.

"Are these lovely ladies friends of yours?" he asked. Definitely respectful and in no way a come-on. Also in no way belaboring a Q and A with Fiona.

"Yes." Fiona almost wept with relief. "Casey Woods, Claire Hedgleigh, this is Niall Dempsey."

Casey's brows rose as she shook his hand. "The real estate developer?" she asked.

"Guilty as charged." He smiled. "It's nice to meet you."

"And you, as well."

"Niall was kind enough to offer available apartments in his buildings to out-of-town guests," Fiona said, as Niall shook Claire's hand.

"That was very gracious of you," Claire said in response.

In truth, she was having a hard time responding at all. What she really wanted to do was recoil from the handshake and back away. The surge of dark energy that emanated from the brief contact made her skin crawl. There was something very ugly about Niall Dempsey. Who he was? His past? Both were filled with darkness and shadows.

How dark? Was he a killer? Claire couldn't discern that. The shadows were too obscuring. She'd have to hold his hand for longer than a handshake to try to break through them. And she couldn't—not just because it would look ridiculous but because his very touch was making her physically ill.

"Miss Hedgleigh?" Niall was speaking to her, looking very concerned. "Are you all right? You're white as a sheet."

"I'm fine, just light-headed." Claire was furious with herself for not doing a better job of hiding her reaction. "I think I'd better finish this soda bread. Meeting and chatting with so many people made me forget to eat. I filled a plate of food and barely touched it." She took a healthy bite of her bread. "I apologize if I scared you."

"Nonsense." Niall indicated the sofa in a now nearly empty living room. "Sit down. I'll bring you something to eat."

Claire wanted to refuse, but she'd already screwed up enough. "Thank you; that would be wonderful. And maybe a glass of water, if you don't mind?"

"Of course I don't." Niall strode off.

"What is it?" Casey quietly asked as she and Fiona sat down beside her on the sofa.

"Later." Claire settled herself, retaining the drawn expression that accompanied her claim to be light-headed.

"Are you okay?" Fiona asked anxiously, oblivious to what was really going on. "I feel like a selfish brat. All I'm thinking about is me, and the two of you are about to drop."

"We're just fine," Casey assured her. "Claire just needs some sustenance. It's been a long day."

Niall returned quickly, handing Claire a plate that was laden with a variety of food. He pulled over a side table and placed a glass of water on it. "I wasn't sure what you liked, so I brought you options," he said.

Claire was already forcing herself, not only to eat but to look ravenous as she did. "I so appreciate this." She smiled, taking a few healthy gulps of water. "I'm feeling better already."

He nodded. "You look better." Abruptly, he frowned, reaching into his pocket and pulling out his vibrating cell phone. He glanced down at the caller ID. "My office," he explained. "Would you excuse me?"

"Of course." Fiona was almost sorry to see him go. He'd been a shred of normalcy in an otherwise unbearable evening.

Claire was thrilled to see him go. She inhaled sharply, then drank more of her water and ate enough of her food to make her whole scene believable. All the while, her gaze followed Niall Dempsey, wondering who the man really was and why he was so shrouded in unknown darkness.

Niall would have ignored his regular cell. But this was his private one. It meant Donald was reaching out to him.

Standing in a quiet corner, he put the phone to his ear. "Talk to me."

"Air traffic. Take a different flight."

Frowning, Niall disconnected the call. His computer guy was still trying to get access to Fiona's pictures. But Donald needed to see him on another matter—right away.

Any further communication with Fiona would have to wait. Besides, he'd seen her earrings up close and memorized every detail. And he'd taken care of the other matter he needed to.

Time to say good night.

Claire watched Niall thank Maureen for everything and shake Colin's hand. Clearly, his phone call had required him to leave. That moment couldn't come fast enough for her.

She endured his good-byes with her, Casey, and Fiona, as well as his outwardly sincere offer to help Fiona in any way he could.

"You're welcome to stay in one of my buildings until your town-house has been restored to livable conditions," he said.

"Thank you so much." Fiona clearly liked and respected the man. "I'm staying at my brother's. But if the work takes longer than expected and Ryan gets tired of having me underfoot, I might just take you up on your generous offer. Hopefully, I won't need to. The workmen are moving quickly."

"Well, if anything changes, the offer stands. Just give me a call." Niall pulled out a business card and handed it to her. "All my contact information is there."

He gave them all a parting smile. "Good night."

Claire felt her whole body relax as he walked away.

That relaxation didn't last long.

Abruptly, she was accosted by a different but equally powerful sense of awareness, one that drew her gaze to the wall where the tapestry panel with the Galway sheep hung. It was just as she remembered it. Ostensibly, nothing had changed. So she wasn't sure what her awareness was all about, but it eclipsed her lingering reaction to Niall Dempsey and compelled her to act.

"Excuse me for a minute," she murmured. She put down her plate and walked across the room to the tapestry, stopping to study it up close. The intensity of the pull she felt was so strong that she almost gave in and touched the woven fabric. But there were still guests in the room, not to mention Maureen McKay, who would *definitely* not appreciate Claire putting her hands on the panel.

Still… Claire's gaze was drawn upward until it settled on the rod from which the tapestry hung.

It was askew. Just a little. Not enough to attribute to anything but a guest bumping into it.

But no guest had bumped into it. Claire's flashes came fast and furious. Someone had touched it, rubbed it between curious fingers. And photos. They'd taken photos of the panel.

Why? Did they know something about the tapestries' significance that FI had yet to figure out? Was it Niall Dempsey? Was that why she'd reacted so powerfully to him? Or was that assumption based only on the fact that these two onslaughts of awareness were so closely timed? Niall's darkness had been deep, but it encompassed his past. That didn't mean he wasn't also guilty of more. But was he?

Claire was being assaulted by a barrage of questions—questions to which she had no answers. But she had to take the next logical step to find some.

She glanced back at Casey and Fiona, signaling that she needed to use the powder room. Fiona gestured toward the hall where that was. Her brows were drawn together as she looked curiously from the tapestry panel to Claire and back. Casey showed no such puzzlement. She merely nodded, realizing that Claire was doing what Claire did best.

Claire headed off, grateful that, given the traditional layout of the house, the hall bath was near bedrooms. Because her real destination was the master bedroom.

It was time to see—and this time to study—the only tapestry panel she had yet to set her eyes on. Had it been handled and photographed tonight, too? She didn't have a clear sense of that. All she knew was that it was time to complete the circle of viewing all the panels that made up the full tapestry. And this time, she'd have the chance to truly scrutinize one of those panels—and whether or not the pull she felt for it was as strong as the pull she felt toward the one in the living room, she'd take advantage of her solitude and touch it.

She was taking a major risk and she knew it. If either Maureen or Colin found her in their room, there'd be no explaining why she was there. And if they caught her with her fingers on the tapestry, Maureen would be furious. But she had to take that chance.

Because if the killer had been here and if he was one step ahead of Forensic Instincts, Claire intended to close that gap. And if Niall Dempsey was that killer, she intended to channel all her own energy into figuring that out, too.

Locating the master bedroom was easy. It was larger than the other rooms clustered around it—those obviously being the children's bedrooms before they'd grown up and moved out.

Claire crossed the threshold, her eyes searching the semi-darkened room even as she did. Basic furnishings—a queen-sized bed with nightstands on either side, a double dresser, an armoire, and a small unit with a TV set and DVD player. A wall mirror hung over the dresser. And directly across from the bed, Claire could make out the outline of the tapestry panel. Clearly, it was the first thing Maureen wanted to see when she woke up and the last thing she wanted to see when she went to sleep.

In one bold move, Claire flipped on the overhead light—and held her breath, waiting.

The distant voices of the lingering guests in the living room were all she heard—that and Maureen McKay's voice as she chatted with them.

So far, so good.

Claire pivoted, and her eyes widened as she caught her first real glimpse of the tapestry panel. No wonder it was Maureen's favorite. It was, quite simply, magical.

Artistically breathtaking, it depicted a crystal bowl nestled inside a flowing lotus blossom. The blossom had leaves of violet, pink, and cream in a variegated pattern and its edges were curled around the bowl like loving fingers. Knowing Ryan and Fiona's family, Claire would bet that it was a Waterford bowl, since the Irish brand of crystal was so world famous. The bowl itself had a crackle effect with tiny fissures as the texture. Unusual for Waterford, but uniquely beautiful. A pale blue background with the same soft green border and symbols that graced the other panels Claire had seen. The images, the panel as a whole—it was like one masterpiece inside another.

Claire also didn't miss the influence this tapestry had on the earrings Fiona was wearing tonight. The shape of the earrings' pearl teardrops matched the shape of the lotus leaves wrapped around the Waterford bowl and the whites in the leaves had the same pure cast as the pearls. Fiona's interpretation was a tribute to her great-grand-mother's creation.

Walking right up to the tapestry, Claire waited a heartbeat to see if any images flashed, if any energy emanated from simply viewing the panel. When that didn't happen, she acted without hesitation, lightly placing her palm against the woven fabric.

First came a sense of stillness. No one had touched or photo-graphed this panel. Whoever had done so to the Galway sheep panel either hadn't wanted to risk exploring the rest of the house or wasn't aware that another panel was hanging elsewhere.

On the heels of that awareness, a different energy flowed from the panel to Claire's hand. A sense of urgency. A story being told—one that *had* to be understood. A piece of a jigsaw puzzle stranded, waiting for its counterparts to interlock with it so as to be united into one. A plea. A search.

And an absolute awareness that nothing else would flow through Claire's senses until all the panels had been assembled.

She turned away, frustrated, and her gaze fell on the four-poster bed.

Her heart began slamming against her ribs.

Danger. Imminent. Personal. Invasive.

Maureen and Colin.

Whoever had tampered with the panel in the living room was coming back, not just to touch but to take. And to use whatever means necessary—violent or otherwise—to learn where the other panels were.

***

Claire made her way straight to Casey, not even aiming for subtle.

"We have a problem," she said quietly, tension underlying every word. She glanced at Fiona. "Don't react to what I'm about to say. It's a matter of safety and urgency."

"You're scaring me," Fiona said, her eyes wide.

"*Please*," Claire replied. "Let us do our job."

She didn't wait for Fiona's nod, although she got it.

"Casey, we have to call Patrick and get additional security for Maureen and Colin. One-on-one when they're out and reinforcements for Al when they're home. The house is being watched. Someone's coming back for the tapestries—all of them."

Fiona's hands balled into fists, pressing deep into the sofa cushion. But she forced herself not to cry out.

"Done," Casey said, already reaching for her cell phone, simultaneously rising to find a private spot. "Is there more?"

"We can't leave, not until all the guests have gone. We need to talk to Fiona's parents alone. We *must* convey the danger involved and convince Maureen to let us take the panels with us tonight. And when we do take them, we want to do it openly, so whoever's watching the house will see us and know the panels are no longer here."

"That'll ensure they look elsewhere—most likely at FI once they see who takes them—so the house won't be a target anymore. But that won't do anything to protect Fiona's parents from people who want answers," Casey replied. "You're right; we need one-on-one security for them. I'll call Patrick." She half turned to Fiona, whose entire face was drained of color. "Your job is to get the guests out of here. I don't care how you do it. Just do it. We need your parents alone."

That snapped Fiona into action. "They'll be gone by the time you get back."

18

Niall was in a foul mood when he walked into Kelly's, having yanked on his canvas jacket and Yankees cap in the car.

He'd barely accomplished anything at the McKays' house tonight. Fiona's earrings hadn't given him any new information. The Trinity knot was one of the most common Celtic symbols; it was sold on random pieces of jewelry everywhere. And the two women he'd assumed were just her friends? They'd ended up being part of the Forensic Instincts team. Bad enough that Fiona's pain-in-the-ass brother was involved, now the whole damn company was safeguarding her like one of her precious pieces of jewelry. He'd done his best to befriend them, right down to rescuing Claire Hedgleigh from a near faint. And their president, Casey Woods, had been affable enough. But at best, that meant he'd steered them away from viewing him as a suspect. It did nothing to stop them from interfering with his search.

He scanned the tavern and saw Donald was tied up with some effusive customer who was praising one of his famous dishes. Niall knew the bar owner saw him because he shot Niall a quick look and tipped his head toward the back room.

Fine. Niall would go back there and wait. He needed to think anyway and whatever Donald had urgently called him down here for was undoubtedly going to further piss him off.

He shut the door behind him, tossed his cap aside, and sank down at one of the booths, elbows on the table, fingers massaging his temples.

He'd become a man obsessed.

The first seeds of that obsession had been planted thirty-six years ago, although he hadn't known it at the time.

A raid he'd made in Belfast. A tout that had to be dealt with. Niall had hated the bastard, knowing that he'd been responsible for the deaths of Niall's mates from his previous unit. He'd come forward, eager to do the job. The request was granted.

He'd broken in through the back door and entered the house wearing a balaclava over his head and carrying a baseball bat studded with tenpenny nails.

The TV set was on and he could hear the family talking and laughing in the living room, the clinking of silverware telling him they were eating their dinner at the same time. He edged forward until he could see them, eating their food on TV trays, absorbed and off guard. The tout. His wife. Two young kids.

Niall waited just long enough to make sure there were no comings or goings that would surprise him and interfere with his task.

Reassured, he went straight for it, trying to block out the screams and cries of the rest of the family as he went for the tout. He'd beaten the shit out of him with his bat, blood splattering with each successive strike... breaking first his legs and then one arm.

Screaming in pain, the tout had fumbled under the chair with his one good arm, reaching for a gun.

Stupid fuck.

Niall had whipped out his own pistol, putting a hole in the tout's forehead in one quick move, watching him crumple to the floor, dead.

He shouldn't have stayed, not even for those brief moments. It violated all his training, went against all his instincts. But he'd never killed a man in front of his wife and kids. His sniper hits were always faceless, his target being his only victim, killed from a distance.

This was different. Seeing the tout's wife and children—God, they couldn't have been more than four and six years old—hearing them sob with grief and terror as they huddled together, staring wild-eyed at the lifeless body, he'd felt his gut twist with remorse, not for killing the tout, but for leaving his family alone and scarred for life by this memory.

They'd looked up and seen him pause. Reflexively, they'd cowered, certain he was going to kill them next.

He shook his head, lowering his pistol so they'd know he meant them no harm. Simultaneously, he'd raised his gaze so as not to see the agony on their faces.

That's when he saw the painting.

A Viking battle. A body of water. A monastery. Graves with Celtic crosses. A slain king lying in his own blood. A wealth of riches spilling alongside him. And the words *The Battle of Bawncullen* scribbled in Gaelic at the base.

Odd that those images registered so vividly at the time.

Even odder that a deeper, more comprehensive visual memory had evidently sunk in, because, decades later, he'd recognized the painting when he saw—and purchased—it.

But in that initial moment back in Belfast, he'd just torn his stare away, regained his self-control, and gotten out of the house the same way he'd entered.

He knew he'd never forget that kill.

The entire scene was etched in his mind and his soul forever.

"Sorry to make you wait." Donald's entrance interrupted Niall's dark musings. "Couldn't get rid of that guy." He sat down across from Niall, planting his elbows on the table and leaning forward, his gaze dark, tension rippling through him.

Niall knew that look, that intensity. Whatever Donald was about to convey was big and it was ugly.

"What happened?" Niall demanded.

"The new kid I hired called in, sounding like a scared rabbit. Said he went to relieve one of the guys watching the McKays' house and saw him talking to a stranger. The stranger slipped our guy a handful of cash and disappeared into the shadows."

"A *stranger*?" Thunderclouds erupted in Niall's eyes. "Give me a description."

"Don't have one. It was too dark and the stranger wore black and a cap pulled low on his face. I dragged our traitor to a warehouse to *encourage* him to talk. Turns out he's a junkie. He'd do anything to get cash for his next fix, including selling us out."

"How did we not know this?"

"He checked out fine. Must keep his habit well hidden. I didn't pick up on it, and I always do."

"I know." Niall gestured for him to continue.

"After a couple of broken kneecaps, he told me that the stranger knew he'd been part of the break-in at Fiona McKay's place. He gave him two hundred bucks for information on what specific pieces of jewelry he saw there."

Niall shot up like an arrow. "How the hell would this stranger know about the significance of Fiona's jewelry?"

Donald's shoulders lifted in a shrug. "Don't know. But I do know what our ex-employee told him. He said he saw a pair of earrings made up of some old, foreign-looking coins and a bracelet with pebbles and green stones. That's all he remembered, except for a bunch of loose jewels."

"Shit." Niall slammed both fists on the table, ignoring the stab of pain that sliced through his scarred palm.

"I take it that's significant."

"It fucking well is. I need to get more than you did. I know what I'm looking for. You don't."

"That's why, instead of killing our guy, I left him bound and gagged until I could get you down here. You can take over from here."

Niall was already on his feet. "Take me to that warehouse."

***

The lock on the warehouse door had been easy to pick.

He hadn't wasted a moment of his precious time. His attack had been brief and brutal and most enjoyable to watch.

He'd used what he always used—his .22 caliber pistol that shot long rifle rounds. He'd put the pistol behind the useless kid's ear—a spot he'd long ago chosen for his victims since it was the soft part of the skull—and fired two shots.

The shots killed but never exited the body. They ricocheted so the pain was unbearable and death was welcome.

The junkie's screams of agony were muffled by the gag still in his mouth.

At last, the writhing and screaming stopped and the body went limp in death.

Cobra stood back and smiled.

19

The final guests had all left the gathering, and Casey, Claire, and Fiona had just finished transferring the tapestry panels from the McKays' house to Casey's car.

Casey laid the last of the tapestries flat on top of the others in the trunk and took an extra minute to make sure they were secure before placing a blanket over them. She then slammed the hatch shut, walked around to slide behind the steering wheel, and shut the door.

"Well done," Claire said from the passenger seat, intentionally looking straight ahead so whoever was watching them wouldn't realize they'd been made. "Open and visible. There's no doubt we have the tapestry panels with us."

"Nope." Casey turned over the ignition, waiting as Fiona gave her mother another hard hug and some quiet reassurance. "And it certainly helped our cause that Maureen followed us out, wringing her hands in distress over parting with the panels. It was clear she'd never let us take them unless it was absolutely necessary, both for their safety and for FI's investigation. It was an all-around win."

As Casey spoke, Fiona jumped into the back seat.

"All set," she said. "I don't think my mom is going to get any calmer than she is now. Until this insanity is resolved and we're all out of danger, she's going to worry. Parting with the tapestries freaked her out more because of *why* we're taking them, not so much *that* we're taking them. Our talk with her hit home, even if we kept the information to a minimum."

What they'd told Maureen was a microcosm of the truth: that she and Colin were in immediate danger and that someone wanted their tapestries badly enough to become violent in order to get them. Even though they'd avoided the word *kill*, Maureen had made the connection.

"Fiona's townhouse... Rose's murder... and now this..." she'd said, her face drained of color. "They're all connected." She hadn't waited for a reply. "But why the tapestry panels? They're not valuable. I don't understand."

"Nor do we," Casey had replied. "But we'll figure it out."

Maureen had clasped Casey hands between hers, clearly aware that there was much being left unsaid. "Please keep my children safe," she'd begged, first and foremost a mother—a mother who was putting aside her concern for herself and her husband and focusing on her children.

"We'll keep *everyone* safe," Casey had promised.

They'd gone on to fill Maureen and Colin in on the security detail watching them at home and following them whenever they went out, and concluded by giving strict instructions for how they should behave and how to contact Al and his arriving backup if they so much as suspected they were being watched or followed.

Both the McKays had listened and nodded grimly.

There was very little Casey could do to ease their concern.

"Your mother is a very smart woman," she said to Fiona now, pulling out of the parking spot to start their drive back to Tribeca. "She's already trying to put together the pieces."

"So am I," Fiona muttered. "And I know a lot more than she does—like how every time I touch my laptop or cell phone, I'm being tracked through spyware."

"Speaking of that, Ryan pinged me a few minutes ago," Casey said. "He wanted to know where the hell we were and what we found out."

Fiona rolled her eyes. "Impatient as ever."

Casey shook her head. "That's not impatience, that's worry. I've never seen Ryan so unhinged."

"He's freaking out," Claire confirmed with that utter certainty that said she wasn't guessing.

Fiona sighed. "I know. I hate that everyone is so focused on my safety. Any news from the FI end of things?"

"Nope. But they're all still at it."

"I never doubted that. What did you tell Ryan?"

"That we'd be back soon and we'll talk then." Casey slanted a sidelong look at Claire. "Because there's a lot even *I* don't know yet—Claire?"

Claire leaned back against the headrest, visibly drained. "The two panels inside the house were revealing," she said. "Each for a different reason."

"Stop," Casey said, holding up a palm. She knew Claire and her gift, and how it sometimes sucked away all her energy. That was visibly the case right now. She looked like hell. "You're exhausted. There's no point in going through this now when you're going to be doing the same thing in an hour when the whole team is gathered around the conference room table."

"Thanks." Claire shut her eyes. "Someone handled the Galway sheep tapestry," she murmured. "They took photos. They didn't touch the panel in the master bedroom because they didn't know it was there."

"But *you* did—and I said to rest," Casey replied firmly.

"So much dark energy." Claire was zoning out. "If I relax and let my mind wander now, more might come to me. The images are still fresh."

"Then relax. I'll let you know when we're at the brownstone."

***

The warehouse door swung open with barely a touch.

"Someone picked the lock," Donald said, glancing over his shoulder at Niall.

Both men pulled out pistols and Donald pushed open the door with his foot.

Silence greeted them as they marched inside, weapons ready.

Donald flipped on the light and they both saw the crumpled body lying in a puddle of blood on the floor.

"I didn't do that much damage," Donald muttered, sweeping the place before determining they were alone and then lowering his gun. "He's dead. Someone got to him."

"That stranger he was working with shut him up for good." Niall walked straight over to the body, kicked it with his foot. "Which means we'll never know…" He broke off, abruptly squatting down and staring at the dead man's skull, his entire body going rigid with shock. "*Fuck*." He kept staring, as if trying to make the obvious go away. "*Fuck, fuck, fuck.*"

"What is it?" Donald was at his side in three strides.

Niall pointed at the hole behind the dead guy's ear. "That's Cobra's work. The stranger is Cobra." He came to his feet, rubbing the back of his neck as the implications shot through his mind. "Peter was right about him being here. Is this why he came? Is he hunting for the same thing I am? Or does he know who I am and is enjoying toying with me before he kills me? Or both?"

Donald was just as thrown as Niall. "You were the only one to get away," he muttered. "Probably the only failure the sociopath ever had."

With Cobra here, Niall was in grave danger. Everything had changed, and all their priorities had to shift. Rose Flaherty's death, Fiona McKay—all of it had to take a back seat to protecting Niall's life.

Clearly, Niall wasn't thinking along those lines, because, abruptly, his head came up. "Maybe our guys weren't lying when they said they didn't kill Rose Flaherty. Maybe she *was* already dead when they got there. Maybe Cobra killed her."

Donald processed that thoughtfully. "If he did, it wasn't in his usual style."

"That's probably because he wasn't ready to be recognized."

"But he is now—by you." Donald pushed to get inside Niall's head, to make him realize what really mattered. "If what you're saying is true, it's all the more reason to think that Cobra knows that Sean Donovan, a.k.a. Silver Finger, is now Niall Dempsey. And that his signature kill here is a taunting announcement of that."

"Yeah. Yeah." Niall nodded, more combative than afraid. He'd faced death before, too many times to count. He'd defied them all. He wasn't about to die at Cobra's hands. Quite the opposite. He'd finally get his chance to have his revenge, to torture and kill his brother's killer. Cobra had made a fortune betraying his IRA mates to the RUC. He was too greedy not to want the treasure that Niall himself was hunting, even if his ultimate goal was to kill Silver Finger. Niall could use that to his advantage, use his findings as bait, and ultimately reel in his quarry.

"Don't get any stupid ideas," Donald cautioned him. "If we're right, he knows who you are. You have no idea who he is."

Niall ignored the warning. "I'll use all my resources. I'll find him. And then I'll blow his head apart."

***

"Okay, Claire. Before we even get started here, why did you react so violently to Niall Dempsey?"

Casey cut to the chase as the entire FI team gathered around the conference room table, standing and waiting for Fiona to lay out the thirteen tapestry panels. "You turned sheet white and reacted as if you'd been scalded when you shook his hand."

Claire grimaced. "I really screwed up. I'm sorry. I hope he didn't make the connection."

"You covered nicely with the whole about-to-faint thing," Casey reassured her. "Judging from his response, I doubt he suspected anything. I, on the other hand, was pretty stunned. In situations like that, you're always able to hide your emotions. Obviously, this time whatever you picked up on was too intense to contain."

"So much evil," Claire murmured. "A black past shrouded in secrecy." Her shoulders lifted in a frustrated shrug. "I can't tell how much of that evil bleeds into the present. And even if it does, I can't tell if it relates to Rose's death or anything else about this case. Maybe if I'd lingered with the handshake…"

"That wasn't an option." Casey waved that away. "You couldn't stand there holding the man's hand for fifteen minutes. That would have been a whole lot weirder than your pulling away. Maybe when you handle the tapestries there'll be a link to him."

"I hope so."

"Hey," Ryan interjected. "Would you mind filling the rest of us in on what you're talking about?"

Claire proceeded to tell them everything she could about Niall Dempsey, as well as her experiences touching the two panels at the McKays' house.

"Do you think Niall Dempsey is the one who moved the Galway sheep panel?" Patrick asked.

Another shrug. "I just don't know, at least not yet."

Marc looked at Fiona. "How well do you know this Dempsey guy?"

"Not very well," she replied. "Obviously, I know what everyone else does. He was born in Ireland—I have no idea where or when, or when he came to New York. Somewhere along the line, he built a multimillion-dollar real estate development business. Besides that, I know he collects antiquities and that he was a frequent customer of Rose's. She was very fond of him; he gave her that expensive bottle of whiskey she was drinking when she…" Fiona broke off, swallowing. "Anyway, that's pretty much it. He's always been nice to me, like tonight when he offered me one of his vacant apartments to stay in until my place is cleaned up. I've never seen the evil Claire is talking about. Then again, he and I are just acquaintances. So I have no real knowledge of him as a human being. And I certainly know nothing about his past."

"I'll rectify that," Ryan said. "I'll dig into Niall Dempsey until we know everything down to what toothpaste he uses." He tipped his head toward the conference room table. "We've got a shitload of stuff to do. So let's speed things up and scrutinize the tapestries."

With that, everyone watched as Fiona laid out the thirteen panels, the large one in the center.

Casey shook her head in amazement. "How exquisite. Your great-grandmother was an incredibly talented woman. I've never seen such attention to detail. I saw just the one panel in your parents' living room, and even that I saw from a distance. But seeing these all up close—the workmanship is astonishing."

"Thank you," Fiona replied. "And, yes, she was amazing. I've seen these tapestries dozens of times and I still catch my breath each time." She finished her task and stood back.

"I've placed these randomly since I have no idea what order they should go in," she said. "Although some of them seem to be grouped together." She pointed. "This old brick farmhouse surrounded by the green fields is clearly set in Ireland, so I'm guessing it belonged to my great-grandparents. They lived in a tiny village in County Kilkenny. My great-grandfather was a stonemason, so I'm sure he had a hand in building that stone wall out front. See the artistry of the wall and the farmhouse being cast half in light, half in shadows? That's what gave me the name of my new collection."

"The Galway sheep would belong in that grouping, too," Casey noted.

Fiona nodded. "So would the panel of the stones in a field. All part of the landscape."

"And these two crosses." Marc pointed at another panel. "One smaller than the other, the smaller in front, creating that light and shadows image you're referring to. The greenery and rolling hills suggest they're in Ireland."

"They're Celtic high Irish crosses." Fiona had studied all the tapestry panels long enough to have done her research. "One of the best-known symbols of Ireland. They're ornamental stones that were cut from either sandstone or granite and are over eight hundred years old." She pointed. "They have geometric carvings, which are hard to make out here because of the woven material. But they're truly beautiful, and, yes, that puts them in the Ireland grouping."

Ryan leaned over her shoulder. "The panel of the passenger ship on the ocean—which I'm assuming is the Atlantic—and the panel of the Statue of Liberty obviously illustrate our great-grandparents' journey to the US."

"And the awesome evening skyline panel is of Manhattan," Emma said. "Maybe it's the first thing they saw as they arrived. Regardless, it's got to be grouped with the journey to New York panels."

"That makes sense." Casey was staring from one panel to the next. "Then come all the random depictions. The Waterford bowl and lotus leaves, which are stunning but tell us nothing. A gravestone with a tiny border woven into it and a tree beside it, a long, dark corridor lit by torches leading who knows where, a decorative stone carving that obviously means something but I have no idea what, and some ancient coins from who knows what civilization."

"Viking," Fiona supplied. "I based a pair of earrings on those coins."

"That's interesting… but it doesn't fit anywhere in particular." Emma sighed in frustration. "So even with the couple of groupings we have, we're still clueless. How do all these panels fit together?"

"Before we can figure that out, we need to interpret the significance of each panel," Marc answered. "That way we can start to determine the order in which they fit together. After that, we'll get to why they're so important and what they lead us to."

Claire tucked a strand of hair behind her ear. Nothing else specific about the tapestries had come to her since she left the McKays' house, but she was still in heightened sensory mode.

Her gaze was drawn back to the center panel. The shield. The Tree of Life. The bejeweled crown. And the tiny fist clutching either a trophy or a goblet.

"The end goal is shown in the large center panel—but we can't get to it without understanding the whole of what we're looking at." She reached out to touch it, then changed her mind. "I can't do this process half-assed. I need to take all the panels to my yoga room and handle each of them, one by one, and then maybe collectively. So let's all do our thing together first, and then I'll go do mine alone."

"As a team, I think we've gone as far as we can with the tapestries for now," Casey said. "My recommendation is to turn things over to you."

Claire nodded, turning to Fiona. "No great revelation at this point, but the jewelry from your new collection has made you a walking target. Whoever has you in their sights gets the connection between Light and Shadows and the tapestries. That's part of why he had guys break into your townhouse—not only to install that spyware and to search for the tapestries but, if they didn't find them, to take photos of everything in your workshop—particularly all the pieces in your new line." Claire paused thoughtfully. "Were the pearl-drop earrings you're wearing tonight out in the open during the break-in?"

Fiona nodded. "Why?"

"Because that means they have photos of them. And yet, I'm not sensing they've made the connection to the Waterford panel. Somehow I don't think they've seen that one yet."

"But my texts to Ryan, and his to me..."

Claire looked to Ryan for corroboration. "I don't think they've gotten far enough along in the analysis of Fiona's hard drive to find those photos. Is that possible? Because when I touched the Waterford panel, I sensed that I was the first one seeing it, other than the family."

"More than possible, it's probably a sure thing," Ryan replied. "You weren't in my lair when I changed the password on Fee's iCloud account to something extremely long and random that would take even a professional hacker considerable time to crack. So my guess is we stopped them before they could see the photos and now they're SOL."

Marc's brows were knit as he continued to study the tapestry as a whole. "Interlocking pieces of a puzzle. Why do I feel as if we're looking at not only a story but a pictorial map leading to… something?"

There was a long moment of silence as the significance of Marc's observation sank in.

"You're right," Claire breathed in a vital moment of realization. "That's exactly what we're looking at."

"Wow. It must be some big-ass discovery if someone's willing to kill for it." Ryan frowned. "Which makes absolutely no sense. Fee's and my great-grandparents were poor immigrants with virtually nothing when they got to the States. So what could they possibly have been leading us to? And why didn't they just keep whatever it is themselves? Why hide it? And if they did hide it, why not tell my grandparents where it was? Why put it in code and wait for an arbitrary generation of McKays to discover it?"

"No answers yet," Patrick said. "Not to any of it."

"So what do we do?" Emma asked.

"We go back to the basics of what we have," Casey responded. "We reread the book pages and the Post-it that Rose sent to Fiona while looking at the tapestries. We call the right professional contacts of Rose's and see what they can tell us about the research she was doing for Fiona. Even if they don't know the answers, they'll know the questions she was asking."

"I never had a chance to talk to Glenna," Fiona said. "I forgot all about it when my place was trashed. Other than coming to my mom's gathering, she's been staying at her sister and brother-in-law's house in Westchester. I think she feels safer being with family than all alone and vulnerable. And she's got nieces and nephews to keep her focused on something other than the murder investigation."

"It doesn't matter," Ryan told her. "I accessed Rose's contact list and pulled the names of her most recent phone calls to fellow antiquities experts," Ryan said. "There were a bunch of repeat calls. To University College Dublin—which, incidentally, is where she went to school—to London, and to New York. All the calls were made the week before she died."

"That's the direction we were headed in before this evening side-tracked us," Casey said. "Ryan, send me the names and the numbers. I'll get in touch with all of them and see what I can find out. I'll try the New York number now, in the hopes that this person is a night owl. It's the middle of the night in Dublin and London, so I'll have to wait before reaching out to them. Maybe I'll get lucky and they're early risers."

She glanced around the table. "In the meantime, I suggest that Ryan goes down to his lair and researches Niall Dempsey. Marc, Patrick, and Emma resume reviewing the files Yoda set up for us. Once I've made my New York call, I'll join you guys in the War Room."

She turned to Claire. "You take the tapestries up to your yoga room and see what happens."

"I've been itching to do that since I first saw them." A respectful glance at Fiona. "May I?"

"Please." Fiona gathered up the panels, placing one on top of the other, and handed them to Claire. "If you pick up on anything, no matter how small, please come and get me. I know a ton about my family history. Something that might not seem significant to you could mean a lot to me."

"I will." Claire stiffened as the tapestries touched her palms. "So much energy." She was already walking out the door. "I don't want it to fade."

Casey watched Claire disappear around the corner to the staircase, confident that they'd soon have more to go on.

"Fiona, I think you should get some rest," she said. "We're trained to go twenty-four seven. You're not. Plus you're wiped. Take a nap."

"Not a prayer," Fiona replied, shaking her head. "I'm not wiped, I'm wired. I need to be part of this process, for the same reason I just gave Claire. I'm personally connected to everything you're poring over. I may have answers you need." She forced a smile. "Plus if my cranky-without-sleep brother can do twenty-four seven, so can I."

Ryan rolled his eyes.

Casey chuckled. "Actually, you haven't seen your brother when he's in high-gear work mode. He's spot-on with little or no sleep. But I have a feeling you'll also hold up just fine. So to work it is."

20

Niall paced around his living room, a glass of whiskey in his hand. It was his second since arriving home. He needed to be alone, to think, to clear his mind and come up with a strategy.

How much did Cobra know? Certainly not all that Niall did, not when he'd made a career out of studying the legends of Irish hoards. Those hoards were secreted treasures from centuries past, stolen or coveted, buried to be recovered later—a later that often never happened, leaving the hoards hidden and unclaimed. His fascination for them had increased as the years passed and he'd become a collector of ancient pieces of jewelry, coins, and other valuable artifacts. He read incessantly about them, following their history the way some people followed the stock market. He was well aware that the majority of the legends were just yarns passed down from generation to generation. Still, a large enough number had been recovered over the years— enough to make studying them both fascinating and purposeful.

Then came those two mind-blowing events that had taken place a year ago, one right after the other, too powerful to be coincidental.

The first occurred when he was browsing the streets of SoHo where an art fair was taking place. Everything from the works of small artisans to higher-priced works were on display. He never knew whether it was pure chance or divine providence that made him round the street corner and turn his head at that moment. But there, among the other canvas paintings, was the one he'd seen in Belfast.

His initial reaction was a knife in his gut, as the memories cut through him. But there was another, more overriding feeling, based on years of research and a knowledge that hadn't been there before.

He didn't take the time to scrutinize the details to ensure authenticity. Too risky. Someone else might purchase the painting and he couldn't let that happen.

He'd bought it on the spot and brought it home, where he could look as he saw fit.

On the heels of his purchase came the second startling interaction.

He'd been having a Guinness at Quinn's, minding his own business, when he'd heard a bunch of mates drinking at the bar, laughing and talking about some hoard that turned out to be nonexistent after countless people had spent decades turning their lives upside down trying to unearth it. The guys had all agreed that much of this hoard talk was a crock of shit, and they'd gone back to their drinking.

But at the far end of the bar was a weathered old sailor, drunk as a skunk, who kept muttering that they were wrong, that the hoard with the king's treasures was real, that the Vikings had stolen it and buried it, that he knew it was true, that he knew the hoard was real, that someone had found it, taken it… He kept repeating the last part over and over, going on to mutter about spilled rubies and emeralds and diamonds, and Niall could have sworn he heard the word *chalice* slurred in the long string of phrases. But he couldn't be sure.

He'd slid onto the stool beside the old guy and bought him another pint, then asked him what he'd been talking about. What treasure had the Vikings stolen? What hoard had been dug up? And how did he know about it?

The sailor had downed the beer, looking at Niall with bloodshot eyes and heavy lids. "The hoard's real, all right," he'd muttered. "Heard it from m'daddy. Came over from Ireland in 1920. The hoard was there."

"There? On the ship? Did he see it?" Niall's heart was pounding. "Did he actually *have* it?"

The sailor barked out a laugh. "Would I be sittin' here, poor as a church mouse and drinkin' a hole in my gut if he had?" He shook his head, half falling onto the counter as he did. "No, but he knew it was on the ship he came over on and that whoever had it planned on settlin' down in New York. Good listener, my daddy. He knew."

Niall had mulled that over carefully. The timeline fit. The hoard had reputedly been whisked away and brought to New York in the early 1900s. No one knew where it had been found or by whom. Or where it was now.

If it was the hoard he'd been reading about all these years.

"You said rubies, emeralds, diamonds, and a chalice?"

"Yup." Another healthy swallow. "Other stuff, too. Don't remember it all."

"Did this hoard have a name?" Niall asked.

"'Course. They all do. Even the fake ones. But this one's real." A few deep swallows of Guinness. "The Vadrefjord Hoard."

That was all the validation Niall had needed.

Now, he put down his glass of whiskey and left the living room, going directly to his private study.

The painting was hanging on the short wall hidden by the door. Secreting it there was probably a ridiculous precaution. He met with many real estate people here, true, but not a single one of them would have given the painting a second glance. The awareness of its significance belonged to him.

He clasped his hands behind his back as he studied the painting for the umpteenth time, having long since memorized details that far surpassed his initial viewing of it back in Belfast.

The battle depicted between the Vikings and the Irish was ferocious. One could almost hear the clash of swords and the screams of the fallen. In the background were the ghostly outlines of an abbey, shrouded in fog and mist. Next to the abbey was a small graveyard with the faint outlines of the distinctive Celtic crosses. But it was a lower image in the painting that told the story.

There lay the slain king. His priceless treasure was strewn on the ground, partially hidden by his body. Gemstones, gold and silver coins, pieces of jewelry, all spilling out of a golden chalice and tumbling down a small rise. And there, caught in action, was a dark figure, barely visible and reaching for the treasure, shovel in hand and a partly dug hole.

The Battle of Bawncullen was scribbled in Gaelic at the bottom of the painting, a vivid memory that had been emblazoned in his mind from that first moment in Belfast.

No artist's signature. Just those four words.

Bawncullen, Niall's research had told him, was one of the settlements the Vikings had invaded and claimed during their ninth-century invasion of Ireland. It was located in Waterford, then Vadrefjord, a seaport in southeast Ireland and the country's oldest city.

Niall had found no hint of research that told him the hoard had originally been buried there, or anywhere in the entire County Waterford. The dark figure, shovel, and partly dug hole were clearly symbolic rather than actual. Not that it mattered. If his research, along with the old sailor's claim, was correct, the Vadrefjord Hoard was no longer in its original burial spot, but right here in New York.

And that damn tapestry Rose Flaherty had been researching for Fiona McKay somehow held the key.

The tapestries had to have been bequeathed to her. Her great-grandparents had come over from Ireland in 1920, obviously on the same ship as the old sailor's father. Which meant they either had the hoard or had enough contact with whoever did to weave its story. He was convinced the former was the case. He was equally convinced that none of the McKays had any idea of this, or they would have recovered the treasure and either bettered their life significantly by keeping it or, more likely, have turned it over to somewhere like the National Museum of Ireland.

Either way, the news of the hoard's recovery would have blasted into the headlines.

So it was still out there. And Fiona was now working with Forensic Instincts. He had no intention of sitting back and following their lead. He had to get a step ahead, so he, not they, would be the one to claim the treasure.

It was time to light a fire under his computer kid's ass.

***

Claire's yoga room was sparsely furnished and utterly peaceful. Shutting her door to the rest of the world, lighting a few soft candles, and sinking down onto her mat in lotus position—the whole ritual was a true Zen experience.

She closed her eyes, taking some time to breathe, to relax, to release the tension that was rippling through her, to ready herself for the task ahead.

When the time was right, she leaned forward, spread out the tapestries on the thicker mat in front of her, and reached for the panel that had been calling out to her from the start—the center panel.

Her fingers lightly traced the woven fabric, literally tingling as they did.

She closed her eyes again, letting the energy flow.

The bejeweled crown. The throne.

She gasped with surprise as a connection she'd never expected took hold.

Violent images. A Viking invasion. A vicious battle. A king stabbed through—a high Irish king, just as Rose's Post-it had read.

Death. Death. Death.

Claire flinched at the jolt of pain that shot through her. Reflexively, she jerked her fingers away and then repositioned them, instead lingering on the gemstones. A veritable treasure. Precious jewels, coins, broaches. All of it spilling out of a chalice and onto the ground, mingling with the high king's blood. A chalice. Not a trophy or a goblet. A chalice—one that glistened like the sun amid a kaleidoscope of color.

So much beauty. So much darkness and death.

Her fingers shifted once again, gliding over the Tree of Life, and abruptly, all the painful images vanished, replaced by a surge of positive energy.

Hope. A bright future. A fresh start. And a sense of immortality.

The border of the tapestry, and its ambiguous funnel shape, commanded Claire's attention, and she moved her fingers there.

It was a continuum of the feeling she'd just been experiencing, and it corresponded exactly with the archeology textbook page Rose had sent Fiona.

The symbol: "light at the end of the tunnel." More new beginnings, fresh starts, endless spiraling into immortality. Interspersed with that was the paragraph on the second page Rose had sent Fiona: *The spiral signifies light and the upside-down U signifies a tunnel or a dark place.*

This center panel epitomized the juxtaposition between death and life.

With a huge intake of breath, Claire opened her eyes and gently set aside the panel. She'd absorbed all she could from this magnificent centerpiece for now.

Still energy-charged, she studied the other panels, pursing her lips as she chose the one to handle next. It had to be one she had yet to touch. Not only because it would hopefully bring a fresh perspective but also because the two panels that had been hanging in the McKays' house were tainted by her earlier reactions. She intentionally wanted to experience this first round of tactile explorations as they were meant to be conveyed by Fiona's great-grandmother, not as they were defined by Rose's murder and the events that had followed. She might find she had no choice, as her insights came at will, but she had a better chance of accomplishing her goal with the panels that had been stored away in the attic, unseen and untouched—for now.

Her gaze fell on the panel with the Viking coins.

She now understood their connection to the center panel. The Viking battle and coins.

But what was their connection to the rest of the tapestries?

She pulled the panel closer and put her hands on it.

A flash of greenery. A brick farmhouse. A stone fence. Loose stones. The outline of a shovel. And then she was abruptly engulfed in darkness, unable to breathe. Panic surged through her, but she held on, trying to go with it. It was impossible. Her lungs were screaming for air and she had none to offer.

It was as if she'd been buried alive.

She yanked her hands away, sweat trickling down her back, as she dragged huge breaths into her body.

It took long minutes for her breathing to resume and for the pounding in her chest to ease. Both were replaced by a deep, wringing fatigue.

She couldn't move on to the next panel, not now. She was way too drained to absorb anything more. On the other hand, she had no intention of giving in to sleep. She had too much to report to the team.

She glanced at the time, stunned to see that two hours had passed.

On shaky legs, she rose, glancing ruefully at the tapestries.

Then, she walked out, headed for the War Room.

21

FI's War Room was the complete antithesis of the sleek, structured, orderly layout of the main conference room. With floor-to-ceiling whiteboards on three of the four walls, "flexible furniture" like rolling chairs and small movable round tables, and sticky flip charts for Post-its and print-outs—both of which now filled the charts—the room practically vibrated with activity, a buzzing hive filled with worker bees.

Ryan was marching around and talking to the team when Claire came in and sank down into a chair. He took in her depleted state and frowned. "You look like hell. What happened with the tapestry fondling?"

"A lot." She brushed damp strands of hair off her forehead, giving him a quizzical look. "Before I get into it, did you find out anything on Niall Dempsey?"

"Some, but there's a huge roadblock there," he replied, still eyeing Claire with concern. "Ostensibly, he's pretty much as Fee described. But I'm finding a huge hole—lots of info on the Niall Dempsey of today, almost nothing on the Niall Dempsey of the past. It's like he deliberately erased his life in Ireland."

"That doesn't surprise me. But I couldn't get a clear picture of how or why."

"Neither can we," Emma said. "That's as much as Ryan's gotten so far." Her brows drew together. "What do you mean by erased his life?"

"He came over from Ireland thirty-five years ago, in 1985, during the Troubles." Ryan was referring to a particularly violent time in history when the Irish were battling the British for a unified Ireland. "He was twenty years old at the time. No red flags there; many people fled the country during that time. Plus, all that information is written up in articles about him in various business publications. It's the before part I'm not getting any hits on."

"Nothing at all on his pre-immigration years?" Marc asked, seeking clarification.

"Just the bare basics. It's like searching for scattered bread-crumbs—breadcrumbs that were planted. A place and date of birth, complete with a birth certificate. That lists his mother's name only, and it appears she's deceased, with no background info of any kind. No reference to additional family—a father, siblings, anything. No milestones like residences, schooling, or jobs. I'm still researching to find specifics on his voyage over, but even there, I'm not finding a manifest that lists his name."

"So he has something in his past to hide," Casey said.

"Sure seems that way—and he's doing a damn good job of hiding it."

"Where was he born?" Patrick asked.

"Belfast—which would certainly explain why he was desperate to get out of the country. The fighting there was intense."

"I'd like to hear his brogue," Patrick responded. "As you know, I have an Irish background myself. If he's really from Northern Ireland, he'll speak quickly and with a more pronounced accent than, say, if he were from Dublin." A shrug. "Then again, I'm sure he's thought of that. My guess is he's too smart to give himself away on something so simple. Still… Belfast is a big place. It's like one of us saying we were born in New York City. That's five boroughs and millions of people. Easy to get lost. You said the birth certificate named his mother. What about the hospital he was born in?"

Ryan shrugged. "One that doesn't exist anymore and whose records can't be found. So, yeah, it doesn't take a rocket scientist to suggest he's hiding from his past. Which would gel with Claire's assessment that there's something dark there. I just don't know what—yet. But I will." Another glance at Claire, who had sunk down into a chair. "You're really not okay, are you?"

"I'm fine, just drained," she said. "And I have a lot to tell you guys, too."

Casey had already crossed the room and grabbed a bottle of water from the fridge. Ryan's report had spawned a seed of an idea—one she wasn't ready to get into with the team yet. She had to handle this just right. Besides, it was time to shift the focus to Claire.

"Drink," she instructed as she handed the bottle to her, more concerned than usual because this was the second time tonight that Claire had been reduced to this state. She needed to hydrate, and she needed to regain her strength. Unfortunately, the recouping would have to wait. She knew it and so did Claire. So she didn't insult her by suggesting it.

"You're sapped," she noted ruefully. "I wish I could tell you we can put this conversation off."

"That's not an option," Claire replied, shaking her head. "I want to tell you everything while it's still fresh in my mind."

"How many of the panels did you handle?" Fiona asked eagerly.

"Only two." Claire shook her head in self-deprecation. "I wanted to cover a lot more ground. But after what I experienced from touching those first two, I couldn't go on. I'm so sorry. It's just that nothing comes when my energy is drained."

"Don't apologize." Fiona sat down beside her, her concern as real as her desire to know. "You were in there for hours. Which two panels did you handle?"

"The centerpiece and the panel with the Viking coins." Claire went on to relay everything she'd experienced to Fiona and to the team.

"The farmhouse was the one you suggested belonged to your great-grandparents," she concluded. "And the stone fence—the one he built—and the loose stones were on their property."

Marc was standing, leaning back against a table that had papers strewn all over it, still in the sorting-out stage. "When you say buried alive, do you think there's a dead body down there?" It wouldn't have been the first time Claire had sensed exactly that and had turned out to be right.

She hesitated, weighing her answer. "I don't think so. I didn't sense a body. I felt as if I were in the ground. Which tells me I was experiencing the actual burial—of something, not someone."

"The king's treasure?" Casey asked.

"That would be my guess," Claire replied. "But it's just a guess, not a powerful sense of certainty. Hopefully that will come later, after I've handled some of the other panels, but not yet."

"An Irish hoard," Fiona breathed, her mind alive with realization.

Emma reacted to the excitement in Fiona's tone. "What's that?" she demanded.

"In essence? A buried treasure." Fiona began pacing around, unable to stay still. "Claire's images all fit. I never dreamed... but Rose used to talk about legendary archeological hoards from all different historical periods, treasures that were buried centuries ago and were still out there, unclaimed."

Ryan arched a dubious brow. "Legendary doesn't mean real."

"Dozens of them have been discovered." Fiona shot him a challenging look. "Which makes them very real. Who knows how many of the legendary ones are just as real?"

"Do the real ones have names? Where are they now? Where were they found? Who found them?" Emma was in true Emma form. But in this case, the rest of the team was right there with her, leaning forward to catch every word.

"I'm not an expert," Fiona replied. "But there are a few that are pretty well known, and Rose talked about them. There's the Broighter

Hoard, which consists of all gold artifacts—I think Rose said from the first century BC. And there's the Ardagh Hoard, which experts determined had been deposited around 900 AD. That one also had a chalice among its pieces. Both the Broighter and the Ardagh Hoards were recovered hundreds of years later, the former by a ploughman on a farm and the latter by a couple of kids digging in a potato field. I don't remember which counties they were buried in, but I'm sure you can Google them to find out. As for where they are, I think they're in the National Museum of Ireland."

"This is fantastic," Emma breathed. "It's like living our very own *Romancing the Stone*."

"And you're right." Ryan had been punching information into his iPhone browser. "They are real. Sorry, Fee."

"You're forgiven." Fiona was way too exhilarated to feel smug about exacting an apology from her always-right brother. "Ry, do you understand what this means?" She waved her hands in excitement. "There must have been a Viking hoard buried on our great-grandparents' land—and they discovered it."

Casey had been digesting all this thoughtfully. "Even without Claire's talent, I think we can assume that they didn't turn it over to anyone. They brought it to New York with them."

"Of course," Fiona said defensively. "They sailed here in 1920, probably right after finding the hoard. As for turning it over, the Irish War of Independence was at its peak. They were probably terrified the British would find out about the hoard and fight to claim it. So they took it and fled."

"Yet they never sold any of the pieces." Patrick responded to Fiona's reaction with a soothing reminder of the probabilities. "They wouldn't have lived in Hell's Kitchen as poor immigrants if they had. Nor would your great-grandmother have taken the time and trouble to weave these tapestries. Clearly, they wanted this hoard for their family. And if it was legendary, they most likely hid it for the same reason you just gave. They were frightened that someone would figure out it had been found, where it had been taken, and come after it."

Marc frowned, bothered by the blatant holes in the explanation. "That makes sense, up to a point. But later, when they had a grown daughter, why didn't they just tell her about this hoard and the tapestry panels? Why leave them in the memory box and say nothing? And on another note, how did they manage to get the hoard through customs? I know that, back then, the biggest concern the US had with the arrival of immigrants was disease, but surely a cache of gemstones, jewelry, and ancient coins would be confiscated."

Fiona shrugged. "I don't know the answer to any of those questions."

"I'm going to do a little genealogy research," Ryan said. "I've never been into that kind of stuff, but maybe I can find something to answer Marc's first two questions, because they're valid ones—ones that are bugging me, too."

"I'm going to do a little digging of my own," Patrick added, steepling his fingers on the table in front of him. "I'm really curious to see if I can use what Claire's given us to locate information on this particular hoard. If it's legendary, then it'll probably show up on blogs, even websites that speculate on this subject. If I get lucky, I'll find out more about it, especially what it's called. Irish hoards are generally named after the places they were found, but in this case, that doesn't apply since no one knows where it was discovered. Let me see what I can dig up."

Claire lowered her bottle of water and sighed. "I wish I were making connections to all this. I wish I could regain my energy and find out what other images the tapestry panels offer me, since they might help you both in your research." She rose. "I'm going to bow out of the War Room for a while if that's okay. I need a change of scene to jump-start me. I'll go home, have a cup of herbal tea and a shower. Sometimes my thoughts flow there. I'll come back ASAP, hopefully with some answers and certainly ready to resume my work with a vengeance."

"Go," Casey replied. "In fact, I'm going to reverse my earlier decision about camping out here all night. It's after one in the morning. I think we should take a few hours off. As much as I want to push us all to the max, we're pretty depleted. Twenty-four seven sounds great in theory, but we're not working at maximum effectiveness if we're brain-dead. I'm personally at a standstill. My whole idea about creating a thread from the text and email contacts between Fiona and Rose was a waste of Yoda's time. Glenna wrote all of Rose's emails, since her employer never learned how to use a computer. All their interactions were either in person or on the phone. Hopefully, when I get back to work, I'll have heard from Rose's UK and New York City contacts."

With that, she turned to Ryan, who was rumpled and red-eyed. "You look like death warmed over. Take Claire and Fiona home with you. Have a beer while Claire drinks her tea and Fiona has a well-deserved glass of wine. Then collapse and sleep, all three of you. Your iPhones will wake you up in four hours." She scanned the rest of the room. "That applies to all of you. Patrick, go home to your wife. You, too, Marc. At least remind them what you look like. Emma, get reacquainted with your bed. Hero abandoned us an hour ago for his. We'll reconvene at six a.m."

"At the latest," Ryan replied. "I've got to stay ahead of the bad guys, especially their computer guy."

"Fine. Good night, everyone." Casey shooed them out. "See you before dawn."

Casey waited for the last of them to leave. Then, she locked up and engaged the Hirsch pad, peeking outside just long enough to ensure Patrick's security detail was in place. Yup. As always. Patrick didn't make mistakes like that.

She went up to the third floor, where she locked Claire's yoga room from the outside.

Privacy ensured. Just in case. She couldn't have Hutch walking by and spotting the tapestries. And since she planned on getting him here now, this precaution was necessary.

She pulled out her cell phone and called him.

"Hey, stranger," he answered. "I thought we weren't going to make a habit of these long nights apart."

"That's why I'm calling. Could you come over now, or are you already tucked in for the night?"

Hutch chuckled. "Is this a booty call?"

"That's exactly what it is. I sent the team home for a breather. We're reconvening at six. That gives us a few hours to—"

"I'm on my way."

22

Casey gave a deep sigh and sank into the bed, draping one leg over Hutch's. The past hour had been a wonderful—and highly anticipated—perk to her plan. The problem was that now she was too exhausted to move, much less broach a conversation with a man who could see through everything.

"You okay?" There was a grin in Hutch's voice. "Or did I overtax you?"

"Maybe a little, but that's only because I'm sleep-deprived." Her words were muffled by the pillows.

"Then rest." Hutch pulled the blanket over them and tucked her against his side. "Based on what you told me, you've got less than two hours to sleep. So use them." He leaned over her and scooped the iPhone off her nightstand, pressing a few keys before putting it down. "I set the alarm."

"Thank you." Casey's eyelids drooped. Two hours was good. That would give her enough time to bring Hutch into the fold—sort of.

She let sleep take over.

The iPhone alarm began its wake-up trill, and Casey groaned, reaching over to hit the snooze button. Just as fast, reality sank in, and she glanced at the digits on the clock. Five a.m. The team would be here in an hour. Definitely wake-up time. She turned off the alarm and sat up. Hero picked up his head, noted how dark it was, and opted to get some more shut-eye.

"Well, that was a nice cat nap," Hutch commented from beside her.

Casey wasn't surprised that Hutch was already awake, his tone totally devoid of the cobwebs of sleep. He could do with less rest than even she could, and she was pretty functional without it.

"I guess I can't entice you to stay in bed another fifteen minutes."

"I'd love that, but the team will be here in an hour." Casey dragged her fingers through her tousled hair. "I'm going to jump in the shower. I need to be alert, not just awake."

"Then I won't join you in the shower."

"Unfortunately, I think that's a given."

"Rain check. I'll brew a pot of coffee. It'll get you into high-functioning mode and give us a chance to talk."

"Perfect." Casey was already on her way to the bathroom.

She needed to plan this conversation very carefully.

Ten minutes later, Casey sat down at the tiny counter in her kitchen, gratefully accepting the mug Hutch handed her.

"I hope we can find a place with a bit more breathing room," she said, easing directly into the subject matter. "This fourth-floor conversion wasn't equipped for anything more than sleeping quarters and a pea-sized kitchen. I know we survive on takeout, but it would be nice to have somewhere to eat it besides a cramped counter."

Hutch pulled up the stool beside hers and sat down, simultaneously taking a swallow of coffee. "We will. Judging from the photos the Realtor forwarded me, we have a few good options that include dining areas as well as living rooms. We just can't wait too long. Great apartments in equally great neighborhoods like Battery Park City disappear fast."

"I know," Casey agreed.

Battery Park City was their first choice. After scanning the internet for apartments that met their specifications, they were leaning heavily in that direction. That didn't mean the door was closed to other options, but the Lower-Manhattan neighborhood would be ideal for their needs.

Right now, it was also ideal for Casey's.

"You've done all the groundwork until now," she said. "Contacting the Realtor, picking out a few places as our starting point, and forwarding me the photos and cost breakdowns she sent. I did look at the photos, by the way. I sneaked a peak during the few breathing minutes I had. The apartments are beautiful. I can't wait to visit them with you. In the meantime, I had an idea, and I wanted to run it by you."

"Ah, at last," Hutch said, his tone utterly matter-of-fact. "We get to the real reason you wanted me here—aside from my incredible sexual prowess."

Casey's jaw dropped. "You knew?"

An offhanded shrug. "Of course I knew. I'm just a little surprised. Subterfuge isn't your style."

"It isn't. I just… My idea is a good one," Casey defended, sidestepping Hutch's straightforward assessment, because he was right and there was no way she could explain why she'd handled things the way she had—not without breaking client privilege and compromising the investigation.

She was cornered and she knew it. She'd just have to push on and give Hutch the facts but steer way clear of the circumstances. He'd know she was leaving things out, but her only hope was he wouldn't press her.

Yeah, right, she thought. *Who am I thinking about?*

"Your idea?" Hutch prompted.

Casey tried to read his expression, even though that was about as successful as reading tea leaves. "One of the apartments you forwarded me is in a building owned by Dempsey Real Estate Development. I've met Niall Dempsey before and I was wondering what you thought of my getting together with him for a cup of coffee and maybe getting an inside track on the right apartment."

"Meaning getting pushed to the top of a waiting list."

"Exactly."

"And you don't want me there why? Because you plan on charming him into helping you out?"

"Of course not. I just thought—"

"That I wouldn't guess this has something to do with the case you're working on." Hutch set down his mug and looked Casey straight in the eye. "Nice try, sweetheart. But checkmate. And by the way, it's good that subterfuge isn't your thing, because you suck at it."

Casey sighed, but she didn't avert her gaze, nor did she lie. "Fine. Checkmate it is. Still, you have to admit it's a good idea. You and I want an apartment that's probably on a lot of people's dream lists. A little influence from the top couldn't hurt."

"But walking into danger can."

This time Casey did lower her gaze, staring into her coffee.

"How does Niall Dempsey factor into your case and how did you happen to meet him?"

"I'm not sure how or even if he factors into our case. This would be just a fishing expedition," she replied, giving Hutch as much candor as she could. "And I met him last night at the McKays' gathering."

"Ah, in honor of Rose Flaherty." Hutch was doing his own thinking, and Casey watched him assimilating the facts. "So he knew her."

"Yes, from their church and from her antique shop."

"Then I'm guessing he also knows Fiona McKay."

Casey nodded, starting to regret bringing this up to Hutch at all. But she was about to use their personal lives as an excuse to get information for their client. And she felt the need to at least clue him in to the meeting, if not the full basis for it.

"You could tell me what's going on," Hutch said. "On the other hand, I could just run Niall Dempsey's name myself."

"But you won't. I know you better." Casey set down her own mug and spread her hands wide. "Besides, you'd probably come up empty." She shook her head in frustration. "Dammit, Hutch, I've already put us both in an untenable situation. I'm breaking client confidentiality and you now know more than you should."

"You said you have no evidence of Dempsey's involvement."

"And that's the truth."

"Then I have nothing I feel compelled to report—even if I'm sure the NYPD detectives have zero awareness of your suspicions." Hutch seized her hand. "Casey, I love you. I worry about you. This isn't a case of one-upmanship. I just don't want you socializing with a potential murder suspect."

"We have no facts that say he's a killer. I promise you that."

"Which means you're reacting to something Claire sensed."

Casey rolled her eyes. "You're relentless. Let me do my job. And in the process, I might land us a great apartment."

"Fine." Hutch blew out a frustrated breath. "Just tell me this—does Patrick have security detail on you?"

"Yes."

"Good. Now tell me you'll meet Dempsey in a public place."

"I will." Casey interlaced her fingers with Hutch's. "I'll be just fine."

"You'd better be. I'm not happy about this case. You're being way too cryptic. You're always direct. You either fill me in or shut me down."

"It's not intentional," she replied. "Frankly, I'm not sure what I know and what I don't. This case is like a moving puzzle. We have to fit pieces together to solve it. And right now we don't understand the pieces, much less how they interconnect."

A hint of a smile curved Hutch's lips. "A puzzle, huh? Well, no one's better at solving puzzles than you. You beat my ass at Anagrams every time we play."

"True." Casey smiled. No matter how many apps they downloaded, nothing beat the good old board game they both loved. "It's great to be quicker than you at some things. I sure did a lousy job of that last night. Although I promise you the booty call part was for real."

"Never doubted it. As for the rest, I understand your predicament. And I appreciate your trying to be honorable about meeting with Dempsey. It's our lives you're discussing, even if it is to help solve your case."

"It's not that cut and dried," Casey assured him. "Do I want to suss the guy out? You bet. But do I want to gain his influence to land us the apartment we want? Without question. The man is a powerhouse. That's a fact. Everything else is supposition."

"Then you're forgiven." Hutch leaned over and kissed her. "By the way," he asked, taking a final belt of coffee, "before you reconvene, can I meet Fiona?" He held up his hand to ward off her oncoming protest. "I don't mean in an official capacity. I'm just curious what kind of a sister could put up with Ryan."

"A very tolerant one." Casey swallowed the last of her own coffee and rose. "And as an aside, you're not fooling me any more than I fooled you. While you're meeting Fiona, you'll be assessing her body language, her state of mind, and who knows what else. Well, you're not going to find anything but a terrific young woman who's strong but scared, both of which she should be. So I'll introduce you, but only if you promise to be my boyfriend and not SSA Hutchinson. At least not overtly."

"I can manage that." Hutch put down his empty mug, as well. "I'll grab a shower. Then I'll wait up here until the team arrives and you've had a chance to give them a heads-up. Once you give me the okay, I'll leash Hero up and just say hi as I take him out for a run. Deal?"

"Deal." Casey reached up to give him a kiss. "FYI, Fiona is gorgeous. Don't make me challenge her to a duel."

Hutch threw back his head in laughter. "Not a chance, sweetheart. With the way I feel about you, you can put away your pistols."

***

Kelly's was dark when Niall and Donald settled themselves in the back room.

"Our computer guy cut through a lot of personal bullshit on Fiona McKay's hard drive, but all her photos are stored on iCloud. He said there's a password he needs to crack and it's not the same as the one our guys found on that Post-it in her townhouse," Donald said. "There are also no emails between the old lady and the girl—I guess the old lady was behind the times. So this process is obviously going to take a lot longer than we had hoped. To be honest, I'm getting the feeling from this kid that he's talking more *if* than *when*. Which means you may never get those pictures."

Niall swore, pulling out his cell phone and scrolling through the two grainy pictures he had: the panel Rose had been researching and the Galway sheep panel that had been hanging in the McKays' living room. Not much to go on. Then again, he knew exactly what he was searching for. Forensic Instincts most likely didn't.

He made a decision.

"I researched everyone on Rose's contact list," he told Donald, tearing off a corner of a napkin and scribbling down some information, after which he stuffed the paper in Donald's hand. "And this professor emeritus at the University of Dublin is the most noted expert in what I need. Get him here right away. Do whatever it takes to make that happen."

23

"Your boyfriend is hot," Fiona said as soon as Casey had made the introductions, Hutch and Hero had taken off, and the team was reconvened in the War Room. "Why did he blow out of here so fast?"

"Because he's FBI," Ryan answered. "He follows the rules. We don't. That puts him in a shitty position. So he respects our privacy, and when we're working a case, he keeps his distance. Which he didn't this time, actually. How come?"

Casey sucked in her breath. "Because I asked him to come over. And I don't think you're all going to be too pleased with me when I tell you why—or how not well it went."

The team was quiet, just watching her and listening as she laid out all the details, not sparing herself in the process.

Unsurprisingly, Emma popped up and rushed over to Casey. "Moving in together, wow, that's so awesome!" She hugged her. "I'm going online and shopping for housewarming gifts right away."

Despite the gravity of the situation, Casey found herself laughing. "Hold off on the shopping; we haven't even found a place yet. But thanks, Emma. I really needed that right about now."

"And you should have it." Claire was the next to chime in. "Congratulations on the perfect next step for you and Hutch."

The rest of the team were equally kind, each member offering their warmest wishes on a happy announcement that shouldn't have had to be back-burnered by the circumstances.

But it was.

"Thank you, all," Casey said, her eyes a little moist. "Your support means a lot. But it's okay to beat me up now."

"Why would anyone beat you up?" Fiona asked. "You didn't exactly pull out the tapestries and show them to him. And as an aside, I think your news is wonderful, too. I know I just met Hutch, but you two look so right together. So congratulations."

"I appreciate your cutting me so much slack." Casey wasn't letting herself off the hook, as she knew the team wouldn't. "But I'm the president of Forensic Instincts and I broke one of my own fundamental rules. If anyone on the team had done this, I'd be all over them. So let's have it, guys. Give me your best shot."

"This is a tough one." Marc was the first to respond, as Casey had expected. He was her right-hand, go-to guy, as he had been since Casey first opened the doors of Forensic Instincts.

He steepled his fingers together, resting his chin on top of them thoughtfully. "You did violate a cardinal rule. On the other hand, given how principled a person you are, you were caught between a rock and a hard place. Using your personal life as a basis to meet up with a potential suspect and not mentioning it to Hutch is just as unethical as letting him in on a piece of our investigation. So this falls between the cracks. I'm not sure I could have handled it any better. But I sure as hell would have known Hutch would see right through me. And you? He can read you like a book."

Casey gave a rueful nod. "I'm not usually so stupid."

"You weren't being stupid," Claire countered instantly. "You were being honorable. That has to factor into our reaction."

"The end result still sucks." Ryan frowned. "You should have run this by us as a team—*before* you did it. Sorry, boss, but you would have ripped me a new one if this had been me."

"You're right, I would have. And you're also right, I should have. The truth is you were all so exhausted that I didn't want to get into yet another debate before sending you home—but that still doesn't excuse my actions."

"Well, for the record, I would have told you to go ahead and fly with it." Claire's tone was more adamant than usual. "My reaction to Niall Dempsey screamed evil. We need to find out who he really is—and was—ASAP. So far, Ryan's come up empty. So I'd have voted yes."

"Thanks, but I'm sure there'd be dissent," Casey replied. "And I would have hammered home my point ad nauseam to make the vote unanimous. Just know that I wasn't trying to avoid a team vote. You have my word on that."

"That never occurred to us, and I agree with Marc," Patrick said. "You were trying to achieve optimum results by walking a very fine line. It backfired, slightly. But I don't see this as a major blow to the investigation. As Fiona said, you didn't show him the tapestries, or even mention them. In fact, you didn't mention anything other than the fact that Niall Dempsey could be a bad guy. Not even a potential killer, which would be the only reason Hutch would feel compelled to step into this."

"Which ultimately might not be a bad thing." Marc was still thinking. "Let's say our research into Dempsey leads us to believe that Claire's instincts about him being the potential killer are right. At that point, we might want to ask Hutch to go ahead and run his name for us."

Ryan scowled. "And if he got a hit?"

"Then we'd have reason to turn it over to the cops," Marc replied. "Let them get the credit for catching the bad guy. Who cares? Our job is to keep Fiona safe, which she would be. And Alvarez and her team would still be in the dark about the tapestries, since there's no way the killer would cough up details that would incriminate him, or give away specifics about a treasure he still hoped to find."

"Yeah, I guess you're right," Ryan conceded. "If the killer's locked up, we can relax about Fee and get on to the fun stuff."

"Yup." Marc glanced back at Casey. "Smart of you to lock Claire's yoga room. Because Hutch can't know about the tapestries. He'd consider them to be material evidence."

"That much at least I did right." Casey gave him a rueful smile. "So what's the verdict? Am I going ahead and calling Niall Dempsey or is punishment about to be rendered?"

There was a chorus of "call him."

"What punishment?" Emma was looking around at all of them as if they each had two heads. "Casey just told us this amazing news about moving in with Hutch, and you're all pissed off that Hutch knows we're digging around about Niall Dempsey? He's a millionaire real estate developer who made his way up from nothing. I seriously doubt his hands are clean. If they're dirtier than your standard developer, we'll figure it out. But right now we know nothing except for the fact that he skeeved Claire out and that her instincts tell her he's got an ugly past. Like I said, big surprise."

Marc's lips twitched. "Emma does have a point."

"Yes, she does," Fiona agreed. "I'm the client and I have no problem with what Casey did. So let's get to the upside, which Claire just touched on. What a great idea, going to Niall directly and seeing what you can find out about him. And what more natural reason to give than trying to get an inside track to an apartment that's in high demand."

"I wish I could be at that meeting," Claire murmured. "But there's no justification you could give for my tagging along. Plus, I don't think I could keep it together in that man's presence, and I'm certainly not going to tip our hand." She paused. "Where did you plan on meeting him?"

"I hadn't decided on a place to suggest." Casey's brows drew together in question. "Why? Is there somewhere in particular that would help you?"

"Not some*where*, some*thing*," Claire replied. "If there's any way you can bring me back an item that belongs to him, I might be able to make a sensory connection to—"

"I'll go with you and pick his pocket," Emma jumped in eagerly. "Just say the word. I'll pose as your PA. I can take notes and lift his wallet at the same time."

Casey rolled her eyes. "You're not going and you're certainly not lifting his wallet, which he'd notice the minute he reached for it." She turned back to Claire. "Why don't I suggest we meet at his office? That way, I can find something innocuous, like a pen, that won't be missed but that he's handled. Would that work?"

"That would be ideal, except you did promise Hutch that you'd meet Dempsey in a public place," Claire reminded her.

"Yes, I did." Casey frowned.

"Believe me, you wouldn't be breaking that promise," Ryan said, eliminating that potential roadblock. "The penthouse Dempsey uses as an office is the size of Grand Central and he's got a revolving door of meetings, not to mention a full-time PA, a receptionist, and a healthy bunch of in-house employees. I should know. With all the research I'm doing, I've read more articles about the guy than I can count."

"Thanks," Casey replied gratefully. She studied Ryan's face. "Still pissed at me?"

"Nah." He waved it away. "I'll just use it as ammo if I ever screw up, which I never do, so it's moot anyway."

"And there's that ego again." Fiona shook her head in exasperation. "Say that once more, and I'll publicly name the list of times you've screwed up."

Ryan shot her a withering look and then abruptly steered the conversation back to their case. "I've got to get down to my lair. Casey, I'll try to get you all I can on Dempsey. And I'll also do my genealogy homework. The clock is ticking."

"Patrick and I will go back to our analysis." Marc lifted his shoulders in a shrug. "Although we've already established a solid reverse chronological view of Fiona's life through the folders Yoda supplied—photos, Word documents, Photoshop files, iMessages, and emails. Fiona clarified and enhanced our scrutiny as needed. We've pared things down only to the data that relates to this case. And frankly, all pertinent data seems to be encapsulated in those tapestry panels, which hopefully the bad guys haven't seen."

"I'm going to my yoga room and picking up where I left off," Claire declared, coming to her feet. "If there are insights to be had, I've got to pray I have them. Time is not our friend here. Nothing new came to me these past few hours, but I did regenerate, unclutter my mind, and open up my sensory awareness. I'm hoping that's enough to move us forward."

"Good." Casey nodded, glancing down at her iPhone and scrolling through her emails. "Right before you all got here, I got return messages from four of the five antiquities experts Rose contacted in London and Dublin. The two London experts had the same information we do and hadn't yet provided Rose with any additional reference material. The same applied to two of the Dublin experts, although the second one referred me to a retired professor—Doctor James Blythe—who's evidently the foremost authority on archeological finds in Ireland and, as luck would have it, on hoards. Dr. Blythe also happens to be the last name on Rose's list—the one I'm having trouble reaching via email. I'll give it another shot, and then I'll call his number at the university. As for Rose's New York expert, she hasn't responded yet—no surprise given it's not even dawn here. I'll keep checking. So those are my assignments, followed by a meeting setup with Niall Dempsey. I'll give you an update as soon as I have one."

She headed for the door, pausing at the entrance and turning to regard the team as a whole. "Thanks for the congratulations and for giving me a pass. Next idea I have will be run by the team before I see it through, especially where it involves Hutch."

***

Niall sat silently in Donald's back room, answering his emails, scrolling through his to-do list, and waiting until his friend returned a few hours later.

"Everything is in place," Donald assured him. "There was a sudden cancelation in first class on a flight from Dublin landing in JFK tonight. Your professor will be taking that seat. He's being well compensated for our urgency and any inconvenience it causes him."

"Good." Niall was already planning his approach when the professor arrived. Imparting too much information could be dangerous, but keeping secrets would impede the expert's ability to help. Niall would have to find the best way to ensure the old man's silence while pushing him to piece together everything Niall needed without the benefit of the tapestry panels.

Despite his bravado, he was worried about how much Fiona McKay and Forensic Instincts were figuring out. What was depicted on the other eleven panels? Had they guessed that what they were seeking was an actual, not merely a legendary, hoard? Did Fiona know of the Vadrefjord Hoard? Did she recognize any of the images from family rituals, like places they'd visit for special occasions or stories that had been passed down through the generations?

He'd love to get his hands on the damn girl and beat it out of her. But his hands were tied on that score, too. There was so much security guarding both Fiona and her parents, not to mention the additional security on the members of the Forensic Instincts team, that he would have a hell of a time getting his hands on any of them.

If necessary, he'd find a way around that. But for that, he'd need help. Help that could make things happen. Help he could feel secure about bringing into his confidence.

It was time to stop keeping Donald in the dark.

Slowly, he raised his head, meeting Donald's gaze. "I've trusted you with my life. It's time to trust you with my quest."

"*Finally.*" Donald pulled up a chair and straddled it. "I had a hell of a time getting your professor over here without giving our contact something besides money and high-end apartment accommodations to entice him. Frankly, he seemed more motivated by the idea of hunting down that Vadrefjord Hoard you jotted down—whatever the hell that is—and restoring it to the National Museum of Ireland. It's a good thing he's poor. He had actually wanted to be at Rose Flaherty's funeral but couldn't afford to make the trip. Now he can come and pay his respects."

"You're right. I put you in an untenable position, and not just to get Professor Blythe to New York City. But also to watch my back, the way you always have, especially now with Cobra here and breathing down my neck. So here goes."

Omitting nothing, Niall filled Donald in on the hoard and his search for it, including his purchase of the painting and the incidents that brought him to it, and how the McKays and the tapestries factored into the hunt.

Donald listened carefully, his brow furrowed in concentration. "All of this now makes sense. That's where this professor factors in."

Niall nodded. "He's an expert on Irish hoards. He wrote a book on the subject, which I've read cover to cover multiple times. He's also an archeologist, with two PhDs and a lifetime of teaching others about the subject. Not to mention being an amateur treasure hunter. I casually mentioned his name to Rose Flaherty the week before she died, and she said he was a genius, that they went to school together and that he signed a first-edition copy of his book to her. I was half tempted to call him myself…"

"It's a damn good thing you didn't." Donald looked grim. "He's a professor emeritus at the University of Dublin. Even if you used an assumed name, it would be too risky. The rules are clear: no contact with our country whatsoever. You have enough danger hovering around you as it is, with Cobra in our own backyard, prepping for some lethal strike."

"That's why I didn't make the call. Plus, I was originally on the fence about letting this old guy in on what I was looking for, and the fact that it's here in the Big Apple. But now I'm feeling the pressure of staying a step ahead of Fiona McKay and Forensic Instincts. And that means taking a chance by involving this Professor Blythe." Worry creased Niall's forehead. "I'm sure Forensic Instincts has his name, as well as Rose's entire contact list. That's why we have to get him on that plane before they reach out to him."

"I doubt that'll be a problem," Donald replied. "I learned a lot about your professor in the past few hours. He lives in a cottage on campus. He rarely visits his office, does all his research at home. His university email address stops right there since he doesn't use email. Even his cell phone is antiquated. So it's going to take a while for Forensic Instincts to track him down. We'll have him out of his house in a matter of hours, maybe less."

"Make it less. Spring for a big dinner before his flight. Come up with whatever you have to. Don't underestimate Forensic Instincts."

On the heels of his words, Niall's cell phone rang. He stared at the caller ID, saw a number he'd recently memorized, and then shot Donald a wary look. "Speak of the devil. It's Forensic Instincts. What the hell do they want?"

Donald looked as stymied as Niall. "I guess there's just one way to find out."

24

"Ms. Woods, what a pleasant surprise."

Having ascertained that it was indeed Forensic Instincts' president on the phone, Niall focused on keeping his tone even and his words calm. "What can I do for you?"

"I apologize for calling so early," Casey began, "but I have a favor to ask."

"A favor? Now I'm intrigued." Niall took out a handkerchief and patted the perspiration from his brow. "How can I help you?"

"My boyfriend and I are looking for an apartment. He works at Federal Plaza and I'm in Tribeca, and we want to find the right place that's both upscale and convenient to our respective workplaces. I was hoping to set up a meeting with you to get your advice and to discuss potential opportunities."

Niall's brows rose. Whatever he'd been expecting, it hadn't been this.

"I realize you're a very busy man," Casey continued, "so I'll try to work around your schedule. But sooner would be much better than later. I can come to your office, since I'm sure that's most convenient."

Niall's wheels were turning. Most convenient didn't matter. Most opportune did. And Casey Woods had just provided him with a potential opportunity to see the tapestries.

"Will your boyfriend be joining us?" he asked.

"Unfortunately not. He's buried in work." There was a smile in Casey's voice. "But he trusts my opinion. So he agreed to leave the research to me."

"A smart man." Niall chuckled. "Are you at your office now?"

"I am. Why?"

"Because I'll be in your neighborhood in about an hour. Why don't I just meet you there? I can look around to get a sense of your taste in living quarters and then I can steer you in the right direction."

A hint of a pause.

"Is that a problem?" Niall knew damn well it was, and why.

"Only in that my team is hard at work in all four corners of our headquarters," Casey replied, impressing Niall with her quick recovery. "It might be hard to take a tour or find a quiet space to talk."

"I'll be unobtrusive and discreet. And I'm sure we can find a meeting room in a four-story brownstone. This would be the fastest way to accomplish your goal. And you did say you wanted to expedite this, right?"

"I certainly did. Okay, let me clear the way for our tour and our talk." She gave Niall FI's address—an address, like its phone number, that he'd already memorized since events dictated it.

"Excellent," he replied. "I'll be there within the hour."

***

Casey swore as she ended the call. This was not the way she'd planned it at all. This entire morning had been a bust. She hadn't reached Professor Blythe, either by email or by phoning his office. And now Niall Dempsey was coming to her, rather than the other way around.

She was already on her feet, clearing the conference room table and scrutinizing the room. Confident that it was data-free, she headed straight for the War Room. She had to regain the position of power here.

"What's up?" Marc asked the instant she appeared in the doorway. He knew her well. And he knew that expression. "Is Blythe a dead end?"

"No, just an impossible man to reach." Casey shook her head and cut to the chase. "It's Dempsey. He's coming here in an hour. Somehow he's 'in the area' and I couldn't persuade him to meet in his office rather than the other way around—not without supplying a good reason, which I don't have."

Marc gave a thoughtful nod. "Interesting, his desire to visit here. He didn't say why?"

"Oh, he said he wanted to get a feel for my taste in living quarters, yammer, yammer, yammer. But the way he pressed me—or manipulated me is more like it—tells me that's bullshit. For starters, how did he know I live where I work? And even more telling, how did he know our offices were in a four-story brownstone? I never mentioned that. But *he* sure did."

"You think he's keeping tabs on us," Patrick said. "That would certainly imply he's got an agenda when it comes to our current case."

"An agenda like getting eyes on the tapestries." Marc's brows knit. "Ryan can't find anything about this guy's past. And we aren't sure if the evil Claire picked up on involved who he is today, not just who he once was. We're already viewing him as a suspect. This makes his guilt an even greater likelihood."

"The question is, does he realize we're onto him, that I'm setting up this meeting to check him out, just like he's checking us out?" Casey asked. "And if so, I'd better be shrewder than he is, or this is not only going to tip our hand, it's going to be a complete standoff."

"That's not even debatable." Marc dismissed that in a heartbeat. "You'll know his shirt size before he's sure what you're looking for and how much you know." A quick glance around the room. "Let's use this time to prep the place. Patrick, Emma, and I will stay behind these closed doors."

Casey nodded. "I already swept the conference room. Now I'll head to the yoga room and tell Claire to lock herself and the tapestries in there. From there, I'll go upstairs and hide everything in my apartment that's even remotely case-related out of plain sight. I'll also bring Hero down to the War Room. I don't want him with me when Dempsey shows up. Hero's senses are way too keen. He'll pick up on the negative energy, and it might make him react."

"I'll go down to Ryan's lair and fill him in," Fiona said, visibly unnerved.

"Stay with him," Marc instructed, Fiona's rattled state being just one of his reasons for saying that. He gave her the other reason, since it would be far better received. "It's best that Niall not see you here, even though I'm quite sure he knows you've hired us."

Fiona shot him an I'm-not-stupid look. "That's a good idea—and not just for the reason you just gave but for the one you didn't. I'm really thrown by all this. I know you're investigating Niall, but I guess it never sank in that he could actually be a killer. The last thing we need is for him to pick up on my nervousness or to ask me any questions. I'll hang out with my brother, who's probably researching Niall right now anyway. Do what you have to. But please let me know the minute he's gone—and what you found out."

"Of course." Casey turned to leave. "Once I bring Hero down to you, I'll lock the War Room door behind me. I'll keep Niall to the same areas our clients see, along with my apartment. We'll talk in one of the small meeting rooms on the first floor. And come hell or high water, I'll find a way to get something of his for Claire. Even if all I can manage is the coffee cup he drinks from."

***

Niall had left the bar immediately after filling Donald in on the phone call.

There was no time for them to brainstorm in preparation for this meeting. He'd have to do it on the fly. He needed to get home, shower, shave, and dress as if he'd just left a business meeting, not spent the night hanging out in the back room of a bar.

But his mind was racing a mile a minute. Despite the coup he'd scored by getting his foot in the door where the tapestries were, the way he'd managed that was by being approached by the enemy. True, Forensic Instincts could be checking out everyone who was closely associated with Rose. On the other hand, he'd be a fool not to worry that he'd somehow found his way onto their short list of suspects.

He had to assume the former and be ready for the latter.

Niall barely acknowledged the doorman as he strode into his building on Park Avenue in Midtown East. His home was the penthouse, although he spent very little time in it. The biggest draw that brought him home most nights was his two beloved Irish terriers, Pope and Martha, who were either walked and cared for by Timothy McGrath, his full-time pet sitter, or who accompanied him to the office if it was going to be an exceptionally long day.

He could hear Timothy preparing their meal as he opened the door. But the two spry terriers heard him, as well, and raced out to greet him. He squatted down to affectionately scratch their ears. Normally, he would spend more time with them, but this morning was not going to afford him that opportunity.

"Mr. Dempsey, I wasn't expecting you," Timothy said as he came out of the kitchen. He'd been instructed to spend the night here and given no notice that Niall would be returning now.

"I won't be staying," Niall replied, rising to his feet. "I'm only here to get ready for a business meeting." He smiled at his pets. "Later, little laddie and little lassie. You go eat your breakfast." He glanced at Timothy. "I'll call and let you know my plans."

"Yes, sir." Timothy rounded up the dogs, who left the hall reluctantly and only because of the tantalizing smells of their home-cooked meal.

Thirty minutes later, Niall slipped into his suit jacket, left the penthouse, and took the elevator down to his waiting limo.

This was going to be one helluva meeting.

***

Professor Emeritus James Blythe settled himself in his first-class airplane seat, pushing his eyeglasses back up on his narrow nose and placing his cane by his side before leaning back to rest his snow-white head against the seat cushion.

His head was still reeling from the events of the past hours. A special courier arriving at his home with an offer that stunned him—an urgent offer that had to be accepted on the spot and acted on in the moment. Given what he was being hired to do, his answer had been an emphatic yes. Then packing, gathering up the necessary texts and research material he expected to need, and being raced to the airport—given his sedentary life of quiet retirement and his body's aged state, he should be exhausted.

Yet he wasn't. In fact, he'd left his cottage on the University of Dublin's lovely green campus that afternoon feeling younger and more excited than he'd been in years.

The Vadrefjord Hoard.

How long had he been researching that treasure? Years. He'd even gone on an archeological dig to find it. Eventually, his research had told him the rest of the story—that the hoard was gone, having been dug up and whisked away to American soil. Thus, its name being coined from the place it was stolen from, rather than the place it was found, since no one was certain where that would be.

James had his suspicions. He knew more about the hoard's history than any scholar, and not only because of his expertise but because of his fascination with where it currently was and his determination to recover it and restore it to its rightful home in the National Museum of Ireland.

The hoard originally belonged to the high king of Ireland Cynbel Ó Conaill, in the ninth century during the Viking invasion. The Vikings had made Vadrefjord, now Waterford, one of their permanent settlements. There had been a fierce and bloody battle—the Battle of Bawncullen—in which the high king was killed and his valuable treasure stolen. Somewhere there was a painting depicting that battle. James would be intrigued to see it, to see how many of the details matched his knowledge base. But his focus wasn't on the painting, it was on the hoard itself.

When Rose had called him and described the tapestry panel she was researching for Fiona McKay, James had listened carefully. Rose's research had already led her to a high king, although she wasn't sure which one. But that information, together with the description of the gemstones, the crown, the Celtic symbols—but most significant of all, the chalice—that had been enough for James to fill in some of her blanks and begin researching anew.

For perhaps the first time, he wished he knew how to use a computer. But that ship had sailed a long time ago, and frankly he hadn't had the slightest incentive to rectify it—until now. So he'd asked a favor of one of his younger colleagues—one he knew would be enthused by this—and she'd happily delved into what he'd requested.

In her report to him, she'd conveyed that Fiona McKay's great-grandparents had lived on a small farm in Owning, County Kilkenny, which was now only a thirty-five-minute drive from Waterford. A long hike by foot, but still reachable, as it would have had to be in the ninth century. So the proximity was established. Next came the fact that the McKays had left the country in 1920 and sailed to New York City.

End of research for James's colleague, but just the beginning of a thought process for James.

Was it possible the hoard had been buried on the McKays' property and they'd found and fled with it to New York? It was the only explanation for the tapestry Fiona was researching. But why a tapestry? And why such a cryptic one? Why hadn't her great-grandparents just shared the treasure with their family?

James hadn't been able to convey the entirety of his findings to Rose before she was killed. He'd been shocked, brokenhearted, and filled with apprehension at the news. Was her murder tied to her research into this matter? Had she been able to pass anything significant on to Fiona McKay? If so, had the young woman delved into anything more on her own?

James was a poor man. And not terribly strong anymore. He relied heavily on his cane to get around. Most of the time, he was secluded in his cottage, contentedly doing his research, collecting his ancient artifacts, and working on another book. Still, he would have pushed himself and flown to New York to attend Rose's funeral if he had the money.

Well, now he did. Thanks to Niall Dempsey, he could pay his respects to Rose and take over where she left off.

He had no idea how much Mr. Dempsey knew. But his desire to restore the hoard to the National Museum of Ireland seemed genuine, and he was clearly an Irish nationalist at heart. So James would tread cautiously. But the extravagant sum of money Niall Dempsey was offering, along with a spacious apartment in one of his upscale buildings, and a driver who was also an aide to help him get around, was giving him the opportunity of a lifetime.

One he had no intention of squandering.

25

Casey was ready a good twenty minutes before the doorbell rang.

She opened it herself, greeting Niall Dempsey with a pleasant smile and a handshake. "Mr. Dempsey, I'm so glad you could find the time to meet with me."

Niall stepped inside the front hallway of Forensic Instincts. He was wearing an expensive business suit and silk tie, and he carried a leather portfolio. He looked every bit the part of a multimillionaire real estate mogul—one whose gaze was already scanning the rooms that were visible.

"You're very welcome." He smiled back, a smile that didn't quite reach his eyes. He was a man on a mission, one that had nothing to do with real estate. "And please, it's Niall."

"Niall it is," she responded. "And I'm Casey. I'm glad we've dispensed with the formalities." She gestured toward the back of the brownstone. "I set up a meeting room for us to talk in. I can make coffee, tea, whichever you prefer."

As she expected, that wasn't the agenda he had in mind.

"Before we talk, I'd like to take a tour of the place," he said, more a statement than a request. "You work in a traditional brownstone that was built in the nineteenth century. That doesn't mean you'd prefer the same for your next place. I need to see your personal tastes before

I discuss real estate options for you and your boyfriend. It would be foolish for me to focus on a new contemporary skyscraper only to find out you prefer to remain in a building like this one."

Casey's brows rose. "I didn't know you built low-rise apartments."

"I don't. That doesn't mean I'm not connected with developers and landlords who can get you into one, though. Which is why I want to see as much of your space, both working and living, as I can."

"That makes perfect sense." Casey almost laughed at the surprise that flickered in Niall's eyes—a flicker he quickly extinguished. He'd obviously expected her to try to counter his efforts and to steer him into one room so she could begin pumping him for information.

Nope, Dempsey. The first point goes to me.

"Fortunately," she continued, "my team is wrapped up in our current investigation and are either out doing reconnaissance or are in-house doing research. So we pretty much have free rein. And as for my apartment"—her eyes twinkled—"I was smart enough to make the place presentable before you arrived."

This time, Niall's forced smile gave nothing away, although Casey knew in her gut that her last comment had thrown him for a loop. She could hear the wheels in his mind spinning: *Presentable as in neat? Or presentable as in tapestry-free? How much does Casey Woods really know about me and my agenda?*

Aloud, all he said was, "I'm ready whenever you are."

Okay, so he had a pretty good poker face.

Hers was better.

She made a wide sweep of her arm. "Where would you like to begin?"

"With your apartment." No hesitation in his reply. He'd obviously pushed aside his uneasiness. "That will tell me the most about your actual living style. Then we can work our way down, floor by floor."

"Fine." Casey wondered if he realized how absurd this whole charade was. He was a real estate developer, not an interior designer or Realtor. He should want to know her and Hutch's combined income and a description of what they were looking for—not a guided tour of her workplace. His arrogance actually made him believe that she'd buy into this.

Unbelievable.

Continuing to play along, Casey tipped her head in the direction of the staircase. "I hope you don't mind four flights of stairs."

"Not at all." This time he did pause—intentionally—a polite, respectful expression on his face. "Although it occurs to me that I'm a male stranger walking into your apartment alone with you. If it would make you feel more comfortable, we could stop by and ask one of your female employees to join us."

A chaperone. How quaint. And how absurd and antiquated. Still, a try, however feeble. He's groping for a legitimate reason to get inside a room where the tapestries are.

"I can take good care of myself," Casey assured him. "I have no reason to believe you're not a gentleman, but if I'm wrong, I have a pistol, and I'm a very good shot."

Niall did a double take, and Casey did nothing to lighten the moment. *Let him worry about who he's dealing with*, she thought.

"I'm fine showing you my place alone, although I appreciate you asking."

His reaction was not even close to what she'd expected. She assumed he'd either be unsettled or maybe amused, thinking that her comment was just her sense of humor. Instead, the look he gave her was one of sheer admiration, as if she'd just revealed a wonderful asset about herself.

How odd. I'll be tucking that tidbit away for later.

Without another word, Niall followed her to the staircase and climbed the steps behind her. Although she couldn't see him, Casey could actually feel him peering around, as well as pausing a few moments at each landing. And it wasn't to assess her decorating tastes. It was to search for open doors or emerging team members.

Not going to happen, Dempsey. Clearly, you have no idea what a prime suspect you are. And you're looking guiltier every minute.

They reached her apartment level, and Niall followed Casey in. It didn't take long for him to assess the place, especially since there wasn't a shred of work-related material visible. One bedroom, one bath, a tiny kitchenette, and an equally small sitting room. All done in deep browns and creams—very striking but very minimalist.

"I'd love to have decorated more," she said. "But as you can see, the space is limited. Plus, I'm not up here that often. Still, it's obvious that I like stark contrast and I love lots of browns, from chocolate to tan. Also I'm a big fan of some updates I wanted to make and never found time for, like a granite countertop and a heated bathroom floor."

"Duly noted."

Yeah, and something I could just as easily have told you during our meeting.

"What about your boyfriend?" Clearly, Niall had decided that Casey wasn't foolish enough to leave her casework lying around for outsiders to see, so he was headed in a different direction: find out more about the boyfriend to see if he might be Casey's confidant and a potential source of information. "What are his tastes?"

"Very similar to mine."

"A like-minded couple. Very refreshing. What profession is he in?"

Casey kept her face carefully blank, although she couldn't wait to answer this one. "He's with the FBI."

Niall did a double take. "The FBI?" Apparently, he hadn't dug that deep into Casey's personal life, only her professional one.

"Yes, Supervisory Special Agent Kyle Hutchinson. He works in the New York field office." *Now you can go look him up. You'll find less on him than you did on me.*

"The FBI," Niall repeated, and Casey could swear there was a fine sheen of perspiration on his brow that hadn't been there before.

"You sound so surprised," she said.

"I suppose I am." Niall's comeback was smart, if not quick. "Given what limited knowledge I have of Forensic Instincts, you don't always tow the legal line."

"No, I suppose we don't, although we try. As for Hutch, we have a solid personal relationship, but we don't pry into each other's work lives. It's an ideal arrangement for us."

Niall inclined his head thoughtfully. "It must be difficult to shove all your work-related material away every time he visits."

"I've gotten good at it. And Hutch doesn't intrude." Casey's tone was perfectly innocent, but the point she was making was *not*.

Niall wasn't stupid. He quickly abandoned that tactic and returned to safe ground. "So, judging by what I'm seeing and what you've described to me, you want a contemporary place. What size building?"

Casey pursed her lips, as if considering the question. She knew very well the kind of apartments Niall built, and ironically, they suited her and Hutch's tastes well. "The brownstone itself is timeless but, as you said, very nineteenth century," she said. "What Hutch and I are really looking for is a skyscraper in a place that's equidistant to both our workplaces—like Battery Park City—with lots of open space, two bedrooms, including a large master, some great amenities like a private gym, and maybe even a little outdoor greenery that gives our home a bit of a suburban feel and where we can exercise my energetic bloodhound."

"Your description sounds very much like Dempsey Towers," Niall said dryly.

"I do my homework."

"Then you also know there's a long wait list for apartments in that complex. They're brand new, extraordinarily spacious, and the complex has a private park, a roof terrace, along with a pool, a gym, and a residents' lounge."

"And pets are allowed," Casey added. "As I said, I do my home-work. And, yes, I'm fully aware there's a wait list, no doubt a very long one. What I'd like to do is to explore a way in which Hutch and I can bypass it."

Niall's brows rose. "No one can accuse you of not being straight-forward."

"No one ever has."

"So your plan is to incentivize me?"

"Not in the way you mean." Casey put that implication to bed at once. "I'm not about to suggest bribing our way to the front of the line. That's not my style."

"Then how do you intend to accomplish your goal?"

"By having a conversation with you in the meeting room I've set up. Hopefully, once you've heard my idea, you'll be amenable to it. That plan sounds a lot more sensible than wasting your time visiting every room in the brownstone."

Niall's lips thinned in barely concealed annoyance as his last filaments of hope went up in smoke. There'd be no seeing the tapestries or picking up tidbits on FI's investigation into Rose Flaherty's murder.

Checkmate, Dempsey.

He gave her a tight nod. "Of course. Lead the way."

Casey did exactly that, and Niall followed her back down to the first floor, slanting one last curious look around as he did. But whatever he still hoped to spot wasn't going to appear. And he wasn't stupid enough to overplay his hand.

He settled himself in the first-floor meeting room, straighten-ing his tie and placing his portfolio on the end table alongside his cream-colored leather tub chair. "Now here I can see your contem-porary taste," he noted aloud, taking in the chrome and glass.

"Yes, I decorated this room." Casey was standing at the JURA coffee station, turning to give him a questioning look. "Would you prefer tea?"

"Not in America, I wouldn't," he said with a chuckle. "It's rare I've found real tea since I left Ireland. Coffee is fine. Black."

Casey wasn't about to let that opportunity go.

"How long have you lived in the States?" she asked as she brewed coffee for them both.

"Thirty-five years," he replied. "All of them in New York. I was a kid when I arrived, and the city offered me the opportunity to make something of myself. I've never regretted settling here."

A response straight from the magazine articles written about you.

Casey walked over and handed him a cup, along with a linen napkin. "I apologize for not having breakfast to go with the coffee. Our meeting was too impromptu for me to make arrangements."

He waved away her apology, taking both the cup and the napkin with a nod of thanks. "I'm not much of a breakfast eater. I generally work until my stomach growls."

"I can relate to that." Casey sat down on the love seat across from him, crossing her legs and sipping at her own coffee. "I've only visited Ireland once. Their tea is in a class by itself."

"No arguments."

"What made you come to America, especially at such a young age? Did your parents have family here? Or did they find a great work opportunity?"

Niall didn't miss a beat. "Neither. I came over by myself. I was young, but not that young—I was twenty. I didn't exactly have an easy life. And I had no family. So I took a chance. It paid off."

"Wow. You must have been incredibly strong to accomplish all you have with no family to lean on."

He shrugged. "You learn to be strong when you're on your own in Belfast during the Troubles."

"When did you lose your parents?"

Calmly, Niall sipped his coffee, then replied, reciting a speech that was so smooth, he'd clearly committed it to memory long ago. "My father was never in the picture. My mother died when I was a kid. I lived on the charity offered by the parents of my mates. They'd each take me in for a few months at a time, and I'd give them most of the wages I made at whatever menial job I had. I went from delivering newspapers to washing dishes to working on farms—all the while praying that neither I nor anyone who mattered to me would get killed."

Casey's expression was the epitome of compassion, only a portion of which was fake. While her instincts told her that a lot of what Niall was recounting was total BS, they also told her that there were elements of truth woven in.

"What a terrible life for a boy to lead," she said. "And you managed to save up enough money to emigrate by the time you were twenty?"

"I did." Another sip of coffee. "I'd done some carpentry work at a few of the farms I just mentioned. That's how I got my start in New York, as a common carpenter." The pride in his voice was genuine, and Casey had no doubt that he'd worked his way up from nothing to the powerful businessman he was today. Then again, his life here in the US was well documented. He hadn't given her a single concrete lead about his life in Ireland.

"Your story is inspiring," she said. "I'm sure your friends back in Belfast are cheering for you."

"I haven't stayed in touch." Niall stared down into his coffee, a muscle working in his jaw. With his head lowered, Casey could spot a jagged scar at his hairline, one that had probably stayed hidden until middle age caused his hairline to recede. Faded but pretty ugly-looking.

She channeled her energy back to what he was saying, which she sensed was important.

"The person closest to me was killed," he said. "After that, nothing was ever the same."

Okay, now that's definitely the truth. Finally. Something I can work with.

Casey leaned forward, gently touching the left sleeve of his suit jacket. "I'm so sorry. That kind of loss must have been excruciating."

Niall raised his head, and Casey saw the moisture in his eyes—a confirmation of her suspicions that the loss he was describing was real. "It was. And I thank you for your kind words. I try not to dwell on the painful memories in my past."

Casey didn't press, at least not about his friend's death. He'd never supply details, and she'd only succeed in getting him to shut down completely. She couldn't let that happen.

"Of course," she said. "I apologize for prying."

"No apology necessary."

Niall set down his coffee cup, reaching over with his right arm to get his portfolio. Business time. He was striving to take control of this meeting. But Casey sensed he wasn't quite himself yet. Which meant she had a small window of opportunity while he was still vulnerable. She had to grab this moment because she wasn't going to get another.

She removed her hand from his sleeve, ready to ask her next question when she caught a quick glimpse of his left hand.

Her entire body stiffened. His hand was a disaster. Not only were the joints on his fingers badly swollen, but his palm had faded patches of blotchy-white scar tissue that made it look like the lunar landing surface.

Casey fought the urge to stare, instead averting her gaze entirely. This was significant. If Niall caught her so much as noticing the scars, she'd be screwed.

Scooting farther back on the love seat, she returned to her original plan.

"What about Ireland do you miss the most?" she asked offhandedly, a far more general and nonthreatening question. "I mean, your childhood in Ireland. I'm sure you've been back there many times as an adult." Actually, she doubted he had. The way he'd spoken, she suspected he'd closed off that avenue forever. And if he had a dark past, he certainly wouldn't want to revisit it.

A hint of a smile, as he hunted through his portfolio. "Hurling. I was a champion before I was sixteen."

Casey's brows knit. "Hurling?"

"It's the most popular sport in Ireland, similar to your football, but far more challenging. Google it. You'll be fascinated."

"And you were a teenage champion? That's pretty awesome."

"I was very impressed with myself. Then again, I've never been known for my humility."

Which is why you're talking about it now. Your colossal arrogance trumps your desire for secrecy. Plus, you probably assume that this fact is so insignificant, there's nothing we can do with it. Think again.

Evidently, she was spot-on, because Niall was totally composed and not the least bit unnerved by having said what he did.

"You mentioned having a bloodhound," he said as he pulled out a few brochures, along with room layouts, pricing, and various wait list numbers.

"Is that a problem? Because if any of these residences don't allow pets—"

"All of my buildings allow pets," Niall interrupted her with a kind wave of the hand. "I have two dogs of my own."

Okay, this was safe territory. "What breeds?" Casey asked.

"Irish terriers, siblings actually. Pope and Martha. So I wouldn't think of offering a residence that didn't invite pets." He handed Casey the material he'd extracted from his portfolio. "Most of this can be found online," he said. "But not as detailed, and certainly not the length of the wait lists." He also gave her a printed page of the names and addresses of several building complexes. "These aren't mine, but they are places I thought you might want to consider. I know the developers. I can certainly reach out to them for you."

Following his lead, Casey switched over to all business. She scanned everything, concentrating mostly on Dempsey Towers and its wait list.

"Wow," she said. "This is even worse than I expected."

"Exactly. So I'm looking forward to hearing your suggestion about how to bypass that without being unethical."

Casey lowered the pages to her lap. "Simple. I remember that at the McKays' gathering for Rose Flaherty, you offered the out-of-town guests accommodations in your vacant apartments. I'm hoping some of those vacant apartments happen to be in Dempsey Towers."

Niall looked impressed with her deduction. Impressed but not taken aback, and not at a loss for an answer. It was as if he'd already thought of this idea himself.

"I keep three or four move-in-condition apartments available in all my buildings," he said. "That way when important colleagues fly in, they have an option other than a hotel."

"And I'm assuming not all of these move-in apartments are one-bedroom."

"You assume correctly. New York City is a desirable city to visit. My colleagues often bring their families to enjoy the sites while we're working."

Casey met his gaze head on. "Would you be willing to part with a two-bedroom apartment in Dempsey Towers that happens to have a great view of the city? Hutch and I could provide a substantial security deposit and not compromise your wait list."

Niall leaned forward and pulled out one of the pages he'd handed her—one that had a full layout of a two-bedroom apartment.

"That would be the one you're interested in," he said.

Clearly, her instinct had been right. He'd run through the same thought process as she had. But their motives were entirely different.

She wanted to rent that apartment.

He wanted to own her.

She stared from the floor plan to Niall and back, forcing herself to look stunned. She had to go this route. If she didn't, he'd be suspicious.

"This is perfect," she said. Pausing, she pressed her lips together as if waffling over whether or not to say what was on her mind, and then blurting it out. "I hope I'm not looking a gift horse in the mouth, but I have to ask—I was expecting to do a lot more to plead our case, maybe tell you how long Hutch and I have waited for this opportunity and how many miles have separated us since we became a couple. But you not only made this easy, you actually came prepared for the very thing I was about to ask for. Please don't think I'm ungrateful, but..."

"But you want to know why," Niall finished for her.

She nodded.

"I don't know if Fiona McKay told you or not, but her family and I go back many years," he said, providing a ready—and well-rehearsed—explanation. "We're all congregants at the same church with a longstanding friendship. And Fiona and I were also both regular customers of Rose Flaherty's. I appreciate what you're doing to help them. So, if I can help you, I'm glad to."

Not to help us. To keep an eye on us. Smart move. Too bad it won't work.

"Thank you so much," Casey said with all the fervor she could muster. This man was definitely scum, or worse. Renting an apartment from one of his buildings wouldn't stop her from digging into his past, and it sure as hell wouldn't stop her from throwing his sorry ass into jail if he was a killer.

She rose, extending her hand to shake his. "This has been an ideal meeting. Again, I truly appreciate your doing this for us." She whipped out her iPhone and called up the calendar. "Now, when can we schedule our tour and the finalizing of our rental?"

Niall shot her an admiring look, simultaneously pulling out his own cell. "Remind me never to try to one-up you."

Too late, Dempsey. You already tried. And you lost.

***

Casey waited only until she'd shown Niall out and watched his town car pull away.

She then retraced her steps to the meeting room, pausing to get what she needed from FI's equipment closet.

Pulling on her latex gloves, she carefully bagged the coffee cup and the napkin, storing them in a cold, dry place.

Time to discuss her plan with the team.

26

Niall paced the length of his living room floor, pausing occasionally to stare out of the panorama of windows, only to retrace his steps and start anew.

He'd had his driver take him home, rather than to Kelly's. As much as he wanted to run the details of his meeting with Casey Woods by Donald, he wasn't walking in there in a designer suit. He'd stick out like a sore thumb. Plus, he wanted to sort things out in his own mind before he discussed them with the one person he trusted. Donald had already left him a cryptic message implying that Professor Blythe was now airborne. So that piece was in place.

Now came the conundrum of Forensic Instincts, and how much they did and did not know.

He felt a lot more uneasy now than he had walking into the brownstone. He'd obviously underestimated Casey Woods and her team. Somehow, he'd believed there'd be some kind of opening, whether it be conversational or actual—like running into Fiona, who'd be more transparent than the FI team—that would have allowed him to get a hint of insight into where things stood on their analysis of the tapestries. He'd even allowed himself to hope he could lay eyes on the panels himself, maybe during a teammate's comings or goings. After all, they had no idea those panels meant anything to him.

Or did they?

He'd prepared himself for the fact that Casey Woods might have an agenda when she called him, one that extended beyond her wanting his influence in getting her and her boyfriend an apartment. After all, everyone on Rose's contact list was a suspect, and he was just another one who had to be crossed off their list. But after her pointed comments and her aggressive approach, he had to wonder if he was more than just one of many.

Did Forensic Instincts have reason to believe he was behind Rose's murder and the danger Fiona was in? In addition to that chilling thought, how much did they know about the tapestry and its history? Did they know about the hoard? Was Fiona aware of the link between her tapestry panels and the stolen treasure? Were they actually searching for it, and if so, how far ahead of him were they in their search?

There had to be a way for him to find his answers and get ahead of the game. And that way was Professor Blythe—Blythe and a trusted mate to play the part of the frail professor's driver and physical aide.

Niall whipped out his phone and made the call.

Even as he did, the hair on the back of his neck stood up, and he turned to scrutinize his apartment, only to pivot back around to stare down at the street below. He knew this feeling. He'd had it many times before. But it had been particularly strong these past few days.

He was definitely being watched.

***

Casey knocked lightly on the door of the yoga room, hoping Claire wasn't in deep meditation or on the verge of making an important connection. "It's me," she said quietly, her lips close to the door. "Bad time to intrude?"

A rustle of movement and the door opened. "I wish." Claire looked tired and frustrated. "I hope you have something for me. Because I'm still stonewalled."

"I have some paperwork." Casey held out the pages Niall had given her from his portfolio. "He handled every page. I hope they'll be enough, because I kept his cup and napkin for DNA testing."

Before she could continue, Claire recoiled from the papers. "It's more than enough. Dempsey's aura is so dark and powerful that it reaches me even before I make contact with him or anything he's touched." She glanced up. "DNA testing. We both know he won't be in the system as Niall Dempsey. He's too smart for that. Which means you're looking into his previous life. Has Ryan dug up answers on that?"

"Not yet. But he will."

"I'm sure. Once he does, I'm assuming that means we're bringing Hutch in on our investigation."

"Would you object?"

"Of course not. If Dempsey has a record, we need to find it."

Casey nodded. "I'm about to broach the subject with the team."

"I'm sure they'll agree." Tentatively, Claire reached out and took the pile of papers, shuddering as she did.

"Are you going to be okay?" Casey asked.

"I'll be fine." Claire's jaw set. "I'm doing this no matter how painful it is. Niall Dempsey is an evil man. I need to know how evil so I can help move our investigation along."

Casey nodded. "Then I'll leave you to your work."

From the yoga room, Casey walked down and knocked at the War Room door. "It's me. I'm alone."

Emma unlocked the door a crack and peeked out to confirm that what Casey had just said was the truth. Then she opened the door for her boss.

Casey walked in, looking amused. "You didn't recognize my voice?"

"Of course I did," Emma replied, wearing her Super-Sleuth expression. "But what if you couldn't speak freely? What if Niall Dempsey was holding a gun to your head, demanding that you let him into the room with us and the tapestries? What if he figured out—"

"Okay, okay." Casey held up her hand, laughing even as she did. "I see your point."

"I still think you watch way too many movies," Marc informed Emma. "Dempsey isn't an idiot. Even if he was sure we had our sights set on him as the key suspect—which I don't think he realizes—he's not going to march in here with a weapon and accost Casey or us. He'd go straight to prison, having accomplished nothing. Start watching game shows instead."

Emma made a face at him. "Boring."

With a good-natured eye roll, Marc turned his attention to Casey. "Well?"

"Well, Hutch and I are getting a great apartment in Battery Park City," Casey said dryly. "And all because of Dempsey's alleged bond with Fiona and her family. In real terms, he's buying himself a connection to me and, as a result, to FI. Whatever we figure out, he wants to know."

"The question is, how much does *he* know?" Patrick mused.

"My guess?" Casey said. "Less than we do in some ways, more in others. Let me give you some insights I came away with." She proceeded to tell them about Niall's obvious probing, his odd reaction to her skill with a pistol, the pieces of his life he'd mentioned that rang true to her, and most of all, the scars on his forehead and his hand.

"The zigzagged scar on his forehead could have been from something as simple as a bar fight," Marc said. "But the description of his palm and his fingers, not only is that gruesome, but it speaks to something bigger than a broken beer bottle." A thoughtful pause. "Let me make a few phone calls. I might be able to come up with answers."

Casey nodded. She never questioned it when Marc made this kind of request. It always paid off.

"By the way," Patrick added. "I heard Dempsey's voice, and his brogue. Definitely Northern Irish."

"No surprise," Marc said. "It's far easier to invent fiction that has its roots in fact. Advertising that he's from Belfast and then having a Dublin brogue would be stupid."

"Which is one thing that Niall Dempsey is not." Casey gave Patrick a grateful look. "Still, I'm glad you thought to do that. I'd totally forgotten."

Patrick shot off a salute. "Just doing my job. As you did yours. It sounds like you managed to keep things more than civil with Dempsey, which is a pretty tall order, given the circumstances."

Casey grimaced. "I'd hardly call us best buds. We were like two cats circling each other. Oh, incidentally, he's a dog lover. That was a surprise. He's a pretty cold guy. But he definitely warmed up when he spoke about his two Irish terriers, Pope and Martha. Because of his bond with them, all his apartments are pet friendly. I guess even the hardest people have a soft spot or two."

"Pope and Martha?" Patrick's forehead creased in thought. "Why do those names sound familiar?"

"I doubt you've socialized with Dempsey's pets," Casey replied with a grin. Her grin faded as she studied Patrick's expression. "What is it?"

"I'm not sure. But I think I have a few phone calls to make, as well."

As with Marc, Casey didn't question Patrick's request. "Then make them. You, too, Marc. I'm going down to the lair to lay all this on Ryan. Maybe the timing of Niall's best friend's death—which he made clear was a violent one—plus the timing of his pre-sixteen hurling championship can provide new leads to run with." She paused. "One last thing. I bagged Dempsey's cup and napkin for DNA testing."

Marc leveled his gaze on her. He knew the way Casey thought, and how far ahead that thinking went. "You're moving toward bringing Hutch in."

Casey nodded. "I am."

"You're getting way ahead of yourself. We're still gathering evidence."

"I realize that. Obviously, I'd wait until we had enough proof for Hutch to have something to work with. But we do have the bagged items. So as soon as Ryan comes through—"

"Forget the idea of going to Hutch with the cup and napkin." Marc cut her off. "He won't be able to access CODIS for DNA testing." The whole team was familiar with the FBI's Combined DNA Index System. "The evidence wasn't collected at a crime scene, so it can't be analyzed at the FBI laboratory. We'll have to go to a private lab for the analysis."

"You're right." Casey digested that thoughtfully.

Marc shifted forward in his chair, exchanging a quick glance with Patrick. As former FBI agents, they both knew the strict protocol the bureau followed—a protocol that Hutch would have to navigate very carefully.

With his customary candor, Marc laid that out for Casey. "Even if the DNA results go our way and Ryan turns up solid evidence, Hutch is going to have major obstacles. There's no open case on our side of the pond. Whether or not Ireland has one remains to be seen. No matter how we play this, Hutch is going to be fighting the tide."

"More so than I realized." Casey frowned, then met Marc's gaze. "Can we involve Aidan?"

"That's where my mind was going," Marc replied. "He's gotten us fast turnarounds on DNA analyses in the past." He paused, choosing his next words carefully. Casey knew only the tip of the iceberg about what Aidan Devereaux, Marc's older brother, did. Marc was privy to it all.

A former Marine captain, trained and skilled in both communications and intel, Aidan was now a communications expert at the largest financial firm in the world. At least officially. Unofficially, he headed up the Zermatt Group—a covert team of military, corporate, and spy agency operatives who searched the data stream and took on emergent crises before they appeared on law enforcement's radar.

Marc had been in the dark about Aidan's other life until recently, when Aidan had called upon him to assist in a rescue op with him and Zermatt. A kidnapped college student being held in Croatia for a ransom that would have tilted the balance of the world's technology.

Casey knew only that she'd loaned Marc to Aidan for a secret mission of some kind. Ryan and Emma had also been called upon, each for different reasons, both in lesser capacities and on a need-to-know basis. Marc was aware of how much Aidan admired FI. But until he opted for full disclosure, Marc remained silent.

Now all he added was, "Aidan has overseas connections who can assist Hutch."

Casey arched a brow. After Marc's return and the simultaneous news reports she read, she'd put two and two together to get at least a nuts-and-bolts four. "I realize that. Aidan and his clandestine team span the globe. Don't worry. I won't pressure you to divulge information. If Aidan won't talk to me, I'll let you handle it—but not until Ryan gives us something solid on who Niall Dempsey really is."

"That's the necessity here," Patrick said. "Until Ryan does that, we have nothing to trigger an investigation. Let's hold off on approaching Aidan about a DNA analysis, and certainly on talking to Hutch. We won't be losing any time. Aidan has a way of making things happen in a matter of hours. And bringing Hutch in too soon would compromise him and derail us and our investigation. We need to build a comprehensive picture of what we're asking of both men."

"Agreed." Casey's nod was reluctant but certain. "So for now I'll just keep the cup and napkin stored and wait." She sighed, looking from Patrick to Marc and back. "Thanks, guys, as always, for being my voices of reason—even if what you're saying is not what I wanted to hear."

Patrick shot her a rueful look. "Sorry. Like I said, just doing my job."

"Same," Marc echoed.

"And doing them well. Sometimes I'm as impulsive as Ryan. I need you two to be the strings to my kite. Speaking of which…" Casey turned and headed toward the door. "Time to invade the lair."

***

Ryan was frowning at his computer screen and Fiona was talking on her cell phone when Casey knocked, announced herself, and walked into the lair.

Instantly, Ryan swiveled his chair around so he could face her, and Fiona began to talk faster, visibly eager to wind up the call and hear what Casey had to say.

"Fee's talking to her marketing manager about a postcard mailing," Ryan supplied in an irritated tone.

"Is that a problem?" Casey asked.

"No, the problem is, she just spoke to her roommate, Lara. By tomorrow afternoon, their townhouse will be all cleaned up and in move-in condition. I don't want her going back there. She disagrees. She's a pain in the ass."

Casey bit back a smile. "I realize you're worried about her. Don't be. Given the high level of security Patrick's placed on Fiona, no one's getting near her. And, Ryan, she's a grown woman. She's already put her life on hold. She needs some normalcy while we solve this case."

"That's what I told him," Fiona said as she ended her call. "I'll follow all the instructions he's given me about using my laptop, and I'll keep all of you and my security team apprised of my schedule. But I need to get my workshop set up, and I need to start designing jewelry again. I'm enough of a wreck as it is." She ignored Ryan's glare. "What happened with Niall?"

"Quite a bit." Once again, Casey ran through the details of her meeting.

"What longstanding friendship?" Fiona demanded. "We go to the same church, and he and I are—were—both loyal patrons of Rose's. That's as deep as it runs." She sucked in an angry breath. "In other words, he's giving you all that BS and that apartment so you'll look the other way."

"I'd say that's a fair description."

"A best friend who was killed and a pre-sixteen hurling championship," Ryan muttered, ready to get back to his computer. "I'm on it."

"Marc's making some phone calls. He has an instinct of some kind and I told him to run with it."

"Good," Ryan replied with a nod. "Because the more I dig into this guy's nonexistent past, the more I'm convinced he only first became Niall Dempsey when he got to New York. No one is so invisible that I can't find them. Any leads Marc can bring me are welcome."

"Claire is in high gear, as well," Casey said. "I gave her the paperwork Dempsey gave me on all his available apartments. She's determined to lock in on something specific, something more than just the aura of pure evil she keeps picking up on."

Again, Ryan nodded. "I'll take whatever she can add to the mix."

"I bagged the cup Dempsey drank from and the linen napkin he used. I want to turn them over to Aidan for DNA analysis. He can handle that and a whole lot more." Casey shot Ryan a knowing look. "You probably have greater insight into how far his reach is than I do."

Ryan neither admitted nor denied that. "You might as well wait on that till I turn up something. Dempsey's not stupid enough to have a criminal record here in the City."

"I totally agree." Casey held up a finger, seeing that Ryan was about to move on to the next subject. "One question."

"Shoot."

"Do the names Pope and Martha mean anything to you?"

"Yeah, they're Dempsey's dogs," Ryan replied. "There are photos of them in a magazine spread on him. Why? Is that significant?"

She shrugged. "I'm not sure. But I'll let you know if that changes."

"Okay." Ryan pointed at the computer screen. "Meanwhile, I've been doing that genealogical research I said I'd do and coupling my findings with some blanks that Fee is filling in. She spent more time listening to our grandmother's stories than I did. Anyway, I think I can answer Marc's questions as to why our great-grandparents didn't tell my grandmother about the hoard and the tapestry panels, and why they left them in the memory box without an explanation."

"Yes, this stuff's fascinating," Fiona interrupted. "Based on the data Ryan turned up, our great-grandfather wasn't just your average stonemason. He was super skilled, and helped on the construction of some cathedrals in Ireland. So when he and our great-grandmother arrived in New York, he got stonemason work without any problems."

Casey glanced at Ryan, her eyes narrowed in a how-is-this-relevant look.

"Fee is all pumped up about the aesthetics of our family history," he answered her with an eye roll. "I'll stick to the pertinent facts. He did do everything Fee just described. But the significant piece of information is that he died just a few months after he and our great-grandmother arrived here."

"Meaning the secret stopped with her," Casey said.

"Which is probably why she wove that secret into the tapestries," Fiona added. "According to the stories our grandmother told me, our great-grandmother was a force to be reckoned with. She wasn't a pathetic widow. She was pregnant with my grandmother when they arrived in New York, so she'd be more determined than ever to protect and preserve the family. I have no idea if she knew that the treasure they found was an ancient hoard, but she certainly knew it was valuable, which meant others would be looking for it. She obviously decided to hide its whereabouts in the tapestries until my grandmother was old enough to pass the secret along to."

"Clearly, that never happened," Casey said.

"No," Ryan replied. "According to the records, our great-grandmother died in 1931. My grandmother was ten, pretty young to handle such a huge secret. She wound up living with some distant relatives I never even knew existed until I did this research."

"I knew she grew up with third or fourth cousins or something like that." Fiona looked annoyed at herself for not having asked more questions about this when she could have.

"They're no longer alive, so it's irrelevant," Ryan told her. "Besides, it yielded one good result. If things had been different, she would never have met our grandfather."

"That's true." Fiona brightened a bit. "Anyway, back to the subject. My grandmother always said that her mother's death—a massive heart attack— was not only sudden but it was totally unexpected, given how robust she was. So, obviously, there was no time for her to rethink her decision and tell her young daughter the truth."

Casey sighed. "So she put the panels in the memory box, which was passed down to her daughter, and the secret remained hidden."

"Yeah." Ryan scowled. "Everything was safely dormant until Fee whacked at the hornet's nest."

"And I'm not sorry." Fiona's chin came up in a show of defiance. "This mystery needs to be solved." Her tone and her expression softened. "My only regret is Rose. It's because of all this that she was killed."

"Hey." Ryan's tone softened, too. "Don't start blaming yourself for Rose's death. You had no idea that what you were asking her to research was dangerous." He raked his hands through his hair. "Look, let's put all the emotional stuff aside. We now know why Fee is the first McKay woman to understand that the tapestry panels are telling a story and what that story is. We also know that Niall Dempsey is our prime suspect. My job is to find out who he really is and what that tells me about who he's become. It's all well and good to find out what a lowlife he was back in Ireland, but I also need to figure out if he's the one who's putting Fee's life in jeopardy."

"You'll have help from Marc and Claire," Casey reminded him. "And you're right. That's priority number one. But secondarily, we have to beat him to the punch when it comes to uncovering this hoard. We have the tapestry panels. He doesn't. That means the clock is ticking. We have to figure out the significance of those panels and follow the treasure map."

As she spoke, her phone gave a quick chirp.

"An email," she murmured. "I left my phone on because I'm waiting for a reply from Dr. Blythe." She glanced at the screen. "It's him. Finally." She opened the email and read through it, her frown deepening as she did.

"Well?" Ryan demanded.

Casey looked up, an odd expression on her face. "It wasn't from the professor. It was from his assistant. Evidently, he doesn't do email or come into the office much. So his assistant is part-time, as well. She retrieved my messages and is advising me that the professor left the country today on a business matter. He didn't leave a return date."

27

Professor Blythe arrived at the JFK terminal, where Peter—or Thomas Murphy, the fictitious name Niall had provided—was waiting for him at the gate. He knew the professor had been briefed on Thomas's role as his driver and physical aide, so he just introduced himself, took the professor's luggage, and assisted him to the town car Niall had gifted him. This new part Niall had asked him to play was certainly a lot more stimulating than making midnight visits to buildings to ensure they were properly locked down.

He drove Blythe directly to one of Niall's beautiful Midtown skyscrapers, where an apartment had been made available for the professor. In fact, this building was the one where Niall himself lived, and Niall's driver was parked in the circular alcove right outside. Peter pulled up alongside the other car, lowering the passenger window to give his friend a surreptitious thumbs-up. Niall partially lowered his tinted glass window to acknowledge and to nod his thanks. Peter then backed up and parked behind Niall's car and, per instructions, escorted James up to the apartment.

Peter didn't make conversation other than to give Blythe a quick tour of the place. He then accompanied the professor to the bedroom, placed his suitcase on the bed, and told him that Mr. Dempsey would be right up.

Blythe thanked him, and Peter retreated to the unit's hallway. He didn't have long to wait.

Niall showed up moments later. He stepped inside the apartment but kept the door ajar—a clear message to Peter that his job was over for tonight.

"Thank you, mate," he said. "Now I've got to lay the groundwork."

Peter nodded. "Ten o'clock tomorrow morning?"

"Yes."

"See you then." With that, Peter took off.

Having heard voices, Professor Blythe came out of the bedroom, leaning heavily on his cane, and inclined his head. "Mr. Dempsey?"

"Niall, and it's a pleasure to meet you, Professor." Niall walked over and extended his hand. "Thank you for coming all this way."

The professor met Niall's handshake, his eyes twinkling. "It was my pleasure. And it's James. I'm not in the classroom, I'm with a colleague."

"Then James it is." Niall gestured toward the living room sofa. "Please, sit. You've come a long way in a very short time. What can I offer you? The refrigerator is fully stocked."

James limped gratefully over to the sofa and sank down, propping his cane alongside him. "I was well fed on the plane, but thank you. Just some water would be fine."

Niall fetched two chilled bottles, handing one to the professor before walking over to the club chair across from his guest and taking a seat. "I hope this apartment meets your needs." He'd intentionally situated James in this building, just a few floors down from his penthouse. They'd meet here. That way, there was no chance of being seen together. Their meetings could remain as clandestine as he intended them to be.

A chuckle. "I can't imagine whose needs it *wouldn't* meet. The bedroom is larger than my cottage."

Niall smiled back. "I own many buildings, but I have a special fondness for this one. It's where I call home."

James took that in. "I must confess, I'd never heard of you before your courier arrived. I now understand that you're a prominent real estate developer. If your other buildings are as impressive as this one, I can understand how you could offer me such a generous consulting fee."

Niall was more amused than annoyed by James's obviously insular existence. Actually, his purely cerebral nature served Niall's purposes quite well. The less James knew about his life—other than his patriotic search for the Vadrefjord Hoard—the better.

"I take great pride in the construction and design of my buildings," he stated simply. "So, yes, I'm blessed to have the means to pay for your expertise and your assistance."

"Frankly? I would have offered you both just for travel and living expenses. The Vadrefjord Hoard is my greatest fascination. If I can help in its recovery and return to Ireland, it would be the greatest honor of my life."

"Then we share the same goal." Niall could see that James was exhausted, but he had to set the stage, discuss tomorrow's agenda, and to earn some goodwill before they said good night.

"You were close to Rose Flaherty," he said in a gentle voice. "She mentioned you often, especially recently with the research she was doing for Fiona McKay. Her death was tragic."

That made James's shoulders slump. "Her *murder*," he corrected, his eyes moist. "And, yes, Rose and I go back many, many years. Do you know if the police have learned anything about who killed her?"

Niall kept his sad face on. "Not as far as I know. It's still an open investigation. But I don't know who'd want that wonderful woman dead. She didn't have an enemy in the world."

James blinked back his tears. "Clearly, that wasn't the case. And I keep asking myself over and over if her murder had anything to do with the research you referred to. Did she uncover anything after she and I spoke? Did that knowledge put her in danger?"

"I've asked myself the same questions, multiple times. And I fervently hope that the police find the answers. Like you, I was very fond of Rose. I not only did quite a bit of business with her, I also learned from her more about the treasures of the world than I can recount." Niall paused. "Rose and I were both congregants of the Basilica of Saint Patrick's Old Cathedral. I've spoken with the monsignor and arranged for you to visit Rose's burial site tomorrow morning at ten thirty. Thomas will take you. You're free to spend as much time as you'd like honoring your dear friend."

James took out a handkerchief and dabbed at his eyes. "Thank you. That means a great deal to me."

"Of course." Niall uncapped his water and took a few swallows—long enough for James to compose himself. He'd established the goodwill. Now came the stage-setting and the description of tomorrow's agenda.

"Before we begin, I need you to agree to two things," Niall said. "One is that anything we discuss remains between us. I realize that requires trust. I'm hoping that our mutual devotion to Rose is enough to establish that trust. Because we both want to quickly accomplish our shared goal and restore the hoard to our country."

"I understand," James replied after mulling it over. "However, I'll need to probe a few things with you before I can agree. But tell me, what is your second requirement?"

"My anonymity. Under no circumstances do I want my name used. I'll work closely with you and provide any assistance you need, but behind the scenes."

That gave James pause. "And why is that?"

Niall didn't intend to lie about this. It would only come back to bite him in the ass if he did. "Because despite my national pride, I'm fundamentally self-interested. Otherwise, I wouldn't have accomplished all I have. Rose's murder has widened in its scope. Fiona herself has been threatened. She's hired private investigators to help her find the killer. I can't have my name associated with a murder investigation. It would throw too much unwanted media attention in my direction. Especially since the McKays and I are congregants of the same church and go back many years together."

James paled. "Threatened? Has someone tried to harm Fiona McKay?"

"Not yet." Again, the truth. "But her townhouse was broken into and the entire place was turned upside down. I have to assume that whoever did this was looking for something connected to Rose's findings." A poignant pause. "Such as the tapestry panels."

A heartbeat of silence. "So you *do* know about the tapestries."

Niall nodded. "Rose was very excited about this project. She showed me the panel Fiona was having her research."

"I see. Well, that certainly answers one of my questions." James inclined his head. "Were the panels stolen during the break-in?"

"I don't think they were ever at Fiona's house. When I went to her parents' gathering in honor of Rose, I saw one of the panels hanging on the living room wall. My guess is that all the panels were there."

"*Were?*"

Niall nodded. "Knowing Fiona, she would never put her parents in danger. So after her own home was torn apart, I suspect she moved the panels to the offices of Forensic Instincts—the PIs she hired."

James blew out a breath. "That poor girl."

"I agree. That's another reason I want to solve this puzzle quickly. It would take Fiona out of harm's way."

"So I'm here to help you do that, by offering her my assistance and, as a result, by tying the tapestries to the location of the hoard."

"Precisely." Niall set down his water bottle and leaned forward. "I'll lay out the specifics in a minute. But first, you said you had questions. Ask them. I want us to be of one mind when I leave this apartment tonight."

"As do I." James set down his own bottle and tapped the head of his cane. "You've already addressed one of my questions. You're aware of the tapestries. So I have only one other. How is it you're also aware of the tapestries' link to the Vadrefjord Hoard, as well as the McKays' connection to it? I hadn't had time enough to share that information with Rose, so she couldn't have discussed it with you."

"Like you, I've been fascinated with the Valdrefjord Hoard for years." Niall stuck with facts he was quite sure James already knew. "As I said, Rose showed me the tapestry panel she was researching for Fiona and told me there were twelve smaller panels that interwove with that central one. Based on what I was seeing—particularly the chalice—not to mention the allusions to royalty, the gemstones, and the Celtic symbols, I came to the conclusion that the secret to the hoard's location was somehow hidden in these tapestries."

"You're saying you came to that conclusion just from viewing a random tapestry with similarities to the hoard's contents?"

"Of course not." Again, Niall stuck to candor. "I've long since suspected that the hoard was dug up from its original location and transported to New York. I had a reliable source—one whose father came over on the same ship as those who carried the hoard—who convinced me of that, as well as of the date this happened. I did some digging. It turns out that the McKays arrived in New York on that same ship on that same date. So once I saw the tapestry, it was easy to connect the dots."

That obviously satisfied James, because he visibly relaxed. "I can tell you more about the hoard's history if that would help."

"I'm sure it would, but let's get to that tomorrow. Right now, I want to finish our conversation and let you get some sleep." Niall could wait for the history. All he needed now was to go over tomorrow's plan. "After you finish at the church tomorrow morning, Thomas will take you to see Fiona. I'll have checked up on her anyway, just to make sure she's okay, so I'll know where she is—which will probably be at Forensic Instincts. Once you tell her who you are and why you're there, she'll be eager to accept your help interpreting the symbols and the imagery on the tapestries. Thomas will be there, both as an escort and to ensure you're steady on your feet and not overtaxing yourself. You and I will meet back here once you're finished."

James's hesitation was slight but present nonetheless. "Somehow I feel I'm being deceitful by acquiring information and passing it along to you without saying a word about it to Fiona."

"I respect your integrity. However, I've already told you my reasons for staying in the shadows." Niall was prepared for this annoying possibility. "Plus, as I said, the McKays and I go back many years. They're very proud and honorable people. If they know I'm assisting you, they'll feel indebted to me. That's the last thing I want. It will complicate our search and slow it down by adding an emotional component."

James was still visibly waffling.

"This is where the trust I referred to comes in," Niall said. "But if you still have doubts, I'll be blunt. I'm a multimillionaire. I don't need the profits from the treasure, no matter how great they are. My only motivations are my fascination for the Valdrefjord Hoard and my desire for it to be found and returned to Ireland. Between your expertise and my resources, we can make that happen. And once it does, I'll expedite the process of transporting the hoard to the National Museum of Ireland and provide full disclosure to the McKays—and, in the process, take the target off Fiona's back. Is that enough for you?"

This time, James gave a definitive nod. "It is."

Niall rose. "Then I'll let you get some rest. Thomas will be here at ten."

***

After a day of playing phone tag, Patrick got hold of his former colleague, had the answers he was looking for, and promptly called a team meeting. Everyone gathered in the conference room—all except Marc, who was uncharacteristically absent.

Patrick shot Casey a should-I-wait look, and Casey nodded.

"Marc has been on the phone all day, talking to I have no idea who," she said. "But when I poked my head into his office and motioned to him that we're having a meeting, he held up a just-a-minute finger. So let's give him time to wrap up his call and join us."

As she spoke, Marc walked into the room and shut the door behind him. "Did I hold things up?"

"Nope," Ryan informed him. "We were just getting settled. Fee is with Hero in the War Room. I practically had to tie her down to keep her away. But until I know what we're dealing with, I don't want her involved."

"She wouldn't be allowed to get involved," Casey reminded him, taking her seat at the head of the table and setting down her coffee mug. "First and foremost, she's our client, despite the fact that she's your sister. Meetings like these are closed. We'll fill Fiona in as need be."

"Good point." Ryan took a belt of coffee. "I'll be sure to use it when Fee pounces on me after we're done."

Casey glanced from Patrick to Marc. "Who first?"

Patrick assessed Marc's expression and gestured for him to take the lead. "You go ahead, Marc. We've both spent the day playing phone tag. I have the strong feeling we've been barking up the same tree from different vantage points. In which case, my findings will corroborate anything you've turned up."

"Yeah, great minds and former FBI agents think alike," Marc said drily. "But thanks." He turned his attention to the entire team. "First, I tracked down a buddy of mine who was a former Navy doctor. Having served in the military, he'd obviously seen injuries like the one you described Dempsey having. I told him the exact details you provided. His immediate response was to say that it was likely caused by a bomb or ordnance going off in close proximity to his hand." Pausing only to take a swallow of coffee, Marc continued. "After that, I reached out to one of the BU's best bomb techs, who confirmed that, in a training video, he'd seen an interview of someone with an injury matching my description who'd had a detonator explode in his hand."

"That fits," Claire said quietly. "Given all the explosion images I keep getting off the pages Casey gave me—that and a whole lot more—everything you're saying concurs with what I'm sensing."

"Let's cut to the chase," Casey said. "Dempsey's old life was with the IRA. It's crossed all our minds. Now it's taking shape. The problem is we have no proof."

"But a great deal more food for thought," Patrick responded.

Casey's gaze instantly moved to him. "It's your turn. Go."

Patrick bent one knee and crossed his leg over the other. "For some reason, Dempsey naming his two dogs *Pope* and *Martha* just rang an alarm bell and it was really bugging me. Having heard your description of Dempsey's hand, thinking of the fact that he left Ireland during the Troubles, I came to the same conclusion: IRA. I needed to connect the two things. So I spent the day reaching out to FBI colleagues I had—some retired and some current—who worked terrorism in the eighties, in those days through the Intelligence Division. The Counterterrorism Division wasn't created until the late nineties. Are any of you familiar with the Omagh bombing?"

"Of course," Marc said. Comprehension began to dawn in his eyes.

A few head shakes, and Emma said, "I was born in the nineties."

A corner of Patrick's mouth lifted. "Ouch."

"Sorry," she replied sheepishly.

"Don't be. All of you are too young to have seen the original TV footage or read the news at the time."

"I saw the documentary that was made about it," Casey said. "But I'm clearly missing something. So go on."

Patrick recounted the facts: that on August fifteenth, 1998—four months after the signing of the Belfast Agreement—a dissident republican car bomb exploded in the market town of Omagh, County Tyrone, Ireland. Twenty-nine people were killed.

"How horrible," Claire murmured.

"Yes, it was." Patrick's expression was sober. "The terrorists phoned the Ulster Television newsroom with a warning of the bomb's location and the time it would be detonated." A pause. "The callers used the Real IRA code word. It was Martha Pope."

A long silence filled the room.

"Shit," Marc broke the silence to say. "Dempsey is openly celebrating an IRA terrorist attack."

"Yeah, he's a real prick." Ryan looked like he wanted to punch something or someone.

Casey was assimilating all she'd just learned. "The problem is that none of this is hard evidence. The use of Martha Pope certainly labels Dempsey an IRA sympathizer, but that's still a leap from being an active IRA member—even with the likelihood that a detonator exploded in his hand."

Ryan swore under his breath. "It's urgent that I figure out who this son of a bitch really is. Because Niall Dempsey sure as hell isn't his real name." He pushed back his chair. "Are we done here? Because I'm itching to get back to my lair. I had just come up with an avenue to pursue. It's not going to be quick. But if it works, we'll have our answers."

Casey responded in a word: "Go."

28

Ryan leaned forward in his chair and started the process.

"Yoda," he summoned his AI system.

"Ready, Ryan," was the response.

"You have the photo of Niall Dempsey I uploaded to the server."

"I do."

"I want you to run a reverse age progression on him. Search all the Irish newspapers, primarily the ones in Northern Ireland. He's now fifty-five. Focus on 1980 and 1981, when he was fifteen and sixteen. Only go back as far as 1978, when he was thirteen, and stop when you hit 1985, when he was twenty. That's the year he immigrated to New York and when Niall Dempsey suddenly came into being."

"Very good," Yoda said. "Are there any other parameters I should adhere to when searching for a match?"

Ryan pursed his lips thoughtfully. He had to narrow this down as best he could, otherwise Yoda's search could take days. "For now, let's stick with sports references in local newspapers. Concentrate on pre-sixteen hurling championships. That's a big deal in Ireland, so I'm counting on there being team photos of the winners and maybe an article to go with them, or even just a list of names from, let's say, left to right."

"I'll begin immediately."

"Good," Ryan replied. "And keep me posted along the way."

***

Hours passed.

It was after one in the morning when Claire showed up at the lair.

The door was partially ajar and she peeked inside, scanning the room to see if they were alone.

Ryan had just finished his umpteenth update from Yoda and was feeling frustrated and impatient. He dragged both hands through his hair, swearing under his breath.

"Bad time?" Claire asked.

He glanced up and swiveled around in his computer chair. "I suck at waiting," he replied.

"That's not exactly a surprise."

"Yeah, I guess not." Ryan eyed her more closely and frowned. "You look like hell."

"Thank you." Claire stepped inside the room. "Where's Fiona?"

"Upstairs, supposedly asleep, which I highly doubt is what she's doing." He took in Claire's tear-stained cheeks and visible agitation. Judging by her question and her ragged appearance, he realized that she wanted it to be just the two of them.

He also realized this was no booty call.

"It's just us," he said simply. "Even Yoda's tied up now. He's got a major assignment to tackle. So lock the door and have a seat." He paused as Claire did just that, settling herself on the well-worn futon that they'd made use of many times, for far more pleasurable reasons than the one she was dealing with now.

"I probably should have gone to Casey." Claire gave a baffled shake of her head. "It's absurd that I'm coming to you when you doubt everything I say. But here I am, nonetheless." She gave Ryan a belated quizzical look. "You said you're working on something with Yoda. Are you deep into finding something out about Dempsey? If so, I'll go radio silent and pray that you come up with answers."

"It's still a work in process and Yoda and I haven't turned up anything—yet. But that could change at any given moment. And by the way, I don't doubt everything you say. I just question it. That's the way my mind works."

Ryan rose and went over to sit beside Claire, wrapping an arm around her and pressing her head to his shoulder. "You're freaked out. What happened?"

"It's what keeps on happening. Every time I touch those pages Casey gave me, I sense death, explosions, gunfire. I see bodies, bloodied and mutilated." She paused. "And I see silver bullets fired with precision, one after the other. Like people are being targeted and killed. And just now"—she shuddered—"I got a quick glimpse of Rose with terror on her face, backing away from something... somebody..."

"Do you sense that Niall is there?" Ryan asked quietly.

He felt Claire shrug against his arm. "I don't see him. I don't sense him. I don't know. And it makes no sense. Rose wasn't shot. Her shop wasn't blown up. And yet the aura of danger is so acute it's painful. But it's like a parallel line drawn next to the other connections."

"Maybe what you're sensing is Dempsey's past and present traveling side by side but not overlapping?"

Claire looked up at Ryan in surprise. "That was very astute or, dare I say, intuitive."

Rather than being irked, Ryan felt a grin tug at his lips. "Maybe you're rubbing off on me... which is an image I kind of like..."

His answer was a small smile and a slight easing of the tension that was knotting Claire's shoulders. "I think that's why I came down here instead of going to our boss. You have a way of taking me down a notch. I have nothing concrete to share, but I'm a total mess from this." She raked a hand through her hair, which was damp with perspiration. "I actually had to race to the bathroom at one point, because I knew I was going to be sick. So much blood... so many bodies... so much death..."

"Sh-h-h." Ryan kissed the top of her head. "Try to let it go—at least long enough to regroup."

He eased away from her and stood up, handing her the blanket that was draped over the back of the futon and then heading over to a cluttered tabletop that contained mostly crumpled granola bar wrappers plus a few basic kitchen-like essentials.

"I'm about to do the unthinkable," he announced. "And that's to make you a cup of herbal tea. You're going to drink it and lie down for a while. I'll keep working and I'll wake you if I come up with anything."

"Thank you," Claire said softly.

"No problem. But if you ever tell anyone I poured you anything other than wine, I'll deny it."

"Your secret is safe." Claire inclined her head, more in interest than in question. "Do you even know how to brew herbal tea?"

He gave her a horrified look. "I said *make* not *brew*. I'll use my coffee pot to produce hot water and rip open one of those packets I keep stored for you down here. I hope brewing tea isn't a deal breaker."

This time, Claire actually laughed. "No, I can handle the tea brewing. Just don't expect me to chug a beer from that scary-looking machine your father has."

"A kegerator. It's a fridge for his Guinness. My dad has it rigged up to dispense draft beer straight from the attached faucet. It's the real deal. But not to worry. I won't suggest that he brings you into the fold. My mom's not a big beer drinker, either."

"Ryan." Claire stopped him before he'd filled up the coffeemaker. "You and your dad need to talk. He's ready to let the past go. You need to be, too."

That came out of left field, and Ryan slowly lowered the coffeepot, staring straight ahead as he processed Claire's words. "Is that a guess or some kind of metaphysical awareness?"

"It's a gut feeling. A strong one. Once this case is solved, I want you to sit down with him. Speak your mind. Listen to what he has to say." A small pause. "Do it for me."

The significance of Claire's stipulation wasn't lost on Ryan. *Do it for me.* That took things to a whole new level.

Surprisingly, he didn't feel boxed in. He felt... touched.

He turned to meet her gaze. "It's that important to you?"

"Yes." She kept her gaze locked on his, clearly aware that she was pushing boundaries that were still delicately being formed. "It's essential for you and for your dad. You need emotional closure, and so does he." She wet her lips with the tip of her tongue, and Ryan could see she was weighing her next words. "I'm asking this of you because I care."

Ryan got it. She was stripping away a layer of her own emotional protection, giving back what she was asking for.

"Okay, Claire-voyant." He winked at her, intentionally lightening the moment. "If it means that much to you, I'll give it a try. But no promises. Years have passed and the differences run deep." He resumed his task of tea making.

"Fair enough." Claire settled herself on the futon and tucked the blanket around her. "I'll drink my tea and try very hard to relax. But promise to wake me if you find something."

"You'll be hearing a lot of back-and-forth between Yoda and me for a while. But when this research of mine pans out, you can bet your life I'll wake you. Hell, I'll scream the house down until everyone comes running. Trust me."

"I do."

***

Niall lay on his back in bed, his arms folded behind his head.

Tomorrow, while Blythe was meeting with Fiona, he had to get down to Kelly's and talk to Donald. He'd pushed the other crisis situation in his life away for the past few days because of all he needed to accomplish, but it was time to take precautions. His past may have been erased, but his sharp instincts hadn't.

Someone was following him, keeping eyes on all his activities. And that someone had to be Cobra.

Clearly, the traitorous bastard didn't plan to kill him right away. Which meant he wanted to get his hands on the hoard first. It would be the ultimate victory, getting hold of the treasure Niall held dear and then finishing what he'd started thirty-five years ago.

Niall thought of Kevin, bleeding to death in his arms, and he gritted his teeth so tightly his jaw nearly snapped.

Oh, someone will definitely die, you sick fuck.

But it isn't going to be me.

***

It was nearly dawn when Yoda issued his final report.

Ryan scrutinized it, leapt up, and pumped the air, shouting, "*Yes-s-s!* I've got you, you miserable prick."

Claire scrambled to her feet, all semblance of restless sleep having vanished. "What is it? What did you find?"

"Exactly what we need." Ryan was practically vibrating with excitement. "Yoda, start a search with that name. I want anything and everything that turns up, starting with birth records and working your way up."

"I've initiated the search, Ryan," Yoda responded.

"Good." Ryan pressed the Contact All button on his phone, simultaneously grabbing Claire's hand and pulling her toward the door. "Full team meeting," he said into his cell. "*Now.*"

***

The conference room was full in under five minutes, everyone at their seats around the table. No one even stopped to grab a cup of coffee, despite how badly they needed it, given the whole team had been pulling yet another all-nighter at the brownstone and were craving the caffeine.

Casey had stopped on the third floor, checking to make sure Fiona had dozed off, which, fortunately, she had. So there would be no interruptions. Ryan's urgent tone had left no room for distractions.

Emma was the last one in, and she automatically locked the door behind her and scooted over to the table. No chocolate croissant jokes were made.

"Go ahead, Ryan." Casey didn't waste an instant.

Ryan nodded, gesturing toward the screen of monitors that filled the long wall of the room.

"Yoda, display the visuals," he instructed.

Instantly, two photos appeared on the screen, followed by a third photo, this one with a lengthy caption underneath.

"The first image on the left is, obviously, Niall Dempsey as we know him today," Ryan said. "The second is the same man, as he would look at fifteen years old. Yoda and I created that second image by using a sophisticated reverse-age-progression program. And the third visual is a newspaper clipping—a photo and a caption—originally posted in a local Northern Irish newspaper, dated April twenty-ninth, 1980, but that wound up pretty much everywhere for reasons you'll understand right away."

As he spoke, Ryan studied the last image, ensuring it was entirely visible for the team to see and to read. He was very pleased by the clarity of both the article and the photo. Obviously, Yoda had visually enhanced them to reduce the graininess.

"What you're seeing was captured on film during a hurling competition between two winning teams vying for the pre-sixteen hurling championship," Ryan clarified in order to save time. "Just so there's no confusion, the *pitch* is what the Irish call what we call the *field*. Read. Look at the photo. You'll see why this went viral *and* why it gives us exactly what we need."

The team complied.

A huge fight broke out on the pitch, the caption read. *One lad struck another with his hurling stick. The savage blow cracked his skull and nearly killed him. But in an astonishing show of skill, the lad who was struck, blood flowing over his right eye, still scored and won the championship before collapsing. What a tough kid, that Sean Donovan!*

The photo of a bloodied but triumphant boy, hoisted on the shoulders of his teammates, was the same boy as the fifteen-year-old Niall Dempsey in Ryan's second visual.

"Damn," Marc hissed between his teeth.

Casey pulled her gaze away from the monitors. "We've got a name. Finally. Great work, Ryan." She gave him a questioning look. "I'm sure you've initiated a search for all things related to Sean Donovan."

"Yoda's been on it since I left the lair. By the time he's finished, we'll know more about Donovan than he remembers about himself." Ryan was still flying on the significance of these results. "I'm sure we'll get hits left and right. You can bet a crazy-ass kid like this will have a record. I'm hacking his juvies. Whatever crimes he committed as an adult will be easy to dig up. Between the two, I'll find an IRA connection. We're going to nail this scumbag to the wall."

"It's time for me to talk to Aidan," Marc said. "He'll get the DNA test run on the cup and the napkin. He'll also make calls that have to be made. Getting search results is imperative, Ryan, so work fast."

"That's the only way I know how to work," Ryan replied. "Tell Aidan we'll have Donovan's life story in an hour, two tops."

"I'll tell him."

Casey's mind had been racing, and she now gave voice to her thoughts. "Once Ryan finds an IRA connection, which we all know he will, I have no choice but to bring Hutch into the fold, even if the end results mean tipping our hand to the NYPD. I'll do whatever I can to prevent that from happening, including reminding Hutch that the only concrete proof we have on Dempsey is his IRA connection—nothing that labels him a suspect in FI's current investigation. But I can't make any promises. You know how ethical Hutch is. But the point is moot. If Dempsey is an IRA terrorist, the Irish government will want him. It's beyond illegal for us to sit on our findings."

Marc's gaze was steady. "That's one of the reasons I want to talk to Aidan. You'll call Hutch the minute Ryan turns up what we need. But the avenue I'm discussing with Aidan—let's just say I can make Hutch's job easier."

"Can you call Aidan now?" Casey asked. "I realize it's not even dawn, but…"

"I can call him."

"Do it."

29

Marc locked his office door, propped his hip on the edge of his desk, and made the call.

His brother answered on the first ring. "Your hours are getting to be as bad as mine."

"Yeah, tell me about it. Are you home or elsewhere in the world?"

"Home. Abby's preschool play is later today. She's playing the Little Engine That Could. I'll be in the front row, wearing out my phone battery taking a twenty-minute video and whatever before-and-after pictures she'll stand still long enough for me to take."

Marc chuckled, visualizing his precocious four-and-a-half-year-old niece taking center stage and wowing the audience. He adored the little hellion, and as for Aidan, Abby had him wrapped so tightly around her little finger that the string might snap.

"I'm sorry I'll miss it," Marc said ruefully. "If I could get out of here for an hour, I would."

"I know." Aidan paused. "Which means FI is in the middle of something big and you need my help."

"Not just yours. Philip's, too." Philip Banks was one of the Zermatt Group's core four. He was British, retired MI6, and now either working a case for Zermatt or being wined and dined by beautiful women in an enviable life only Philip could make happen. It helped that he looked like a fiftysomething James Bond.

"I'm listening."

Marc laid it out for his brother, sticking to the international aspects of the case so as not to break client privilege—other than to mention Dempsey's name, which was necessary.

Aidan whistled. "Niall Dempsey. That's a pretty big fish."

"Uh-huh."

"And he's obviously a threat to one of your clients, or you wouldn't be probing the IRA connection."

Marc fell silent.

"Got it." Aidan didn't push any more than Marc did when their roles were reversed. "I can get you reliable DNA testing results in less than two hours. And Philip can connect up with his contacts at MI5 and at the Police Service of Northern Ireland, ask the right questions, and put a bug in the right ears."

"I need Philip to do that now, as in yesterday." Marc was pushing this where it needed to go. "I realize we're doing this ass-backwards, because Ryan is still digging up the proof we need connecting Donovan with the IRA. But Philip has to finagle things ahead of time and find out if Irish law enforcement has an open case file on Sean Donovan. I'm willing to bet they do, even if the case has gone cold. We've got to be ready to have them connect with the FBI's London legal attaché as soon as we have Ryan's results, while we simultaneously hand those results over to our FBI contact ASAP. If we ask for his help, he has to work this case as an assist to an open international case. He can't open a file himself, not when the DNA wasn't processed through the proper channels and not without breaking way too many bureau rules."

"Makes sense," Aidan agreed. "And knowing Ryan, he'll have a full criminal dossier on Donovan by the time you and I hang up, ready to pass on to me and to your FBI guy. I'll call Philip now. You get that coffee cup and napkin over to me. I'll have word back from Philip and the DNA results in your hands before I leave for Abby's play."

***

Nine a.m. brought with it a flurry of activity.

At the same moment that Aidan's messenger was placing the DNA results in Marc's hands, Ryan burst upstairs from his lair, having just bellowed into his phone that it was time for the team to reconvene. He reached the first floor and spotted Marc, who was opening the envelope.

"Call Aidan," he said. "Tell him I just uploaded a shitload of stuff tying Sean Donovan to the IRA, and that I sent him a link to the file. He needs to look at it while we're having our meeting."

"Done." Marc was already whipping out his cell, ready to catch Aidan before he walked into Abby's preschool. "And you tell Casey to call Hutch and have him on standby."

"What's going on?" Fiona walked out of the den and grabbed Ryan's arm as he rounded the second-floor landing and turned to head to the conference room.

He shook himself free. "We're close, Fee. So don't screw things up by going into a whole drama queen speech about why you want to be in this meeting. You're not invited. Deal with it if you want us to solve this crime."

Fiona blinked in surprise at the uncharacteristic sharpness of Ryan's order and quickly chose not to argue. "Okay. I'll hang out in the den. But as soon as I can know anything—"

"You will."

Ryan blew by her and beat everyone else into the conference room.

"Yoda, call up everything we turned up and display it on the screen," he instructed.

"Yes, Ryan."

Half turning, Ryan looked at Casey as she sprinted in and headed for her seat, scanning the monitors even as she did.

"Call Hutch and tell him to expect us to contact him within the hour," Ryan instructed. "He'll have what he needs and then some, given whatever Aidan is doing."

Casey punched in Hutch's private line and spoke quietly into the phone before disconnecting the call. "He didn't ask questions. But he's waiting to hear from us." She turned to the rest of the team, who'd hurried in behind her and who were all studying the monitors. "Everyone, sit," she instructed.

"I've got the DNA results." Marc waved the open envelope in the air as he took his seat. "All the i's are dotted and the t's crossed. It'll be admissible for our purposes."

"Good." Casey turned her attention back to the wall of screens. "Looks like we have plenty to discuss."

Ryan nodded. "We sure as shit do. Yoda, run us through this."

Yoda complied. "On your left, you'll see a full personal profile on Sean Donovan."

The team's eyes all shifted in that direction and read:

Sean Donovan
Born: 12 August, 1965. Town of Lurgan, County Armagh, Northern Ireland. Moved to Dundalk, County Louth, Republic of Ireland in 1976.
Mother: Margaret Donovan
Father: Unnamed
Siblings: One brother, Kevin. Again, Mother, Margaret Donovan. Again, father unnamed. Born 3 September, 1967. Died: 28 February, 1985.

The profile showed Sean's birth certificate and driver's license and went on to list the schools he'd attended, the hurling teams he'd won championships on, even the details of his report cards—including his poor grades and equally poor behavior.

"Stop or go on?" Ryan asked the team.

"Stop." Casey held up a palm. "Look at the date of Kevin Donovan's death. It's the same year his big brother left Ireland and became Niall Dempsey. I keep remembering how emotional Dempsey got when he spoke of losing the person closest to him. Maybe that person wasn't just a friend. Maybe that was his brother."

"Good catch." Ryan's tone said he'd already made that connection. "I dug up all I could on Kevin Donovan's death. It was the result of a shooting, but where it took place and under what circumstances are suspiciously omitted. However, based on what I turned up on the funeral attendees, it sure as hell looks like he had an IRA funeral. And in reference to what you just said, interestingly, I see no record of Sean Donovan having attended."

"He was forced to take off beforehand," Patrick concluded aloud. "That means he was tied to what had to be an IRA-related shooting and had to flee Ireland fast. That had to cut deep—another reason for the pained reaction Casey saw."

"I'm not finished poking around into Kevin Donovan's history," Ryan said. "Including if his brother was on the scene when he died. But I don't want to diverge—not yet. It's Sean himself, not Kevin, who we need immediate answers on. So let's get to the legal stuff Yoda and I turned up."

Casey nodded. "Please continue, Yoda."

"Yes, Casey," Yoda replied. "On the next monitor to your right, you'll see Sean Donovan's juvenile records. Twice he was arrested on auto thefts. Twice he was detained under the suspicion of being an IRA lookout."

"IRA block kids," Ryan clarified. "They literally stood at the end of the streets where the IRA was conducting illegal activities and kept watch. Any sign of the RUC—the Royal Ulster Constabulary—and those block kids' jobs were to bang trash can lids as loud as they could to warn their counterparts to take off."

Marc's eyes narrowed as he studied the monitor. "Detained," he repeated. "No IRA-related juvie arrests?"

"Nope." Ryan scowled. "Just grabbed and questioned. No proof, no arrests."

"Then it's of no help."

"Be patient." Ryan indicated the rest of the monitors. "Go on, Yoda."

"Everything else you see on the monitors pertains to Donovan's record as an adult," Yoda reported. "As you can see, he was picked up five times for questioning along with others who were known IRA leaders. His name is consistently linked to them all."

"Still not proof," Marc said.

"The arrests you're looking for are next, Marc," Yoda advised him. "Sean Donovan was arrested on two separate occasions for car thefts in which the cars were used for IRA crimes. And last, and most significant, he was arrested for and found guilty of aggravated assault, along with two other men, in what was officially labeled an IRA crime."

"Bingo." Marc gestured at Casey. "You and I have to talk to Hutch on speaker phone. I got what I needed from Aidan—and I'm not referring only to the DNA test. There are things Hutch has to know up front—things that will allow him to do what has to be done."

"Does that include killing me?" Casey asked dryly.

"Hopefully not. Not if he hears me out."

***

Casey and Marc went into her private office and made the call.

Hutch listened very quietly as Casey filled him in on everything the FI team had learned in the past few hours.

"Did you already know that Dempsey had an IRA connection?" he asked when she'd finished, his voice steely.

"I had my suspicions," she replied with total candor. "But nothing to back up those suspicions—not until this morning when Ryan filled our entire wall of monitors with the information he'd found. But before I even read the details, I called and asked you to be on standby."

She paused, instinctively assuming her role as the president of FI even though she knew Hutch would definitely explode.

"Please, Hutch, I don't want the NYPD to be privy to this information. We still have no proof that Dempsey is involved in the murder case threatening Fiona. Is there any way…?"

"Dammit, Casey." He didn't surprise her with his reaction, and she could hear his fist strike the desk. "The man is a terrorist. He lives in Manhattan and is now a viable suspect in a New York City homicide. There's no legal way I can sit on this—"

"Yes, Hutch, there is," Marc interrupted to say. "If you keep the federal case file restricted, you limit access to all the reports, letters, etc. to those people you designate."

"Cut the crap, Marc," Hutch snapped, clearly livid. "I don't have a case file, nor can I open one. Nothing you're passing along to me was conducted using FBI personnel and FBI procedures. You're former bureau. You might not follow the rules anymore, but you sure as hell know them."

"You're right. I do. Which is why I'm asking you to listen to me for a minute. There's a legitimate way you can handle this through proper FBI channels."

"I'd love to hear it."

Marc began by telling Hutch about what his research had turned up about Niall's hand injury, as well as Patrick's figuring out the Martha Pope connection.

"So you did know he was IRA."

"Patrick and I were pretty sure of it, yes. Casey knew only that we were checking out some leads. Any suspicions she had were purely that."

"Go on."

"I jumped the gun before Ryan supplied the proof. Suffice it to say I have connections overseas, including a former MI6 agent." Marc made no mention of Aidan, Philip, or the Zermatt Group. "He has friends at both the Police Service of Northern Ireland and MI5. He made some calls for me and found out there's an open case file on Sean Donovan. After thirty-five years, the case has gone cold, but Irish law enforcement would jump at the chance to resurrect it."

"Which they could do if an agency across the pond could provide them with something tangible." Hutch was starting to calm down. "You're suggesting I work this case as an assist."

"Yes. That way, you can not only work on that case file, you can legally interact with the Irish authorities via the bureau's legal attaché in London—who, incidentally, will be contacting you today since she's already been apprised of the situation by MI5."

Hutch absorbed that unexpected piece of information. "You've certainly been busy."

"That's my job. Now you can ethically do yours."

"There was no DNA testing thirty-five years ago. Does the PSNI—which was then still the RUC—have something of Donovan's we can use to determine a match?"

"They do. It was already obtained out of the evidence vault for testing."

"So, I provide them with your test results, via our Legat, and they do the comparison."

"Uh-huh. At which point you can legally collaborate with them to bring Sean Donovan, a.k.a. Niall Dempsey, to justice." Marc paused, surprising Casey by leaning forward and pressing the mute button.

"I had a quick talk with Aidan before joining the team in the conference room," he told her. "That's the only reason I didn't share this next part with you in advance. Sorry."

Before Casey could respond, Marc unmuted the conversation.

"A quick update," he said. "An anonymous source at MI5 just passed along some intel on Sean Donovan. Evidently, he was an IRA sniper—an ace who was used for high-level hits. His real name was known only by IRA leaders. His code name was Silver Finger, and that name alone made the RUC shake in its boots. He was at the top of his game when he was ID'ed and ambushed by an RUC informant, at which time he abruptly disappeared off the grid."

"Which is when he flew to New York and became Niall Dempsey. No wonder Irish law enforcement wants him back so badly." Hutch was back to his usual take-charge, level-headed self. "The DNA match will be quick. After that, I can put surveillance on Dempsey, make sure he doesn't flee." A pause. "And, yes, I can keep this case restricted so it doesn't screw up your investigation—under one condition. If you should find even a shred of evidence that Dempsey is involved in any ongoing criminal activity on US soil—including the murder of Rose Flaherty—you apprise me ASAP. At which time I'll lift any case restrictions and, with regard to your investigation, provide full disclosure to the NYPD. That's as far as I'm willing to bend. Do we understand each other?"

"We do," Casey replied, not happy with Hutch's tone but knowing full well it was warranted. Still and all, she aimed for the impossible. "I don't suppose FI can be part of that restricted list?"

A sharp intake of breath. "Casey, don't push me."

"I had to try."

Hutch sounded *almost* as if he were biting back a grin. "Yeah, Madame President, I know."

30

It was almost noon and the Basilica at Saint Patrick's Old Cathedral was quiet.

Slowly and painfully, James left the columbarium and the niche that held Rose's cremains. He dabbed at the tears in his eyes with a handkerchief and made his way inside the magnificent chapel to bow his head and say a prayer for his dear departed friend.

Peter waited respectfully at the entranceway doors. His car was parked right outside, thanks to the handicap parking permit Niall had given him to hang in the window. Parking in the city sucked. And Professor Blythe was in no physical shape to hike to the closest garage, whether that permit was legally obtained or not.

As soon as Peter saw the professor lift his head and reach for his cane, he turned away and pulled out his cell phone, pressing Niall's number.

"We're finished here," he informed his friend.

"Good," Niall replied. "Fiona McKay's security detail is outside the offices of Forensic Instincts, which means that's where she is. I'm texting you the address. Please take the professor there after he calls her and arranges a meeting."

"She'll see him right away?"

"Immediately—as soon as she hears his name."

"Done." Peter disconnected the call. Niall had told him enough to know who their target was and where Niall wanted Blythe to meet with her. Fortunately, the scenario was working in their favor.

He turned and walked forward to assist the professor back to the car.

***

The FI team was in the conference room, discussing the unsurprising but unpleasant visit they'd just had from Detectives Alvarez and Shaw, who were "just checking in" to see if FI had anything new to report.

"You don't think Hutch said something, do you?" Ryan asked.

"Not a prayer." Casey gave an adamant shake of her head. "Hutch is a man of his word. If he said he wouldn't contact the NYPD, then he didn't."

"It was a fishing expedition," Patrick said. "Plus a chance to needle us. Sort of like: 'Hi, remember us? We're watching your every move.' They're not going to let up, so expect more visits until we solve this case."

Marc nodded, clearly unbothered by the detectives' drop-in. "So let's solve it. The IRA facet of the investigation is now in federal hands. Time to turn our attention back where it belongs—to Rose's murder, to the threat to Fiona, and to finding that hoard before the killer does."

"Why don't we stop calling him 'the killer'?" Emma gave an impatient wave of her hand. "We all *know* that it's Dempsey."

"All signs point to him, yes," Casey replied. "But until we have proof, he's still a suspect."

"A scary one," Claire murmured.

"Which is why Patrick is now having him watched." Casey was clearly ready to move on from the IRA connection. "Plus, he'll soon be under FBI surveillance. So let's concentrate on what he wants and what we have: the tapestries. The closer we get to figuring out the location of that hoard and moving in on it, the more likely Dempsey will do something reckless in order to beat us to the punch. And when he does, we'll be ready to stop him. We'll bring him down and find the McKay treasure all in one fell swoop."

Claire rose to her feet. "I'll collect the tapestry panels from my yoga room and bring them down to the conference room so we can view them through fresh eyes." She took a few steps, then paused. "We should bring Fiona back into the fold in our analysis. And not only because she's jumping out of her skin. But because her insights are invaluable."

"Absolutely." Casey nodded. "This isn't a closed team meeting. Fiona has been part of this aspect of the investigation from the start. Stop by the den and ask her to—"

Casey was interrupted by a loud banging on the conference room door.

"It's me," Fiona announced urgently from the other side of the door. "I have to see you guys *right now*."

Claire walked over and yanked open the door. "Are you all right?" she asked, concern knitting her brows.

"I'm better than all right. I'm psyched!" Fiona waved her cell phone at them as if it held the answers to their questions. "I just got a call from Professor Blythe. The reason you couldn't reach him is because he was flying to New York to pay his respects to Rose. And now he wants to meet with me to discuss the research he was helping her with and the tapestries."

The entire team looked stunned.

"That's either perfect timing or a very abrupt and bizarre coincidence," Casey said. Reflexively, she shot an inquisitive look at Marc.

"Let's assume it's the former," he replied. "Because I don't believe in bizarre coincidences, and certainly not abrupt ones."

"Nor do I," she replied. "The man is an expert on hoards. Could he have followed up on Rose's research, figured out both the existence and the value of this particular hoard, and then decided to fly to New York to help Fiona—motive being he could be part of the discovery and be handsomely compensated for his efforts?"

"He's a good man," Claire said softly. "He's not driven by greed. And he's deeply mourning the loss of his friend."

Casey accepted Claire's intuitive statement without question. "Then let's not dissect possible ulterior motives—at least not until we've met the man." She turned to Fiona. "Ask Professor Blythe to come to FI's offices. That way, he can not only help you, but he can meet with us all. He needs to know that our knowledge base has grown dramatically since your original research request to Rose."

"I know. I already asked him to come here. I told him I'd hired FI to protect me and to help the police solve Rose's murder. He's on his way."

***

Any thought that Professor Blythe was insincere in his affection for Rose or duplicitous about his commitment to helping Fiona decipher the tapestry panels for honorable reasons vanished the instant Casey met him. Not only met him but looked him straight in the eyes—eyes that were damp from having just visited the columbarium that housed Rose's cremains.

The slight, elderly man emanated nothing but kindness and wisdom, and Casey took an immediate liking to him. He introduced himself and Thomas Murphy, his driver and physical aide, and shook everyone's hand in turn, simultaneously apologizing for his emotional state.

"You've suffered a tragic loss," Casey said. "I'm so sorry."

"Thank you, my dear."

He turned to Ryan and tilted his head quizzically. "McKay. Is that a coincidence?"

"No." A corner of Ryan's mouth lifted. "Fiona is my younger sister. Prepare yourself for a deluge of questions fired at supersonic speed."

The moment of levity was perfectly timed, and James chuckled. "From what Rose said, I'd expect no less. In fact, I welcome it." He turned to Fiona, the emotion back in his gaze. "Rose told me how special you are. I'm sure you miss her as much as I do."

Fiona nodded, sadness flickering across her face. "Terribly so. But her Mass and service were a wonderful tribute to her. I wish you could have been there."

"As do I." He swallowed hard. "I had to gather the strength and the funds to make this trip. I just couldn't do it fast enough—"

"You're here now, and that's all that matters," Fiona interrupted quickly, sensing that the poor man was going to break down.

"I appreciate your kindness." He squeezed her hand. "That she's gone is painful enough. But that someone murdered her…" Again, he swallowed, shaking his head in noncomprehension.

This time it was Fiona who squeezed his hand. "I know," she murmured. "But this incredible team you just met is going to find her killer."

James cleared his throat and turned to Casey. "You're private investigators," he said. "I'm afraid that's all I know."

"We'll fill you in." Casey gestured toward the first-floor conference room. Because of its larger size, the main conference room had already been set up, but having noted both the professor's cane and his frail condition, Casey had abruptly changed plans. "Let's get settled and then we can talk."

James murmured his assent, and "Thomas" stepped forward to assist him down the hall.

"Marc, can you and Patrick show the gentlemen down to the small conference room and set up the tables to accommodate the tapestries?" Casey asked.

"Absolutely." Marc understood instantly, as did Patrick, who joined Marc at the head of the group.

"Please," he said. "Follow us."

Once the professor had walked far enough away to be out of earshot, Casey pulled Emma and Claire aside. "Emma, please bring down the breakfast tray. I'll set up the JURA and make Professor Blythe whatever he wants to drink. And, Claire, please get the tapestries."

Without question, both women hurried upstairs.

Soon after, everyone was settled on the leather tub chairs and love seats in the smaller conference room. Marc had moved the large oval coffee table closer to the love seat where Professor Blythe sat and put an additional table beside it. Between the two, all the tapestry panels could be spread out and viewed.

"Thomas" had been escorted to a comfortable interviewing room adjacent to the conference room. Emma made sure he had ample refreshment and a stack of reading material, although he'd assured her he had phone calls to make and work to do on his iPad. She then joined the others, shutting the door behind her.

Peter waited until he heard the telltale click of the conference room door having closed.

Then he set aside his plate and his cup and came to his feet. He didn't want the piss-poor coffee anyway. What he wanted was a real drink, actually a few. But there'd be time for that later. Right now, he had a job to do. He had to assume that Niall hadn't counted on this PI team being included in whatever Fiona McKay was consulting with the professor about. Plus, Niall couldn't be sure that this old man would remember all the details of what now looked to be a major meeting.

The scenario was definitely a monkey wrench in Niall's plan. So it was time for Peter to step in. Whatever these smooth investigators learned, he'd better learn, too.

The brownstone was quiet, reinforcing what Peter had already guessed: that the entire investigative team was closeted in one room, so there was no one out and about and no chance of being spotted.

On that thought, he walked quietly to the closed door and leaned his head against it to listen.

31

Professor Blythe couldn't help but admire the intricate beauty of the tapestry panels before he even began examining the pieces or applying his knowledge to the process. He wiped his spectacles with a handkerchief and then pushed them back on the bridge of his nose as he leaned forward and stared from one exquisitely woven piece to the next.

His gaze settled on the center panel.

"What Rose sent me was an electronic photo of this." He gently touched one edge. "We both needed assistance in the communication—she in taking and sending the photo and I in viewing it. What you young people can do with technology is a mystery to me." He shook his head in wonder. "But I digress. Seeing this in person, studying its detail—it truly comes alive. Fiona, your great-grandmother was an extraordinary artist as well as a gifted storyteller."

"Thank you," Fiona said. "But I really need to understand the story she's trying to tell, not only through the center panel but through all the panels combined. Can you help me?"

He sat back and pursed his lips. "Forgive me for being blunt, but I'd expected this conversation to be strictly between you and me. How much of what we're about to discuss is Forensic Instincts privy to?"

"All of it. Their investigation into Rose's murder includes the significance of the tapestries." Fiona didn't miss a beat. "And before you ask, let me tell you what we already know, or at least what we think we know."

She proceeded to lay out the details: that the tapestry panels joined together in a specific order they had yet to figure out, but that led to a mysterious hoard discovered by her great-grandparents on their property in County Kilkenny—a hoard they'd secretly transported to New York in 1920.

"We know they hid the treasure and want us to find it," she added. "And we've taken a stab at deciphering the meaning of some of the panels. But we don't have your knowledge of Celtic symbols or archeological expertise. And we're floundering."

Professor Blythe's brows had risen. "Not nearly as much as I'd expected you to be. I was only aware of the fact that you'd been researching the tapestries for your new jewelry line. Clearly, you've come a long way since then. In fact, you've answered some questions I myself still had." He folded his hands in his lap. "Do you know why neither your grandparents nor your parents were able to find the hoard, or why your great-grandmother chose to weave the secret into tapestry panels?"

"Yes." Fiona quickly filled him in on the genealogy research Ryan had done.

"That makes sense." James nodded. "All right, it's my turn. Let me supply you with some of the legendary facts of the Valdrefjord Hoard."

"Is that the name of the hoard?" Fiona asked eagerly.

"It is."

"I could find nothing on it," Patrick said. "And I scoured the internet."

"That's because, as you know, hoards are named after the places where they're discovered. And since this treasure was never officially unearthed, it remained unnamed and was referred to only as a vast legendary hoard. To those of us who were passionate about its contents and history, as well as about determining its whereabouts, we referred to it by the name of the town where it was originally stolen—Valdrefjord, now Waterford." James tapped the panel that held the crystal bowl cradled by the lotus. "That would lend meaning to this panel. Clearly, your great-grandmother knew her history."

"The lotus blossoms wrapped around the crystal symbolize the fact that the treasure is hidden, safely nurtured," Claire murmured.

James cocked his head in her direction. "That would be a good supposition."

"Claire doesn't suppose," Fiona said. "She knows. She's a clair-cognizant."

Rather than looking skeptical, the professor looked intrigued. "That must be both a blessing and a curse."

"It is," Claire replied simply.

"You'll have to share some of your other insights with me as we go through this process. In the interim, here's the history I was referring to."

He went on to tell them about the high king of Ireland Cynbel Ó Conaill and how his treasure was stolen in the ninth century during the Viking invasion, during the Battle of Bawncullen.

Fiona hung on to his every word. "Waterford isn't far from Kilkenny," she said. "It would have been reasonable for the Vikings to hide the treasure on what became my great-grandparents' farm in the hopes of returning later to claim it."

"Precisely. Which obviously never happened."

Casey pointed to the panel groupings, arranged the way they'd puzzled them out. "We assumed Fiona's great-grandmother was telling the story in some sort of chronological order. So we put the Irish imagery here." She indicated one area on the coffee table. "And the New York imagery here." She pointed to the section beside it. "Of course, all this is up for interpretation. Plus it leaves us with gaping holes—panels that don't clearly fit into either category."

James pushed his spectacles higher on his nose and leaned forward again, studying the Irish panels one by one. "The farm seems to be self-explanatory; it's where the hoard was found and where the McKays' story began. The stones probably have a double meaning—the farm's landscape and the hoard's contents."

"Do you know what those contents are?" Fiona asked.

"I know there are over two hundred pieces in it, including coins, beads, loose stones, and jewelry, some pieces more valuable than the others."

She gasped. "That many!"

He nodded. "However, as legend has it, the chalice itself is worth a fortune. Although your great-grandmother depicted it in crude form on her tapestry panel—my guess would be as a precaution in case someone outside the family were to see it—the real chalice is solid gold, small, hammered, and hollow, with a fitted lid. Even the stem is hollow in order to accommodate all the small items concealed within." He warmed to his subject. "I've read differing descriptions in my ancient archeological volumes, but they all agree that the chalice has a raised design of Celtic knots and spirals in the body and the lid. One text highlights that the lid has a ruby in the handle with intricate woven gold designs around it. Another source claims that there are gemstones in the base of the chalice, including rubies, emeralds, and sapphires, again with woven designs."

"It sounds exquisite," Fiona breathed.

As she spoke, James's trained eye was captured by the panel featuring the decorative stone carving. "On the subject of chalices... this is fascinating," he murmured. He brought the panel closer to his face. "Are you familiar with the Ardagh Hoard?"

"Yes," Fiona replied instantly. "In fact, I told the FI team about it when we first realized we were dealing with our own hoard. I know the Ardagh Hoard was buried sometime around 900 AD and that there was a chalice among its pieces. I think it was copper. I don't know where it was discovered but I do remember it was found by a couple of kids digging in a potato field."

"County Limerick," James supplied. "And you're correct about everything except the exact composite of the chalice. It's an astonishing work of art. Some consider it to be the most beautiful of all Irish artifacts. It's a mere seven inches tall, nine-and-a-half inches in diameter, and its bowl is four inches deep."

"That's much smaller than I realized."

"Indeed. Yet it consists of three hundred fifty-four parts, six metals, and forty-eight different designs. Copper is one of those metals, but there's also gold, silver, bronze, brass, and lead." James continued staring at the panel in his hands. "The Ardagh Chalice has many embellishments, but one in particular has always stood out to me: there are two gold medallions, both of them center points on the front and back sides of the chalice."

"And how does that relate to the panel you're looking at?" Marc asked. "Are you saying it's a medallion, not a stone carving?"

"I believe it's both." James ran his finger along the different contours on the panel. "The shorter, separate color yarn that defines the sharp outer angles conveys the appearance of a stone carving. But the actual image is a woven replica of one of the medallions on the Ardagh Chalice." He pursed his lips, intent on his study.

"Like the Ardagh Chalice, the weave is depicting a gold medallion outlined in silver with four silver petals inside. The gold areas have scroll patterns. At points north, south, east, and west, four small cloisonné enameled jewels are represented. And at the center of the medallion is another enamel of an ancient medieval design. I've seen the same design on a famous brooch in the British Museum. Fiona's great-grandmother clearly knew of the Ardagh Chalice. I suspect she was showing you the parallel between the two hoards. Although legend has it that the Valdrefjord Hoard is even more valuable than the Ardagh Hoard."

"It is also a stone carving, though. It actually exists," Claire breathed softly. "It's a decorative wall piece of some kind. Its image keeps flickering in and out of my mind." She gave a slight shake of her head. "I just can't get an insight as to where it is.

"This is all great," Ryan interrupted. "But putting aside symbolic and metaphysical interpretations, we're talking about what sounds to me to be a priceless treasure, one that would prompt an onslaught of people to go after it." He gave James an apologetic look. "I'm sorry, Professor Blythe. It's not that I don't appreciate artistic beauty, it's just that I'm the pragmatist in the family. As much as I enjoy learning about the hoard, I'm more worried that someone is willing to kill for it—and that my sister is the next target."

"No need to apologize," James replied. "You love your sister. That's as it should be. I'm sure your great-grandparents would be proud." He smiled faintly. "But you want me to get back to my analysis so you can find your answers. And so I shall." He lowered his head to study the panels again. "We've covered the farmhouse, the stones, the coins, and the stone carving," he murmured.

"And the Galway sheep not only herald Ireland, but their colors are those of gemstones," Fiona added.

"What about the high Irish crosses?" Casey asked, her puzzle-oriented mind hard at work. "That panel has been bothering me. I realize those are religious symbols, but how do they relate to the hoard? Their colors don't seem to be significant. And why two crosses, one smaller than the other? That panel just doesn't seem to fit. Ryan and Fiona's great-grandmother was a woman with a mission—to lead the family to the hoard. Why weave an entire panel with no connection to the hoard, but just to herald their country, especially when they were fleeing it? Is there some meaning I'm missing?"

"I see your point, but I have no answer." James gave an apologetic shrug. "All I can do is interpret meanings where I see them. I'm afraid the problem-solving is up to you."

"Why don't we skip to areas that fall under your expertise," Marc suggested, cutting to the chase. "The Irish crosses and the New York symbols are our problem. So is this long, dark corridor lit solely by torches, since I see no symbols woven on it. Let's get to the others. Also, we have to explore the light at the end of the tunnel symbol that appears repeatedly on all the panels."

Again, James smiled faintly. "Another pragmatist. Very well, I'll try not to digress. Judging by the name you just ascribed to the symbol, I'm guessing Rose was able to pass that information along to Fiona before she… departed."

Fiona produced the two text pages and the Post-it Note Rose had sent her. "This is all I know."

A quick perusal. "It's all I know, as well. I considered that the symbol might be figurative—meaning that by finding the hoard, you'd make your way through the darkness and into the light. On the other hand, I considered that the symbol might have a more tangible meaning—that the hoard itself is buried in a place of immense darkness."

"Maybe the meaning is even less abstract than that," Ryan said impatiently. "Maybe the hoard is actually buried in a tunnel. That would explain the corridor panel Marc was talking about."

James looked dubious, but he asked, "There are several large tunnels in New York City, are there not?"

"Large, traffic-jammed ones, yes," Patrick replied. "The Lincoln Tunnel, the Holland Tunnel, and the Midtown Tunnel, for starters. But none of them existed in 1920."

"Plus, we're veering away from the truth." Claire shut the door on that theory. "The concept of a tunnel is significant but not literal."

"Significant how then?" Ryan demanded.

"I don't know." Claire dragged both her hands through her hair. "I just don't know—at least not yet."

"What about this panel?" Emma asked, pointing to the gravestone shaded by the tree. "Does this mean the hoard is in or close by a cemetery? Cemeteries are dark. And is the tree important?"

"Another reference to the Tree of Life," James murmured. "Growth, strength, connection to family. And in this case, with the tree being tall and eclipsing the gravestone, I'd say life triumphing over death, new beginnings triumphing over endings."

He picked up the panel and placed it on his lap. "I must say that this is the panel I was most looking forward to studying. Not because the hoard is necessarily hidden in a cemetery but because the gravestone is being used to discreetly show tiny symbols woven around its arch." He pointed, running his finger around the entire arch.

Casey rose and went to stand behind him, leaning forward, her gaze following the area he was designating. "I assumed they were an embellished border that Fiona's great-grandmother wove into the panel."

"No, they're definitely symbols." James squinted. "You wouldn't by any chance have a magnifying headset or even an old-fashioned magnifying glass?"

Casey shot a questioning glance at Ryan.

"I've got a magnifying headset somewhere in my lair," he replied, half rising. "I'll just have to scrounge around—"

"Don't bother." Fiona jumped up. "It'll take you an hour to find anything in that clutter. I have one. It's with my stuff in the den. Give me two minutes."

She was back in less time than that, shooting an odd glance over her shoulder as she came in. "I think your aide is either restless, bored, or hungry. He was pacing around when I blew by."

Emma stood. "I'll go check. Don't have any great revelations till I get back."

James chuckled. "I'll try not to."

"Here you go." Fiona handed the headset over to James as Emma dashed out the door.

"Excellent." He immediately settled the tool on his head and peered through the lenses at the now-magnified symbols. "Fascinating.

Four symbols in all, three of which are repeated on either side of the arch and a sole one at the top." He placed the panel in the center of the table. "I have old eyes. You all have young ones. I'll describe what I'm seeing, and once you focus on them as symbols and not a random design, you'll be able to view them without the magnification."

"I can do better than that," Ryan said. "Yoda," he instructed, "please display this panel. Zoom in on the archway of the gravestone and follow the professor's descriptions by indicating each symbol he describes."

"Yes, Ryan," Yoda responded.

The poor professor nearly leapt out of his seat. "Who was that?" he asked, his voice shaky.

Claire leaned forward and placed a gentle hand on the professor's forearm. "Yoda is our artificial intelligence member," she said with a smile. "I don't understand him much better than you do. But Ryan built him and he's pretty close to omniscient. He'll make your job easier."

As she spoke, the zoomed image of the arch on the tapestry panel appeared across the broad stretch of monitors covering the far wall, directly across from the love seat where the professor sat.

"See?" Claire urged him to look in that direction.

James removed his headset and blinked in amazement. "It's like magic."

"I think so," Ryan complimented himself.

"Let's get down to business." Casey swiveled her tub chair around, gesturing for the rest of the team to reorient themselves so they were all facing the monitors.

Emma popped back into the room just as everyone had finished resituating themselves. "Mr. Murphy was just stretching his legs," she announced. "He's working on his iPad now." A quick glance at the screens. "What did I miss?"

"Nothing," Claire assured her. "We're about to hear the professor's insights into these symbols."

Emma scooted over and perched behind Casey's chair.

James was still murmuring in disbelief, although he was visibly relieved at the much larger view.

"There's that medallion again," Casey said, eyeing the top of the headstone. "It's the only symbol that's not replicated elsewhere on the arch. So either the stone carving or its similarity to the Ardagh Hoard must be significant."

"I agree," James said.

Patrick's brow was furrowed. "And there's the Waterford bowl with the lotus leaves, one on each side. Another reminder of the name Valdrefjord Hoard, along with the fact that it's hidden away and protected."

Casey's gaze was shifting rapidly, and a puzzled look crossed her face. "What's that odd symbol that also repeats itself on either side of the arch?" She pointed at the symbol, which was three thick lines of different lengths. Two were intersecting at forty-five degree angles. One had a pointed tip; the other was squared off on each end. And bisecting those two lines was the third line, which went straight up and down and had a stubby rectangular shape on top.

"Is this an emblem of some kind? Because that's what it looks like."

"And the vertical image looks like a shovel," Ryan said. "Could that be a reveal about how our great-grandfather buried the hoard? And where? Underground?"

A pensive look crossed James's face, and he stared intently at the symbol. "I've seen that particular symbol before," he murmured as Yoda zoomed in closer. "Fifty years ago, when I was a young man and a newly hired professor teaching art history."

"You remember fifty years ago?" Emma asked, her eyes wide with astonishment. "I can't remember what I wore yesterday."

James chuckled. "I have somewhat of a photographic memory." He paused, deep in thought. "Now the significance… give me a moment."

He let the images come, rolling through his mind like an old movie reel, playing backwards in time.

And suddenly, there it was—total recall.

"Ah!" he exclaimed. "Three images, the basics of a stonemason's tools. A chisel, a straight edge, and a mallet. The emblem is ancient yet current, since those tools haven't changed for centuries."

Fiona frowned. "Why would my great-grandmother weave that symbol into the gravestone arch?"

"To put emphasis on her husband's trade?" Patrick suggested. Even as he spoke, he shook his head. "That would seem to be superfluous, since your family all knew his occupation."

"She's telling us something," Claire said, leaning forward to let her fingers brush against the tapestry panel. "A stonemason, gemstones, a stone carving—they're all related somehow."

"That makes sense," James said. "Now we have to figure out how." He took off his spectacles and rubbed his eyes.

The gesture wasn't lost on Casey. It was obvious the elderly man was getting tired. And she wanted as much of his expertise as possible before her instincts told her it was too much for his health and his strength.

He'd gone back to gazing at the tapestry panel, his mind clearly preoccupied with something he saw. "The final image totally mystifies me. It also appears on either side of the arch." He waited as Yoda zoomed in.

"It's a series of four intersecting lines," Marc noted. "It looks like an asterisk." He squinted. "And there are two vertical wavy lines on either side of the asterisk. What does that symbolize?"

"Nothing I know of," James replied. "Which makes it even more puzzling. Not to sound immodest, but there are few ancient symbols, even obscure ones, that are totally foreign to me. It makes me suspect that Fiona's great-grandmother created her own symbol here."

"Yes." Claire continued to run her fingers over the actual panel. "Not a true symbol, but symbolic. The image is a sum of its parts."

"You have more insight in this case than I do." James's voice was starting to fade, as was he. "I wish I could tell you more."

"You've already told us a great deal, for which we're grateful," Casey said, rising from her chair. "It's been a taxing day for you, and I can see how spent you are. I'll ask Mr. Murphy to take you back to your hotel."

James's nod was reluctant, although his eyes widened when he took out his old-fashioned pocket watch and saw the time. "My goodness, it's after three. I didn't realize we'd been talking for so long."

"The complex analysis you were doing here was far more intense than just talking," Casey amended. "Given how emotionally taxing your morning was and how mentally exhausting your afternoon was, it's no wonder you're so depleted."

"Nevertheless, I apologize for my limited strength. I feel as if there's more I might be able to do for you when I'm rested. May I come back?"

"I'd be so grateful if you would," Fiona replied, her expression torn between compassion for the elderly man and her fervent desire to continue this interpretation session right now. "Please call my cell any time of the day or night."

"I shall." The professor reached for his cane, and Casey helped him rise, signaling Emma with her eyes to go get Mr. Murphy.

Moments later, the aide was helping James walk to the door, simultaneously explaining that his car—along with its handicap permit—was parked right outside FI's offices.

Still, the entire team stood and watched until James had been settled into the comfortable back seat, and with a friendly nod, Thomas had climbed into the driver's seat and eased away from the curb.

"You were right, Claire," Casey said. "He's a good man. Now it's time to take his analysis and do some of our own."

32

Hutch had spent a good chunk of his day researching Niall Dempsey, trying to come up with some telltale evidence that he was currently linked to or funding the Provisional IRA.

He'd come up empty, frustrated, and worried sick about the reality that Casey was focusing her investigation on a probable IRA terrorist.

Sure enough, just as Marc predicted, the FBI's London Legat had contacted him several hours after his conference call with Casey and Marc to say the Police Service of Northern Ireland and MI5 were requesting his assistance in locating Sean Donovan, a.k.a. Silver Finger. The Irish authorities had already set the wheels in motion, having taken the bloodied shirt that belonged to Donovan out of its evidence locker for DNA testing. The results were expected to be in sometime tomorrow. In the interim, Hutch had forwarded the lab results on Niall Dempsey to them so the comparison could be made ASAP.

Hutch had followed all the rules to a tee. He should be pleased. He wasn't. This case involved a lot more than identifying Dempsey and matching him with his real name and the crimes he had committed. That alone couldn't happen fast enough to suit Hutch, so he could be an official part of the investigation.

But he already knew what the results would be. Because he knew Marc, and given what he'd told him and the certainty with which he spoke, FI had all but conclusive evidence that Niall Dempsey was a former IRA assassin.

What was driving Hutch crazy was the fact that—despite his promise to keep the NYPD out of his investigation for now—his every instinct was screaming that that prick was also Rose Flaherty's killer, plus a threat to Fiona McKay.

Which made him a threat to Casey.

What the hell was she opening herself up to this time? How effective could Patrick's security team be when pitted against an acclaimed assassin—a sniper who took people out with one bullet?

And how in God's name could Hutch keep her safe?

He shoved back his chair and rose.

Technically, it was too soon for him to provide FBI surveillance on Dempsey. However, that didn't mean he himself couldn't keep an eye on the man. Yeah, it meant jumping the gun and bending the rules, but when it came to Casey's safety, he'd done that before and he'd doubtless do it again.

No updates would be forthcoming from the UK until tomorrow.

Which freed up the rest of his day.

He knew exactly how he planned to spend it.

***

Peter frowned as he helped the professor settle himself on the sofa in the apartment's living room. The old man had nodded off twice in the car, intermittently muttering aloud about stonemason tools and crisscrossing lines. He was now half-asleep, already lying down and pillowing his head on the cushioned arm of the sofa.

He'd be of no use to Niall now.

"I have to call Mr. Dempsey," James murmured, confirming what Peter already knew. "We're supposed to meet here, now."

Making an executive decision, Peter went over and scooped up a folded blanket, shaking it out and covering the professor with it.

"You're too tired for an in-depth conversation," he said. "An hour or two's wait won't matter. I'll call Mr. Dempsey for you and explain. If he disagrees, I'll wake you so you can meet with him right away. Otherwise, I'll let you sleep. I'll go out and bring back some dinner. By then, you'll feel rested and ready to tell Mr. Dempsey all the details of your discussion."

James nodded, removing his spectacles and placing them on the end table beside him, propping his cane up against it.

"Thank you, Thomas." His lids drooped. "I didn't expect the day to be so draining. Please tell Mr. Dempsey—Niall—that I appreciate his patience."

"I will." Peter was already heading for the front door.

He'd make the call from the hallway and see if Niall wanted to be filled in in person, which Peter would gladly do. But after that, he was heading out to a decent pub to buy himself a couple of pints before picking up the professor's dinner and returning to the apartment to make sure the old man was awake and clearheaded enough to meet with Niall about this insanely valuable hoard.

This assignment was getting more intriguing by the minute.

***

Niall had spent the hours that Blythe was with Fiona at Kelly's, filling Donald in on the fact that he was being watched—unquestionably by Cobra—and arguing about what steps they were going to take.

Donald was furious that Niall hadn't mentioned this before. Jaw tightly clenched, he waved away Niall's protests and began making phone calls, talking to his contacts and hiring the right guys—guys who had the experience and the ability to safeguard Niall and to deal with armed killers.

The whole time Donald was talking, Niall was slamming around and cursing. He'd only given in because he knew Donald was right—he needed this level of protection where it came to Cobra.

That didn't mean his own plan had changed. The minute he figured out the identity of the traitorous tout, he'd find him and put a bullet in his head.

Niall had only been home for a short while when his cell phone rang. He didn't bother looking at the caller ID. The flip phone he'd given the professor was a dinosaur.

"Hello?" he answered.

"It's me," Peter replied. "Your professor is out cold on the sofa. My suggestion, given how much he has to tell you, is that you let him regain his strength. Trust me, he's of no use to you right now."

Niall ingested what Peter said as well as its implications.

"You know what Blythe and Fiona McKay discussed?" he asked carefully.

"I made sure to know. Because it wasn't just Fiona and Blythe. The entire Forensic Instincts team was closeted in there behind locked doors. Whatever the girl was privy to, so were they."

"Shit." As pissed as Niall was, he wasn't surprised. "I had a feeling this might happen. She's probably told Casey Woods and her people everything she knows so they can solve their damn murder investigation and recover what I want." He paused, weighing his next words. "How much did you overhear?"

Peter sighed. "Enough so you can stop keeping me in the dark, mate. I stood outside the door and listened. I only got bits and pieces. But I heard enough to know there's some legendary hoard that's buried here in the city and that there are a bunch of tapestry panels leading to it. It's clearly worth a fortune. Obviously, you want to find it—and not to return it to some Irish museum."

Niall blew out a breath. There were only two people on this earth that he trusted: Donald and Peter. Out of necessity, he'd already told the entire story to Donald. It seemed he was about to have to do the same thing with Peter. There'd been no reason to involve him until now. But circumstances had changed.

"I should have told you sooner," he said. "The truth is I'm still used to counting on no one but myself. Thanks for having my back. Tell me what you heard. I'll fill in the rest later. And of course, I'll share the wealth with you, once the hoard is in my hands."

"I won't lie and say I wouldn't love a portion of that amount of cash. But I'd help you anyway. You know that."

"I do." Niall felt a surge of gratitude and of relief. Not only could he now be open with Peter and ask for his help, but he didn't any longer have to fabricate reasons to supply Peter with money. Even though he still intended to keep the hoard in its entirety rather than selling off its pieces—something Peter probably hadn't thought about—he could still give his friend a seven-figure cash payment for his part in the recovery.

It was a win-win.

"Where are you now?" he asked.

"Right outside the professor's apartment. Do you want me to come up?"

"Yes, right away."

"I'll be there in a minute." Peter chuckled. "But after that, I'm headed to Quinn's for a pint or two before I pick up dinner for the professor. All those hours of eavesdropping gave me quite a thirst."

***

Despite his exhaustion, James found himself tossing and turning on the sofa. His eyelids were heavy and his body ached. But his mind wouldn't shut down. It came as no surprise that he was overstimulated from the hours he'd spent at Forensic Instincts analyzing the symbols on the tapestry panels. He hadn't wanted to leave, not without answers. Partly because of his fascination with finding the Valdrefjord Hoard, but even more so to help Fiona and to aid Forensic Instincts in finding Rose's killer.

Still, pragmatism told him that in order to be of help to them, he needed to recoup his strength. In addition, he needed a clear mind to meet with Niall. And right now, he had neither the strength nor the clear mind.

He pushed himself to a sitting position. He'd make himself something warm and soothing to drink. Then, he'd turn off the end table lamp that Peter had left on for him. He always slept better in a dark room.

After picking up his cane, he made his way into the kitchen and looked around. Niall had gone to the trouble of having everything from Assam tea and a teapot, so James could take authentic Irish tea, to coffee and a coffeemaker, should he prefer that.

He smiled as he saw the apologetically tucked-away boxes of herbal tea. Niall had doubtless left those in the event that James wanted something quick, easy, and relaxing. And in this case, that idea was spot-on. As much as James loved his true Irish tea, he hadn't the strength to start the process of steeping and preparing. He glanced at the boxes of herbal tea, spotted chamomile, and within minutes, was limping his way back to the sofa to enjoy a cup. He draped the blanket across his lap and sipped until he felt the slumbering effects of the tea. Then, he set his teacup down on the coffee table and lay his cane alongside him on the floor. He removed his spectacles and reached over to place them on the end table and to turn off the lamp.

The glittering of metal caught his eye. He pushed his spectacles back on his nose, leaned over, and peered at the floor. A slim object of some kind was wedged between the sofa and the end table.

"What's this?" he murmured.

He worked his fingers down until they closed around the object and he was able to pull it free.

By the light cast by the still-lit lamp, he could see it was a badge of some kind, most likely a cap badge given its construction.

He studied it thoughtfully. White metal that used to have a brass coating, now worn away. Not precious metal but some kind of plating. And an interesting shape—round, but with edges that looked like wings around a seven-sided star.

"Fascinating," he said aloud.

Cobra's cell phone vibrated in his front pocket. He pulled it out and glanced at the screen. Sure enough, it was the surveillance app he'd created—the one linked to the bug he'd planted in the old Irish guy's apartment. No easy feat, given the building security. But as always, he'd found a way around it, coming in through the parking garage under the building. He'd worn a black sweatshirt, with a hood pulled over his head and shielding his face so the camera couldn't catch him.

His surveillance app had opened a window, which meant a conversation of some kind was going on.

Cobra tapped the Listen button.

It seemed the old guy was talking to himself.

And it didn't take him long to figure out the object of his mutterings.

Unaware that he was being monitored, James continued scrutinizing the badge and talking aloud.

"The raised writing is Gaelic," he muttered. "Óglaıġ na hÉıreann." A pause. "Soldiers of Ireland," he translated. "Astonishing. This must date back to the early 1900s. An antique that was dropped by its owner. I must give it to Niall so he can return it."

James turned the badge over in his hands. "Cobra," he mused. Someone had proudly taken the trouble of having the word engraved on the back.

"Perhaps this was a gift." James set the badge down carefully on the end table, yawning as he did. "A half hour," he murmured. "Just to rest. Then I'll call Niall."

He settled himself on the sofa, pulled the blanket over him, and shut his eyes.

Cobra was enraged, as much by his own carelessness as by the old man's discovery.

He'd carried his good luck charm for decades now, ever since he'd killed that MI5 fuck who'd been working undercover in Northern Ireland and had used that cap badge as part of his cover. It had belonged to one of the original uprising leaders in the 1916 Easter Rising, and the MI5 guy had gotten his hands on it, using it as part of his street cred to show the IRA that he was legit. But the IRA had dug deep enough into his cover to make it unravel. Then they'd called on Cobra to do the hit. Hell, he'd been working for the RUC, and the instructions from his handler were to let any RUC source or MI5 undercover agents go and make it look like the information on them was bad. Screw that. The thrill of the kill was too great, and besides, he'd hated the guy anyway. So he'd beaten him senseless, shot him twice behind the ear, and watched him die an agonizing death.

He knew the risk he was taking by keeping the badge as a souvenir—even more so after he'd engraved it with his code name. But it had become a trophy for his most risky kill. No one killed an MI-5 agent and lived to tell about it. No one but him. This was his private medal, his self-bestowed badge of honor. He wasn't letting it go despite the fact that both the RUC and MI5 knew his signature kill, so if they ever got wind of the badge's whereabouts, they'd manage to find him, at which point he'd be a dead man. Besides, he knew the IRA would quietly make him a hero for this hit, and he just couldn't resist the lure of being the focus of so much admiration.

And now, he'd set himself up, stupid shit that he was. He must have dropped the badge when he installed the bug.

He had to get it back.

33

Niall had spent the past few hours trying to relieve his stress by roughhousing with Pope and Martha.

His conversation with Peter had been telling enough for him to know in his gut that Forensic Instincts would take what the professor gave them, combine it with analyses he couldn't generate without having the tapestries, and make inroads toward finding the hoard.

His hoard.

He'd taken precautions to make sure that didn't happen. He'd contacted Donald and asked him to surveil the Forensic Instincts team. He wasn't worried about when one of them went out alone. He was focused on any indication that the team was heading somewhere en masse. Should that happen, he needed to know exactly where they were going. And whether or not it turned out to be a false alarm, he'd follow them.

He glanced at the clock on his mantel. Despite the specifics that Peter had been able to pass along, he'd only heard snatches of the meeting from outside the door, not to mention that his understanding of what he'd overheard was limited. There was only one person who could explain the full extent of what had taken place, as well as what it all meant.

The professor had been asleep long enough. It was time to wake him up so they could talk.

***

Niall glanced both ways as he made his way down the corridor. All was quiet. He reached the professor's apartment door and raised his hand to knock. He frowned when he saw that the door was slightly ajar. Peter would never have made that error.

No sounds coming from inside, so there were no visitors. Which left open the possibility that the professor had gone out.

Why? More unsettling: with whom? Had someone from Forensic Instincts been here to collect the old man while Peter was out?

Niall wasn't waiting to find out. He shoved opened the door and strode inside. "James?" he called out.

He was greeted by nothing but silence.

Shit. Where is he?

Niall was on his way to the bedroom when he caught sight of his answer. Crumpled on the floor at the far end of the living room, blood still oozing out of his head, lay the professor.

Even as Niall hurried to his side and squatted down, he knew the man was dead. Just as he knew what he'd find when he examined the body.

Two shots behind the ear at the soft part of the skull. No exit wounds. Fired, he knew, by a .22 caliber pistol that used long rifle rounds. An excruciating death.

Cobra.

"*Fuck*," he ground out, forcing his teeth to stay clenched to muffle the sound. The last thing he needed was a swell of apartment dwellers to rush in and see that a murder had just taken place in his building. "*Fuck, fuck, fuck!*"

"Niall?" Peter's voice came from the entranceway. "Why are you on the floor... *Shit.*" Having walked close enough to see what his friend was examining, he tossed aside the bags of takeout food he'd been carrying and hurried over to squat down beside him.

It didn't take him long to assess the situation, not when this signature kill was common IRA knowledge.

"What the hell—*Cobra*?" he exclaimed in disbelief. "Why...?"

"He's after the hoard." Niall waved away Peter's questions, rising quickly to his feet. "No time to explain." He tossed his apartment keys at Peter. "Go upstairs and wait for me."

"You're not taking care of this body alone."

"I'm not taking care of it at all. Just do as I say."

Hearing the steely edge in Niall's tone, Peter nodded, grabbing the keys and taking off.

Niall waited a heartbeat. Then he pulled out his private phone and called Donald.

"He's been here," he said tersely, aborting code words in light of the urgency involved.

"Victim?" Donald asked.

"Blythe. His apartment. I need cleaners—now."

"I'll take care of it. Just get out of there."

***

Niall joined Peter in his apartment, where they'd met mere hours ago.

Peter perched at the edge of the living room sofa, scratching Pope's and Martha's ears as he watched his friend pace furiously around the room.

"So you knew Cobra was in New York," he said.

"Not when you told me, but later," Niall replied.

"You said he's after the hoard."

"Yeah." A long pause. "And he knows that Niall Dempsey is one step ahead of him."

Peter's brows went up. "How?"

Niall sank down into a chair, propping his elbows on his knees and steepling his fingers beneath his chin. He had to be careful. There was one piece of his life as Sean Donovan that even Peter couldn't know. And that was his identity as Silver Finger. No one but Donald could ever know that.

"I'm not sure how he figured things out," Niall answered with as much candor as he could. "Certainly not about the existence or whereabouts of the hoard. As for the rest, I can only speculate. I was a regular customer of Rose Flaherty—the antiquities expert whose cremains you took Blythe to visit this morning. She was researching the tapestry panels for Fiona McKay. And I was keeping a close eye on that research, paying frequent visits to Rose's shop and asking lots of questions. For all I know, he was there. I have no idea what he looks like or what identity he's assumed."

"You think he killed Rose Flaherty?"

"Without a doubt. He probably got whatever information he could out of her and then gave her a good hard shove. No need to waste fanfare on the old woman."

"You're a high-profile guy who was showing interest in the tapestry. He must have interrogated her about you. She could have told him anything before she died." Peter paused, then carefully spoke the words Niall had been anticipating. "He must know what you did back in Ireland. Otherwise, why would he kill your professor the way he did—shoving his signature style in your face?"

"He definitely knows I'm former IRA." Niall didn't skirt the question or sugarcoat his response. He owed the truth about Cobra to Peter. Regardless of his friend's ambivalence toward the prick, he'd lost friends to his lethal hand, as well. "This is the second such kill he's taunted me with," Niall said. "The first was one of the guys I'd hired to stay on top of Fiona McKay and Forensic Instincts. I found the body. That's when I knew you were right about his being here. The fucking tout wanted to leave his calling card to let me know he was after what I wanted."

"So this is a double victory for him—part personal and part greed."

"The personal part's a sick game to him. But the rest? He wants that hoard and the fortune that goes along with it. And somehow he knows I'm close to finding it." Niall's eyes glittered with hatred. "The question is, what did the professor tell him while he was begging for his life? And how much of it did Cobra even understand? He knows the tapestries exist. But there's no way he'd make sense of the babblings of a terrified old man. No, he's counting on my leading him to his prize."

Peter nodded slowly in agreement. "So what now?"

"Now we lie low while the professor's body is disposed of. By sometime tomorrow, Forensic Instincts is bound to reach out to him. And they're going to get suspicious and alarmed when they realize he's vanished."

"Can they tie him to you?"

Niall shook his head. "Not a prayer. The only name they have is the fake one you used. So let them wear themselves out. As long as they keep looking for the hoard. Which, no matter what, they will. And we'll be right there to take it from them."

***

Claire awakened with a strangled cry.

The whole team had gone to their respective chill-out spots in the brownstone and conked out for the night, having worked on their assignments for hours. It had been days since any of them had slept, and as Casey had decided, they need to recoup.

Tossing and turning on the futon in Ryan's lair, Claire had been unable to fall asleep, plagued by a dark feeling that had pervaded her since early evening. Now she gave a strangled cry, bolting upright with sweat dripping down her back.

"Claire, what is it?" Ryan jolted awake beside her, pivoting to gently grip her shoulders and turn her to face him. She looked dazed and terrified—a state he'd seen her in before. And it didn't bode well.

"Death," she whispered. "Violent death."

Ryan swallowed hard. "Who?" he asked.

Her eyes filled with tears as she looked at him. "Oh, Ryan, I think it was the professor." She could barely speak. "His face keeps flashing in and out of my mind, interspersed with flashes of blood, fear, and suffering." She squeezed her eyes shut, trying to block out the image. "So much pain."

Ryan felt bile rise in his throat. "Is Dempsey there? Is he the killer?"

"I… I can't see." Claire was trembling like a leaf. "I never can when it comes to that bastard. It's like there's a cloak covering him, even now that I know his past."

Ryan held her for a moment. Then, he eased her away. "Let's assemble the team."

The conference room was dead silent as Claire spoke.

Fiona, who'd been included in this emergency meeting, began to openly weep. "If it is the professor, it's my fault. He came to help me."

"He came to pay his respects to Rose and to search for the hoard he'd been fascinated by for decades," Marc responded, trying to assuage Fiona's sense of guilt.

Ryan had been pounding away at his laptop. "Do you know how many Thomas Murphys there are in Manhattan?" he muttered. "If we knew a damn thing about this aide, I could narrow down my search. But I've got a whole lot of nothing."

"Maybe he'll contact us," Emma suggested. "When he goes to the professor's hotel and doesn't find him…"

"What hotel? Do we even know where he was staying?" Patrick interrupted. He was clearly angry at himself for not having put security on the elderly man.

Casey gave a grim shake of her head. "It's not just you who screwed up this time, Patrick. We all did. We didn't ask a single question. Not about where the professor was staying. Not any details about his aide. Not about a damn thing."

"His cell phone's dead," Ryan announced. "That number was the only tie we had to him, other than his contact info in Ireland."

"And Thomas Murphy," Marc reminded them with a frown. "Does anyone but me wonder if it's a coincidence that the professor's aide has such a common Irish last name?"

Patrick met his gaze. "You think he was a plant." He nodded in answer to his own question. "My instincts say the same. Fiona found him wandering around outside our closed meeting door. He said he was stretching his legs. I'd say he was eavesdropping."

"I'll be willing to bet he was working for Dempsey," Ryan said. "In which case, I wouldn't waste time waiting for his frantic phone call saying the professor is missing. We can check the footage from our outdoor cameras to see if they caught his license plate. If so, I'll do some digging. But I wouldn't hold my breath. The plates were likely fake."

"I agree," Claire said, her eyes still damp. "It's not an insight, but it feels true. This was all a setup. Maybe I would have gotten a sense of that if I weren't so focused on the professor helping us with the tapestries."

Casey's sadness was laced with frustration. "Not only is this a tragedy, but there's almost nothing proactive we can do. We can't hunt for a body—we don't even know for sure that the murder has taken place or, if it did, where. And we can't call the police with nothing to go on but a feeling from Claire." She pursed her lips, considering what steps might be taken. "Ryan, when we're done here, follow up on those license plates. Emma, call the professor's assistant at University College Dublin and see if she's heard from him. Chat her up enough to casually ask if he has any family. Don't send up any red flags."

"Okay." Emma nodded, coming to her feet. "I'll report back the minute I have something."

"Thanks." Casey turned up her palms. "Is there anything I'm not thinking of?"

"No." Marc shook his head. "Unfortunately, after that, we're stuck between a rock and a hard place—at least until we can prove Niall

Dempsey is both an IRA terrorist and a killer. Once he's been arrested, then we'll get our answers."

The whole team looked grim.

Heartsick or not, Casey rose to her leadership role. "In the meantime, the best way to honor Professor Blythe is to finish what we started. Let's go back to the tapestries, use what he told us, and find that hoard."

Hutch got a call from the FBI's London attaché just before nine a.m.

The facts were indisputable.

Sean Donovan and Niall Dempsey were the same person.

In addition to that, the PSNI's forensic team had found two separate blood samples on the shirt they'd tested—samples that had shown DNA elements that were close enough to indicate that Donovan was related to the other victim.

MI5 had collaborated with the PSNI, providing Hutch with the necessary intel. Donovan, a.k.a. Silver Finger, had a brother, Kevin, who'd been the spotter on his older brother's final assignment. The RUC's top informant, code name Cobra, had alerted his handler to the planned hit. Reinforcements had arrived. The mission had been aborted. Shots were fired. Silver Finger had survived. His brother had not.

From that moment on, Sean Donovan had disappeared off the grid—until now.

Hutch read the long list of Donovan's hits, and his gut clenched. This conscienceless assassin was the animal that was at the heart of Casey's ongoing case.

And Hutch's role in what was an official, highly classified bureau investigation meant he couldn't say a word to her about what he'd learned. Not that it mattered. His silence would tell her all she needed to know. And it wouldn't do a damn thing to stop her or FI from following through on their work.

As for the federal investigation, this would be just the beginning. An arrest warrant based on information from Ireland would take a long time. Plus, the Irish authorities wanted to build an airtight prosecution case. If there were other IRA terrorists connected to Dempsey or who had, in fact, escaped the way he had through a network of sympathizers here in the US, it was essential that that be discovered. Dempsey was not a flight risk. He was a well-respected member of the community. More would be gained by taking the time to surveil him and find out who he met with and if they, too, had IRA connections. In addition, it would be essential to investigate his financials and see if funds had been sent to support IRA causes that might be simmering beneath the surface.

The good news was that Hutch could now officially initiate surveillance on the bastard.

And Hutch planned on being an integral part of that surveillance himself.

34

The FI team gathered in the main conference room, the tapestry panels spread out across the table.

As expected, Emma's phone call had yielded no results.

Professor Blythe hadn't advised his assistant of where in New York City he was staying, nor had he contacted her since his arrival. He'd never spoken of family. As far as the young woman was aware, he was alone and very much a recluse.

Ryan's digging hadn't turned up any living relatives, either. And as expected, Thomas Murphy's license plates had come up bogus.

So there was only Claire's awareness and a deep sense of grief that drove the team back to their work. Until they had the facts they needed, they'd honor the professor by following the path he'd paved for them.

They began where they'd left off—with the gravestone archway.

Yoda projected it across the wall of monitors, ready to zoom in as need be.

Casey was the first to speak.

"I think the most pressing thing for us to figure out is what James regarded as a huge question mark—the symbol Fiona's great-grandmother created. Yoda, please zoom in on that asterisk-looking symbol with the wavy lines on either side." Casey waited until he'd complied. "I feel as if that asterisk is kind of like an embellished *X* marks the spot."

"Yeah, but what spot?" Ryan asked. As usual, he was the most frustrated member of the team, pacing around behind the seating arrangement and gazing at the monitors. "We're not even sure the hoard is in Manhattan. It could be anywhere."

Fiona shook her head. "Our great-grandparents were poor immigrants who settled in Hell's Kitchen. They wouldn't have been able to travel outside a small radius."

"The wavy lines around the asterisk are driving me crazy," Casey said. "How are they connected to the asterisk? Or are they?"

"They're an organic whole," Claire replied. "So, yes, they're connected." She leaned forward and ran her fingers over the actual symbol. "I can feel them running through me."

Those particular words brought Casey up short. "Running through you? You mean, like rivers?"

Claire's eyes widened. "Curving. Meandering. Yes, rivers."

"The East River and the Hudson River," Marc said. "Definitely Manhattan."

His gaze was drawn back to the tapestry panels they'd arranged in the NYC category. "Maybe we shouldn't be so quick to lump the New York panels together. Maybe there's something here."

"Like what?" Ryan asked. "The ship crossing the ocean is self-explanatory. The Statue of Liberty can't be confused with anything else."

"What about this last one?" Marc pointed at the panel of the New York City skyline. "It doesn't fit."

Ryan glanced at it and shrugged. "Maybe they were sightseeing and the skyline impressed them enough to include in their New York story."

"That would be a waste," Marc replied. "This isn't a pictorial journey; it's the equivalent of a treasure map."

"I agree," Patrick said. "And if Fiona's great-grandmother were simply telling the rest of their journey to New York, she would have woven a view of Hell's Kitchen—which this certainly is not."

Emma took a bite of her chocolate croissant and studied the monitor. "Actually, it kind of looks like Lower Manhattan."

"It is." Fiona sat up excitedly, touching the panel and outlining a building with her finger. "Yoda, can you zoom in here?"

"Of course."

An instant later it was done.

"See this Romanesque Revival architecture?" Fiona asked. "I think it's the Puck building. It's a landmark now, but it would have been pretty new in the twenties."

"You're right." Emma nodded. "I recognize it because it was in a bunch of movies. And I know it's in Nolita," she added, referring to the Manhattan neighborhood whose shortened name came from *North of Little Italy*.

"Nolita looked a whole lot different in the twenties than it does now," Patrick reminded them. "We can't be sure what they were focusing on."

"Oh, yes, we can." Casey bolted to her feet. "The clues are staring us right in the face, but we haven't been seeing them." She studied the Nolita skyline for one last second. "Fiona just said that the Puck Building was a landmark. Well, whatever place in which her great-grandparents chose to bury the hoard had to stand the test of time, as well—and she'd realize that." Casey didn't bother instructing Yoda, just pointed at the asterisk again. "X marks the spot. Eliminate the X and what do you see?"

"A cross," Fiona breathed. "Churches stand the test of time."

"Right. Now look at the twin high Irish crosses, the ones we thought belonged with the Irish grouping. Two religious symbols, one big, one smaller—with the smaller one in the forefront." She looked at the team, triumph glittering in her eyes. "Two Saint Patrick's Cathedrals, the smaller one being highlighted."

"Oh my God." Now it was Fiona's turn to jump up. "The hoard is buried at Old Saint Patrick's. X marks the spot is the crossroads of Mulberry Street and Prince Street."

"Shit." Ryan stared from one panel to the other. "I don't believe this. How could I not have figured that out?"

"Because it's like any other puzzle," Casey said. "You can stare at it and stare at it and see nothing. And suddenly, it's all there, right in front of you. Speaking of which…" Casey tapped the final panel they had yet to examine—the long, dark corridor. "Now that we know the hoard's location, we need to fit this corridor into the picture. Fiona, have you ever seen a corridor like this at Old Saint Patrick's?"

Slowly, Fiona shook her head. "I don't think so."

"It's not there anymore," Claire murmured. "But it used to lead to"—awareness dawned in her eyes—"to the light at the end of the tunnel. I just don't know what that is."

"I do." Fiona was practically vibrating with excitement. "Old Saint Patrick's is the only church in New York with catacombs beneath it. The entrance is inside the church. But there was an original entrance that was torn down when the new one was rebuilt."

"Yes," Claire breathed. "Underground crypts." Her gaze grew brighter still. "And many of those crypts have stone carvings outside them."

"That's all we need." Ryan glanced around the room at everyone. "Prep before we leave?"

Fiona held up her palm. "Wait. We have either the perfect opportunity or a major roadblock. You'll have to tell me."

"Go on," Casey said.

"The Basilica now offers tours of the catacombs to the general public a bunch of times a day. Tommy's New York gives them. Hang on." Fiona pulled out her iPhone and entered that information. "Here it is. Three times a day—at eleven, one, and three o'clock—seven days a week. Each tour is an hour and a half long." She looked up. "So the catacombs won't be deserted, and when they are, they'll be locked tight."

Ryan looked stoked. "Who wants deserted? We can just join in the three o'clock tour—the final one of the day—and then just kind of stay behind. It'll get us down there no problem." A corner of his mouth lifted. "I bet you never thought I'd be so psyched to go to church, huh, Fee?"

"Nope. But there's a first time for everything. And this is definitely it." Fiona turned to Casey. "It's not even noon yet. We have plenty of planning time. I'm the novice here, so I'm all ears."

"For starters," Casey said, "we're not all going. Fiona's a congregant and Ryan's a McKay, so it would look odd if they went on a first-time tour of the catacombs."

"I'm not missing this," Ryan stated flatly.

Casey shot him a take-it-easy look. "I wasn't asking you to. This is your and Fiona's family. You both have every right to be there when we find the hoard. What I was going to say is that we have to make it seem as if the two of you are bringing a few of us along for this unique experience."

"Which means that some of us have to stay back," Claire said with a nod of understanding. "That would be Emma and me." She waved away Emma's protest. "This isn't a thrill ride. It's real. The people we need there are Marc and Patrick. Casey, you're our leader and you have a carry and conceal permit and a pistol, as well."

A current of communication passed between Casey and Claire.

"Guns?" Fiona asked, definitely taken aback. "Why?"

"Because we have to keep Dempsey in mind," Casey responded, trying to keep it light. "Just in case he knows more than we think he does…" She paused, intentionally omitting any mention of the professor.

"That's still five people," Ryan pointed out. "Three, if you exclude Fiona and me from the tourist list."

"I'll be outside," Patrick replied. "I'll drive you in my car so it won't be the FI van that's parked outside the church. I'll have your backs—just in case. No one will get by me."

"I never doubted it," Casey said. "Which is all the more essential given there's probably little, if any, cell reception in the catacombs."

Marc was nodding his head. "This works. It'll only be Casey and me being shown around. Just a couple of Fiona and Ryan's friends."

"Exactly." Casey moved aside all the panels—all but one. And that was the panel they'd originally determined to be of merely a stone carving but that Professor Blythe had told them was also a woven replica of one of the medallions on the Ardagh Chalice.

"Yoda, I need you to zoom in as close as possible here." She waited until it was done. "It's time to study every detail of this panel and to recall everything the professor described about it. Claire, you said you sensed the carving was a decorative wall piece. That means it must be hanging somewhere in the catacombs. I'm sure the walls down there are filled with decorative pieces. So we all need to take a photo of this panel and simultaneously memorize precisely what we're looking for in case there's no opportunity to check our iPhones. Obviously, the carving marks the spot where the hoard is secreted. We won't have much time. We'd better know how to use it."

***

It was drizzling when Patrick got behind the wheel of his car and the others climbed in.

Fortunately, he drove a decent-sized sedan, so Marc, Ryan, and Fiona fit comfortably in the back seat, with Casey in the passenger seat up front.

"All set?" he asked, glancing in the rearview mirror.

"Buckled in and ready to go," Fiona replied eagerly. She was practically vibrating with excitement. So was the entire team, each member aware that the end goal was in sight.

"I've got the tools we might need right here." Ryan patted the camera bag beside him—a bag that actually contained no photography equipment at all, but instead held just what they'd need to work with. To complete the charade, he had a thirty-five-millimeter camera hanging around his neck, ostensibly to take photos that were more professional than a cell phone could produce.

"Then we're off." Patrick pulled away from the curb.

As he did, Casey glanced out the window. She knew in her gut that they were being watched and that their observers were probably going to follow Fiona to their destination.

Hopefully, that destination would appear to be totally innocuous.

The caveat would be if Niall Dempsey knew more than they thought he did.

Even so, they'd be ready for him.

***

Niall was showing Peter the painting of the Battle of Bawncullen when his private cell phone rang.

"Talk to me," he answered, his blood pressure already through the ceiling. Donald had called him hours ago to say that the professor's body had been disposed of. So this was either news about Cobra or about Fiona McKay and the Forensic Instincts team.

"An unusual outing," Donald replied, speaking much less cryptically than usual. That told Niall that this was a time-is-of-the-essence situation that precluded a trip down to Kelly's bar.

"I'm listening."

"Four of them and our target in a private car."

Niall's antenna went up. "Stopped where?"

"Your church. On some tour."

"A tour?" Niall frowned. He knew about the tours conducted three times a day for tourists. "They're in there now?"

"With a large group, yes."

Odd enough to be disturbing, but not to trigger the alarm bells—yet. The McKays were proud of their church. Maybe Fiona was introducing her new friends to its beauty. It was possible they were stalemated right now without the professor's help to continue their analysis of the tapestries—help that was never going to come. So, yeah, this could be a diversion to keep them from going crazy. Still, he had to be extra vigilant when it came to Forensic Instincts. They knew he was having Fiona followed. This could be a decoy stop, after which they could try to slip out and head elsewhere.

"Eyes on them," he told Donald. "If they go anywhere other than back to their office once the tour ends, I want to know."

35

The catacombs were located deep beneath the church, and the walk through them was the grand finale of the tour.

The guided exploration began in a large outer room with a gleaming tiled floor and one wall of layered stones. Two great wooden doors marked the entrance to the crypts. Each of the thirty or so tour registrants took one of the proffered LED candles, and the guide opened the doors, instructing them to watch their step as they followed him.

They all stepped into a dark, low-ceilinged, vaulted corridor, their candles flickering as one. Combined with that pale illumination was the reflected red lighting from the modern-day exit signs, all of which melded together to give the catacombs an eerie glow.

The effect was both exhilarating and chilling.

As they had throughout the tour of the grounds, the chapel, and the Erben organ, Casey, Marc, Ryan, and Fiona stayed at the back of the group. Given the tight quarters, the number of people, and the singular focus of the group, positioning themselves would be a piece of cake.

Casey carefully scrutinized her surroundings. Even at first glance, it was obvious that modern renovations had been made, and yet the historic feel remained, as, she suspected, did much of the original stonework.

"Awesome," Ryan muttered, looking around and snapping some photos with his camera. "I can't believe I've never been down here."

Fiona arched a brow. "I'm not even sure if you made it to my first communion, much less toured the catacombs."

"Very funny."

"Lots of stone," Casey said, scrutinizing their surroundings. "I wonder if some of this is your great-grandfather's handiwork."

"I asked myself the same question," Fiona said. "To think that his masonry might be melded into these walls forever—a kind of immortality."

"Lots of stone also means lots of study for us," Marc reminded them. He nudged them forward. "Let's keep up—for now."

They followed along the dimly lit hallway, plaster walls revealing embedded headstones, marking the internment of people long past, some famous, some not. Some of the niches were more extravagant than others, as was customary in cemeteries around the world. Most were plain, but others marked more elaborate burial chambers that held the dead from several generations of an entire family. These were marked by plaques, carvings, beautiful tile, and ironwork.

The tour guide pointed out each detail as the group progressed slowly, and the crypt corridors made several turns—turns with squared-off corners that would be optimal for later concealment. Other than noting that, the team had only one goal in mind—finding that stone carving.

It was a long time in coming, but it happened.

Casey spotted it first, and she seized Fiona's arm.

"There," she whispered, tipping her head toward the crypt over which hung exactly what they were seeking.

"Oh my God." Fiona clapped a hand over her mouth and stared.

It was just as the professor had described, and what they'd memorized on their own—sans the enhancement of colors, but beautifully crafted nonetheless.

A medallion. Four petals inside. Scroll patterns. Tiny dots representing the four small cloisonné enameled jewels. And at the center of the medallion, another tiny design, a tip to the ancient medieval design they'd seen on the actual tapestry panel.

"How exquisite," Fiona said. "I can't believe the attention to detail."

"And I can't wait to see what's inside," Ryan replied, his Indiana Jones spirit alive and kicking.

"How much longer is the tour?" Marc asked Fiona.

"We're winding up," she said. "My guess would be about ten minutes."

"We wait five," Marc instructed. "Then we retreat to that brick corner we just passed and flatten ourselves against the outer wall. We don't budge or make a sound until the last person leaves and the doors are shut. Agreed?"

They all nodded in unison.

Reluctantly, they continued walking, very slowly, gradually putting a small distance between themselves and the rest of the group—not enough to notice, but enough to position themselves for a swift backward motion.

The wooden doors loomed just ahead.

***

Again, Niall's cell phone rang.

"Tour's over," Donald told him. "Crowd's gone. But they're still inside."

Niall's brows drew together. "In the chapel? The office? With the monsignor?"

"Nowhere our guys can see. And one of them went in to check. No sign anywhere."

Niall was now on high alert. "Did they sneak out?"

"All exit doors covered. And their car hasn't budged."

"Then the only place they can be is... *Fuck!*"

Pieces rapidly dropped into place in Niall's head. Stone carving. Dark tunnel. Irish crosses.

"The fucking hoard is buried in the catacombs," he said, speaking to Donald but tilting his head toward Peter.

He couldn't wait to hang up.

"Call me if anything changes," he barked into the phone.

"I'll have our guys watching you," Donald replied. "Remember, you're not the only one who wants this."

Cobra, Niall thought, disconnecting the call.

"You armed?" he asked Peter.

"Always." Peter patted his side.

"Then we're moving—*now*."

***

Marc was crouched low, his strong back being used as Ryan's work platform so Ryan could easily reach their target. The chisel and hand sledge were already in play, as Ryan very carefully chiseled out the mortar between the carving and the wall.

"Don't destroy the carving," Fiona said fervently. "You have to preserve our great-grandfather's work."

Her brother shot her an irritated look. "That's the plan. Why do you think I'm working at a snail's pace when we all know I want to shatter this thing to bits and grab what's inside?"

He went back to his task, whacking the hand sledge firmly but measuredly at the chisel.

Pieces of mortar began falling away.

Success was almost within reach.

***

Hutch leaned forward in his parked car, peering intently through the window. From the start, he'd appointed himself the "eye" in this surveillance operation, keeping a perpetual view of his target unless traffic or stoplights interfered. During this trip, he'd almost lost Dempsey once on Fifth Avenue but had gotten him back in his sights quickly enough that he didn't have to radio his surveillance team for one of them to take over.

His entire team—eight agents in their nondescript sedans—had all been staked out at various places around Dempsey's apartment building and were now at the scene of the Basilica at Saint Patrick's Old Cathedral in Nolita.

Intently, Hutch watched as Dempsey and another guy went inside. No visible weapons. No covert movements. No evident danger.

Given that, he knew he couldn't compromise the operation.

He instructed his team to situate themselves and stay put, covering all the exits but not making any moves. This was a house of worship— Dempsey's house of worship. There was no cause to suspect foul play.

Still, Hutch had a very bad feeling in his gut.

***

Patrick had a similar feeling—but in his case, he knew exactly why.

The FI team was inside the church as Dempsey and the guy they knew as Thomas Murphy made their way in. And unless Dempsey and his crony had a sudden urge to pray, that could mean only one thing.

They knew the hoard was in the catacombs and that FI was down there recovering it.

Patrick acted instantly, unaware that he was parked halfway down the block from Hutch or that there was an FBI surveillance team on the scene.

He quickly group-texted the team. He had to retain his position outside, slumped down low in the driver's seat. Dempsey had been tailing both Fiona and FI all week, so he must have other men in place. Hopefully, they hadn't noticed the fact that Patrick had hung back, remaining in the sedan rather than joining the others. He couldn't screw that up by abandoning his cover and heading into the church.

He only hoped that by some miracle his text would go through.
But the catacombs were isolated underground.

He didn't hold out much hope.

∗

It took time and patience—neither of which Ryan had—until finally
he wriggled the carving free, removing it as one piece, intact.

"Gotcha," he said triumphantly, quickly peering into the hollow
stonework. "There's definitely something inside."

"Yeah, well, Fiona's going to have to take over from here," Marc
said. "You've used me as a springboard long enough, plus we all deserve
to be part of this discovery—especially your sister."

"Thanks, Marc." Fiona gave him a grateful look, reaching up as Ryan
reluctantly handed down the stone carving. "Careful," he said. "It's heavy."

She nodded, holding tight to their prize and waiting for Ryan to
jump down beside her.

Ryan took back the carving, holding it steady as Fiona reached
inside.

Her brows knit in puzzlement as she pulled out what looked like
a crude piece of plaster.

"What the hell?" Ryan didn't react well. "It's a lump of nothing.
It looks like some kind of animal. Is this a joke?"

Fiona turned the heavy piece over in her hands—and awareness
darted across her face. "A Galway sheep," she breathed. "A crude version
of one, but that's what it is."

She held out the half-finished object for them all to see.

"The perfect place for concealment," Casey said. "And an ideal way
to smuggle something valuable into the country. I always wondered
how your great-grandparents managed to do that without the treasure
being spotted. Now we know." She gestured at the sheep. "This I think
we can shatter with your great-grandfather's full approval."

With an eager nod, Fiona struck the plaster sheep against the wall, pulling away pieces as she did.

Inside shone an exquisite golden object, small but perfect.

The chalice. A chalice that once belonged to a king.

It was a hammered solid gold piece with a raised design of Celtic knots and spirals both on the body and the lid. On the lid was a ruby surrounded by intricate woven gold designs. Sparkling gemstones—rubies, emeralds, and sapphires—were set in the base of the chalice, with the same woven designs surrounding them. Much like the Ardagh Chalice, this one was about seven inches tall and maybe nine or ten inches in diameter, with a bowl that was about four inches deep.

"My God," Fiona breathed. "This is breathtaking." She lifted the lid, peering inside the chalice, whose body and stem were both hollow, and got her first look at the numerous pieces that comprised the Valdrefjord Hoard.

With care and awe, she lifted out a few of them—a gold necklace, three solid gold coins, and two sapphires and a ruby, along with several semiprecious gemstones.

She was just reaching inside again when a hard, cold voice sounded behind them, accompanied by the click of a trigger.

"Don't bother savoring your find," Niall Dempsey said. "You won't be keeping it long enough to examine the pieces."

Fiona jolted with shock, and her head snapped around in time to see Dempsey pointing a pistol at her, backed up by the man she knew as Thomas Murphy.

Niall shifted his weapon, aiming it at Marc. "You—Navy SEAL—take out your gun very slowly and kick it over here. That applies to you, as well, Casey. After all, you were kind enough to tell me what an excellent shot you are."

As they complied, Niall stepped forward to quickly frisk Ryan, after which he sneered. "Nothing, tech guy?"

"Fuck you." Ryan took a protective step toward Fiona. "And don't lay a hand on my sister."

"I didn't plan to." Niall turned his pistol on Fiona. "Give me the chalice."

Fiona looked helplessly at Casey, who nodded her head. "Give it to him," she said.

Shaking violently, Fiona shoved the chalice in Dempsey's scarred hand. She looked like she wanted to spit at him but was too terrified to do so.

"Good." Niall stepped back again, his finger on the trigger as he swept the group. "Now, all of you, facedown on the ground, hands behind your backs. One move and I won't hesitate to make it your last."

"Why bother?" Casey asked, as the four of them did as Dempsey had directed. "You're going to kill us anyway."

"There are different ways to die. Plus, I'd rather not desecrate the church, not unless I have to."

He waited until they were all lying on the floor execution style before turning his attention to the treasure he'd searched so many years for.

"At last." His eyes glittered as he cradled the chalice. "The Valdrefjord Hoard."

As he spoke, there was another click of a trigger, this one behind him, and a pistol was jabbed in his back.

"Now *you* can hand it over, mate."

"What?" Niall froze, looking totally baffled. "Peter?"

"Surprised?" Peter laughed—a sound that held an unnatural darkness inside of it. "Did you *really* think I was nothing more than your piss-ass flunky?"

He leaned forward and snatched the chalice from Niall's hand, stuffing it into the deep pocket of his jacket. "We've come full circle, haven't we, mate? From the beer-guzzling hours down at the docks to now, the moment when you're finally realizing what an asshole you've been. This belongs to me. I own it, and I own *you*."

"What are you talking about?" Shock and confusion echoed in Niall's voice. "I told you I'd pay you whatever you want."

Peter swore, shoving the barrel of the gun harder into Niall's back. "You still think this is about your fucking real estate fortune? You're an even bigger idiot than I thought you were. Turns out, between the two of us, I'm the genius. First, the entire hoard is now mine. Second, who do you think got rid of that doddering old woman and your expert of a professor so *this* could happen?" He pressed his hand triumphantly against the pocket that held the chalice.

Niall's breath was coming faster, his mind racing to put together the pieces. "What are you talking about? Cobra killed those…"

All the color drained from his face.

"Yeah, he did, didn't he?" Peter mocked with another chilling laugh. "He killed all his victims, including the ones the RUC told him not to kill. He even had the pleasure of torturing and executing his son-of-a-bitch father. Can you imagine the sense of power he felt? The feeling of playing God? Of course not. You were a fucking sniper. You never got to experience the thrill of watching someone die at your feet, hear their cries of pain, see them writhe like eels before they bled out. You were just the prize pet of the IRA—their celebrated *Silver Finger*. You told me so yourself. So proud. So drunk. Back in those days, I was sober. I held my booze a hell of a lot better than you did. We were mates. Close to brothers. You babbled out the truth. And I listened. I remembered. And when the money was good enough, when my hatred for you was strong enough, I finally got to do what I was born to do—hand you over to the RUC."

Peter jabbed the gun still deeper into Niall's back, enough to make him wince in pain. "But you didn't die. Only your weak, pathetic brother, Kevin, did. Instead, the Provos got you out of the country. And here you are, the rich and famous Niall Dempsey. Can you imagine the joy I felt when I found that article? Saw your face? Knew I had another chance? This time, *mate*, you're not getting away. This time Cobra will make his record a perfect one hundred percent." He shifted his pistol to the back of Niall's head, just behind his ear.

Tears of betrayal had been gathering in Niall's eyes—until Peter mentioned Kevin and Niall felt the telltale positioning of his gun. Then, it was like a light switch had been flipped.

Bitter hatred etched in every line on Niall's face, tightened every muscle of his body and, with lightning speed, he acted.

In one smooth motion, he yanked out a second pistol—this one from a holster in his belt that was beneath the front of his untucked shirt. Moving his head to the right and down, he whipped around, using his left hand to knock Peter's weapon away. With his right hand, he fired two shots to Peter's chest, watching as the man who'd turned out to be his most loathed enemy crumpled to the floor, shouting in pain as blood seeped through his shirt.

Niall took two steps forward, murder glittering in his eyes as he stood over the dying man.

"This one's for Kevin—*mate*," he said, raising his gun and putting one final bullet through Peter's head.

Cobra died at his feet.

Fiona screamed, but Niall barely heard her. For a fleeting instant, he stared down at Peter's lifeless body, swallowing convulsively. His best mate. His detested enemy. How could they be one and the same?

Forcibly, he shoved away a reaction that would have to be dealt with at a later time. He had to deal with the here and now.

He gave a quick glance behind him to ensure his captives hadn't moved. Satisfied, he bent down, fished in Peter's pocket, and retrieved the chalice—reclaiming what was his. He then gathered up all the

weapons, holstering one of his and gripping the other as he pocketed
Peter's. He straightened to plan his exit.

Casey's pistol was closer to the team than Marc's was.

The moment Niall had bent down, she'd swiveled herself around
and begun crawling toward her weapon. Her fingers were about to
close on the barrel when Niall spotted her.

He kicked the gun out of her reach, steadying his own aim back at
her. "Nice try, lass. But I'm harder than I am sentimental. I've cheated
Death more times than you can imagine. You're not going to be the
one to do me in." He squatted long enough to seize both her and
Marc's guns. A smirk twisted his lips. "I seem to be very well armed."

Casey sat up. "Do you honestly believe you're walking out of
here with that hoard a free man, Silver Finger? We know who you
are. We've dug up your whole past. And we didn't come here alone."

"Again, nice try. But you heard all that blather for the first time
just now."

"Did we?" Casey arched a brow. "Then explain how we also
know you're Sean Donovan? I don't recall your best mate, Cobra,
mentioning that part."

Niall did a double take, then a spark of admiration lit his eyes.
"You really are a resourceful group, aren't you?" He paused. "Who
did you bring with you besides Patrick Lynch? His extensive security
network?" Abruptly, his eyes narrowed. "Or are there others—like
your boyfriend?"

Casey had to tread carefully. She wished she could blurt out that,
in addition to Patrick, they'd brought not only his security guys but
an entire FBI SWAT team, all of whom would be on him the minute
he stepped outside the church doors. But not only was that way over
the top, the truth was she had no idea how far along Hutch had gotten

in his efforts, if he even had a surveillance team in place. And if she pushed Dempsey's buttons too hard, he might decide to shoot them all here and now and then take off.

As long as they were alive, there was hope.

"I only wish he were," she fired back, as if his question had caught her off guard, causing her to answer honestly. "And if I had a shred of concrete evidence on you, he would be."

As expected, a look of relief darted across Dempsey's face. "So it's just the formidable Forensic Instincts team I have to deal with. Good to know." He tapped the barrel of his pistol thoughtfully. "Still, it would be foolish of me to underestimate Lynch or his men. They're all former bureau and NYPD. Therefore"—he stalked forward and jerked Casey to her feet—"it appears I'll need a shield to safeguard me. And while we're in church, you'd better pray that Lynch is smart enough to put your life ahead of my capture."

He shoved Casey in front of him, yanking her arms behind her back and aiming the pistol at her head. "Now let's take a little walk."

He paused only to address the group as a whole. "Think about it before you try any heroics. Is it worth risking Casey's life to come after me? Stay put and you'll all live. The hoard and I will vanish. As you know, I've done it before. And this time I have a lot more money to help me out. If you've researched me as thoroughly as you claim, you know the level of my marksmanship. I don't miss. So enjoy the catacombs. Your fearless leader will be back with you as soon as I'm free."

36

Hutch saw the front door of the church start to open at the same time as Patrick did. But it was Hutch who froze with shock at the sight of Casey being led out at gunpoint, a pistol pressed to the back of her head.

What the hell... Forensic Instincts was in there, too?

"Shit." He hadn't been expecting this, hadn't geared up. And there wasn't time enough to do so now. He was already inching open his car door, talking briefly into his radio to alert his team.

"Subject is exiting the front door of the church holding a hostage at gunpoint," he reported. "Hostage is a white female, red hair, blue shirt. I'm on the move."

He signed off. His team would know what to do—close in and wait for the opportunity to act. But he was the closest agent on the scene and the only one with something—or some*one*—to lose.

He climbed out of the car and squatted down behind it, making his way from one vehicle to the next as he drew nearer to the church.

He was diagonally across from where they stood when he spied Patrick, who was also crouched down behind a sedan. He obviously knew Casey and other FI team members were inside the church and was acting as outside security. And now he was in the same position Hutch was, poised to act but unwilling to risk Casey's life.

"Greetings, Mr. Lynch," Niall called out, shoving Casey forward with his every step, the barrel of his gun shifting to her right temple. "I'm not certain which car is yours, but it hardly matters. I suggest that you and your men hold your fire unless you want me to put a bullet in this lovely lass's head. I'll send her back to you as soon as I'm securely gone. That might take a while, so you'll have to be patient. Just bear in mind that I have little interest in whether or not she lives or dies, but I suspect you do. So the choice is yours. Make it."

He stopped, waited.

All was still.

"Wise choice," he said, continuing to move Casey along.

Casey's gaze was shifting up and down the street. She spotted Patrick's car and, although he was concealed, she knew he'd be crouched down behind it. What she didn't know was that he wasn't the only pro on the scene.

Hutch had waited until Niall stopped talking and had taken a few steps. Then, he'd shifted away from the back of the car he was perched behind, barely and briefly—hoping Casey might see him. And he knew the moment when she did. Her gaze widened, locked on his for a heartbeat before she averted it.

He quickly ducked back behind the car. Step one accomplished. Time for step two.

He pulled a coin out of his pocket and tossed it the three-car-length distance between himself and Patrick.

With the tiniest clink, it landed on the street near Patrick's knee, and Patrick looked up, his head swiveling in the direction where the coin had come from.

His searching stare met Hutch's.

A current of communication ran between them, and Hutch signaled Patrick by tilting his head in Niall's direction and tipping his gun toward Patrick.

Retired or not, right then Patrick was all FBI. He got the drift immediately and nodded his understanding.

Ever so slowly, he rose, just until his sight—and his gun—cleared the top of the car. Resting his elbows on the hood, he shouted, "Drop your weapon, Dempsey."

Taken by surprise, Niall veered immediately toward Patrick's voice, spotting him and instinctively turning his gun on him.

Before he could fire, Casey kicked him in the arch of the foot with the heel of her shoe as hard as possible. As she wriggled free, he growled in pain and groped for her. She sidestepped quickly.

And in one fluid motion, Hutch rose and fired two bullets into Niall's chest.

Niall cried out and fell to his knees. Hutch took no chances, following up with a shot straight to Niall's forehead.

Niall crumpled onto the pavement, dead.

The FI team had crept up from the catacombs and reached the front door of the church—where Marc had stopped them once he saw Hutch and realized what was about to go down. Now, they rushed out, all heading straight to Casey to make sure she was okay. Hutch was already holding her, and Patrick had loped up the steps to join him.

Fiona stood with the others, arms wrapped around herself, shaking and still in shock. She just stared from Casey to the dead body beside her—the second one she'd seen that day.

"Hey." Ryan pulled her to his side and gave her a hard hug. "I know this is rough. But the good guys just won. Hang in there."

"I'm trying." She swallowed past the horrible taste in her mouth. "I guess you're all used to this."

"You never get used to this." Gently, Ryan attempted to turn her away from the ugly sight.

Abruptly, Fiona straightened, realizing that she had to use the precious few minutes when Hutch was preoccupied with Casey, and when his team was first blasting onto the scene, to do what she had to do. It was irrational and she knew it. And touching a dead body was going to make her even sicker than she already was. But neither of those things was going to stop her.

"Fee?" Ryan was totally at sea.

Fiona moved forward and, fighting back nausea, bent down over Niall's lifeless body—just long enough to rummage in his pocket and retrieve the chalice. Then she scooted back. She didn't shove the chalice in her purse. Hiding it was not her intent, nor would she be able to anyway, since the FBI guys were already eyeballing her and would be confiscating the chalice in about a nanosecond. But this was *her* family's gift to Ireland, it was happening in front of *her* church, and she couldn't bear the thought of that precious treasure lying on the corpse of a horrific, blasphemous killer—not even for an instant.

She extended her hand in offering as one of Hutch's men approached her.

"Here, sir," she said respectfully. "This is what Niall Dempsey was after. I'll leave it in your custody. But please, be gentle with it—it's an Irish treasure."

The special agent looked a bit puzzled, but he nodded as Fiona transferred the chalice—and its contents—over to him.

In the distance, the wail of sirens heralded the arrival of the NYPD.

"Uh-oh," Ryan muttered, looking away from the FBI team to the red lights of the approaching police cars. "Now we're *really* in deep shit."

EPILOGUE

The FI team had a quick debriefing late the following morning.

They'd spent half the night with the FBI and the NYPD before going home and collapsing for a few hours of much-needed sleep. Fortunately, their smoothly polished explanations had been enough to get them off the hook with only a modicum of hostility and the ability to tell their attorneys that they didn't need to stay on standby.

Now they sat around the conference room table, munching on egg sandwiches and inhaling tall mugs of coffee.

"I guess we were pretty convincing," Ryan said with a wide grin. All ego and triumph, he polished off his second sandwich, leaned back in his chair, and folded his hands behind his head. "Law enforcement bought our story."

Marc arched a brow. "Think again, smart-ass. Alvarez knew we were spouting half-truths. She wanted to rip us a new one, and she and Shaw would have been thrilled to put us out of business, toss us in a cell, and throw away the key. The fact is, they had no solid evidence that we were actively checking out Dempsey or that we were impeding their investigation. The bullshit we fed them—that we were unknowingly on the same treasure hunt as Dempsey, that we were using Fiona's tapestries to guide us, and that we had no idea the tapestry panels were the reason Rose Flaherty was killed, was just that—bullshit. But there was no way to prove it, and likely little political will to spend the resources unraveling our tale. So don't begin to think the cops bought into any of our story. They just had no choice but to swallow it.

"As for the bureau, we got lucky there, too. Hutch never mentioned our part in his investigation. The international terrorism case against Dempsey was initiated by the Police Service of Northern Ireland and MI5. Period. So we can congratulate ourselves for, once again, being great at covering our asses. But not for putting one over on law enforcement. That didn't happen any more this time than it did the last dozen."

"Fine," Ryan muttered. "So we're just good bullshit artists. But you're really a buzzkill."

"Marc's right," Patrick said. "It also didn't hurt that both the FBI and the NYPD got all the credit for bringing down Silver Finger and Cobra, plus solving a local homicide—actually three, given the professor and Cobra were killed here, as well. Law enforcement's approval ratings will skyrocket."

Emma's grin was a lot like Ryan's. "Maybe, but did you see today's news reports? The media caught us on the scene. They know our reputation. And let's not forget we found a legendary Irish hoard worth a gazillion dollars. That'll put us center stage—again—especially since we're a lot more colorful than law enforcement." She took an enthusiastic bite of her egg sandwich. "Sweet."

Casey set down her mug with a hint of a smile. She'd been pretty shaken up after her near-miss, but she'd gotten through the questioning with the rest of the team and, after a few quiet hours alone with Hutch, was now very much herself—although those quiet hours had been preceded by a *very* stern lecture from the man she loved about recklessness and putting her life in danger. She hadn't argued. But they both knew this would happen again, and probably again after that. Forensic Instincts—and all it entailed—was in her blood.

"We've got more than enough to celebrate," she said now. "But none of that's about outwitting law enforcement. Marc's right; that's never happening. Suffice it to say we're great at dancing as fast as we can. So, instead, let's celebrate the successful conclusion of the case. Fiona is safe and moved back into her townhouse. Two international killers are dead. Plans are underway to transport the Valdrefjord Hoard to the National Museum of Ireland."

Casey's eyes twinkled. "And Hutch jumped on a new listing—an apartment in Battery City that's even better than the one in Dempsey Towers. All the same amenities, but with additional square footage and no connection to that despicable killer. Hero and I swung by early this morning and he gave it his sniff of approval. The lease signing is late this afternoon."

"That's wonderful!" Claire exclaimed, leaning forward to give Casey a warm hug. "Tell us when moving day is, and we'll all be there to get you and Hutch settled to start your new life together."

"And I can *finally* start shopping for housewarming gifts," Emma added with a squeal of excitement.

They were all toasting Casey and Hutch with their coffee mugs when Yoda announced, "Fiona McKay has arrived."

Marc inclined his head at Casey. "I think we're done here."

Casey nodded. "She called a little while ago and asked to come by. She's early, but, yes, our debriefing is officially concluded."

"Great, I'll let her in." Emma took off in a flash, her heels clicking on the steps and picking up speed as she neared the entranceway.

Three minutes later, she returned with Fiona beside her.

"I know I'm early," Fiona said, glancing hesitantly around the table. "Am I interrupting?"

"Nope," Patrick said. "We just wrapped up. Case closed."

Fiona let out a sigh of relief. "Thank heavens—and thank *you*." She assessed Casey with concern. "Are you okay?"

"It took a bit. But now I'm good as new." Casey returned the assessing look, giving a happy nod when she saw that Fiona was herself again, too. "Grab a cup of coffee and an egg sandwich," she urged, patting the back of an empty chair. "Then have a seat."

Fiona did as Casey suggested, bringing her sandwich and coffee to the table and getting settled—pausing only long enough to slide her Longchamp backpack off her shoulder and gently setting it on the rug beside her chair.

That done, she shot an immediate, puzzled glance at Ryan. "I called Mom and Dad to fill them in on everything, but apparently you did it for me—and really well, by the way. Mom was actually composed, even proud and excited about what our great-grandparents—and we—accomplished, and honored about being part of the restoration of the Valdrefjord Hoard. She was really touched by the fact that she and Dad were being allowed to see the hoard before its return to Ireland, since it was found on their ancestral property. Sure, she was worried about both you and me, but she was far from the emotional basket case I expected."

A corner of Ryan's mouth lifted. "What can I say? I'm just the natural soothing type."

Claire almost spit out her herbal tea as the rest of the team laughed uncontrollably.

Fiona still looked puzzled. "You lost rock, paper, scissors last time. It was my turn to help them deal with this one."

"It was too huge and complicated for you to handle," Ryan answered her frankly. "Bad enough to hear that Dempsey almost killed us and that he *did* kill Rose—the second part of which was as close to the truth as I could give them. There's way too much about Dempsey's previous life and the FBI investigation that *can't* be said. As it is, you know a hell of a lot more than you should."

"You're right." Fiona shuddered. "And I'm not sure where the public and classified info part ways. So I'm glad you took the problem out of my hands. Truthfully, I'd rather forget everything about last night—but I never will."

"No, you won't. But at least you know that Mom and Dad are relatively fine." Ryan's grin widened. "Hearing you're okay from your incredible big brother holds a lot of weight."

"And so the ego lives on," Marc noted dryly.

"Did you doubt it?" Claire asked, visibly torn between exasperation and laughter.

Fiona wasn't done questioning her brother. "Dad said the two of you were meeting up for a beer. What's that about?"

Claire sat up straighter and met Ryan's gaze.

A current of communication ran between them.

"Nothing special," he told his sister. "Just playing catch-up."

"Whatever that means." A momentary flash of sadness crossed Fiona's face. "I went back to church this morning and lit a candle for the professor. I lit a second one from all of you."

"What a lovely thing to do," Casey said. "Thank you. He was a fine man."

They all grew quiet, offering James a unanimous moment of silence and appreciation.

It was Fiona who shook off the somber mood.

"I come bearing gifts," she said, reaching down to get her backpack, which she promptly placed in the center of the table.

Unzipping it, she pulled out eight velvet jewelry bags, all emblazed with the logo *Fiona McKay Jewelry* in gold, and each one labeled with one of their names, Hutch and Hero included. She passed them out, making sure to include Hutch's when she presented Casey with hers.

"These are for you—with my love and thanks," she said simply. "Each one of these pieces has a special meaning to me, and each one just felt right for the person who's receiving it. I hope you agree. Open them one at a time—Casey first."

She watched as Casey untied her pouch and slid out a long, thin silver chain on which hung a Tree of Life medallion that was studded with tiny jewels.

"It's exquisite," Casey said, admiring each tiny stone.

"In your case," Fiona explained, "it symbolizes strength, family, and resilience—all of which you embody both as a person and as the president of Forensic Instincts." She tipped her chin toward the pouch with Hutch's name on it. "The silver cuff links I chose for Hutch match your medallion—just as you two match each other."

"Thank you so much." Casey looked moved to tears.

With a smile, Fiona turned to Marc. "You next."

Marc complied. "Wow," he said, admiring a handsome pair of square sterling silver cuff links. They had a raised border and an engraved series of intertwined Celtic knots.

"The threads are all interconnected, symbolizing continuity," Fiona explained. "You're the rock of the FI team, Marc, and you epitomize the essence of loyalty, faith, friendship, and love—all of which are reflected in that design."

"I'm honored," he replied, still studying the elegant knots.

With that, Fiona turned to Claire, urged her to open her pouch.

Claire slipped out a stunning ring that depicted an all-seeing eye set in a triangle shape in twenty-two-karat granulation. "Oh, my," she breathed.

"I think that one's self-explanatory." Fiona watched her expression with pleasure. "Your insights are as unique as you are."

"My turn?" Emma asked eagerly.

Fiona laughed. "Absolutely. Go for it."

Emma yanked open the cord and pulled out a beautiful pair of sterling silver earrings. Each earring was a delicate spiral symbol and each had a tiny ruby set in the center.

"My birthstone," Emma exclaimed.

"I do my homework." Fiona loved watching Emma's open display of joy—a joy that was just a natural part of Emma. "The symbols there stand for growth through transition," she said. "And if that's not you, I don't know what is."

She turned to Patrick. "Now you."

As asked, Patrick removed his own unique pair of silver cuff links, these with a different pair of Celtic symbols in silver repoussé. "These are very handsome," he said, admiring the unusual design.

"Those are the Celtic symbols for grounding force," Fiona told him. "And that's exactly what you are to this team—and to me."

There was a softness to Patrick's expression as he nodded his understanding and his thanks.

Fiona inclined her head in Ryan's direction, grinning as she saw the scowl on Ryan's face as he fiddled with the pouch.

"It won't bite," she teased him. "And, yes, I know you don't do jewelry. But you'll do this." She gestured at the pouch. "Open it."

"Okay, but no promises," he said.

"Fair enough." She waited while Ryan pulled out his gift: a round medallion on a long, heavy silver chain. Its image was a raised design showing three legs all in the position of a marathon runner about to take off. Each leg extended outward from a central hub, like spokes of a wheel.

His brows knit. "This is kind of cool," he said cautiously, although he was visibly intrigued. "What does it mean?"

"It speaks to the wearer, who represents perpetual motion, fierce independence, and competitiveness. That describes you to a T."

"Awesome," he clarified, with a nod. "Now this is something I can wear."

"I kind of thought so." Fiona beamed. She leaned over and untied the pouch labeled Hero. "Here you go, boy," she said, pulling out the bloodhound's gift.

Hero, who'd been lying beside Casey on the rug, realized he was being spoken to and picked up his head.

"I just need a little cooperation from you, and I think you'll be very pleased with the results," Fiona told him.

Prior to squatting down in front of him, she held up the gift for the team to see. It was a sturdy, cream-colored leather dog collar with solid chrome fittings and a hefty, rectangular silver dog tag hanging from a loop in the center. The tag had a series of intertwined Celtic knots engraved on its front, and on the back, the name *Hero* was boldly engraved in block letters, along with FI's main telephone number.

Everyone chuckled as Hero sat proudly still while Fiona removed his old collar and then wrapped the new leather one around his neck, finding the correct hole so she could buckle his new collar perfectly into place.

"There," she said, sitting back on her heels. "You look dashing. And I chose your symbol from the many choices out there because, like Marc's, it also represents loyalty, faith, friendship, and love."

Hero seemed to sense that he was being praised because he gave an enthusiastic bark.

"You really went above and beyond," Casey said, still admiring her necklace. "It truly wasn't necessary—but just try to take this away from me."

Another round of laughter.

"You saved my life and restored my great-grandparents' legacy," Fiona said, returning to her chair. "I owe you all this and more. Which reminds me, about payment…"

Casey waved away what Fiona was about to say. "Consider these payment in full." She leaned forward and clicked her mug to Fiona's. "And consider yourself an honorary member of the FI family."

AUTHOR'S NOTE

I hope you enjoyed getting to know Fiona McKay and watching her dynamic relationships with her family (especially Ryan!) and the Forensic Instincts team.

I'm very excited to announce that Fiona has decided to launch her own website, where you can view and purchase some of her awesome jewelry.

You can find it at: **FionaMckayJewelry.com**

And this is just the beginning! New pieces will be added regularly, so keep checking back!

As inspired as I was by the beauty and history of the Basilica of Saint Patrick's Old Cathedral, I would like to ask any of my readers who choose to visit, to respect the sanctity of the church as I did. While the descriptions and essence of the church captured between these pages are very real, the congregants and circumstances within the story are entirely fictional. That said, I encourage you to take a tour and get swept up in the magic as I did.

ACKNOWLEDGEMENTS

During the course of writing NO STONE UNTURNED, I had the privilege of consulting with a small group of FBI specialists who have dedicated and continue to dedicate themselves to stopping worldwide terrorism. My thanks go out to them, first and foremost, for what they do for our country and second (and on a much smaller scale), for their willingness to help me with great patience and professionalism. Any errors or omissions I might have made, however small, throughout these pages are mine and mine alone.

FBI SSA Mark Lundgren (retired), Counterterrorism and Counterintelligence, who gave me enormous amounts of time he didn't have and a history and in-depth understanding of the IRA that helped me create the most authentic backdrop to my story as possible. I affectionately refer to Mark as SSA "Mongoose", because you all know what a mongoose does to a cobra…

FBI ASAC Richard W. Kelly (retired), Joint Terrorist Task Force (JTTF), who brought a wealth of professional experience to life for me, and whose great personality and even greater humility made learning a pleasure for me.

FBI SSA Thomas F. Dowd (retired), Counterterrorism, who was generous with his time and equally generous with his knowledge.

In addition to the above, my deep gratitude go out to the following people, each one of whom brought their unique talents to helping me write this book:

Angela D. Bell, FBI Office of Public Affairs, who (as always) knew exactly which contacts to connect me with, and made those connections possible. Quite simply, no one does it better.

FBI Special Agent Laura M. Robinson, Newark Evidence Response Team Senior Team Leader, who has been a constant source of contacts for me as well as an educator in all things FBI for over a decade.

Nancy Troske, goldsmith extraordinaire, who was my guru in all aspects of Fiona McKay's jewelry-making skills, the talent behind Fiona's spectacular designs, and a teammate I deeply valued throughout my researching and writing of this book. From church visits to ancient artifacts to Celtic symbols, I loved taking this journey with you, Nan! For those of my readers who want to check out Nancy's unique and stunning jewelry, go to: nancytroskejewelry.com.

Jennifer Sarah Frank, New York based private investigator specializing in global criminal and civil investigations, whose areas of expertise are widespread and who kindly introduced me to the NYPD experts I needed.

Tefta Shaska, NYPD 2nd Grade Detective (retired), who shared a wealth of police procedural information with me.

Irma Rivera, Manhattan South Homicide Detective (retired), who educated me on homicide investigations as well as how they're treated by the Medical Examiner.

Detective Al Sheppard, NYPD Major Case Squad, a one-of-a-kind human being who was generous with his time, his knowledge, and his humanity. You'll be deeply missed, Al. Naming a character after you in NO STONE UNTURNED is my small way of honoring your memory.

FBI SSA (retired) Konrad Motyka, who came to my rescue yet again, and put me in touch with just the right NYPD detective.

Charles J. Longi, NYPD homicide detective (retired), who taught me the nitty-gritty facts about New York City homicide procedures, and who is the first person I've worked with who works even longer hours than I do.

FBI SA Robert Wittman (retired), former Senior Investigator and Founder of the FBI's National Art Crime Team, who, once again, shared his bottomless knowledge base of art and antiquities with me.

FBI Supervisory Special Agent Stephen M. Egbert, International Operations Division (IOD), who was kind enough to put me in touch with his lovely wife, who hails from Ireland.

Helen Egbert, who brought Irish culture alive for me.

Susan Lancaster, who shared her childhood Irish stories with me.

Frank Alfieri, Director Rite of Christian Burial, Basilica of Saint Patrick's Old Cathedral, who welcomed me into this spectacular church and provided me with all the resources I needed to capture its beauty and history in my story.

Tommy of Tommy's New York, whose tour of the cathedral is something that cannot be missed.

Last, but never least, to my support system:

Adam Wilson, who goes above and beyond in his role as an editorial partner. I'll skip all the accolades, since there are not nearly enough in my vocabulary, and just say, welcome back, not-so-MOE.

And to my family, who give me the love, the support, and the incentive to give all I can to all I do.